Blood Redemption

by Tessa Dawn

A Blood Curse Novel
Book Five
In the Blood Curse Series

Published by Ghost Pines Publishing, LLC
http://www.ghostpinespublishing.com

Volume V of the Blood Curse Series by Tessa Dawn
First Edition Trade Paperback Published October 31, 2013
10 9 8 7 6 5 4 3 2 1

ISBN-13: 978-1-937223-08-3
Printed in the United States of America

Author may be contacted at: http://www.tessadawn.com

𝖌𝖕
Ghost Pines Publishing, LLC

Acknowledgments

Ever since the pivotal scene in Blood Destiny, where his character emerged in a dirty shed, strapped to a guillotine, Saber's story has been lurking in the shadows, just waiting to be told. Even then, I knew there was something special about this vampire; it was just a matter of when—and where—he would emerge in the series.

I would like to give a special thanks to the Blood Curse Series Street Team for helping to spread the word about Saber's book: You guys absolutely rock, and I am forever in your debt. And as always, to all my fans and readers, you are truly a gift from the heavens.

Dedication

for *Nashoba* ~

Because my love for you knows no bounds!

Because your potential knows no limits.

And because the joy you have brought to my life…is legendary.

Credits

Ghost Pines, Publishing, LLC., *Publishing & Design*

GreenHouse Design, Inc., *Cover Art*

Lidia Bircea, *Romanian Translations*

Mercedes Arnold, *Reading & Critique*

Reba Hilbert, *Editing*

The Blood Curse

In 800 BC, Prince Jadon and Prince Jaegar Demir were banished from their Romanian homeland after being cursed by a ghostly apparition: *the reincarnated Blood of their numerous female victims*. The princes belonged to an ancient society that sacrificed its females to the point of extinction, and the punishment was severe.

They were forced to roam the earth in darkness as creatures of the night. They were condemned to feed on the blood of the innocent and stripped of their ability to produce female offspring. They were damned to father twin sons by human hosts who would die wretchedly upon giving birth; and the firstborn of the first set would forever be required as a sacrifice of atonement for the sins of their forefathers.

Staggered by the enormity of *The Curse*, Prince Jadon, whose own hands had never shed blood, begged his accuser for leniency and received *four small mercies*—four exceptions to the curse that would apply to his house and his descendants, alone.

Ψ Though still creatures of the night, they would be allowed to walk in the sun.

Ψ Though still required to live on blood, they would not be forced to take the lives of the innocent.

Ψ While still incapable of producing female offspring, they would be given *one opportunity and thirty days* to obtain a mate—a human *destiny* chosen by the gods—following a sign that appeared in the heavens.

Ψ While they were still required to sacrifice a firstborn son, their twins would be born as one child of darkness and one child of light, allowing them to sacrifice the former while keeping the latter to carry on their race.

And so...forever banished from their homeland in the Transylvanian mountains of Eastern Europe, the descendants of

BLOOD REDEMPTION

Jaegar and the descendants of Jadon became the Vampyr of legend: roaming the earth, ruling the elements, living on the blood of others...forever bound by an ancient curse. They were brothers of the same species, separated only by degrees of light and shadow.

Prologue

Sunday — before sunrise

Damien Alexiares paced the floor in his underground lair, feeling the confinement of the colony more acutely than he had ever felt it before. His stomach literally hurt, and the helplessness that consumed him made him want to fly off in a rage and commit indiscriminate murder. The sun would rise at six thirty-five AM, and with its arrival, he would lose his eldest living son, Saber.

And there wasn't a damn thing he could do to stop it.

Even if they were willing to go to war, they could not survive the sunlight.

Leaning back against the cold stone wall of his underground lair, he stared at his remaining sons, Dane and Diablo, wondering if the waiting was killing them as much as it was killing him.

Dane bared his fangs and scowled. "Why can't we go get him—before the sun comes up?" He had already asked the same question at least a dozen times. For a 600-year-old male, he was sometimes a little slow to catch on.

"You and whose army?" Diablo said with a scowl.

"The sons of Jadon aren't gods!" Dane stormed, his face twisting with rage. "Why doesn't anyone believe we can take them?"

Damien sighed, determined to try once again to provide his youngest son with an explanation. "Male to male, one-to-one, of course we can. They have no powers we do not also possess—may the strongest soldier win—but as a group? Our colony against their army? It's a different matter entirely."

"Why?" Dane demanded.

"Because they have Napolean, and even under the cover of

BLOOD REDEMPTION

night, he can channel the power of the sun. We can't fight in the daylight, and we can't fight in the light of Napolean's being."

Dane laughed derisively. "The king has never supported an all-out war between our houses, and he won't support one now." He squared his jaw defiantly. "It was different when he came to rescue the princess; she was a valuable commodity, an irreplaceable relic in the house of Jadon, but outside of that one incident, when has Napolean Mondragon ever done anything other than break up the wars and keep both sides from destroying each other and, more important, from killing thousands in the human population? I'm telling you, one expedition will not become a war!"

Diablo pulled his hair in frustration. "It's not just that, Dane. Who in the house of Jaegar will die just to bring Saber back safely?"

"Lots of males will fight to the death for Saber!" Dane was practically incensed now, the veins in his forehead throbbing, his blood beginning to boil. "Saber has led hunting parties for decades, stood as a loyal and faithful servant to the house of Jaegar—hell, that's how he got caught, doing the council's dirty work—don't tell me there is no one who will fight for our brother!" He sprang from his chair, and Damien intercepted him before he could wrap his arms around his twin brother's neck.

"Your hatred is misplaced, Dane. I know this is killing you, but attacking Diablo isn't going to bring Saber back."

"Bring Saber back?" Dane echoed frenetically. "You act as if he's already dead."

Damien stiffened, stilling himself against the pain of Dane's words. It was just too much to bear. Stepping outside of the room for a fresh breath of air, he seriously considered petitioning the dark lords—or even the celestial gods—whichever set of deities might be most inclined to save his son, for help.

And wasn't that just the dilemma of the past eight centuries—as well as the greatest lie he had ever told? The most seditious secret?

Which group of deities was he to petition?

Damien rubbed his palm against the cold, abrasive wall and then scratched a mysterious symbol into the stone with a hardened claw. Placing his palm over the pictogram to hide it, he hung his head in shame, remembering the night of Saber's birth. Recalling everything he had done. Wishing like hell that he could just go back in time and have that moment to do over, he shook his head in confusion: Would he, though, do things any differently, that is?

Damien had brutalized the frail human woman for days, before viciously mounting her in order to sire his first set of twins—surely, there was nothing he would have done differently there. The female had been a small, diminutive woman of little consequence: In fact, he could hardly remember if her hair had been brown or blond. He did remember, however, that she had put up quite a struggle on the sacrificial stone as his twin sons clawed their way out of her fragile body, tearing through her innards, shattering her ribs, and forcing their way into the world. He had been forced to incinerate her corpse almost immediately in response to the horrific smell, and then he had turned his attention directly to his duty: to the requirement of the Blood Curse—sacrificing the firstborn son.

He moaned at the strength of the memory. He had turned his back on the second-born child, the one who would live, for only a second—*just one second*—while he had placed the firstborn child on the altar.

But that one second had been one too many. Far too long.

Why had he set the baby down?

The decision, as he thought back on it, was incomprehensible. Maybe he had wanted to keep his living child far, far away from the greedy clutches of the Blood, lest the vengeful spirit get confused and take them both. Or maybe he had just been so full of hubris, heady from the power of the rape and kill and the ensuing birth, that he had thought himself and his children invincible.

Damien Alexiares had been wrong.

BLOOD REDEMPTION

Dead wrong.

And his remaining son had paid with his life when the human brother of the woman he had violated, a vampire-hunter on top of everything else, had stormed into the cavern and sprayed the child with diamond-tipped bullets, tossing him into the very fire that consumed his sister in his lust for revenge.

Damien had flown into a virulent rage. He had been utterly inconsolable. On one hand, the Blood had come for his firstborn son, taking him in an eternal cycle of vengeance that never ceased, even as, on the other hand, the brother of the worthless piece of trash he had used to incubate his children had put his second son to death.

He had been absolutely devastated—just as he was now.

Rendering himself invisible, Damien Alexiares had shredded that brazen vampire-hunter into a thousand pieces of so much trash, sending him to whatever afterlife his sister now inhabited. Yet even that had not been enough. He had stewed and paced and spat in a red haze of fury, until, in a rare moment of clarity, he had remembered the house of Jadon and the recent Blood Moon: that damnable, taunting sign that appeared in the heavens whenever a son of Jadon was given his *destiny*...and his own twin sons.

In the midst of his grief and rage, Damien had somehow recalled the fact that the sign had occurred exactly thirty days before: The celestial god Serpens had showered his favor on one of the sons of Jadon, giving him thirty days to claim his *destiny*, bear twin sons of his own, and sacrifice the Dark One of the two progeny to the Blood.

It didn't require any divination to figure out who the chosen male was, or to obtain the name of his human *destiny*: Such things were common knowledge in the house of Jaegar, and whenever they could, the Dark Ones used that knowledge to strike out at their formidable enemies of light. Indeed, the male had been a Master Warrior, not yet an Ancient, named Rafael Dzuna; and his destiny had been a human woman passing through the valley by the name of Lorna. A quick trip to the upper hall of annals, and Damien had garnered the name of their surviving son: Sabino Dzuna, born under the ruling moon of the god Serpens, child of light to a sacrificed twin of darkness.

Had Damien's own tragedy occurred only a couple of hours earlier, he might have had a chance to steal the dark twin, the child that was to be turned over to the Curse, but fate had not blessed him so that day.

Thinking of Saber now, how could he wish that? The dark lords of hell could not have given him a better son than the one he had taken on that fateful night.

Sabino.

Saber.

He smiled at the memory, even as his heart wept from the knowledge of his impending loss. Eight hundred years ago, the Light Vampyr had lived in hidden cliff dwellings as well as sparse stone lodgings that were much more spread apart. As attacks from Dark Ones were infrequent, they were generally carefree in their comings and goings.

Taking Sabino—Saber—from his crib had been as easy as taking blood from a human baby, hardly sport at all. But the moment he had looked into those dark eyes, he had known…this was his son for all time.

And so it came to pass: He had brought the light infant back to the colony and passed him off as the child he had lost, a son of his own blood, subject to the approval of the dark lord S'nepres—the twin energy of Serpens, residing in the abyss. When at last he bathed the child in his own blood, and S'nepres consecrated the babe by turning his hair a true crimson and black, like those of the males born to the house of Jaegar, Damien had known it was fate.

Providence.

Always meant to be.

For whatever reason, his true firstborn son had been lost, but Sabino Dzuna, inaugurated with the name Saber, had simply and divinely taken the lost child's place. And 200 years later, when Damien had decided to kidnap and violate another human woman in order to sire more sons, he had been allowed to keep both of the twins: Dane and Diablo.

His family had been complete.

Only now, he would lose one of his own, the most precious to his rotting soul.

Saber.

Damien stared at the symbol he had etched into the wall, the pictogram representing the celestial deity Serpens, and quickly scratched it out, lest the dark lord S'nepres strike him dead where he stood. Would S'nepres answer his prayer now and save Saber? Demons rarely delighted in the giving of life, but if he prayed to Serpens, the true god of Saber's birth, would even Serpens care enough to help the child now?

He hung his head in despair and fury.

By all that was unholy, Saber was going to die.

Saber Alexiares tugged at the ties that bound him to the post, knowing that he was too weak from blood loss to break free or escape. As he glanced toward the eastern horizon, his heart sank in his soulless chest.

The sun.

That great ball of fire that journeyed every day from the east to the west…

Entire civilizations of humans had worshipped it throughout history; many more counted on it to give life to the trees and the plants of the fields today; but to his kind, the sons of Jaegar, it was an abomination, a scourge of nature to be feared above all else.

The sun was dreaded more than the vampire-hunting societies, the Lycans, or even the males in the house of Jadon— for its rays meant certain death. And not an easy or painless passing, but the slow, insidious cleansing of darkness by light. A purging by fire that was said to burn like acid flowing through the veins, like alcohol permeating an open wound, to pierce the skin and the internal organs like a thousand blades of steel, each one sharper and more finely honed than the last, rendering the dying vampire incapacitated by an agony that assaulted his mind, body, and soul without mercy.

It was a final reckoning that no one dared provoke. And even young boys were taught to flee from its light, to dive away from busted windows in desperation, to calculate their comings and goings from the colony with infinite precision for one reason and one reason only: to always, *always* avoid the sun. The fear of the sun was more than ingrained or conditioned; it was instinctive and all-consuming.

Despite his desperate attempt at courage, Saber's heart thundered in his chest, and he refused to meet the eyes of his accusers, not because the warriors in the house of Jadon intimidated him—and not because he gave a damn what they thought—but because his mind was too consumed by primordial terror to focus on who was in front of him. Eight hundred years of conditioning had stricken terror into his soul, and his vision was growing blurry beneath the onslaught of fear.

He hung his head forward, not wanting to meet the sun with his gaze when, at last, it rose over the horizon. From all he had been told, the first rays burned the orbs right out of their sockets, and then it began to penetrate the brain—

"Stop!" he commanded himself, helpless to get control over the fear. "Do not think about it."

In his debilitating state of weakness, he swayed where he stood, hanging from two posts like a sacrificial lamb, and then he prayed to the dark lord of his birth that the demon might take his soul before the sun began to scorch him: Even the tortures of hell were a welcome substitute compared to what would soon be rising over the canyon.

Saber felt a sickening wave of nausea wash over him, and he struggled not to vomit in front of his enemies. And then he saw the faintest glimpse of something he had never expected to behold in all of his 800 years.

BLOOD REDEMPTION

Natural, solar light.

The sun peeking its blazing face over the horizon.

Terror seized him like a vise, and the air rushed out of his body. Every instinct, every ounce of training he had received over the centuries, assailed him at once, demanding flight. Demanding that he flee to the shade.

He had to get out of the sun!

Summoning whatever strength he had left, Saber succumbed to pure hysteria, his mind a red haze of insanity.

Get out of the sun! Get out of the sun!

The light! The light!

The sounds that came from his throat were inhuman; the contortions of his body, as he bucked and pulled and twisted and turned in a feverish attempt to break his bonds, were desperately grotesque. His arms snapped like twigs, and the vertebrae in his spine popped like corn behind the effort, yet he still continued to struggle mightily, his frenzied psyche driving him over a ledge from which he would never return. The flesh on his feet grew bloodied and torn as the appendages tore against the stones on the ground. As he tried in vain to run.

Run!

But the air wouldn't move through his lungs!

His body wouldn't budge—not even when he broke his wrists in an effort to free his hands from the manacles.

Saber could not escape.

As his world became nothing but a living, breathing ball of fire, scorching away even the last remnants of what had been his sanity, Saber Alexiares descended into a world of madness where the sun was the devil, and he was the greatest sinner on earth.

Napolean Mondragon watched in morbid fascination as the macabre scene played out before him. He had sentenced Dark Ones to die in the sun before, and the brutal taking of their bodies by the great ball of fire had never been a pleasant thing to witness, but this was beyond gruesome.

Beyond comprehension.

The male tied to the stake was suffering unlike any other he had ever seen, but not from the sun's rays, and not because his wicked body, soul, and mind were burning.

He was suffering because his flesh remained untouched.

Saber Alexiares was not burning in the sun!

And that simply wasn't possible.

Napolean turned to Nachari Silivasi and the council of wizards who sat beside him on the ground, those with a front row seat to the execution. "What is this?" he demanded.

Niko Durciak shook his head. "Milord, he isn't—"

"Burning?" Napolean clipped, his impatience getting the best of him. *By all that was holy, would somebody stop that screaming?* He had never seen the likes of it. "Why not?" he demanded.

Nachari Silivasi turned his attention inward and began to chant softly beneath his breath, trying desperately to divine what his sovereign lord requested. And then, in an abrupt halt, he raised his head and furrowed his brows. "I heard something, but I don't know what it means."

"You don't know what *what* means?" Napolean asked calmly. He had to keep his composure despite the ghastly display persisting in the canyon.

"The word that comes to me is *Serpens.*"

"Serpents?" Napolean asked, seeking clarification. "Snakes?"

"No, milord," Nachari answered. "Serpens. Like the celestial deity of rebirth."

Napolean spun around, trying to make sense of Nachari's words. He stared at the spectacle taking place before him, his own heart now racing in his chest, while his mind processed what he had been told: *Serpens...the celestial deity of rebirth.*

All at once, understanding dawned, and the earth stood still around him. "Who has the keys to the manacles?" he shouted.

There was a moment of confusion as the warriors searched their pockets and coats. Finally, Ramsey Olaru stepped forward.

"I have them, milord, but why…" His voice trailed off in disbelief. Clearly, he couldn't even form the question because the meaning was so absurd: *Why would they release the Dark One?*

Napolean gestured toward the keys and met Ramsey's stare head-on. "Get him down from there and take him out of the sun—before he kills himself with fright."

"Milord?" Ramsey's voice was harsh with disapproval.

"He isn't from the house of Jaegar, and he isn't going to burn," Napolean explained.

Nachari's eyes widened and he took a step back. "I don't understand."

Napolean blinked several times and slowly shook his head. "Somebody find Rafael and Lorna Dzuna; I believe this male is their son."

one

The red haze of madness that enveloped Saber Alexiares began to dissipate slowly; first, in small increments of lucidity—thoughts and feelings broke through the darkness like distant pieces of a conversation drifting from another room—and finally, in larger blocks of acute awareness, until, at last, he sat up straight on the narrow cot beneath him, swung his aching legs to the side, and stood on unsteady feet.

The room still spun around him, and he grasped his head in both hands. "What the hell happened?" he muttered beneath his breath. Memories began to flood his cerebellum in disjointed pictures: the torture and questioning that went on for days; the sons of Jadon draining his body of blood to the point of veritable weakness, nearly death; being strapped to the posts in the Red Canyon while awaiting his final execution by…the sun.

Oh dark lords, the sun.

He ran his hands furiously up and down his body, testing for substance and injuries: first, his arms and legs; next, his chest and torso; and finally, his back and head.

Nothing.

Everything seemed to be intact, neither melted nor burned.

What was he—dead or alive? Where was he? In the colony or the Valley of Death and Shadows? Instinctively, he tried to reach out to his brothers with telepathy, but the transmission hit a firm, implacable barrier. Something was blocking the wavelength.

He spun around in wild circles, a dangerous predator, confused and alert, trying to scent his enemy. His eyes swept the long, narrow cot beside him, raised to assess the two small windows at the top of the cell—there was light shining through the openings!—and quickly flicked to the thick iron bars, each imbedded with thousands of inset diamonds that locked him into the cell.

A feral hiss escaped his lips as he spun around again, glaring outside the bars at a huge figure pacing back and forth. He would know that six-foot-five, muscle-bound frame anywhere. He should—after all, he had worn it for weeks during his plot to kill Kristina Silivasi and ultimately, Nachari's new *destiny*, Deanna.

It was Ramsey Olaru.

And the cocky, self-important sentinel was standing post as a guard.

"Hey, you," Saber growled, more confused than ever. "What the hell is going on? Where am I? What happened?"

The sentinel turned around lazily, and a slow, derisive smile curved the corners of his mouth. "Well, would you look here; it would appear the dead has risen."

Saber flew at the bars, grabbing two thick slabs with clenched fists and wrenching back. When the iron didn't budge, he spat in Ramsey's direction. "Open the door, son of Jadon! Open the door, and we'll see what has or hasn't risen!"

Ramsey slowly shook his head from side to side, chiding Saber with a tsk-tsk of the tongue: "Really, Saber? Is all that bravado truly necessary?" He sighed, slow and long. "After all, I just watched you scream and holler like a stuck pig in front of the entire house of Jadon." He cringed, his face wrinkling up in disgust. "Extremely unbecoming of a soldier, wouldn't you say?"

Saber took a measured step back from the bars and stared at the ground beneath him. The floor was made of stone and mortar, and there were enough diamonds imbedded in the stones to start a new mine. The sturdy walls, which appeared no less than six feet thick, were made of the same material—there was no way he was tunneling out of the place or using his superior vampiric strength to crash through the barrier. So, what the hell had happened then?

Clearly, Ramsey did not belong in the Valley of Death and Shadows, which meant Saber couldn't have perished in the sun. But why not ? What. The. Hell?

Tessa Dawn

Saber sat down slowly on the cot, realizing he was still incredibly weak. His blood volume felt almost nonexistent, which meant that his enemy wasn't taking any chances—the sons of Jadon were still keeping him drained of life force. His throat felt parched. "I need to feed," he mumbled absently, to no one in particular.

Ramsey approached the bars then, actually sauntered up within clawing reach as if he didn't have a care in the world. "Sorry, Chief: The kitchen is closed for a while. At least for you."

Saber shook his head, wishing he could clear the cobwebs. Something must have gone wrong. Maybe the sun never came up. Maybe the sons of Jadon had decided to keep him a little longer, torture him for more information before offering him to that great fiery orange ball in the sky. He rubbed his temples. *But why?* He could've sworn he had been in that meadow…dying.

Maybe it had all been a bad dream, a terrible nightmare. He groaned as he began to accept the possibility: This meant he would have to do it all over again. Great lords, he would have to find a way to commit suicide. He simply could not endure what he had gone through in that dream: waiting for the sun's wrath, his body giving way to full-fledged panic, his mind descending into an endless pit of insanity.

Ramsey watched him like a hawk, his gold-speckled, hazel eyes flickering with amusement as well as condescension. "I guess this means I'm going to have to start calling you *brother*," he said mockingly, a deep taunting laughter echoing in his throat. "How d'ya like them apples?"

Saber swung both legs back onto the cot and reclined gingerly—he wasn't feeling well.

At all.

He shut his eyes to stop the room from spinning and drew in a slow, deep breath. "What the hell are you talking about, asshole?" He opened one eye and peeked at Ramsey through his peripheral vision.

Ramsey raised one muscle-bound arm above his head, rested

3

it on the outside of the bars, and leaned in toward him. "I'm talking about your predicament, *brother.*"

Saber snarled instinctively, and the pit of his stomach turned queasy. "You got something to say—say it."

Ramsey's face lit up with unbridled anticipation. "Oh, yeah. I've got a whole helluva lot to say, Chief."

Saber shifted back and forth on the cot, trying to find a more comfortable position. He was naked from the waist up, wearing a pair of loose-fitting scrubs on the bottom, and the heavy wool blanket beneath him was scratching his back. "This century?" he mocked.

Ramsey shrugged, his demeanor nonchalant. "This century. Last century. Hell, the last eight centuries, apparently."

Saber frowned. "Quit talking in riddles, Sentinel."

Leaning next to the heavy iron door of the cell, Ramsey pushed off the bars; sauntered along the length of the cubicle; and came to stand directly in front of Saber, across from the cot. He planted his feet and squared his shoulders. "Why do you think you're still here?" he asked. His voice was a mere whisper.

Saber shrugged. "I don't know. Because you assholes haven't killed me yet."

Ramsey shook his head. "Try again. We staked you out in the sun all right. It's just…you didn't burn, Chief. Why do you think that is?"

Saber felt momentarily disconnected from his body, virtually cast away from reality. "What are you talking about?"

"Don't you remember?" Ramsey asked. "We tied you to the posts and watched…waited…as the sun rose high in the sky and poured all those wonderful gamma rays all over you, head to toe. And you? You just screamed and writhed and panicked like a stuck pig, but nothing happened. You didn't burn. Now, I repeat: Why do you think that is?"

Saber opened both eyes and turned his head in Ramsey's direction. So, it hadn't been a dream then. He shook his head, confused. "I…I…" His voice trailed off.

"You didn't burn because you aren't who you think you are."

Ramsey's voice was strong with insistence. "Your real name is Sabino Dzuna. You were born eight hundred years ago under the Serpens Blood Moon to your real parents, Rafael and Lorna Dzuna. Apparently, someone from the house of Jaegar wanted a baby and took you." He paused, apparently for effect. "You've been raised all this time with the hyenas, only to find out you were meant to be a lion. Damn, that's rough, brother."

Saber shot off the cot in a rage, his large crimson-and-black wings shooting instinctively from his back as he flew at the cage and swiped a clawed hand at Ramsey.

The sentinel simply backed away. "Don't blame me; I'm just the messenger."

"You're a lying piece of—"

"Whoa, brother." Ramsey held both hands up in front of him. "I'm a lot of wicked things, but a liar isn't one of them."

Saber hissed and snarled, wishing like hell he could come through the bars, if only for a second. He would tear the miserable bastard to shreds. Sabino Dzuna—what the hell kind of name was that? And what the hell kind of game were these fools trying to play? He ran his hands through his thick mane of hair—hair filled with characteristic red and black bands—the signature coronet of the Dark Ones, the crown of the King Cobra. The irrefutable proof that he was exactly who he knew he was: a son born of Damien Alexiares and some unfortunate human wench. A soldier in the house of Jaegar. "You're full of it, *brother*," he mocked in return.

Ramsey remained undaunted. "All right, believe what you want, but tell me then—why didn't you burn, Saber?"

Just then, a powerful male rounded the corner just outside the cell and began to walk in Saber's direction. His purposeful gate, regal shoulders, and the way he held his head up as if the earth and moon would bow down to him at will left no question as to who the male was: Saber Alexiares was staring at the ancient king of the house of Jadon, the formidable warrior who had lived from the time of the original Blood Curse, Napolean Mondragon, himself.

5

Despite his anger, he stepped away from the door. When Napolean simply passed through the bars without bothering to unlock the cage or open the door—the king moved through the considerable diamond barrier as if it wasn't even there!—Saber took a healthy step backward.

Holy crap.

He had never seen anything like that. The male was immune to the absolute powers of diamonds. Unheard of.

"Greetings," the ancient king said. His long black hair, with silver stripes of antique highlights interspersed throughout, swayed ever so slightly as he moved, and his predatory eyes flashed like molten fire. "Sit," he said, gesturing toward the cot.

Saber was not one to take direction so easily. Under any other circumstances, he would have told the male where to go and how to get there, but there was just something in the powerful leader's eyes that backed him up, something that said not only could Napolean kill him with a glance, but he wouldn't hesitate if Saber defied him. Scowling, Saber took a step back and sat on the cot.

Napolean glided forward, his harsh, ancient eyes boring into Saber's. "I am your king, whether you know it or not, and you *will* avert your gaze when you are in my presence."

Saber blanched. *What the hell?* Had the entire world gone mad? What he wouldn't give to rip those haughty eyes right out of the king's head. Still, discretion was sometimes the better part of valor, and he was at too great a disadvantage right now. Hell, he didn't even know what was real. He lowered his head and stared at the floor, all the while seething in his soul.

"Better," Napolean said. He walked right up to the edge of the cot, not even remotely concerned that Saber posed any threat, and squatted down in front of him.

Squatted down in front of him.

Making himself vulnerable.

Was he really that sure of himself?

Such a thing was like holding an arm behind one's back while facing a tiger; reaching out to slap a towering grizzly bear;

6

or exposing one's belly to an alpha wolf—the ancient king was in the most vulnerable position imaginable, and he was obviously doing it for effect, to make a point: *I can and will destroy you at will, and I don't even have to feign concern.*

Saber swallowed hard, feeling his Adam's apple bob up and down, and his lips turned up in a sneer. Still, he held his tongue.

"Good boy," Napolean said. "Now then, our wizards have been able to discern a great deal of information over the past hour or so." He paused to let his words sink in. "Eight hundred years ago, following the Serpens Blood Moon, a child from the house of Jadon was stolen out of his crib following the Blood Sacrifice of his dark twin by his father, Rafael Dzuna. You were that child, Saber, and it would appear that your abductor, whom we now know was Damien Alexiares, beseeched the Dark Lord S'nepres to consecrate you into the house of Jaegar." His eyes swept over Saber's hair. "Perhaps this is why you have crimson-and-black hair—we don't fully understand the extent of the dark magic that was performed on your behalf." He glanced around the room absently before meeting Saber's gaze once more. "We do know, however, that you still have a soul"—he swept his hand out in a derisive gesture—"such as it is, or you would have surely perished in the sun." He reached out his powerful hand and clasped Saber's face boldly by the jaw. "What we don't know is if there is anything worth saving inside of you; if your soul is not beyond redemption."

Saber jerked away, his sharp fangs instinctively shooting forth in his mouth, even as his lips curled back in a snarl of warning.

Napolean didn't react. "My sentinels will take you to shower, and you will clean yourself up." His nose turned up in disgust. "Remove this stench. And we will keep you here, for a time, in this cell, alive but weak...harmless. You will be given enough blood to sustain your life, but not enough to rejuvenate, while we consider—while I consider—your fate. Is that understood?"

Saber had never wanted to destroy anything in all his life—to kill anyone—more than he wanted to kill this haughty being in front of him. There was no way he was going to agree to such absurdity. He knew who he was, and the entire house of Jadon could be damned. Bring on the sun…again. Bring on the Valley of Death and Shadows. He was Saber Mikhael Alexiares, firstborn son to Damien Alexiares, brother to Diablo and Dane, and soldier in the house of Jaegar. Nothing, absolutely nothing, would ever change that. And these light vampires, these scourges of nature who strutted around as if they were entitled to all the favors the gods had bestowed upon them, they could weave all the fanciful tales they wanted trying to convince him otherwise. He knew better.

Saber Alexiares was the devil's son, and that's who he intended to remain.

Forever.

"You may as well kill me now," he snarled. "I'd rather descend into the pit of hell to live as a slave to demons than ascend to this mockery of manhood you call the house of Jadon. I don't believe you. Not one word. And given half a chance—any chance—I will kill the first of your kind that I can: man, woman, or child. It makes no difference to me."

Napolean looked off into the distance before slowly turning back to regard the Dark One. He nodded slowly and then smiled ever so faintly. *Smiled.* "Perhaps," he said coolly. "Perhaps. But the hour of your death—or the content of your life—will be up to me, not you." With that, he reached out and grabbed Saber's forearm. When Saber tried to wrench it away, his entire body froze, paralyzed; and he was suddenly seized by indescribable pain, racked with an agonizing sense of nothingness, the utter absence of personal power.

As the infamous king of the house of Jadon slowly released his fangs and bent his head to Saber's wrist, everything in Saber's soul rebelled. *No!* This could not be happening. This simply could not be real.

Please…

Two lethal canines sank deep into Saber's wrist, Napolean's jaw locking down with such force that the radius bone beneath it split in two, while the unyielding king drank Saber's blood.

The room spun in maddening circles.

The pain brought him up short.

The power that swirled around him crashed against him in violent waves of nausea, yet he sat there, helpless, locked in the compulsion of the greatest being to ever walk the earth, as the king took his due from what he believed to be one of his subjects.

When at last the king withdrew his fangs, licked his taut lips, and released Saber's arm, a scourge like fire burning through a grass field coursed through Saber's veins.

"I carry the blood of every child born into the house of Jadon in my veins," Napolean explained. "And you are no exception." He leaned forward then, and his piercing eyes flashed with an intensity Saber had never seen before: a clear and unmistakable warning. "Know this, Sabino Dzuna. The sun cannot kill you. Its rays cannot scorch you, but should you harm one hair on the head of one of my subjects, I will destroy you one cell, one strand of DNA, at a time; you will pray for mercy, but none will be forthcoming. You believe you know what pain and suffering are, but you do not. Pray you do not have to find out." With that, the ancient king rose, nodded his head as if they had just been talking about the weather, and strode to the edge of the cell, without ever looking back.

Saber watched in horror as the king passed through the bars once more, without bothering to open the door, and then the ancient one turned to Ramsey Olaru. "Get him cleaned up."

Ramsey's head declined in a nod, and the pit bull's ferocious nature seemed all at once subdued. "As you wish, milord."

With that, the king simply vanished into thin air.

two

Vanya Demir rearranged the sundry items on her oak writer's desk and reached for her lavender cell phone. It was late in Colorado, she knew, but her homesickness was getting the best of her. She simply needed to hear her sister's voice. Dialing the digits slowly and carefully—these modern devices were vexing at best—she waited for someone in the Silivasi household to answer.

When at last Ciopori picked up the phone, she sighed with pleasure. It was so nice to hear her sister's voice. "Princess," Vanya said by way of greeting.

Ciopori chuckled in response. "Princess," she said.

Vanya smiled. "You sound wide awake—I thought you might be sleeping."

Ciopori groaned. "No such luck, Vanya. Nikolai has been up all night, bouncing around the house like a beach ball—I think Marquis played with him long past his bedtime." She sighed. "It is so lovely to hear your voice. How are you, sister?"

Vanya tried to keep her voice cheery. "I miss you terribly, Ciopori. And Nikolai." She paused. "I know I've only been in Romania for eight weeks, but I fear it is time for a visit just the same."

"Have you changed your mind about living there?" Ciopori asked, sounding hopeful. "You know you are always welcome with us. Marquis would be happy to—"

"No...*no*," Vanya interrupted. "My work here is important, as well as fulfilling—it is truly where I belong. But I think I may need to wean off of my family more slowly." She chuckled halfheartedly. "I see no reason why I cannot travel back and forth and still do what is needed for my people." Vanya was referring to the decision she had shared with Napolean: the commitment she had made to use her status as a surviving,

11

original female to teach at the Romanian University, thereby restoring the ancient knowledge of celestial magic, a way of life practiced only by the original females of their kind, to the house of Jadon.

Ciopori's voice came alive with energy. "Of course! I'm so pleased to hear this. We should get out our schedules and plan something soon then."

"That isn't necessary," Vanya said. "I have already seen to the arrangements."

"What do you mean?" Ciopori asked.

Vanya tittered softly. "I mean I will be there late Monday, around midnight."

Ciopori was quiet, obviously trying to digest Vanya's words.

"It's eight AM here," Vanya said absently, knowing that her sister intuitively knew the time difference; Ciopori was a celestial princess, after all, intimately connected with the stars and the moon and the planets. "I've chartered the house of Jadon's private plane," Vanya offered by way of explanation, "and I will be departing within the hour. I can sleep this night on the plane, and I should arrive at the Dark Moon Vale airstrip around midnight tomorrow, your time, of course." She sighed. "As you can see, my bags are packed, and I'm eager to travel."

Ciopori cleared her throat. "Wow…well, that is unexpected. However, it is wonderful news. I trust you will stay with Marquis and me?"

"For most of the time," Vanya said. "I don't wish to interfere with your household—you are still newlyweds, you know."

"Yes," Ciopori agreed, "newlyweds with a five-and-a half-month-old baby, hurricane Nikolai."

Vanya laughed wholeheartedly. "Oh, I can't wait to see him. Is he getting big?"

"Growing like a weed," Ciopori said. "Just yesterday, he latched onto a lock of Marquis's hair with his fist and refused to let go. Marquis could not pry his hand loose without hurting his tiny fingers, and by the time it was over, Marquis had a bald spot at the crown of his head." She laughed. "It's already grown back, but it was quite an episode to behold."

Vanya giggled conspiratorially, her reaction a bit too appreciative. "What a spitfire, that one." She regained her composure. "So, it is settled then? I will come directly to your home…for a time."

"Of course," Ciopori answered, and then her voice grew somewhat serious. "Although, you know, Vanya, maybe you should wait a week or two, just to be safe."

"Safe?" Vanya asked, her voice revealing her concern. "Why wouldn't I be safe?"

"It's just…" Ciopori sighed. "I mean, it isn't anything serious, but there is a Dark One in our midst now, and I must admit, the whole thing is a bit creepy."

Vanya inhaled sharply, not liking the sound of her sister's words. "A Dark One? Whatever for? I thought Napolean's hunting teams were exterminating them whenever possible." She breathed uneasily. "I mean, I understand that the dynamics have changed considerably, ever since the Dark Ones have become, shall I say…*emboldened*, but I really don't think that has anything to do with me or you. Our king will keep us safe. Not to mention Marquis."

Ciopori sighed. "Of course. *Of course.* It's just this is an entirely different situation. The warriors captured a Dark One two weeks ago—he was plotting against the house of Jadon as usual, trying to use Kristina in order to get to the Silivasis."

"Oh, my!" Vanya exclaimed. "Is Kristina okay?"

"Yes…well, she is now. He certainly hurt her when he went after both she and Nachari's *destiny*." Before Vanya could ask, Ciopori added, "It's a very long story. I will fill you in on the details when you get here. Just suffice to say that Nachari is back, he is mated, and he has a beautiful son, Sebastian; and the Dark One who tried to destroy him survived an execution by sun just earlier this morning."

Vanya started. She shifted uncomfortably on her bed, and her mind began to race. "Sister! Why haven't you called me?

There is so much going on!"

"I know, I know. I'm sorry. I was going to pick up the phone this week, but like I said, there's just been so much going on."

"And email or text?" Vanya asked, her voice taking on a slight note of chiding.

"Yeah, I know. I'm sorry. Still not my favorite modes of communication."

"No," Vanya agreed, "I suppose they aren't mine, either." She flashed back to Ciopori's recent words. "But this Dark One, you say he survived an execution by sun? How is such a thing even possible?"

Ciopori whistled low beneath her breath, sounding a bit like her brother-in-law Nathaniel. "Because, as it turns out, he wasn't really born to the house of Jaegar." She quickly explained all they had discovered since that morning, while Vanya sat in stunned silence.

"Wow…I hardly know what to say," Vanya finally said.

"I know," Ciopori agreed. "It's bizarre to say the least."

"I imagine Napolean has his hands full then."

Ciopori grew silent, as if unsure about how to proceed. They both knew that it was a touchy subject: Vanya and Napolean had shared a brief but very intense…connection …before the king had found his *destiny*; and there would always be a special place in Vanya's heart for the ancient male, independent of his position as ruler of the house of Jadon.

Finally, when the silence had lingered to the point of becoming awkward, Vanya said, "Well, I don't see how that places either of us in jeopardy, let alone myself. I'm sure I will have nothing at all to do with this…new member of the house of Jadon."

"Of course not," Ciopori agreed. "I just…the thought of us keeping him alive, perhaps allowing him to move in and out of the valley—among our people at some point—it just really causes me concern. I mean, how will we ever trust him? And if we have to kill him…his poor parents. They will lose him twice."

"Indeed," Vanya said, feeling more than a little sympathy for all the players involved. How much hurt, suffering, and pain had been caused by one act of selfishness? "His mother must be so relieved…scared yet hopeful. *Appalled*." She closed her eyes and said a gentle prayer to Andromeda, the goddess who had birthed six sons in Greek legend: *Please, if it is your will, touch the hearts of this family and redeem the soul of this lost one; surely, his life must still have value…to someone.*

Just then, an odd tingling sensation settled against her breast, and her heart skipped a beat. She shook it off, thinking perhaps the goddess had heard her prayer. "Now then," she said to Ciopori, "I won't hear another word of it. I have complete faith in our warriors and the benevolence of the gods. Whatever is happening with this poor, misguided male has nothing to do with me or our family, so I will not hear another word of it. I will see you on the morrow, yes?"

Vanya could practically envision Ciopori's smile as her warmth radiated through the phone. "Yes," Ciopori agreed. "I will have your room ready, and I can't wait to see you."

"Very well, to my uneventful homecoming then."

"To your much anticipated homecoming," Ciopori corrected. With that, she hung up the phone.

three

It was late Sunday night, nearly 11:15 PM, when the outer door to the Chamber of Sacrifice and Atonement flew open, crashing into the wall behind it, and a short, diminutive woman with medium brown hair and the most compassionate dark brown eyes Saber had ever seen flew through the threshold. She stumbled into the guard-check area, barely catching her footing as she stopped between the chamber and Saber's cell.

Ramsey intercepted her immediately. "Whoa, wait a minute, Lorna. Slow down." He restrained her by her arms, his broad chest and wide shoulders blocking her view of the prisoner. "This isn't the boy you remember."

The female struggled mightily to break free, rocking back and forth from one foot to another in a desperate attempt to get a glimpse beyond the warrior's shoulders. "I understand, Sentinel. I do. Let me go." Her voice was insistent.

Ramsey slowly released her. "Stay away from the bars," he warned.

The woman nodded several times and then immediately headed toward the cell, flanked by both Ramsey and his brother Santos, the long, flowing ruffles of her knee-length skirt rustling as she walked. She stopped just short of the bars, raised her gaze to appraise the prisoner, and then gasped in surprise, both hands flying up to her cheeks. "Oh, my gods," she whispered, her kind eyes brimming with tears. "It *is* you."

Saber rotated on the cot nervously and glared at the gawking woman. "Who the hell are you?" he barked defensively.

She smiled, her narrow cheeks softening with joy. "I'm...I am your mother...Lorna."

Her voice was barely audible, but Saber heard her clearly. He recoiled and shuffled back on the cot, and then his eyes shifted to Ramsey and flashed with anger. "Get this woman out of my face!"

The female paled, but she held her ground. "It's okay," she said to Ramsey as he held out a hand, prepared to escort her out of the room. "Give us some space."

Ramsey eyed Santos warily, and the two took a slight step back, maybe about an inch.

"Sabino," she whispered, measuring him quickly from head to toe. "How are you? Are you in pain? Do you need anything?"

Saber chuckled loud and haughtily then, his dark, angry eyes narrowing with contempt. "What the hell do you want?"

"Just to…" She had to stop and collect herself. "Just to see you, to know that you're really…alive."

Saber shrugged and rolled his eyes, amplifying his disgust. "Well, there you go. Alive and well and living above the surface in Dark Moon Vale." His lips twitched, and he didn't bother to conceal a hint of fangs. "As for all this mother-son bullshit, let me make this easy on you, okay ? You're not my mother." He smiled a wicked, incorrigible grin. "My *mother* was a slab of meat on a sacrificial stone that gave my *father* hours and hours of pleasure before he killed her. You are just a scrawny, misguided female who doesn't belong here. Now get out." He released his fangs fully and slowly licked his lips. "Before I get…ugly."

Lorna drew back in surprise and visibly swallowed her fear. As her face melted with disappointment, she brushed a single tear from her eye and shook her head. "I'm sorry," she mewled, "I just—"

"Look, woman; what part of get out—"

The ground beneath the cot rumbled, and the air grew dense with fury, both occurrences cutting Saber off in midsentence; and then a tall, formidable-looking male strode into the guard room with long, measured strides. He stepped all the way up to the bars and glared at Saber with murderous contempt in his eyes. "Watch your mouth, boy!"

"Rafael, don't!" Lorna exclaimed, placing her open palm on the male's chest to restrain him.

Saber stood up and approached the bars. Far be it from him

to retreat from a challenge. If this fool wanted to play, then so be it. He was just about to release his claws and swipe at the warrior's jugular, certain he could move faster than the old geezer could get out of the way, when he caught a really good look at the male's face. The visage brought him up short.

Saber's jaw parted. And his brow furrowed in disbelief.

The male before him was about six feet tall. He had cropped black hair and deep, dark eyes the color of coal, but what really stood out were his features: His nose was straight and prominent with an ever so slightly rounded ridge on the end, just like Saber's; and the vicious look of contempt on his face, the snarl that tugged only at the upper corner of his right, top lip, was an exact match to the snarl Saber had seen in the mirror a dozen times before.

Saber Alexiares was staring into his own reflection, and no one with two eyes in their sockets could deny it.

He cocked his head to the side and studied the male's physique next: tall, muscular, but in a sculpted, sinewy way. Strong but lean. And his narrow hips were more square than V-shaped. His knees turned out *just barely*, as if he had almost been born bowlegged but it hadn't quite happened.

Saber straightened his own legs on impulse, trying to hide the identical condition in his own gait.

What the hell is going on?

The male's eyes flashed with anger. "How dare you speak to your mother like that!"

Saber took the man's measure. "And you are?"

"Rafael," he snarled. "Your father."

Despite his cool indifference, the words struck Saber like the grill of a Mack truck, and Saber backed away. Quickly catching himself, he planted his feet and stared the male down. "My father is Damien Alexiares; I have no idea who you are, old man."

Rafael sneered in disgust, and then he wrapped his arm around Lorna's shoulders—she was rapidly coming unglued, tears streaming down her face, her chest shaking with rising sobs. "Just how many women and children have you murdered?" Rafael snarled. "How many females have you raped?" He shoved Lorna behind him and gripped the bars in two angry fists, practically daring Saber to make a move in his direction. "How much flesh have you consumed, Dark One?"

Saber shrugged his shoulders casually. "Enough."

Rafael spat in disgust. "Well, at least we can agree on one thing, monster; you aren't the child I lost so many years ago— you're no son of mine!"

Lorna gasped and nearly swooned, and Santos had to step forward and catch her. "Oh, gods," she cried inconsolably, "please, Rafael, stop! You don't know what you're saying."

Saber flicked his gaze to hers and shrugged. "Nah, Lorna," he whispered. "It's all good. At least the family reunion is over, and we can all drop the bullshit now. Why don't you go back to your happy little home in your prim, puritan world and mourn the loss of whatever baby you think you once had. Wasn't me then. Isn't me now." He winked at her, returned to the cot, lay down on the mattress, and crossed his feet at the ankles. As he leisurely folded his arms behind his head, he regarded them both through the corner of his eyes.

"Come on, Lorna," Rafael said, his voice brooking no argument. "Let's leave this monster in his cell."

Lorna sidestepped around her large mate and boldly stepped up to the bars, where she leveled a devastated gaze at Saber. "Napolean is a just king; he rules with a fair and steady hand. He will not deny you basic comforts." She raised her chin. "I will not allow him to." She swallowed hard and pushed on. "If there is anything you need, send word through the sentinels, and I will try to get it for you." She placed her hand over her heart and brushed away another falling tear. "You're alive; that is all I need to know." She smiled faintly then. "It is enough." With that, she turned and rushed out of the room.

Saber didn't stir.

He didn't move a muscle.

Not only was he completely disinterested in the whole overly dramatic scene, but frankly, he didn't feel a thing.

Nothing.

Whatever these vampires thought—whatever they referred to as their souls—his had long ago been extinguished. He was, indeed, a monster. If not born, then bred. And he still refused to believe he came from anything other than Damien's seed and a tragic human life. Staring blankly ahead at the one called Rafael, he could appreciate the full measure of hate in the male's eyes.

That he understood intimately.

As the warrior regarded him with silent contempt, Saber sank deeper into the mattress, and something in the pit of his stomach stirred.

He couldn't quite name it—it was too unfamiliar.

And it only lasted a moment.

Nevertheless, it stirred.

four

Dane and Diablo stormed into their father's lair, leaving the heavy wooden door open behind them. Their faces were flushed with anger, their eyes wide with disbelief.

"Have you heard the news?" Dane practically shouted, his wild, dark eyes dazed with confusion. "They say he didn't burn! *Saber.* They say he's still alive."

"What the hell happened?" Diablo demanded.

Damien buried his head in his hands. *Dark Lords, how am I going to talk my way out of this one?* A piece of his heart rejoiced—Saber was still alive—yet the more rational part knew his own days were numbered now that his treason was certain to be uncovered. "I don't know," he mumbled. "I'm still trying to gather information, myself."

"What the hell do you mean, *you don't know?*" Diablo sneered. "Father, what is going on?"

Before Damien could come up with a plausible answer, a band of five soldiers stormed into the room, each bearing the official tattoo of the colony's formal guard on his upper arm. The large circular tattoos undulated like snakes wrapped around hard muscle as each guard clutched his weapon in his right hand and dangled a diamond choker in his left.

The tallest of the five, a seven-foot male named Achilles Zahora, squared off to Damien and cleared his throat. "Damien Alexiares, we have been ordered by the Dark Council to detain you and your sons."

His second-in-command, a shorter, barrel-chested male by the name of Blaise Liska, stepped forward to flank Achilles's side, the gesture issuing an immediate threat to Damien.

Dane spun around in a fury, jumped in front of his father, and pushed Damien behind him. "What the hell are you talking about?" he stormed, impulsive as always. "Back up!" He released a wicked set of fangs and snarled. "I'm not playing with you, Blaise. Back. The. Hell. Up!"

The guard didn't budge, and he was quickly joined by the remaining three soldiers. "Dane..." He softened his voice. "We can do this the easy way or the hard way."

Diablo strolled into the mix then, taking a place beside his brother. "What is *this*?" he asked. He turned to look at his father. "Dad?"

Damien held both hands out in front of him, palms forward, in a gesture of surrender. "Soldiers, please." He drew in a deep breath and gestured toward his sons. "This has nothing to do with my sons; I will go with you peacefully. Just leave my family out of it."

Dane gasped in disbelief, but before he could speak, Achilles stepped forward. "Sorry, Damien. No deal. The council said all of you." A scarlet lock of the soldier's chin-length, black-and-red hair fell forward, blocking his left eye, and he let it hang, undisturbed. His right eye shone by contrast like a laser in the night sky, the oddly pale yet rich citrine color illuminated against his bronze complexion. He held out a pair of diamond-studded handcuffs.

"What are those for?" Diablo demanded, his own ire clearly rising to a dangerous level. The tension in the room could have been sliced with a knife.

"Diablo, don't," Damien said cautiously. He turned to regard Blaise with pleading eyes. "What does the Colony Guard want with my boys?"

"Sorry," the soldier answered. "Not privy to that information. The council speaks; we act."

Damien shook his head in frustration. So, this was what it had come to?

For the briefest moment, he considered fighting, knowing that his boys would have his back. The three of them could take out at least as many soldiers, maybe one more, but ultimately, they could not defeat Achilles or Blaise. The males were too seasoned as soldiers, trained to the nth degree in mortal combat as a way of being—hell, of breathing. The pair would get militant, and Damien and his sons would be subdued. He tried to reason rationally: What could they possibly want with his sons, other than to question them? This calmed him down a bit. *Of course*, questioning; that's all the council wanted. After all, Oskar Vadovsky and his protégés had no idea what had happened eight hundred years ago. All they knew was that a member of the house of Jaegar had been staked to a post in the red canyons, sacrificed to the sun by their enemy, and the male hadn't burned. They weren't stupid. Two plus two was usually four—Dark One plus sun usually equaled death.

They knew Saber was an imposter.

And they wanted to know how…when…why.

Who knew?

Damien would give the chief of council the information he needed, clear his sons of all wrongdoing, and deal with the hand he was dealt afterward. It was his mess to clean up, after all. Looking at his sons, he made an instant decision. He wasn't going to lose anyone else, not today. They were safer surrendering. He held his wrists out in front of him. "Damien, Diablo,"—he put more than a fair amount of authority into his voice—"don't fight this." He eyed them sternly, each one in turn. "I mean it." He paused, considering his next words. "There are some things…about your brother…you don't know. Some questions I need to answer for the council. Your names will be cleared in all of this as soon as I'm through. Trust me. Just go along, for now." He leveled a threatening glare at the soldiers, hoping to make his intent crystal clear, if not implicit: *You can have me, but if you mess with my boys, I will kill each and every one of you with my bare hands.*

A wry smile curved along the corners of Achilles's mouth, no doubt in response to the unspoken threat: Dark Ones didn't take well to challenges, and they were always eager to fight.

Dane shook his head in utter bewilderment, his own need to lash out barely bridled beneath the surface. "What are you talking about, Dad?" He watched in disgust as the soldier snapped the cuffs on Damien's wrists and locked them in place. "Is that really necessary?" he snapped.

"Orders, my man," Achilles responded.

Diablo sneered at the guard, and a low, answering growl rumbled in the guard's throat. He swept his angry gaze to Damien. "What don't we know about Saber?" he asked, his voice betraying his mounting dread.

Damien simply shook his head. As the soldiers displayed two more pair of handcuffs, Damien nodded with authority at his sons. "Submit...I mean it."

"Talk, right now!" Diablo said, tucking both of his arms behind his back to avoid being cuffed. The male was *this close* to starting a fight the Alexiares clan could not ultimately win.

Damien shut his eyes. *Dark Lords*, he had never meant for this to happen. He raised his head, squared his jaw, and reopened his eyes, commanding the attention of both his sons. "Know this," he bit out in a raspy yet remorseful voice. "Saber is your brother. He has always been your brother. He will always be your brother. That is all you need to know." He swallowed his angst and gestured at the extra pairs of handcuffs. "Go ahead. They will not resist."

"You bastard," Dane whispered, his voice barely audible. "What did you do?"

Damien spun around angrily then, glaring at the youngest of the two twins. "I did what I had to, and I would do it again in a heartbeat."

Diablo exhaled a reluctant breath and slowly shook his head. "It? What's *it*, Dad?"

Damien drew from a waning well of courage and opened a private family bandwidth in order to communicate telepathically with his sons. He would not share his humiliation with the guards. Not now. Maybe not ever. *Eight hundred years ago, when I set out to sire a family, to fulfill the demands of the Blood Curse, something went wrong. I was able to sacrifice the firstborn as required, but before I could stop it, the second child was murdered by the human woman's brother: a vampire hunter.* He swallowed hard and pressed on. *Saber had just been born thirty days before*—the words nearly got stuck in his psyche, but he forced them out—*to a couple in the house of Jadon.*

Diablo literally recoiled. His face turned pale, and he nearly staggered back. "Stop!" He spoke out loud, obviously hoping to halt the words before they became irretrievable.

Dane's mouth fell open. "What did you do!" He rushed the words, sounding nearly hysterical.

Damien continued to speak telepathically. *I was grief-stricken. I—*

Stole an effin' child from the house of Jadon? Diablo supplied incredulously.

Dane shook his head in disbelief. *Tell me it was at least the Dark One, the evil twin that you took?* he demanded.

The unnamed one had already been sacrificed...or I would have. If it were possible to whisper telepathically, Damien's words would have been barely audible. *But,* he added quickly, *Saber was consecrated by the Dark Lord S'nepres; he was ushered in to the house of Jaegar by the twin demon lord of his birth—you've seen his hair. He is truly one of us! I swear, down to the soulless cavern in his empty chest, by all that is unholy, Saber is your brother. He is my son!*

Dane covered his mouth with his hands.

Diablo stared down at the ground.

And silence overwhelmed the dark lair.

The guards grew restless and shuffled their feet, yet still the silence lingered.

When, finally, enough time had passed for the males to process what they had heard, Diablo looked back up and regarded his father with disgust, the betrayal in his eyes as stark as it was unbearable to look upon. "You need to keep your mouth shut, Father. You need to ask for legal counsel before your head ends up on a pike...or worse. Do you understand?"

Damien nodded, feeling utterly helpless. "Yes, yes, of course. And the two of you—you don't need to worry. You won't be implicated. How could you be?"

Dane laughed then, loud and sardonic, the sarcasm in his voice echoing throughout the lair. "Have you lost your damn mind?" he snarled. "Do you not know who we are? Where we are?" He looked around the room, gestured at the garrison of soldiers standing before them, each male born and bred from evil since the day he was born, all of them immersed in a world where mercy and compassion were mocked as weaknesses. "Forget your eight-hundred-year-old logic. This is the house of *Jaegar*. We are *his* blood descendants. Our bodies have no souls; our lives have no value; and our brethren have no duty outside of obedience to the code of this house. You violated that code, and should Oskar Vadovsky get a wild hair up his ass to exact vengeance, just for the hell of it, we are all as good as dead."

Damien nodded, almost unconsciously.

He watched as each of his sons was handcuffed in turn, restrained, and led to the door of the lair, surrounded by enemies of their own kind; and he couldn't help but wonder: Was this the last time the three of them would ever gather together as free vampires?

Had he really lost *everything*?

Dear Dark Lords of Hell, *what had he done*?

Saber Alexiares awoke in a rage. He shot up from the cot, momentarily disoriented, and rushed toward the bars. He didn't know what was driving him, but something was wrong.

Terribly wrong.

His face flushed, his skin heated, and he felt his eyes change, the pupils growing narrow and more severe. "My brothers!" he shouted to no one in particular.

Ramsey Olaru rose slowly from a wide, leather armchair and sauntered toward the cell, regarding the prisoner warily. "Come again?"

Saber snarled, feeling almost mad with rage. "Dane…Diablo." The words were nearly incoherent as he murmured them. "My brothers."

Tessa Dawn

Ramsey stopped short in front of the cell door. "You need to calm down, Chief." He assessed Saber from head to toe. "You're too weak in your current condition to put off this kind of aggression."

Saber drew back on his haunches and hissed at the warrior, wishing for all he was worth that he could come through the bars. Of course he was too weak—they were keeping him drained of all but a few drops of blood, and he was virtually entombed in diamond. "Let me out, and we can talk about it," he clipped.

Ramsey chuckled, although there was no humor in the sound. "Can't do that, friend."

Saber stalked slowly toward the cell door, his glare holding Ramsey's in an unbroken glower of fury. "Sure you can," he whispered. He gathered all his remaining strength; and then, moving as swiftly as he could, he released his claws, forced his arm through the bars, and swiped at the warrior's face.

Ramsey drew back in the nick of time, just barely avoiding the wicked gashes that would have otherwise been left in Saber's wake. "What the hell—"

"I want to see my brothers!"

"What?" Ramsey spat the word. His face was a mask of incredulity.

"My family! I want to see them. Call Napolean—let him know."

"Yeah," Ramsey said mockingly. "'Cause that's gonna happen."

"You bastard!" Saber snarled. "Keeping me in here like an animal, locked away from everything and everyone who matters!" He practically snorted in his fury. "You wanna kill me? Fine! *Do it!* But if not, then let me see my brothers."

Santos Olaru rose from his languorous position in a matching armchair across the room. He traversed the space in a wide, vulturine circle and slinked to his brother's side. "What's the problem here?"

"Your boy is having a sudden bout of homesickness. Wants

29

to see his *brothers*."

"Dark Ones?" Santos asked, frowning.

"You know of any others?" Ramsey asked.

Saber hurled himself at the bars. He grabbed hold of the slats for all he was worth and began to tug and pull, howling his rage like an animal, spitting curses and threats like a demonic creature. While the bars didn't move, the heavens above them did. The moonlit sky gave way to utter darkness, revealing the fact that the clouds were starting to grow restless, and then the cosmic show began: Thunder roared in the heavens. Lightning crackled in the sky. Wind began to howl outside the windows.

"Get me a sedative." Ramsey's voice was like a dark echo in a narrow tunnel, assaulting Saber's ears from far away. His brain was too consumed with fury to decipher the meaning of individual words. He simply kept after the bars. He would break through eventually—or die trying.

Before he could register movement, the door to his cell swung open, and he leapt indiscriminately in the direction of his captors, his lethal fangs extended in preparation for attack.

The bite felt exquisite.

Did the blood belong to Ramsey or Santos? he wondered as he gulped it in hungry, desperate pulls. No matter. His jaw was locked down like a pit bull's, and his feral growls were only interrupted by primal slurps and drunken swallows. Just then, he felt a sharp pain in his upper arm and thought he registered a syringe sticking out from his exposed flesh. He didn't care.

Nothing mattered.

There was only blood.

Damien...

Diablo...

And the madness.

He began to stumble as his thoughts grew sluggish and the room began to expand and contract in great waves of illusion.

"Did you get it into him?" one of the sentinels asked the other.

"Yeah, I got him." It sounded like Santos.

"Son-of-a-hyena! I think he ripped half my neck out!"

Saber drew back to look at his handiwork, the hanging, fleshy tissue around Ramsey's throat. Yeah, it was Ramsey's. And…and…why was the floor shifting like that?

For a second, his mind grappled with the question, trying to grasp hold of the answer: a sedative?

His captors had drugged him, but then…

The thought dissipated.

Along with his conscious awareness, the world around him collapsed into a cavern of pressing darkness and ghostly silence.

And then his body hit the ground.

five

Saber felt like an infant, curled up into a fetal position, staring up at flashing colors.

Moving shapes.

Dipping objects.

They swirled around his head as some funky music played in the background. Childish sounds.

Lullabies?

His stared wide-eyed at a soft green object: fluid, moving, twisting like the wind. It was covered in frogs—what the heck?—and little blue dragons. Was he hallucinating? He opened his mouth to speak, and the sound that came out was garbled and unintelligible.

Nonsense.

Random syllables.

He leaned forward and stared even closer at the object.

Ah, yes; it was a blanket. And he was somehow tangled up inside of it. He started to wiggle and squirm in a desperate effort to get the creepy thing off of him, when all at once, he was startled by the sound of loud, disturbing voices.

"Rafael, no! *Please*...I'm not ready."

A high-pitched voice, the female, the one called Lorna was rushing toward him—how was she doing it? Could she fly?—and she looked like a giant. *Great Evil Lord S'nepres, he had to get free from this green and blue restraint!*

He started to cry.

No...to wail.

The sounds were just too much, too loud, the vibrations spinning all around him as the woman argued with the man. He told her it had to be done, and she begged him not to do it. He told her that the Blood would come for the unnamed one and claim him, too, if he didn't hurry, and she bawled like a ninny.

BLOOD REDEMPTION

Saber cringed.

The one called Rafael was gone now. He had simply left the inconsolable woman kneeling on the floor in a pile of her own grief, pleading—nice guy—and now... now she was slowly pulling herself up and approaching—

Approaching what?

A bassinette?

Him?

Saber reached up to grasp his head, and his tiny arms flailed wildly instead. Holy Demoness of the Night, he had no control over his body whatsoever. Shit! What was this?

As the giant figure of the woman loomed closer and closer, he folded in on himself in a panic. He had to get out! Get away! Stop her!

Wake up!

"Wake up!" Ramsey's thunderous voice pierced the vapor of confusion, and Saber shot upright on the cot.

He was lying in his cell covered in sweat, his feet loosely bound by diamond-studded leather straps to the end of the cot.

"Bad dream, Chief?" Ramsey asked, his husky voice cutting through the haze. "You've been asleep for about ten hours—didn't think you were coming back."

Saber's eyes flashed to the sentinel's, measuring the distinctive hazel orbs for signs of truth. Ten hours? What in the world?

Last he remembered, he had been feeding on someone's neck. He turned to regard his captors; there were two of them present: Ramsey and Saxson Olaru. Last time, it had been Santos, right before the duo had...drugged him.

Still gasping for air, he made a point of slowing down his breathing, and lay back on the cot. The sentinels had drugged him, and he must have been dreaming.

As relief began to wash over him, a funny feeling prickled his spine. Wait a minute. Had he been dreaming...or remembering? He swallowed a lump in his throat and ran a tired hand through his matted hair. Damn, he needed another shower! The woman

34

he had seen, Lorna, had she been real or imaginary? Had he imagined the whole awful scene, or had he recalled something while in a drug-induced sleep?

Impossible, he thought. He couldn't recall anything between Lorna and Rafael Dzuna, least of all the night they sacrificed one of two twins to the Blood—unless…he had been there. And how was that even possible?

He bit a hole in his tongue, as if the action could cut off the thoughts.

No.

Absolutely not!

"What's going on?" Ramsey asked, as if the sadistic bastard gave a crap. "You look like you've seen a ghost."

Saber stared at him blankly, trying to process all the madness converging in his mind. He was Saber Alexiares, firstborn son of Damien Alexiares, brother to Diablo and Dane, soldier in the house of Jaegar, descendant of the offspring of humans and dark lords. He wasn't anybody's punk, and he hadn't been raised to hide like a pitiful human from things that went bump in the night.

Hell, he *was* the thing that went bump in the night.

And he'd be damned if he didn't face his enemy—any enemy—head-on.

"Can you…can you check something for me?" he mumbled, hating that he was reduced to asking Ramsey Olaru for help. But what else could he do?

The six-foot-five, muscle-bound sentinel raised his sculpted eyebrows—and wasn't that just a walking contradiction, a lethal-looking vampire with the sculpted features of a print-model. Funny that. "Like what?" Ramsey asked suspiciously.

Saber exhaled slowly. No point in dragging it out. "That family—the Dzunas—was there a blanket?"

"Excuse me?" Ramsey said.

"A blanket," Saber repeated. "The night of the sacrifice, before their son was taken; did the kid have a blue and green blanket?" He braced himself for the laughter and scorn he knew was coming, but to his surprise, Ramsey's face tightened with intensity, and his light eyes grew dark with contemplation. "Anything else?"

Saber shook his head from side to side in disgust and tried not to virtually hiss the words. "Frogs or dragons…whatever! Just find out about an effin' blanket."

The brutal warrior leaned back on his heels and dropped into a casual, indifferent stance; whatever concern had shone in his eyes was now gone. "I'll think about it," he grunted.

Saber nodded. That was all he could ask.

It wasn't like the information would matter one way or the other.

Vanya Demir retreated once again to the private cabin toward the back of the plane. She closed the shade over the small cabin window and reclined on the slender compartmental bed. She was travel-weary, and her sense of time was all muddled. She had twelve more hours of flying to go; and although it would be around noon in Colorado, it was still around nine PM in Romania—no matter how she turned it, she was exhausted.

She fluffed the pillow, flipped it over, and fluffed it again. Then she tossed and turned on the semi-comfortable bed in an attempt to find a better position.

The problem wasn't really the accommodations: The house of Jadon kept an incredibly nice private plane. It was her restless, beleaguered mind that kept her from sleeping peacefully, the incessant nightmares that had recently begun to haunt her. Whether sitting upright in the plane's main cabin, or reclining in the sleeping compartment, every time she drifted off, the dream would begin again where it last left off.

Where in the world were these strange images coming from? Vanya wondered. By all the celestial gods and goddesses, what was going on? She hadn't been this plagued by night terrors in centuries. Okay, well, she had no memory of her dreams during The Long Sleep—the term both she and her sister Princess Ciopori used in reference to the 2,810 years they had remained in the ground, cocooned in the earth, in a state of unconscious limbo, sleeping deep beneath the fertile soil of Dark Moon Vale, awaiting a rescuer to awaken them.

Vanya and Ciopori were the only remaining members of a long-ago race, the two surviving females from a time that preceded the Blood Curse. They were the royal daughters of King Sakarias and Queen Jade, the surviving siblings of the original twins, Jadon and Jaegar Demir, and as all of the Vampyr now knew, Jadon had secretly saved their lives during that fateful, tumultuous time. In a desperate attempt to keep Prince Jaegar's bloodthirsty soldiers from sacrificing the last of the monarchy—every other female in their homeland had already been slain—Jadon had rushed them out of the castle in the middle of the night in secrecy. He had turned them over to a sympathetic convoy of warriors, a covert group of mercenaries led by the powerful wizard Fabien, and Fabien had placed the females in a deep, enchanted sleep far away in the New World, in order to await Jadon's return. Needless to say, Jadon never returned; but thank the gods, Ciopori had been Marquis Silivasi's *destiny*. It was the powerful connection between the two would-be lovers that had awakened Ciopori's resting soul, and Marquis had rescued Vanya in turn.

Since then, a lot had happened: Ciopori and Marquis had fallen in love, mated, and given birth to their firstborn son, Nikolai Jadon Silivasi. And Vanya Demir, having shared a brief romantic tryst with the ancient king, Napolean Mondragon, had decided to return to the University in Romania in order to revive the original theology of the people. She had begun to draft what would soon become the first written texts of the forgotten spells, the Celestial Magick, that had been entrusted to the females of their race so long ago, an invaluable work of restoration and legacy for the surviving males in the house of Jadon.

BLOOD REDEMPTION

Vanya sat up in bed and buried her face in her hands. It was simply no use: sleeping, that is. Her mind would not stop wandering. Perhaps, then, she should take a deeper look at her dream...give it the attention it demanded.

Perhaps if she set pen to paper in a literal sense, she could metaphorically put the images to rest, and her subconscious would give her a break.

Perhaps.

She had hours and hours ahead of her in flight; it was at least worth a try.

Deciding on this new course of action, Vanya rose from the bed, retrieved her journal from her carry-on bag, turned to a blank page, and began to record the nightmare.

The dream always begins the same. I am wandering through the old country when I come across a cave, a place of unparalleled darkness. Something in my soul registers danger immediately, and I am overwhelmed with a feeling of flight. The desire to run. I don't want to go any further or explore; I simply wish to retreat; but something draws me forward.

The cave is eerie and damp; it is covered in moss and stalactites, and I hug my arms to my chest in response to the chill. Yet and still, I push forward.

And that's when I see him—it—the fire-breathing dragon. His eyes are like brilliant rubies at first, rare precious stones which conceal ancient secrets, reflect an uncanny intelligence back at me; but they quickly turn to a pair of hot coals, infused with rage, saturated with contempt, and full of demonic purpose.

I step back in alarm. The creature is fierce, and I know that he will destroy me if I let him. Slowly, ever so carefully, I begin to retreat. My feet are now bare, and the rocky floor is rough against my soles, tearing at my flesh and causing me great distress, but I am too afraid to cry out, lest the vicious beast pounce in response to my fear.

It is then that I notice the treasure.

It is a small chest, ornately decorated, and it rests behind the monster, almost as if he is guarding it. Hiding it. I don't feel as if he is protecting it—perhaps he isn't even aware of it—but he is certainly standing as an impassible barrier to The People, preventing them from discovering it.

38

Tessa Dawn

When I say The People, I mean the Vampyr, the descendants of my brother Jadon's house, those who still retain their souls. And I cannot tell you how I know, but there is something of such great value and significance in this treasure chest, something that belongs to the house of Jadon, something I deeply wish to return to the king.

The dragon levels his fiery gaze on me, and I am hypnotized by those eyes—those hateful, dangerous, glorious eyes. He will not let me get to the treasure; he will not allow me to return it to my people.

I don't know what to do.

Everything in my soul screams at me to flee the beast; yet everything in my ancient memory demands that I unlock the chest. I am torn. Conflicted. Terrified.

And that's when the dragon opens his fearsome mouth and begins to breathe fire, scorching me from head to toe. My thin linen nightgown is ablaze, and I gasp from the heat and the pain.

And then I scream, a piteous, never-ending cry.

And then I awaken.

Vanya wiped her brow and set the journal and pen down on the bed. There. She had recorded the dream. Perhaps, now, her subconscious would give her a moment's peace. Wetting her suddenly dry lips with her tongue, she couldn't help but wonder what the omen meant: She was a celestial princess, a female of a forgotten race, imbued with an ancient wisdom and mystical powers. Surely the gods were trying to tell her something, and whatever it was, it was vitally important to the people.

Frowning, she decided to try once again to get some sleep if possible. Soon, she would be back in Dark Moon Vale with Marquis and Ciopori, yet she knew what had to be done.

She had to let Napolean know about the nightmare…right away.

In fact, the moment she landed, she needed to go to the manse.

Surely the wise king would understand the meaning behind the prophecy.

six

Vanya Demir thanked her limo driver for bringing her to Napolean's home safely, and instructed him to go to the lodge and get some sleep. He would be heading back to the airfield in less than twenty-four hours to return to Romania, and his services were no longer needed at her side. By all that was holy, it was too late to come calling on the ancient king, nearly ten PM in Dark Moon Vale, but she had made a decision and she intended to follow it through.

The vampire pilot, a Master Warrior by the name of Sloan, had landed the radar-deflecting plane nearly two hours early, making unusual progress without any headwinds, and she had called Ciopori and Marquis to let them know there was no need for them to pick her up from the airport: She would procure one of the king's limousines from the airfield, allow the pilot to drop her off at Napolean's compound, and catch a ride to Marquis and Ciopori's home in the morning. Either that, or one of them could come fetch her after they awoke. Staying at the mansion might be a little awkward—okay, so maybe it would be more than a little awkward—but it was late; Brooke and Phoenix would surely be sleeping, should the gods be merciful; and she and Napolean could discuss her dream in private, leaving very little need to get bogged down with conversation pertaining to other, more trivial matters. The visit would be short and sweet, directly to the point.

Vanya sighed, remembering her brief conversation with Marquis. She had called the Silivasi household the moment she had landed, and Marquis had tried to raise holy hell with her over her decision to call on Napolean rather than wait on him and Ciopori. Not that Marquis didn't raise holy hell over just about everything, but she'd had to be very firm in order to get the Ancient Master Warrior to back off. She chuckled to herself;

41

after all, she understood Marquis's objections, even if she didn't agree with them: It was late; the sun had already set; and Dark Moon Vale was a valley ripe with potential dangers and enemies. Nevertheless, Vanya was not a child. She would be at the king's house overnight, and what could be safer, when Ramsey, Saxson, and Santos were, as always, ever near? Not to mention, Napolean Mondragon was not about to let any harm come to one of the original princesses.

Vanya felt quite safe, really.

However, now that she actually stood before the massive, arched doorway at the front of Napolean's compound and prepared to knock on the king's front door, she felt the first real pangs of uncertainty.

She tucked a long, flowing lock of her tousled hair behind her shoulder, straightened her back, and then glanced downward in a last-minute appraisal of her physical appearance.

And then she cringed.

Her dress was a mess; her hair was positively unruly; and she more or less looked like a disheveled vagabond. At the very least, she should have taken the time to braid several locks of her hair, bind the interwoven braids in silk ties, and change into something more formal, perhaps her sapphire-blue gown with the cross-laced bodice and ankle-length hem, in order to make herself more presentable for the king.

She smoothed the front of her asymmetrical skirt—a modest black swirl made of light cotton cloth in a simple layered pattern—and unraveled a thin piece of twisted lace along the collar of the cream-colored vest. She sighed. Was all of this nitpicking really about propriety, or was it about something else entirely?

Perhaps Napolean Mondragon still held a very special place in her heart—perhaps she merely wanted to appear beautiful when the king saw her again, and that was simply wrong.

Not okay.

Inappropriate on so many levels.

The king was happy now. He was mated to a beautiful,

intelligent, independent woman, Brooke Adams, and the two of them had a child, a son they called Phoenix, the future king of the house of Jadon. He deserved to be happy, and she was happy for him. Truly, she was.

Vanya grasped the tattered journal tighter in her hands and tried to summon her courage. It wasn't like she was still a maiden—well, in some ways she was—but she wasn't petty, insecure, or unable to handle the more awkward aspects of life. She winced as she thought about how the king might view her impulsive, nocturnal behavior. It was bad enough that she had ventured into the night alone—Napolean would scold her as mercilessly as Marquis had for daring to be so independent; and that, she could handle—but what if he found her impetuous visit in poor taste? What if he did not see the immediate urgency of her nightmare? After all, she wasn't the only female to ever have a recurring bad dream—why should she demand the attention of the king the instant she felt...unsettled?

What if he viewed her behavior as not only unsuitable but self-indulgent?

Vanya sighed. She knew the dream was significant, *very* significant, and Napolean would see it the same way. Still, what if she woke up Brooke and the young prince? Could this not wait until morning?

Vanya quickly withdrew her hand from the door, placed her palm against her stomach to steady her nerves, and exhaled slowly with relief. Of course it could wait. Stepping slowly away from the door, she sought to formulate a new plan, a compromise that might work better for all.

She opened the well-worn journal to the section she had so recently penned and turned back the corner of the first page. She would not disturb the fearsome leader in the middle of the night, not at his home with his wife and his child. She would simply take it to one of the nearby sentinels and ask them to deliver it to Napolean in the morning with a message: *Contact Vanya the moment you read this.* And then she would ask one of the sentinels to chauffeur her to the Dark Moon Lodge, where she would stay for just one night. She could meet up with Marquis and Ciopori tomorrow, as planned, after meeting with the king in the light—and propriety—of the day.

Yes, that would do just fine.

It was a much better idea.

Turning on her heel, she raised the collar of her vest for warmth and headed toward the Chamber of Sacrifice and Atonement—more specifically, to the guard watch-room, where the Olaru brothers secured the recent prisoner twenty-four hours a day, keeping a careful eye on the holding cell and the newly detained Dark One.

seven

Saber Alexiares sat up on the damnable cot in his cell and stared out one of the two windows above him. It was about ten o'clock at night—don't ask him how he knew, he just did. As a Dark Vampire, he was the descendant of Jaegar Demir, and while Jaegar may have been an evil prodigy from a once-pure race, he had also been the offspring of celestial gods and humans, before he had bowed down to the demons. In other words, evil or not, Saber still belonged to a race of beings who were intrinsically connected to the earth and stars, the planets around them, and no matter how evil or ruthless he had become, he retained each and every one of those otherworldly abilities. Not to mention, he had lived deep beneath the ground in the dark colony for hundreds of years, where no light or reflections ever crept in; and in the process, he had honed his skills of intuition to a tee. He could divine the time of day or night within seconds of any clock simply by feeling the subtle shifts in the universe around him. It was as easy and natural as breathing.

He stared up at the moon and sky and thought of his brothers. Where were they now? Were they deep in the colony hanging out with other warriors, perhaps shooting pool or sparring in the gym—the Dark Ones almost never slept at night; they preferred to take their repose in the day—or were they out hunting, even as he thought of them, prowling the streets of the surrounding towns in search of fresh blood?

He licked his lips, wishing...dreaming.

Oh, what it would be like to call on his youngest sibling, Dane, to feed—just once more. To reject the meager and ridiculous vials of blood he was given by his captors and feast like a lion in the house of Jaegar. He shrugged his shoulders, wondering what the self-righteous males of the house of Jadon would think of the Dark Ones' custom, the way they fed: The youngest sibling in every household was a hunter, and the *hunters* roamed in packs. They stalked their prey from one end of the earth to the next, careful not to leave too many dead bodies in any one city or town in order to avoid detection by humans, and then they gorged on their victims, feeding their feral appetites beyond the point of satiation in order to return to the colony and feed their elder brothers and fathers. It was easier to hunt that way, in smaller, less obvious numbers, and it helped to preserve the population of their prey, leaving more food alive for future generations to consume.

As Saber's thoughts drifted, branching off from one memory to another, he was suddenly drawn to the sky: The image in the window was changing, metamorphosing, becoming something entirely foreign yet eerily familiar.

Saber swung his feet off the side of the cot, stood on slightly unstable legs, and meandered to the nearest window, stretching his neck to see more clearly. Indeed, the sky had transformed into a slate-gray canvas, deepening by the second, until it emerged an iridescent black. The moon followed suit, transforming in dazzling waves from ivory to seashell white; from white to burgeoning rose; and from rose to deep, scarlet red.

Saber let out a full-throated laugh, reacting to the utter absurdity of it all. *Those favored, undeserving bastards,* he thought, referring to the males in the house of Jadon. Like them, he was now waiting like a spoiled child playing with a Rubik's cube, hoping to solve the puzzle: Who would the chosen male be tonight? Which of the cursed celestial gods would bestow some hapless human woman on her new, overbearing, testosterone-laden mate? How would the whole damn Curse play out?

At least it would be entertainment—a distraction in a world that was rapidly becoming unbearable to live in—and what the hell did they plan to do with him anyway? Convert him to the good side? Save his blackened soul? He scoffed irreverently as he continued to stare out the window.

And then he took an unwitting step back.

Tessa Dawn

What. The. Hell.

A globular cluster had appeared across the blackened sky, like a paint-by-number picture filling itself in; and the stars in the cluster were very distinct and familiar: Serpens Caput, the head of a snake, and Serpens Cauda, the tail, both wrapped neatly around Ophiuchus—it was a Serpens Blood Moon.

Saber looped his hands behind his head. He leaned back and roared with laughter. Oh, this was rich! You couldn't even make this shit up—it just kept getting better and better! Glancing over his shoulder, he stared at Ramsey Olaru. The stoic male was staring through a larger window in the watch room, viewing the celestial show from his more comfortable, privileged vantage point. But surely, even he hadn't expected this.

"Hey, son of Jadon," Saber called mockingly.

Ramsey blinked several times, acknowledging that he had heard Saber speak, but he didn't respond or turn in his direction.

Saber gestured toward the window, knowing the sentinel's peripheral vision worked just fine. "What the hell is that?" he chided. He pointed at the sky. "That looks like...hell, I don't know...my astronomy's a little rusty—we don't really study the celestial gods too much down in the bowels of the earth, but..." He cleared his throat and took a step closer to the window. "But I could swear that looks like a snake to me. What do you call that again?" He snapped his fingers several times as if trying to remember. "You know, that one god you worship? Oh yeah, Serpens." He licked his lips in anticipation, and a taunting snarl escaped his throat. "Shit, *brother*, isn't that mine? I mean, if I'm this stolen child you think I am." He leapt from the window to the cell door and snarled at the insolent warrior, his fangs fully extended. "So, where's my wifey then? Who's going to get her for me? Because she has to be close by, right? I mean, that's how the Curse works for you light vampires, true?" He turned around to regard the cell and gestured toward the narrow, unkempt cot. "Can I actually *take* her in here?" The thought made him audacious. "You guys gonna watch? Learn something?"

Ramsey Olaru twitched, almost imperceptibly. The rage in

47

his hazel eyes shone in an emerging, heated glow. He turned his head slowly in a serpentine motion and scowled with disgust. "Glad you're enjoying the show, Chief. Because you know what it means, right?"

Saber shrugged, completely unaffected. "Yeah, I've been blessed by your gods…twice." The sarcasm in his voice was abundant.

Ramsey smiled a sinister grin and sauntered toward him. When, at last, they stood on opposite sides of the bars, their eyes locked in a parody of lethal, spiritual combat. "It means I only have to put up with you for thirty more days." He pointed at the sky through the window. "Napolean will *never* give the likes of you a human woman, a cherished *destiny*; and in thirty days, when the blood comes calling—and oh, I think we can both agree that it *will* come calling—your sorry, meaningless life is going to come to a truly brutal and fitting end." He leaned forward and winked. "How d'ya like them apples, Chief?"

Saber didn't even flinch.

There was no way he was going to give the smug bastard the satisfaction.

So what if his life came to an end? As far as he was concerned, it was over anyhow. He swallowed the rising taste of bile in his throat as he thought about the ritual sacrifice, the way in which the Blood would claim him, the endless pain and torture he would be forced to endure on his way out of this world, and then he drew a deep breath, dismissing the thought.

Whatever.

He would cross that bridge when he came to it.

For now, he was far more curious as to how this whole thing would play out. What had Lorna said? Napolean is a just king who rules with a fair hand. The Ancient One wouldn't be so quick to dismiss tradition and thumb his nose at the will of the gods, and who knew, maybe Saber could play this whole thing to his advantage, work his way out of this claustrophobic cell, spend a few days in the fresh air before he met his final demise.

Right now, there was only one thing burning a hole through

his curious mind: Who the hell was the female?

And where was she?

Vanya Demir stood in stunned silence, her fingers still wrapped firmly around the outside handle of the door to the Chamber of Sacrifice and Atonement. On one hand, she could hardly pull her eyes from the sky, the magnificent splendor of the stars and the unmitigated power of the gods. On the other hand, she could hardly look away from her wrist.

A feeling of overwhelming excitement…and dread…enveloped her.

It couldn't be.

It just couldn't be!

Had the celestial god, Serpens, chosen *her*, an original female from a time so far removed, to be the mate of one of Napolean's males? Had this been her fate all along? Had she been chosen that long ago to be the mate of a vampire? But how was that even possible? She had been born before the Curse even happened.

She released the door handle and clasped her head in confusion. And then she held her arm up once again to stare at the strange, enigmatic symbols etched into her flesh.

Serpens.

The god of rebirth.

There was simply no denying it. But how? Who? Where was the male?

Was he a Warrior, a Healer, or a Justice?

Surely, in her case, he would almost have to be a Wizard. She wasn't sure what she felt, and her body began to sway from the overwhelming emotion and confusion.

She reached once again for the door handle, this time using it to maintain her balance. She was just about to tug on the handle, when all at once, a terrifying voice cut through the silence like thunder. "Do not open that door, Princess!"

Vanya spun around. She would know that alluring tone anywhere. The voice belonged to Napolean Mondragon. She released the handle and squared her shoulders to face the ancient king, her mouth dropping open. "Milord," she uttered breathlessly.

"What are you doing out here…in the night…all alone?" he asked, his tone revealing his disapproval.

"I…I was—" She stopped short, preferring to query the ancient king instead of being interrogated by him. "I believe, the question, milord, is what are you doing out here in the night, all alone?"

Napolean frowned, clearly having little patience for her diversion. "Marquis called me when you arrived at the airfield to let me know you would be coming to the manse. When you didn't show up, I became worried. Then I tracked you here."

Vanya sighed. Of course. She should have known that her family would alert Napolean, and the king would keep careful track of the time. As was his right, the sagacious ruler carried the blood of every member of the house of Jadon in his veins in order to maintain a connection with his subjects, and Vanya was no exception. In fact, he had practically demanded the blood offering as a concession in order to allow her to travel to Romania. As if she could not have pulled rank and insisted. She absently turned over her wrist, remembering the day Napolean had drunk from her vein, and she was immediately reminded of the sky—and the Serpens Blood Moon. She glanced upward. "Have you seen the moon, milord?"

All at once, Napolean looked as if someone had slapped him across the face. Indeed, as if someone had murdered his firstborn child. In a rare moment of unrestrained emotion, he reached out, grabbed her arm, and rotated her wrist. His touch was not at all gentle.

"Your Grace!" she exclaimed in admonishment. "Please."

He dropped her arm as if she had burned him, and then he took an unwitting step backward, his usual calm and regal demeanor disturbed. "Dear gods, Vanya."

Vanya placed her open palm against her chest and fought to collect her breath. "What is it?"

When he didn't answer—looked as if he *couldn't* even maintain eye contact, let alone answer—she knew something was wrong.

Really, really wrong.

Napolean Mondragon was the embodiment of a noble king, an unshakable warrior, and a hardened ruler—nothing fazed the 2,800-year-old male, and there was no challenge he did not meet head-on. Only now, he looked more like an angry tiger than the king of the Vampyr. Almost robotically, he reached out a second time and took the princess's wrist. His grip was softer, almost hesitant in nature, but his searching fingers revealed his confusion. He traced the celestial etchings and lines with disbelief. And then he slowly exhaled, his face a mask of both sorrow and determination. "I am so sorry, Princess...for this."

Vanya drew back in immediate alarm this time. "For what?" she asked. Whatever could *this* mean? "Napolean? What is it—why are you so upset?" Surely, he wasn't angry because she might belong to another male, not now, when he had Brooke. She began to lose her patience then. "I demand that you tell me at once, milord." When he still didn't speak, she raised her voice. "Say something, Napolean; you're scaring me!"

Napolean met her eyes with a steely gaze and held up both hands in an act of contrition. It was as if he were apologizing and trying to calm her down at the same time. His lips parted, as if he were about to speak, but then he obviously thought better of it and looked away. Eventually, he planted his feet and squared his broad shoulders, and when, at last, he met her gaze again, there was a hard, unyielding resolve in his eyes. His jaw was set in a hard line, and his sculpted lips were drawn taut. "Do not be afraid," he whispered. "Everything is going to be fine. You will not be mated under this Blood Moon, and nothing adverse will happen to you as a consequence. I won't let it." He shrugged his shoulders ever so slightly and added, "This may be a rough *thirty* days—indeed, it *will be* a difficult thirty days for many—but your life will not be changed."

Vanya was just about to respond when a beautiful, tall brunette with long, purposeful strides and stunning sapphire eyes approached the two of them, her limber hands working feverishly to finish tying the knot on the heavy white bathrobe she was wearing. Her feet were clad in soft slippers, and her hair was mussed from sleep. "So, you have already sealed the fate of so many?" she said. Her voice was soft but challenging. "You have unilaterally decided that the gods are wrong and you need to overrule them?"

Napolean took her full measure. "Brooke, you shouldn't be out in this cold."

Brooke frowned and shrugged off his words. "Neither should you. Neither should Vanya. But that's neither here nor there." She bit her bottom lip while considering her words. "I was in our room, waiting for you to check on the princess, waiting to talk a bit more about the Blood Moon and the male…" Her voice trailed off, and then she cleared her throat. "And then I started thinking about the Curse, the necessity of proximity, and I put two and two together." Her eyes were full of a deep compassion as they swept briefly downward over Vanya's wrist. "I thought you might need me."

By all the gods, it was still hard to witness the undeniable love and rightness of Brooke and Napolean's union. The king swallowed hard and nodded at his mate. "Thank you."

Brooke declined her head in a gesture that could only be described as stately; and then she turned her attention to the princess. "Hi, Vanya."

Vanya regarded the beautiful mate of the Vampyr lord with a slight nod of her head and tried to maintain at least some semblance of dignity under the circumstances. "Greetings, milady."

Brooke's expression became all at once serious. "How are you?"

Vanya frowned. "Well, isn't that the question…" She eyed

Napolean warily. "I don't really know. Perhaps someone would like to tell me what's going on?"

Brooke appeared completely taken aback, and her hand went up to her chest. "Oh, God, I'm sorry. I thought—" She pressed her lips tightly together and held her breath for a moment, refusing to say another word. When any one of them could have cut through the silence with a knife, she turned toward her mate. "Napolean?"

The king gave his *destiny* a cautionary glance. "Brooke, I appreciate your support—you know I do. But I need to handle this myself."

Brooke nodded her head and took a deep breath. "Okay...if that is what you need, but I think..." She was so very careful with her words: far, far *too* careful. "I think you might want to *sit with this* for a while. There's still time. Maybe slow down. Bring Vanya inside. Let's all just take a step back and analyze the situation together."

The situation?

Vanya didn't know if she should be terrified by the cryptic way they were talking or mad as hell at the way they were treating her with kid gloves. Was it because she was an ancient princess, or was she perceived as a woman scorned? Fire began to stir in her belly, and she leveled her gaze at Napolean. "I would like to know what *situation* your mate is referring to." She tried to soften her tone and failed. "And I would like to know now, milord." She pointed directly at the moon then. "For what it is worth, I am not a half-wit, so I gather it has something to do with the moon"—she pointed at her wrist—"and my arm." She immediately regretted the clip in her demeanor, but truth be told, she was afraid.

Napolean stiffened in surprise, clearly caught off guard by her overt aggression. "Vanya..." He inhaled sharply. "It's not...personal. I'm not trying to avoid the subject." His deep onyx eyes, with their rare silver irises, narrowed in concentration. "I am simply trying to think of a way to protect you, as well as the house of Jadon, and all those with a...personal interest in this matter."

"Protect me from *what*, Napolean?"

Napolean started to respond, but before he could, Ciopori Demir materialized in the courtyard and quickly rushed to her sister's side. She swept an anxious arm around Vanya's waist and laid her head gently on her shoulder. "Sister, are you okay? Napolean just contacted us telepathically; I can hardly believe this is happening."

Marquis Silivasi followed in quick succession, appearing beside his mate with their son Nikolai still squirming in his arms. "We need to get her out of here"—he spoke directly to Napolean while inclining his head toward the door to the chamber of Sacrifice and Atonement, and then he growled— "away from that door...and that male...*now!*"

Napolean cleared his throat. "Watch yourself, Warrior. Remember to whom you're speaking."

Marquis averted his eyes out of respect, but he continued to simmer just below the surface.

Vanya threw her hands up in frustration and snorted. "So, you find it acceptable to converse with my family telepathically about the matter, but not me?" She could hardly believe what she was seeing and hearing. By all that was holy, what were they all so afraid of, and why didn't they trust her to handle it?

Ciopori stepped in front of Vanya. She nervously smoothed the hem of Vanya's blouse with her fingertips, and then she met her gaze with a look of such trepidation that it shook Vanya to the core. "Napolean hasn't told you?"

"Told me what!" Vanya insisted.

Ciopori reached out to take her hand, and Vanya slapped it away, overwhelmed by all the frenetic attention.

Brooke frowned. "Let's all go back to the house," she said. "Let's sit down and discuss this indoors." She glanced nervously at the heavy metal door behind them.

"Discuss what?" Vanya repeated, staring down the beautiful woman whom the gods had so honored with Napolean's heart.

Brooke's eyes softened. "I'm sorry, Vanya. This has got to

appear so incredibly rude: You're absolutely right—someone needs to tell you what is happening. Right away. We are all just a little bit on edge right now. Would you mind coming inside, to the house, where we can all sit down and talk?" She paused to remember her etiquette. "Please, Princess."

Vanya knew she should just go with them inside and talk it out, but the apprehension was getting the best of her. "With all due respect, Brooke, I can very well see what is happening." Despite her attempt at courtesy, she gestured wildly at the sky. "I do have eyes, you know." She held out her wrist. "And I can feel my own skin tingling...and I can even match the shapes with the stars." She glared at Marquis and Ciopori in turn. "What I cannot discern is why the lot of you are acting so defensive and crazy. Surely this is not the first Blood Moon the house of Jadon has ever seen."

Marquis Silivasi took a bold step forward. "The male," he grumbled, "the one the gods have bound you to; it is Saber Alexiares. The Dark One."

The words drifted past Vanya's ears, but they didn't quite settle in her consciousness.

"Marquis," Ciopori groaned.

"We don't know exactly what he is—Dark or Light—or what he's capable of becoming," Brooke added thoughtfully.

"Forgive me, My Queen," Ciopori intoned, "but by any standard that matters, we most certainly do. The male is wholly dark—unapologetically evil—and frankly, abhorrent!" By the look on her face, Ciopori was not about to be challenged on her assessment.

The night seemed to settle into a distant, quiet void, the beauty of the sky a sudden paradox: If the earth had opened up and swallowed her whole, Vanya could not have been more stunned.

Or silent.

Napolean Mondragon growled deep in his throat, and the ground shifted briefly beneath them. He waved an imperious hand in front of them all and spoke three short words: "Stop.

Everyone. *Now.*" His voice traveled like vapor on the wind, wrapping itself around all those who were present and commanding their obedience.

Marquis eyed the king warily, awaiting his next command.

Brooke took a gentle step back, allowing him space.

And Ciopori averted her eyes in a show of submission and respect.

Vanya, however, took a tentative step toward him, her eyes acutely focused on his serious face. "Napolean? Is this true?"

He regarded her gently. "Yes, Vanya. It is."

Her mind felt as if it could handle the revelation, but her body staggered sideways.

Napolean caught her by the elbow. "It is true that you are Saber's *destiny*, but you are not bound to anyone, Princess. We do not have to indulge the gods in everything."

"Really?" Brooke whispered. She lowered her head, pulled her robe tighter around her now shivering form, and began to pad back toward the main house, leaving the others standing there in shocked silence.

Napolean watched her walk away with a look of abject helplessness in his eyes, and then he quickly regained his composure, refocusing on the matter at hand. "Come to the manse, Vanya. Join us inside where it's warm. Let us all talk this out."

Vanya swayed once more on her feet, and Ciopori reached out to catch her. She turned to regard the heavy iron door just beyond her reach, and she imagined the male inside. *How easy it is for Napolean to speak such weighty words, condemn another soul to death,* she thought. A male who had been stolen from his crib as a mere babe, a descendant of Jadon who was now more animal than man. "Very well," she whispered. "There is nothing to be achieved by standing out in the cold." She raised her head and nodded slowly. "Besides, I need to sit down."

Ciopori grasped her hand, linked their fingers, and held on firmly. "We will figure this out, sister. I swear." She clenched her eyes shut as if trying to force a disturbing image from her mind.

"By all the gods, I promise; we will not let that monster near you."

Vanya didn't respond.

It was too much. It was all just...too much.

She looked down at the tattered journal, still clutched in her left hand, and slowly held it up. "Oh, I almost forgot," she whispered, holding it out to Napolean. "I brought this for you. It's why I was here."

Napolean reached out and accepted the book, a look of curiosity in his dark, keen eyes. "What is it?"

"A dream that has been haunting my sleep. I thought I should share it with you...right away."

Napolean frowned. "What kind of dream?"

Vanya chuckled softly then, a sound completely devoid of humor. "A dream about a fire-breathing dragon that is lost to darkness, and a treasure that must somehow be returned to the house of Jadon."

eight

Salvatore Nistor cupped the glowing cube on his nightstand between the palms of his hands lovingly, stroking it like a dark defiler in the night. While the cube had fallen short before—failing to reveal that Marquis and Nachari had murdered his brother Valentine certainly came to mind—it was not failing him now: The afterglow of the Serpens Blood Moon was reflected starkly, and without ambiguity, in the etched glass; and the fact that this Omen belonged to the newest member of the house of Jadon, Sabino Dzuna, better known as Saber Alexiares, was not lost on the ancient sorcerer either.

Sabino Dzuna.

A stolen child of light.

Lifted from his crib by Damien Alexiares after the loss of his own dark, twin sons.

The very idea of it boggled the mind.

Surrounded by the wispy smoke of a dozen candles, each one perched on a stone pedestal, Salvatore released the cube, rubbed his hands together to return warmth to his palms, and rotated on his bed to get a better view of the bloodied prisoner, chained to his lair wall—Damien Alexiares. "Well, would you look at this," he drawled, smiling faintly at the weakened Dark One. "Oh," he sighed and shrugged his shoulders, "I suppose those shackles prevent you from coming this way." He absently licked his thin lips. "No matter. I would be happy to tell you what my cube reveals this night."

Damien struggled to raise his head and focus his blood-caked eyes on the councilman. "Your liege?" he whispered.

"What's that?" Salvatore said.

"Your liege," Damien repeated.

Salvatore laughed loud and hearty. "Your liege," he mocked, "how funny—is that how you address the most powerful sorcerer in the house of Jaegar? Do I look like a dark lord to you?"

Damien tried to shake his head, but the effort was too much. "No, sir...no." He cleared his throat to remove the phlegm. "That's how I address one of my revered council members."

"Ah," Salvatore said. "I see." He rose from the bed and strolled lazily across the floor until he was standing directly in front of Damien; then he raised his pointer finger and slowly lifted the battered male's head. "Look at me, Damien."

The male blinked several times.

"Tell me again: Did your sons know about your deception?"

This time, Damien managed to shake his head. "No, Salvatore." He spat out blood. "I swear by the dark lords, they didn't know."

"Never...after all these years?" Salvatore asked.

"Never," Damien answered.

"Hmm." Salvatore released Damien's chin and touched his own lips, considering. "Well then, maybe they don't deserve execution...as their father does."

Damien practically wilted on the vine. For a 900-year-old soldier, a powerful and dark male in the house of Jaegar who had sired at least four children—two of whom died at birth and two of whom were summarily screwed because of their father's lack of forethought—Damien was a sad sight indeed. The guards had whipped him until his skin peeled back from his flesh; they had broken bone after bone in order to make him confess his crime; and they had threatened him all the while with sentencing his innocent sons to death as part of his punishment.

Salvatore knew the boys were innocent. Dane and Diablo's surprise had been as great as his own, and their sense of betrayal, having learned that their revered eldest brother was indeed an imposter, was almost as deep as his own. But these things called for swift and absolute punishment. If ever there was a cause worth making a lesson out of, an example for all others to see, this was the time, and this was the family.

It wasn't the fact that Damien had stolen the child, after all.

It was the deception. He had brought an interloper into the house of Jaegar, a son of the Light Ones, who could potentially communicate with his own kind. A being that had a soul of all things!

No one could possibly know what dangers that posed to the ancient house of darkness Salvatore so affectionately called home. The bottom line was plain: Damien should have presented his plan to the council in a formal petition, and he should have asked for his brethren's permission. At the least, the house of Jaegar could have approached the abduction as an experiment. At the most, they would have watched Saber Alexiares closely.

Very, very closely.

The supernatural cube on the nightstand glowed momentarily, reminding Salvatore of the recent revelation: the Serpens Moon. "Ah yes," he spoke aloud, taking a step away from Damien to regard him more keenly. "I almost forgot my original point."

Damien held Salvatore's gaze, but he didn't dare speak.

"My cube. Do you see it?"

"Yes," Damien muttered, the sound muffled between broken teeth.

"Do you know what it heralds, soldier? What has been revealed even as we labored in my lair?"

Damien shook his head, and his matted hair swayed ever so slightly. "No."

Salvatore swept his arm out in front of him. "Then allow me to tell you, simple man."

Man.

As in hu-*man.*

Was there any greater slur in the house of Jaegar—except maybe being called a son of Jadon?

Damien swallowed hard and waited.

"It tells me, beloved father of three, that there was a Blood Moon this night. A Serpens Blood Moon to be exact." He spun around and paced toward a computer screen which was now reflecting the image of a satellite feed—the Dark Ones were tapped into NASA's computers; and Salvatore could watch the sky in real time, almost as clearly as if he stood on the earth instead of living deep below it. "It would appear that the celestial god of rebirth has bestowed your *son* with a human *destiny*. Is that not the most ironic, not to mention ludicrous, thing you've ever heard of? Saber...Alexiares? The male would just as soon rape her and kill her as mate her." He snickered. "I wonder if his new family knows this."

Damien bristled in reaction to the words *new family*, and Salvatore knew it was taking everything the male had not to lash out in verbal retaliation. It seemed Damien Alexiares truly loved his *firstborn*...or whatever the hell the male truly was. No matter. "But here's the thing," Salvatore continued. "This new development provides us with a wonderful opportunity to clean up this mess, so to speak."

Damien frowned, his sweat-drenched forehead creasing with concern. "I don't understand."

"Of course you don't!" Salvatore snapped, raising his chin and pitching his own long, black-and-red locks behind his shoulder in contempt. "Of course you don't." He lowered his voice. "But you will."

He sat down in the chair in front of the computer, grabbed the mouse, and double-clicked on some stellular icon in order to bring the picture of the sky into sharper focus. "You see, Saber now has one full moon, or thirty days to be exact, to find, claim, and impregnate his chosen mate. As you well know, one of his two twin sons, the Dark One, unfortunately, must be sacrificed to the Blood in a timely fashion, or the male will meet"—he rocked back on the heels of his chair and grimaced—"well, a very painful and prolonged end."

Damien ground his teeth together and clenched his eyes shut, if only for a moment. "Is there nothing you would do for Saber?" he finally asked, daring to speak as boldly as he clearly felt he must. "After all he's done for you...for this house?"

Salvatore tapped his fingers on the desk three times trying to think of the correct reply—and to restrain himself from killing the insolent, deceitful bastard right then and there.

Treason was treason.

And law was law, even among heathens.

And Damien was treading on very thin ice.

He spun around in his chair to face the prisoner. "Ask not what your council can do for you," he barked with derision.

Damien winced. "Forgive me." It sounded as insincere as it was. "What can I do for my council?" His voice thickened then. "If it will save Dane and Diablo, I would do anything."

Now this appeased Salvatore, at least somewhat. "That's better," he crooned. "Now then, let's see. What can you do for us?" Before Damien could reply, he leaned forward and lowered his voice, not even trying to hide his disdain. "You can convince your two remaining sons—because trust me, Damien, Saber is lost to you forever—to serve your house better than you did." He opened the second drawer on the right of his desk and pulled out a small blue vial of some unfamiliar substance and held it up in his left hand. "Do you know what this is?"

"No," Damien muttered, his arms drooping against his heavy chains.

"Of course, you don't," Salvatore sneered. "No one does." He tossed it back and forth between his hands twice. "Well, allow me to tell you. It is—how shall I say?—birth control of a sort. For males."

Damien's head shot up in surprise, and he stared incredulously at Salvatore. "Birth control?"

"Did I stutter?" Salvatore said.

Damien held his tongue.

Rolling his eyes, Salvatore set the vial down on his desk. "Yes, Mr. Alexiares: birth control. You see, there are some secrets in the house of Jaegar that remain with the council and the sorcerer—they're not meant for the general population." He leveled a hate-filled glare at the traitor and frowned. "Which of course means that now that I've told you, I will absolutely have to kill you. But then, you're already dead, so it really doesn't matter." He picked up the vial and slammed it back down on the desk for effect. "As you know, we have long searched for ways to attack our arrogant cousins, the ones who walk in the sun—the contemptible house of Jadon—and it has been an uphill battle, one we have waged valiantly for centuries with cunning, stealth, and determination. Still, it never hurts to have more potent weapons at our disposal. This, my dear friend"—he pointed at the vial—"is a unique and extraordinary weapon. It makes a male infertile for sixty days." He chuckled at the thought. "Well, that's not entirely true. For at least thirty days, and up to sixty. It is colorless and odorless, and once ingested, the male will perform as always—screw whatever woman he chooses with optimum virility and stamina—but he will, indeed, shoot blanks. As you also know, those born to the house of Jadon must speak a pregnancy into being. Unlike ourselves, they have to *want* a woman to get pregnant, to think it into being or wish for it, or some such nonsense, in order for it to happen." *Unlike ourselves*, Salvatore thought, *we only have to rape, release our seed, and death becomes an absolute certainty, with or without the birth of our children, depending upon whether we kill the female host before the forty-eight-hour pregnancy 'expires' and our offspring does it for us. Clawing their way out of her tortured body.* The thought gave him excited chills.

He stared at the blue bottle with fascination and anticipation then. "Get this potion into the body of a chosen male from the house of Jadon immediately following his Blood Moon, and his ability to fulfill the demands of the Blood Curse is hampered, impossible, really...null and void. In plain speak for dummies—that would be you—his death is a foregone conclusion."

Ignoring the insult, Damien seemed to think about it for a moment, and then he suddenly found his voice, weak as it was. "I don't understand," he mumbled. "How long have you had this potion? If we have the ability to block pregnancy, then why do we go to such lengths to try to keep our kidnapped nannies and female captives alive? Destroying their wombs, killing the very labor we need to raise our infant sons?"

Salvatore frowned. "No, you don't understand, Damien, but

since you are about to die, I will explain it to you." He leaned back in his desk chair and intertwined his fingers in front of him. "We have not had this potion long. It is a gift from the Dark Lord Ademordna, one I have pleaded and prayed for, for decades." He shivered with delight. "The price was two hundred dead human virgins, their hearts carved out while still beating, offered in smoke and fire on a makeshift altar." He sighed in exasperation. "Do you have any idea how hard is to find two hundred virgin females of child-bearing age in these United States these days?" He rolled his dark eyes. "Trust me; it isn't easy." He waved a dismissive hand in front of him. "But that is what our lord required for the formula—I won't share with you the sorcery and spells that had to accompany it—and that is what I gave him. Suffice to say, Ademordna made it abundantly clear that we, his servants in the house of Jaegar, were never, *ever* to use this potion ourselves. To do so would be to deny the dark deities the torture, death, and agony they so enjoy to watch. It would be sacrilege against our very nature, not to mention an intervention that would violate the Blood Curse and surely come back to haunt us. The vengeful females of our ancestors do demand their pound of flesh, do they not?"

Damien licked his cracked lips and croaked out an affirmative sound. "But you can use it on the sons of Jadon?"

"Why not?" Salvatore snapped. "That was the point of all that sacrifice!" He took a deep, calming breath. "Yes, Damien; if we can get it into the bodies of our enemies, we may use it." He smiled then, his flash of anger gone. "And that is where you come in. That is where Dane and Diablo come in."

Damien swallowed a bit of bile, clearly beginning to put two and two together. "You want Dane or Diablo to get Saber to ingest the potion?" He shook his head in confusion. "How? Why would Saber do that? I mean, not only do our males drink only blood for sustenance, but it would be suicide."

Salvatore rose languidly and turned to face his prisoner. "This is true, but Saber will never know that he's ingesting a foreign substance. If the host drinks the potion—and Saber drinks the host's blood—then Saber, in effect, drinks the potion. Do you see how simple that is?" Salvatore knew he didn't need to explain any further. Damien was rebellious; he wasn't stupid. The male would understand exactly what the sorcerer was saying: He was referring to the ancient custom in the house of Jaegar of younger siblings feeding their fathers and brothers.

"But you said the Dark Lords forbade it—our own males taking the potion," Damien said in a weak voice, interrupting Salvatore's thoughts.

"They do," Salvatore replied.

"Then, if Dane or Diablo ingest the poison in order to feed it to Saber—"

"Then Dane or Diablo will die," Salvatore supplied.

Damien nearly shook with anger. Nearly. He was far too weak to pull it off with any aplomb. "You can't ask me to send one of my innocent sons to his death."

Salvatore laughed then. "Oh, but I think I can. You see, your own death is simply a formality, a matter of going before the high court to receive your sentence. Dane and Diablo? Well, they are not yet a foregone conclusion." He strode across the room in three giant purposeful steps and snatched Damien by the jaw, his claws extending and biting into the tender flesh. "You may save *one* son, my treacherous brother: Dane or Diablo. The choice is yours. Choose who will feed Saber and die and who your council will allow to live." He paused for effect, then drew a jagged claw across the male's face, before releasing his hold. "If you do not choose either son, we will feed one the potion anyway and slay them both." His words were final, venomous, and harshly clipped. "But do it soon, *Father*, for we need to get to Saber before he *gets* to his *destiny*, if you understand my meaning."

Damien looked positively pale, aside from being drained of ninety percent of his blood, and Salvatore almost felt sorry for him.

Almost.

It must be hard to lose a son…but then, the sorcerer had

much bigger fish to fry and no time for communal compassion: They had to plot and scheme.

Whether Dane or Diablo acted as host was a small matter. Very small. They still had to find a way to get the potion into Saber, and that would take some doing. It would take a missive attached to a white flag, perhaps in the talons of a falcon, being sent to the fair and just Napolean Mondragon: a brother's plea for a final meeting with his long-lost sibling. A promise of truce between houses that had stood in deadly opposition for as long as the Vampyr could be counted. It would require mercy and diplomacy, a delegation of dark soldiers meeting light warriors underneath the night stars in the Red Canyons that stood as a middle ground between the darker and lighter factions of their kind, a temporary cease-fire that had never before been achieved.

Would the ancient king go for it? Salvatore wondered. Would he allow the newest member of his house to meet with a former brother, *a current enemy*, in order to say good-bye, to find peace...or closure...or whatever the hell a king with a soul would call such nonsense.

Salvatore and the Dark Ones' council would have to make a perfect offer. They would have to get Dane or Diablo close enough to feed Saber, and they would have to convince the male to do it, no matter what occurred, without letting him know that his *brotherly kiss* would, in fact, be a kiss of death for both of them.

Yes, Damien needed to choose quickly, perhaps even wisely.

And then Salvatore and the council needed to act.

Definitively.

And pray for a king's compassion.

nine

Vanya Demir dragged a narrow wingback chair against the door of Napolean's upper level guest bedroom and securely wedged the top beneath the doorknob. Not that the chair would actually stop a determined vampire from entering, but *gods be merciful*, she had to have a moment alone.

She had just excused herself from Napolean's living room, begging a momentary retreat, and she had no doubt that her family, and her king, were still going at it, discussing *her* life.

"We will protect you, Vanya," Marquis had insisted.

"You will need to stay here at the compound where you are more heavily guarded," Napolean had insisted.

"I will not let him anywhere near you," Ciopori had asserted. As if her sister was any match for a Dark One.

Brooke was the only one who had acted with objectivity or restraint, suggesting that Vanya should be allowed to think and decide for herself; and that had caused more than a little friction between the queen and Napolean. No doubt, they would be talking late into the night, long after everyone else went to sleep.

And that wasn't even the half of it.

It seemed like every interested soul in Dark Moon Vale, including a swarm of Master Warriors who had somehow figured it out, had felt the need to weigh in on the princess's predicament, until half of those gathered in Napolean's front room were practically strangers, many of whom were speaking at the same time.

Enough already!

Vanya had needed a break.

It wasn't like she was a child. After all, she was 2,830 years old. Granted, she had spent 2,810 of those years sleeping in the ground, but the point was: She was hardly wet behind the ears. Surely, she could apply some measure of reason and analysis on her own.

So, Saber Alexiares was a dark soul.

A completely rotten, unredeemable fiend who had tortured, slain, and violated innocence his entire long existence—and who knew what those words really meant in terms of the details concerning his abhorrent life. She didn't want to contemplate his history, not right now. But she was able to contemplate the fact that he was born to the house of Jadon, not the house of Jaegar. She was able to consider the fact that Napolean had spared him from immediate execution for some reason—perhaps the king felt he was not entirely beyond redemption. And, she was certainly able to understand that, like the dragon from her dream, he was cornered in a dark cave, having never known the light, and there were too many unknown variables to draw final conclusions just yet. The celestial gods were not idiots by any stretch of the imagination.

Vanya padded across the room and took a leisurely position on the bed, reclining atop the goose-down comforter. She immediately fluffed a small, rectangular pillow and snuggled into the embroidered fabric. Staring up at the coffered ceiling, she took a deep breath and tried to still her racing heart.

Dear gods, she had a mate; she was another male's *destiny*. In her wildest imagination, and especially after the hurtful fiasco that had been her brief relationship with Napolean, the revelation was wholly unexpected.

And yes, she understood full well that this was a dangerous and depraved being. For all that was holy, she had known her brother Jaegar in the flesh...and at his worst. She had witnessed the murder of her half-celestial sisters. She had lived during a time when war was blood sport used to avert boredom, and women were taken and used like chattel. She had known the best and the worst that the soul was capable of, but she could not dismiss the fact that she had also always belonged to someone else. Her family. Her father, the king. Her people and their kingdom. Her duty and her honor...

But never to a man.

Never to a living, breathing, sentient male with flesh and blood and struggles of his own.

She remembered the fire and the passion that had come from Napolean's hands; the gentleness and brutality that dwelled in the same set of fingers; the need and the desperation that had shone in his eyes. The animal beneath the man. The vulnerability beneath the strength.

And she trembled.

What if—just what if—there was something universally male or untouched in Saber Alexiares? What if—just what if—there was some place in the entire vast universe that might belong solely, and without obligation, to her?

Someone?

Vanya had never had a man, a friend, a child...anything...to call her own. She had been born to responsibility and duty. She had been raised to be poised, mature, and regal. She had been reared to serve, to give, and to persevere. Hers was a life that had always belonged to everything and everyone but her. There were no breaks or reprieves, no true sabbaticals from the seriousness of theology and study. There were only her people and her royal blood. Her never-ending sense of purpose. And while that was fine—it was woven into the very fabric of who she was, and she embraced it—was she not also a woman? A person? A living, breathing, feeling entity as well? And what about her dream—the treasure?

Vanya rubbed her slender palms over her face and tried to clear her mind.

Who was this dark, fire-breathing dragon? And why wasn't she qualified to discern the truth of his embittered soul on her own? The more she thought about it, the idea of him reclining on a stiff, narrow cot in an ancient, barren cell, less than a mile away, the more she felt drawn to see for herself.

She didn't need to be a vampire to cloak her appearance, to move as the mist through a dark, tree-filled forest; she had centuries of magic in her repertoire. She was an original female, the daughter of King Sakarias and Queen Jade, descended from a long line of celestial gods and humans—the goddess Cygnus and her human mate Mateo, to be exact—and her powers were formidable. Especially since she had been honing them at the Romanian University.

Swallowing hard to suppress her fear, Vanya summoned her determination as well as her courage: Yes, she would enter the dragon's lair on her own; she would remain quiet as a mouse and equally unobtrusive; and she would see for herself what the Serpens Blood Moon was all about. She would look the devil in the eyes and measure the full blackness of his soul. And she didn't need her king, or her sister, or her brother-in-law, or the house of Jadon's keepers to assist her.

Vanya Demir created a holographic double of her body. She left the double in the guest bed; slipped through the wall like a ghostly apparition; and made her way down the long, narrow hall, with its dimly lit sconces and outrageously expensive carpets, headed for the Chamber of Sacrifice and Atonement, for Saber Alexiares's holding cell.

Before she opened the heavy outer door, she conjured a simple but powerful sleeping spell, the equivalent of sprinkling celestial slumbering dust around and about the bodies of Saber's guards, Ramsey and Saxson Olaru; and the two sentinels were instantly sleeping deeply, long before they had a chance to notice her entry. In fact, Ramsey had fallen asleep so quickly, he was still sitting upright in his comfortable chair, still facing the cell from his vigilant position.

It was late, around eleven forty-five at night, and to Vanya's absolute relief, the fire-breathing dragon was sleeping soundly as well—at least he appeared to be sleeping soundly. As her ethereal form began to take more substantive shape, she tiptoed cautiously toward the horizontal cot, ever so careful not to wake the sleeping vampire, and then she peered curiously at his prone form.

The Dark One was lying on his back, partially turned on his left side, with his left arm bent at the elbow and stretched in such a way that he could cradle his own head. He wasn't chained, either to the wall or the bed, but there were enough diamonds embedded in the stone walls and the floors to keep him restrained without the use of additional manacles. Not to mention, he appeared to be substantially weakened, as one who was missing an extensive amount of life-force or chi. Clearly, the warriors were keeping him drained of vital blood, denying him much needed sustenance. Vanya grimaced—what an awful state of affairs. How sad that such dire measures were clearly necessary.

As she bent to take her first true look at his face, her breath caught in her throat: The sight of the male was jarring, intimidating, in many ways, yet deeply stirring to her own blood and soul. Her mouth felt suddenly dry, and she swallowed convulsively.

Saber's hair was thick and wavy, almost unruly in its mass, and it hung just to his shoulders, as far as she could tell from that angle. And the unnatural highlights—the dense, unmistakable red bands woven throughout the raven tresses—were positively unsettling. *Dear gods*, he looked just like a Dark One, just like a cursed male from the house of Jaegar. And of course, that was what he was—or at least, what he had once been.

She fought not to shudder as she took another careful step forward, and her hand rose inadvertently to cover her mouth.

His nose was as straight as an arrow, rugged yet nicely refined, and perfect in its shape and structure. His cheekbones were positively chiseled, as were his jaw and the slight indentation in his chin. His mouth was set in a harsh, cruel line, almost contemptuous, even in his sleep, but his lips were firm and well filled out, shapely in their own right. Vanya drew back in surprise. By all the gods, he was disturbingly handsome—in the most treacherous type of way. Everything about him screamed danger.

And excitement.

She followed the angles of his face down to his neck, making note of the copper hue of his skin—and just how was it that a male who lived underground maintained such a rich complexion? She paused when her gaze traveled to his raised arm, then narrowed in on the distinct lines of his musculature, all that raw power barely concealed beneath smooth, unmarred skin. It was surprising to see such raw perfection—not that she had expected a mass of scars and warts, but still, she felt as if she were staring at an artist's rendition of an anatomy chart rather than a ruthless male who had lived a life of violence and brutality. The various contours of his build were clearly defined beneath a fine, silken covering, and every striation of his muscles was readily apparent, as if sculpted by a potter's hands, into taut, lean tissue.

Sweeping her long, flaxen hair behind her shoulders, Vanya took a cautious step back.

He was dangerous, indeed.

Lethal, without question.

For more reasons than one.

Saber's spirit radiated around him, and it was a synthesis of fire and lava and dark swirling smoke. This male had known no gentleness in his life, no mercy or kindness—or peace. He was simply ash and stone in a flawless, hardened shell. Feeling the sudden need to draw fresh air, Vanya slowly backed away, picking up her pace as she headed toward the cell door. She had seen quite enough: an outer beauty concealing an inner fury. She would conjure her magic once more and slip through the bars undetected, and then she would quickly retreat—perhaps she would run—back to Napolean's manse, where she would, indeed, allow her loved ones to provide the protection they were offering.

Somehow the fantasy of the male was more glorious, and far safer, than the reality.

As Vanya struggled to remember the words of the

incantation she needed to keep her form fluid and ghost-like, to allow an ethereal transition that would take her safely through the bars, she all at once heard the most terrifying sound imaginable behind her: the soft, almost inaudible rustling of a body rising from its slumber, the low pad of bare feet finding purchase on a stone floor.

And then just like that, Saber was there.

Behind her.

Pushing up against her. His hard, lean body pressing into hers, trapping her against the bars.

She gasped. And she would have screamed...fought...tried to run, except the most vivid images from her dream instantly replayed in her mind: *I step back in alarm. The creature is fierce, and I know that he will destroy me if I let him. Slowly, ever so carefully, I begin to retreat. My feet are now bare, and the rocky floor is rough against my skin, tearing at my flesh and causing me great distress, but I am too afraid to cry out, lest the vicious beast pounce in response to my fear.*

Trying her best to remain calm, she focused on what was happening here and now. By the measure of his chin against her hair, he was a full head taller than she, perhaps six-foot-one, give or take an inch, and his breathing was silent and steady, measured only by the rise and fall of his powerful chest against her much narrower back.

"You must be Vanya," he whispered in a deep, foreboding voice, his warm breath wafting over her ear. His tone was as silken as it was threatening, and Vanya cleared her throat, hoping to sound confident and unafraid.

"And how would you know this?" she asked, a purposeful hint of arrogance in her tone.

He practically purred his words. "How could I not? Jaegar. Jadon. Ciopori. *Vanya*"—he rolled her name off his tongue as he nipped at the lobe of her ear—"your likenesses were recorded in the annals of history...stored in the colony's library."

The thought made her sick—so all the Dark Ones knew her by sight then?

She couldn't dwell on it now. She was too busy remembering

to breathe; recalling her dream; replaying the scorching, excruciating fire and pain...trying desperately not to get burned.

"I see," she whispered.

"Do you?" He tilted his hips forward ever so slightly. "The real question is—why are you here, *sweet Princess?*"

Vanya nearly forgot herself. "Stand back, soldier!" Her tone was too impassioned—too fearful. She immediately softened her voice and murmured, "Please."

He responded to her uncertainty exactly as she knew he would, by becoming more aroused, and as his ardor increased, he deliberately pressed his erection against her bottom.

She didn't dare move.

Dearest goddess of light, please—get me out of this.

He groaned then, his voice a low purr. "I don't believe you answered my question: *Why are you here?*" The words were clipped and cruel, not even mockingly seductive. He placed his right hand on her hip, at the small of her waist, and bent forward to her neck, his lethal fangs scraping against her delicate skin, before he slowly pulled away. "Why would a lamb seek out a lion—unless it wanted to be slaughtered?" He gestured toward the guards, rotating his wrist in front of her so she could follow the motion, and then he slowly shook his head from side to side, his thick crimson-and-black hair spilling across her shoulders. "You even put your saviors to sleep."

Vanya felt as if her heart might just beat out of her chest or, worse yet, simply stop beating altogether. She pushed back against him with her left elbow, trying to wedge some space between them, trying to remove his arousal from her backside before he became too inflamed to stop. "I...I..."

Oh gods, how did she answer this?

"You what?" he snarled, and then he clutched her offending arm with his hand, pushed back with a minimal amount of effort, and easily held it immobile. His powerful fingers clamped down on her elbow then, and they felt like an iron shackle, bruising her tender skin—was he punishing her for her resistance?

And then he froze.

His severe fingers relaxed, and he drew in a harsh, jagged breath.

The orange light from the Blood Moon was streaming in through the narrow windows, and as it poured down over them, a haunting shadow appeared on her arm, illuminating the markings on her skin like light from a fire. *"Dark Lords..."* He spoke the vile words with reverence. "You have the celestial god of rebirth on your arm—*Serpens.*" For a moment, it appeared as if he didn't understand what it meant, as if he didn't know what he wanted to do next...

And then a deep, barely audible growl rose in his throat, and Vanya knew that he had made the connection.

That he truly understood who she was...*to him.*

She thought of her dream once more, and waited with bated breath: *And that's when the dragon opens his fearsome mouth and begins to breathe fire, scorching me from head to toe. My thin linen nightgown is ablaze, and I gasp from the heat...and the pain.*

And then I scream, a piteous, never-ending cry.

Once more, Saber slowly lowered his head until his mouth hovered perilously above the artery between Vanya's neck and her shoulder; only this time, the twin set of fangs elongated until they pressed sharply against her skin. "I want to taste you, Princess," he drawled.

Vanya inhaled sharply. "No! Please—"

He didn't wait for her to finish speaking.

He pierced her skin with amazing speed, striking like a coiled rattlesnake, not caring at all that she was a female or a princess. Her body began to convulse from the shock, and he made a tight seal around the wound with his hard, full lips, taking long, drugging pulls of her blood, funneling her life through his canines. As the pain robbed her of breath, he moaned with pleasure.

And then he reached up to grab a fistful of her hair in his hands. Locking her in place, he used his other hand to stroke her hips and belly.

Vanya wrenched her neck aside so forcefully that she managed to dislodge his fangs, even as she lost several strands of hair. "No!" she shouted, desperate to break free. "Stop this at once! Leave me alone!" She peered back over her shoulder to meet his eyes and immediately wished that she hadn't.

He looked like a wild animal.

A demon.

The kind of thing that should swiftly be put to death—summarily and without mercy.

His eyes glowed feral red; his right lip drew back in an angry snarl; and his jaw clenched so tight that his veins could be seen through his skin. He was lost in bloodlust, a murderous, carnal haze of need, solely unaware of her presence as a separate being with a heart or a soul.

Her heart dropped into her stomach; she struggled to catch her breath; and her knees grew weak beneath her. "Saber, please...stop!" Why was she bothering to plead with him? To speak his name as if that made any difference?

His angry fist tightened in her hair, and he drew back his lips in a threatening gesture of dominance and defiance, his gleaming white fangs gnashing together with rage. "*You are mine.*"

"No!" she bit out. "*No.* It does not work that way!"

"*Mine.*" An inhuman sound escaped his throat, and he practically salivated. "Ah, but I think that it does." The hand that remained on her hip slid forward as he splayed his fingers over the inside of her thigh and tugged her back against him, kneading her flesh in his palm.

That was it!

Something inside of her snapped.

Hot tears of alarm stung her eyes, and she began to twist back and forth violently, trying desperately to force him off her. He wasn't a dragon—he was a man! A rage-filled, crazy, insufferable man.

And she could no longer afford this paralysis.

Summoning every ounce of courage she had, she wrenched her thigh free from his hand, slammed her shoulders into his chest, and stomped her foot into his shin. "Lasa-ma impace!" she screamed, spinning around to face him. *Leave me alone!*

To her surprise, he released her hair and stepped back, fluidly.

Before he could counter her futile resistance, she began to chant in their original tongue:

"Ancient Wind, Artic Rain;
Born of fire, blood, and pain;
Perched upon Lord Serpens' throne;
Blend your power with my own!"

As the words left her lips, her soul gathered power from the four directions. She drew it inward, harnessed its strength, and evoked a primordial force as old as time itself. Vanya Demir built a glowing arc of energy around the tips of her fingers. She allowed it only a second to swirl and build, and then she hurled it at the dragon, sending the full force of impact into Saber's chest.

Saber gasped in pain and flew backward, slamming into the opposite wall. His wild hair whipped around him as if caught in a great gust of wind, and his neck popped, twisting unnaturally, making a horrible, piteous sound, although it didn't appear to be broken. When at last he slumped to the ground, he simply sat there in stunned silence, staring up at the princess with red, glowing eyes, his furious gaze locked with hers in some elemental dance of wills.

He was still as the night.

Silent as a prayer.

Yet tumultuous as the sea.

As she called upon her magic once more to wriggle her way back through the bars, back to a place of safety, she turned to stare at the stunned, disheveled vampire. "I am not a child to be toyed with, Saber! You may be stronger than me, but I have magic you can only dream of." She licked her lips and frowned, still appalled by his animal nature. "Do you enjoy being a monster?"

He shrugged, seemingly indifferent. "Do you enjoy being a princess?"

BLOOD REDEMPTION

"I was born a princess, Mr. Alexiares!"

"And I was *born* a monster, Miss Demir."

"Yes," she whispered. "A fire-breathing dragon." Turning on her heels, she headed toward the outer door, releasing the guards' sleeping spell on her way—the Olaru brothers would both be awake in less than two minutes, neither remembering their repose nor the time that had passed while they slumbered. As she depressed the handle and pushed against the cumbersome weight of the door, she turned around to look upon the dragon one last time: "Tell no one you saw me," she ordered. "And I will do the same." Squaring her shoulders, she raised her chin and regarded him with pity. "You will be dead in thirty days, Saber Alexiares; and the world will be a better place for it."

She could still see the smirk of indifference on his face as she fled into the night.

Saber Alexiares drew his knees toward his chest, filled his laboring lungs with air, and relaxed into the stone wall behind him, staring out into the space where Princess Vanya had just stood.

Her magic was impressive to say the least.

She had mustered courage, defiance, and tenacity: all admirable traits for a being not born to the house of Jaegar. She had even struck swiftly, sending him flying across the room into the damnable stone wall—and didn't that just make his back feel like he'd been run over by a John Deere tractor ? Still, even in his weakened state, he could have summersaulted out of the attack and launched at her before she saw him stir. She would have never known what hit her.

He wondered if she knew just how easily he could have killed her: While she was still summoning the words for her spell, he could have snatched her beating heart right out of her

80

enticing chest. While she was still spinning around to face him, he could have snapped her slender neck with nothing more than a flick of his wrist. Before they even made eye contact, he could have closed her beautiful eyes...forever. Did this brave yet foolish woman truly understand that he could move faster than sound or light? That he could have thrown her on the cot and undressed her before she realized he was on top of her.

She was brave to be sure, but he was a soldier in the house of Jaegar, a dark male who had eight hundred years of savage fighting stored in his repertoire; the princess had been no match for his speed, cunning, or cruelty.

And yet, she still lived.

Why, he wondered, *hadn't he punished her for her insolence?*

True, he had fed from her with calloused indifference, but if he had struck half as hard as he could have, her collarbone would be situated two inches lower right now. No, Saber Alexiares had exercised uncommon restraint.

Enormous control.

He rose from the floor, walked gingerly to the cot, and lowered his body to the mattress, resting his elbows on his knees and his chin in his hands.

Perhaps he was still hoping to survive...somehow. But to what end?

To buy him time until he could escape and return to the colony? After all, wasn't that what he really wanted? To get as far away from the light vampires as possible and return to the life he knew and loved, return to his father and his brothers and the house of Jaegar...if they would still have him.

Perhaps he had handled the whole situation wrong.

Perhaps he had prematurely alienated the one soul he needed in his corner most of all: the one person who could advocate mightily for his life...and freedom. The one person who could bend the ear of the king. Saber Alexiares had only thirty days to live—*unless* he enlisted the princess's cooperation. Perhaps the beautiful female could be made into an ally. At the least, he did not need her as an enemy. Clearly, she was formidable in her own right.

Scrubbing his hands over his face, he sighed, feeling suddenly weary. Well, shit, he had totally screwed that up. What to do now?

The princess was not about to come back and visit him again—not now—not without a great deal of persuasion. Not without a much gentler, far more diplomatic touch. And who in this entire infernal valley of self-righteous vampires would actually advocate for an enemy: a male who had attacked their women and plotted against their house? It was not as if there was anyone he could turn to who suffered any love lost on his account—

Or was there?

Staring out at Ramsey and Saxson, Saber scratched his head. He waited for the males to catch their breath, collect their bearings, and reorient themselves to the room. Clearly, they had no idea what had just happened, other than the fact that there had to be an odd gap of time in their memories—well, maybe not a gap, perhaps just an unfamiliar haze. Far be it from him to enlighten them to the truth.

When at last Ramsey sauntered toward the cell, Saber stood up slowly, careful not to appear too antagonistic. "I have a request," he said, trying to keep his voice low and congenial. He couldn't actually muster respect—never that—but he didn't have to be outright hostile, either.

Ramsey's eyebrows shot up, and he looked at him suspiciously. "Oh yeah," he mumbled, "and what's that." His voice was still gruff from sleep.

Saber swallowed a sarcastic retort. "The woman...Lorna." He spoke evenly. "I would like to see her."

Ramsey cleared his throat as if testing it for metal. "Come again," he snarled.

"The one who came to see me before, the female, I wasn't...*prepared*...for her visit."

"And now you are?" Ramsey asked, his voice revealing his distrust. "Why?"

Saber shrugged his shoulders and tried to appear as cooperative as possible, while still remaining nonchalant. He had to make it believable. "Do I need to articulate a reason?" he replied. "You say she's my mother. Perhaps I just need to...be sure."

ten

The next day

The frail, tiny woman could not have been more than five-foot-six, one hundred ten pounds. Her medium-length brown hair was twisted in a repetitive pattern of S-curls, and her soft, compassionate brown eyes blended into her smooth complexion as she stepped up to Ramsey's desk and waited nervously for the sentinel's instructions.

Saber watched her like a hawk, wishing he knew more acutely what was going on inside of her head—he was almost tempted to take a look, but he didn't want to risk a mind probe, something that might easily be detected by the 815-year-old vampire. After all, Lorna was, at the least, that: a human *destiny* converted to their species by her mate Rafael over 800 years ago. She might be small and unthreatening, but she wasn't a mere weak human, someone to take lightly or underestimate. Not even if she thought she was his mother.

Drawing a slow, deep breath into his lungs, he watched Ramsey Olaru instead. The male retrieved a set of iron keys from a rusted hook beside his desk and made his way directly over to the cage door. He was just about to open it when his nostrils narrowed, and he casually sniffed the air. His eyes shot up to Saber, and he frowned. "You're stronger than you were before," he said, his face betraying his confusion...and concern. "How's that, Chief?"

Saber shrugged his shoulders and shook his head. "Don't know," he said. "Maybe the males in the house of Jaegar are just stronger than the males in the house of Jadon."

Ramsey cut his eyes derisively, the smart hazel pupils flashing amber with disdain. He looked Saber up and down from his head to his toes and slowly licked his lips.

BLOOD REDEMPTION

Saber didn't dare move a muscle. If the male detected Vanya's blood in his system, then it was truly *game over*; trying to get to Lorna would be the least of his worries. After what seemed an interminable length of time, Ramsey finally stepped forward. He reached into the deep pockets of his cargo pants and pulled out a survival blade, with a wicked-looking curve. "Hands through the bars, palms up."

Saber stifled a hiss. The miserable bastard wanted to drain him, some more...*as if*. Everything in him rebelled at the thought, but what could he do? He needed to see Lorna, to be alone with the sympathetic woman, and Ramsey wasn't about to let that happen if he thought Saber posed even the slightest threat. "Fine," Saber snapped. Without hesitation, he stuck both arms out, extended them before Ramsey, and turned his hands palms up.

The ruthless warrior struck with lightning-quick accuracy and force, two swift, deep slashes drawn vertically along Saber's exposed flesh. As the dark crimson blood began to flow in rivulets, staining Saber's arms and dripping on the ground, he stumbled slightly to the side and grasped at a bar with his right hand. "And what if I bleed to death before our visit is finished?"

Ramsey shrugged with apathy. "Oh well."

Saber shut his eyes, counted backward from ten, then reopened them. "Are we set then?"

Ramsey shook his head. "Not quite." He held up the keys to the door in one hand and a pair of iron manacles speckled with diamond dust in the other. "Turn around and link your arms behind your back."

Saber took a step away from the door and did what he was told. Again, Ramsey moved with impressive speed, entering the cell, snapping the cuffs on Saber's wrists, and pushing the male forward with a harsh thrust before Saber could hope to respond in his weakened state. And then the male did something that surprised him: He held out an odd leather device. It looked a bit like a bridle, the kind of headgear a horse might wear, only the metal bit was smaller, and the strap that linked behind the ears was clearly made to fit a vampire's head. Saber snarled angrily then. He couldn't help it. "You have got to be kidding."

"Do I look like I'm kidding?" Ramsey said.

"How the hell am I supposed to talk to that woman with a bit in my mouth?" Saber protested.

Ramsey sneered. "Frankly, my dear, I don't give a damn. All I care about is making sure you don't bite."

Saber snorted so abruptly that he hawked up phlegm. He spit it on the ground and opened his mouth to accept the bit, not bothering to conceal his protracting fangs. They were what they were—an unspoken invitation: *Anytime. Anywhere. The two of us— without all this bullshit.*

"If only I could, Chief," Ramsey mumbled, forcing the bit into Saber's mouth in the roughest manner possible. He over tightened the straps, making sure to catch several locks of Saber's hair in the buckle, just to add insult to injury. And then he looked down at the bloody floor. Waiting about sixty more seconds, he released his incisors, dripped some venom onto the tips of his large, calloused fingers, and smeared the substance over Saber's wounds. The pain began to subside, and the healing began immediately. "Sit," Ramsey ordered, motioning toward the cot. He exited the cell, brought a folding chair back in, and placed it in front of the bed. "You come near this chair, or Lorna, and I'll rip your head off," Ramsey said. "Got that?"

Saber's jaw tightened and he clamped down on the bit. "Yeah," he grunted around the metal—the words sounding garbled. "I got it."

"Good," Ramsey said. With that, he waved Lorna forward and helped her into the chair. "I'll be right outside the door, and it won't be locked," he told her. "He's weak. I can move three times as fast, but he's still dangerous. Keep your distance."

Lorna nodded weakly, her eyes filling up with moisture. "Thank you, Ramsey," she said softly, shifting nervously in her seat. And then she turned to face Saber and smiled faintly, clearly struggling to keep from reacting to what she saw: a monster, cut, gagged, and humiliated in a jail cell before her. She rubbed her hands together awkwardly and swallowed two times. "I...I was so pleased to hear that you asked for me." Her voice was quaking, and Saber didn't know how to respond. Not only did the bit feel foreign and offensive, but the woman was displaying an uncomfortable amount of emotion.

"I wanted..." His voice trailed off as he tried to work his tongue around the bit. "I wanted to ask you some—" *Son of a bitch!* He sounded like an imbecile.

There was no way he was going to be able to pull this off with any measure of finesse.

He might as well end the visit now.

"That's okay," Lorna said, seeming to understand what he was feeling. She reached out slowly and pushed the collar of his shirt away from his neck toward his shoulder.

Ramsey jumped up from his chair. "What are you doing, Lorna?"

She turned around to face him. "We need to be able to talk, Ramsey."

The sentinel stared at her for a while and then finally nodded. "No more than an ounce, either way," he said.

"Of course," Lorna agreed. With that, she released the daintiest pair of fangs Saber had ever seen and slowly leaned forward.

Saber started to back up and frown, but he stopped himself. This woman was more like a mosquito than a vampire. As she slowly sank her fangs into his throat, scoring him more gently than any predator ought to, he held his breath, fighting the disgust. He wanted her off him—away from him—back across the room, preferably, but if this was what it took...

After swallowing a very small amount of blood, she bravely scored her own wrist and raised it to his eye level to show him. "Just a taste," she said.

Saber swallowed convulsively. His feeding instincts were triggered, and he wanted to spring off the bed, pin her down to the ground, and tear her delicate throat out, drinking to his heart's content, but as it stood, he would have to find a way to swallow around a metal bar. She pressed her wrist to his mouth, and his tongue snaked out quickly to lap the blood, three times.

There you have it, she said telepathically. *Now we can talk.*

Saber did not want to consider what he had just done. From this moment forward, he could track Lorna Dzuna at will; and dark lords take pity, the female could track him, too. Well, that didn't matter: If he were ever unrestricted and free, outside of these bars, she would hardly be a formidable enemy.

Thank you, he said, trying to display some manners. *Now then, as I was saying—*

Oh, wait, she interrupted, holding up her hand apologetically. *I didn't mean to cut you off; it's just…* She reached into her large purse and pulled out a soft object. *It's just that Ramsey told me what you asked, and I wanted to show you something.* She set the object down in his lap, sat back in her chair, and looked up at him with a gaze of such unrestrained longing in her eyes that it made him want to…heave.

Saber looked down at the object.

And then he froze, his own heart beating out a frantic rhythm.

His mouth became suddenly dry, and the bit felt like it had grown a couple of inches in diameter. *Great S'nepres, dark lord of his birth, what the…hell?*

It wasn't possible.

It simply wasn't true.

But there it was, in living color, lying right in his lap for the entire world to see: a light blue and green blanket, covered in little frogs and dragons. The blanket he had seen in his dream. The blanket his *mother* had wrapped him in after his birth.

Get it off me! he said, forgetting to exercise decorum. *Move it out of my sight.*

Lorna snatched the blanket with harried surprise and quickly stuffed it in her purse. *I'm sorry,* she muttered quickly. *I thought—* She stopped herself short. *You asked Ramsey about it, so I just assumed…* Her voice trailed off. *I'm sorry.*

Saber felt like the earth was shifting beneath him. Like

nothing he had ever known or believed held true anymore. As if he could embrace a rage so savage, so cruel...

He wanted to murder, feed, and destroy for a millennium.

But he had to pull himself together.

He had to make use of this time—and this woman.

It didn't matter.

Damien Alexiares was his father.

Dane Alexiares was his brother.

Diablo Alexiares was his friend.

He had grown up in the house of Jaegar, and he would return to the house of Jaegar. If anything, this new revelation simply meant that he would be a greater asset to his brothers of darkness than ever before. Nothing had changed, really. Damien had always known Saber's secret; yet he had cherished his firstborn son just the same.

So be it.

The time to think it all through—to process this new information—was later.

Much, much later.

He drew in a deep breath, pushed every thought and emotion aside, and met Lorna's eyes with his own purposeful glare. *Very well. Thank you for showing that to me. It answers...a lot.*

Lorna nodded rapidly and waited. *I am sorry, Sabino; I know this must be—*

Saber! His psychic voice nearly vibrated with rage. *My name is Saber, and it will always be Saber.*

Saber, Lorna whispered. *Of course.* They sat in uncomfortable silence for at least several minutes before Lorna finally dared to speak again. *Was there another reason you wished to see me?* She tried to force a smile. *Is there anything I can do for you—bring for you?*

Saber stared blankly at the woman in front of him; by all that was wicked, she was either the most naive being that had ever walked the earth or the most charitable, forgiving, and compassionate—how could they possibly share DNA? *There is something*, he finally said.

Her eyebrows shot up, and she leaned forward in her chair.

Of course, tell me. What is it? She was far too eager, and it simply made him angrier.

He set it aside.

You know of the Blood Moon?

Lorna's hand went to her heart, and she drew an anxious breath. *Of course, I couldn't believe it.*

Dark Lords, did this female always wear her emotions on her sleeves? Thank S'nepres, he hadn't been raised by such weakness. *Then you've also heard by now that my...*destiny...*is the princess, Vanya?*

Lorna smiled then, at first timidly and with apprehension, but then with tacit approval. *Yes, I think it's...miraculous.*

Of course you do, Saber thought. *Um, I'm going to need some help...getting through to her...to Vanya.*

I'm sure if you just try...a little harder than usual...to show some chivalry, she will be happy to sit with you and—

No, Saber interrupted, unable to stifle his laugh—you truly couldn't make this shit up—*I can assure you that she wants nothing to do with me.* He tried to think of a way to tell her, without actually *telling* her. *I've run into the female before; we have a history. It wasn't pleasant.*

Lorna blanched, unable to conceal her dismay. *And she lived?*

Saber couldn't help but roll his eyes. *Yes...she lived.*

Oh, I see. Lorna smiled for all she was worth then. *Of course she lived—just like Jocelyn Silivasi lived after the incident at the cabin.* She placed her hand lightly on his knee and patted him gently. *You are my son. You are your father's son. No true Dark One—under any circumstances, no matter how dire—would have ever walked away from a kill, or left his enemy with a day's reprieve, not unless it was simple self-preservation. You always had a soul.*

Saber knew what Lorna was referring to, the day he and a group of dark soldiers had run into Nathaniel, Marquis, and Nachari Silivasi in the meadow just beyond the Snake River, the day the lycan Tristan Hart had tried to murder Nathaniel's *destiny.* Saber had been caught off guard and captured by the vampire hunters, along with the crazy boy Braden something-or-other, and the two of them had been bound in a shed, awaiting their final fate. Jocelyn had stumbled across the macabre scene, Saber strapped like a medieval prisoner to an ancient guillotine, Braden nailed like a Roman slave to a cross, and the female had set him free in a calculated move to save her own life.

She had known Saber would attack and kill their mutual enemy if given half a chance; and her gamble had paid off. Later, when he ran into the Silivasi brothers along with Jocelyn, in the meadow, he had made his own calculated decision—to stop the war for the night, forestall another bloody battle, and live to fight another day. It hadn't been as compassionate as it seemed; but truth be told, he had owed the brave woman—Jocelyn—that much. How had she put it? *The enemy of my enemy is my friend.* And while that was hardly the case, even in that meadow, Saber had felt a modicum of respect for the brave female.

A fleeting, retractable regard.

And that was all.

Saber could not have agreed with Lorna less: He walked away from the Silivasi brothers after the Lycan attack because he was tired of fighting; the Dark Ones had dead to gather; and they could always resume another day. Furthermore, he had let Princess Vanya live the night before because he needed her in order to survive. Point blank. Simple. Rational. Strategic decisions.

He measured his next words carefully—he had to be cautious. This woman, with all her desperation, need, and Pollyanna psychology, could confuse him if he let her. *Lorna*, he said, to regain her attention. *The point is: I need you to do something special…unique…affectionate for the princess, something that symbolically comes from me, at least in theory. Something that says, 'I'm sorry.' I need you to convince her to talk with me, sit with me, perhaps go for an escorted walk with me—after sunset, if you don't mind.* He was careful to emphasize the time of day, not that the warriors would ever let him out of that tiny cell, but just in case, he did not ever, under any circumstances, want to feel or see the sunlight again. *I need you to convince her to give me a second chance.*

Tessa Dawn

Lorna placed her hand over her mouth, thinking. *I can do that,* she finally said. And then she regarded him circumspectly. *However, I will not lie for you, Sabino—Saber. So, whatever else you do, you must sincerely mean this apology.*

He nodded slyly. *I do.*

She looked at him cross-wise through the corner of her eye but pressed on. *Maybe. Maybe not.* And then she splayed her fingers on his knee and increased the pressure. *Just the same, I am asking you—I am not telling you like a superior; I am not threatening you like an enemy; and I am not begging you like a subordinate—I am simply asking you as the woman who gave you life: Do not hurt this princess, Saber. If I do this for you, do not dishonor her. Give me your word.*

Saber didn't know whether to laugh, cry, or break free from his chains and try to put the poor, misguided creature out of her misery. Do not dishonor the princess? Do not lie? Do not hurt anyone? Give her his *word.*

As if!

Dear Valley of Shadows; she really did think she was speaking to a male from the house of Jadon. Why couldn't anyone comprehend the depth of his depravity, the cellular makeup of his so-called soul?

Eight hundred years in darkness.

Just as many years serving the dark lords of the Abyss…willingly.

He looked at Lorna, and for the briefest moment, he almost wished he were something else, *someone else*, that she still had the son she obviously wanted and believed in so desperately.

Because this was beyond sad.

This was epically tragic.

Lorna, do this thing for me and you have my word.

He never even broke a sweat.

93

eleven

Later that evening

Vanya Demir glanced up at the spectacular domed ceiling in Napolean's private rectory and marveled at the artistry that never failed to amaze her: the hand-painted mural of Zeus and Apollo. Remembering where she was, and why she was there, she looked back down, shook her head in utter exasperation, and tried to push through her fatigue. They had been going back and forth in Napolean's living room for hours—her, Marquis, Ciopori, Brooke, Napolean, and Ramsey—Nathaniel Silivasi was filling in for the lead sentinel at the guard station with Saxson or Santos, whoever was working the current shift.

The way she understood it, the king had received a missive from the house of Jaegar earlier that day, carried on the wings of a beautiful falcon, and the missive had been arrogant and to the point, dated *Tuesday, the second day of March.*

To: His Grace, Napolean Mondragon, Ruler of the house of Jadon

From: His Excellence, Oskar Vadovsky, Chief of Council for the house of Jaegar

Purpose: To request a meeting of delegates in the Red Canyons

Time: Tomorrow—Wednesday, the third day of March at eleven PM.

Dear Sir, it has come to our attention that there is a matter of some delicacy between our houses. One of your ranks has infiltrated our colony for eight hundred years, and has now been returned to his rightful home. While this imposter is no longer our concern, our High Court has convicted his father, Damien Alexiares, of treason; and the traitor is to be executed at five AM, Thursday morning, the fourth day of March. His brothers have yet to stand trial.

It would appear that Damien's last dying wish is to speak with his unlawful son. In addition, Saber's brother, Dane, would like one last chance to speak with his illegitimate brother. To that end, we are offering a limited truce in order to conduct this matter in peace. The house of Jaegar will provide a delegation of one soldier, both family members, and one sorcerer, accompanied by our High Chief of Council; and we would request an equal delegation of five members from the house of Jadon, including yourself and Saber, of course, to join us. We feel this is a fair and manageable number of participants.

Please be advised that we do not wish to wage war, nor will we make any strategic moves against you, our enemies. On this matter, you have our word.

If this request meets with your approval, we will see you tomorrow night in the Red Canyons. Should you decline our benevolent offer, then we will assume that you have no interest in allowing Saber this one last indulgence, and Damien will be summarily executed along with his remaining offspring: Dane and Diablo.

Sincerely, the house of Jaegar

Marquis Silivasi snorted with derision. "If these hyenas aren't up to something, then I'm not an Ancient Master Warrior. I still say to hell with them. Let them execute Damien, Dane, and Diablo. Three less animals for us to worry about."

Ramsey Olaru, who had been lounging against the opposite wall with his arms crossed over his chest, his right knee bent so that his foot rested against the wall, pushed off from his perch and sauntered over to Marquis's side. Talking around the thin toothpick that was lodged between his lips, he nodded. "I'm afraid I have to agree with Marquis. We shouldn't do this, milord."

Ciopori Demir brushed a stray piece of lint off her skirt and slipped her arm through her mate's, leaning her head against Marquis's shoulder as if exhausted by the conversation. "I, too, agree with Marquis." She paused as if carefully considering her words. "In truth, what difference does it make, my king?"

"We will not allow Vanya to bear sons with that animal," Marquis said in consensus. "So really, he's already as good as dead."

Now this just irritated Vanya—on so many levels.

Shifting ever so slightly in her oversized armchair next to the king's, she turned to face the ancient ruler of the house of Jadon. "Perhaps we should all keep in mind that I am a grown woman, and the ultimate decision still belongs to me." Despite her horrific run-in with the hedonistic male, she still could not completely dismiss her dream—or what it might mean to the people. The idea of a buried treasure being somewhere, anywhere, inside of or connected to that male continued to niggle at her, giving her pause. Deciding the life—and death—of another was no easy matter.

Brooke sat on the arm of Napolean's chair and only spoke sporadically. "I think we need to listen to Vanya," she offered.

Marquis scoffed. Turning to catch Vanya's eyes, he said, "You're free to decide whatever you wish, sister. Just so long as it doesn't include going within five feet of that overgrown piece of donkey dung. Sorry, that's just the way it is."

By the hardened look on Ramsey's face, Vanya could tell the warriors were in agreement. She rolled her eyes conspicuously. "Ciopori," she said glibly, "perhaps you should check your mate...before he over reaches."

Ciopori sighed and glanced away, clearly appearing torn. "Marquis," she whispered. "Gentle, darling. *Gentle.*"

Napolean cleared his throat, and the room went silent. He fixed his insightful eyes on Vanya and regarded her carefully, maybe too carefully. *What all was he seeing?* she wondered. She just didn't know, but to his credit, he held his tongue.

And then he frowned.

He sat back in the large, royal blue armchair and intertwined his fingers. "There are three things I must consider, beyond the obvious concern for Vanya's safety: First, Saber's history in the house of Jaegar, which pertains to his connection to his dark family and the development of his soul. Second, the impact seeing his father and brother might have on him, for good or for evil. And third, the logistics involved in such a meeting, should we choose to go through with it."

Marquis opened his mouth to speak, and Napolean waved his hand ever so slightly to silence him. The noble king was not through speaking. "With regard to Saber's history with Damien, Dane, and Diablo, this is an intricate matter. For the males in the house of Jaegar, there is a strong connection, a code of sorts based on loyalty, survival, and centuries of cohabitation. While the Dark Ones may erroneously call their connections *love*, it is more of an imprinting: Even snakes will bind together in a mating ball to propel their species forward. Such ties are strong and binding. Saber, however, has always had a soul."

Both Ramsey and Marquis growled with disapproval, and Napolean leveled a *cease and desist* gaze at the keyed-up warriors, each one in turn, making it very clear how the hierarchy, at least in the house of Jadon, still worked. "You will hold your tongues…and your reactions."

He didn't await their reply. Rather, he lowered his head, his eyes flashing the slightest feral red, and stared pointedly at Vanya. "Whether he knows it or not—whether he *owns* it or not—Saber Alexiares was born with a soul." He turned his attention to Ramsey. "That means that he was born with the capacity and potential to love." Moving his attention to Marquis, he added, "Whether or not he understands that he possesses this capacity is not the issue I am wrestling with." Clearing his throat, he continued: "After eight hundred years with his dark father and six hundred years with his brothers, there is a very good chance that what *Saber* feels for them is beyond loyalty, imprinting, and survival. There is a very good chance that in his own demented way, he loves these males deeply. And when they are gone, he may grieve just as profoundly as we would, following the loss of one of our own." He chewed his lip in concentration, carefully considering his words. "If we deny him this meeting and his family is executed, they will become martyrs in his eyes; and he will forever blame the house of Jadon for a pain he does not even comprehend." He turned toward Vanya then. "If he is not already lost to us forever—and he very well may be—his rage will most certainly consume him. His loyalty to the house of Jaegar will be set in stone, and any evolvement of his soul outside of their influence will be impossible."

Tessa Dawn

When Brooke brushed her hand lightly along his shoulder in an obvious gesture of support, he visibly relaxed beneath her touch. "There is also the matter of repercussions: What impact will such a meeting of houses have on Mr. Alexiares?" He regarded Marquis with scrutiny then. "I agree with you, Master Warrior, there is an ulterior motive involved—the Dark Ones are always up to something. Nonetheless, we are capable of containing the situation if necessary." His eyes flashed a strange gold and yellow, reminiscent of the sun's rays at high noon, before settling back into a dark, regal hue. "I am more than capable of containing—or destroying—our enemy." He stiffened. "As you know, I don't want to risk the collateral damage of so many human lives should I have to unleash my fury in the valley, but I will if I have to."

Marquis's sharp inhale made it clear that there would be no argument from the Ancient Master Warrior. Napolean's prowess in battle was legendary—his overwhelming facility for lethality and power beyond what anyone in the house of Jadon could even comprehend.

"I…" Ramsey tested his voice before proceeding. "I understand that, milord; however, the cost in human life, in natural destruction—perhaps even to your own health should you have to *go there*—might be more of a risk than any of us are willing to take."

Napolean appeared to be considering Ramsey's words. "Perhaps." He shrugged. "However, if the Dark Ones are planning some sort of subterfuge—a trick or worse, an attack—then it is more than likely against Saber, himself." He absently braced his jaw with his thumb and forefinger. "They do not want this male—who has lived among them, studied their histories and secrets, shared in their customs and ceremonies—waltzing off into the sunset to live among their enemy, knowing he could potentially share all he has learned with our house. Believe me, whether they try something tomorrow night or not, they want Saber Alexiares dead."

Vanya shivered unwittingly, rubbing her arms with her hands

to generate heat.

"This may be the edge we need," Napolean explained.

"How so?" Ramsey asked.

"A chink in the armor, so to speak," Napolean answered. "If they make a move against Saber, then they also make it clear that he is no longer welcome among them. If they actually try to kill him, then he learns that his loyalty, and his unconscious love, are not shared by his dark brothers. They leave us an opening…they leave *him* an opening…to begin absorbing information from a different vantage point: one that at least allows the possibility that he was not born there, and may be other than what he assumes." He rubbed his temples wearily then. "It isn't much. The male is as hardwired as I have ever seen, nurture trumping nature at its max; but just the same, it may be a crucial opportunity if we ever hope to make any inroads with the soldier."

For some reason, the king's words must have triggered a momentary lapse in reason within Ramsey Olaru. He spit out his toothpick—*on Napolean's floor*—and snarled, "I gotta be honest; I've watched the bastard day in and day out for a while now, and I'm not so sure he still has a soul to be saved." His muscles bunched and rippled as he drew to his full height. "Frankly, I'm against all of it. I say the male never gets anywhere near Vanya, and the Dark Ones can take their delegation and shove it where the sun don't shine. Literally." His voice dropped to a lethal purr. "If it please you, milord; my job, *my sworn duty*, is to kill Dark Ones. If you recall, I spend my evenings, or at least I used to before I became a glorified babysitter, arranging hunting parties to troll the local towns and counties, extinguishing dark vampires. Tracking them, hunting them, ensnaring them whenever necessary, so I can deliver their hearts and their heads back to hell. Now, you want your warriors to just stand back and let them waltz into neutral territory, knowing damn well they're planning an offensive, all so we might save this one unredeemable soul." His lips twitched in anger. "Well, I say the cost is too high. The risk is too great. I say no to it all."

The king's jaw tightened, and his own voice took on a dangerous edge. "Your allegiance is to the house of Jadon first, Ramsey."

Ramsey turned on his heel and took an aggressive step toward Napolean. "You're damn right it is!"

"And Saber is *born* of this house!"

"The hell he is!" Ramsey shouted in an unprecedented display of insubordination.

Napolean dropped his own tone to a low, lethal whisper. "At any rate, you will obey your Sovereign."

Ramsey seemed to inhale Napolean's words and swish them around in his mouth, trying feverishly to swallow them, before failing. In a barely audible tone, he murmured, "Maybe. Maybe not on this one."

Napolean's head turned to the side in an eerily serpentine motion, and a terrifying pop, like that of an amplifier blowing a fuse, crackled in the air as the king's ancient eyes bored into Ramsey's like a searing laser of light.

Just like that, the powerful sentinel flew off his feet and landed prone on his back, his body immediately drawing in on itself as he contorted in pain. His complexion grew sallow and his face became gaunt as the ancient king rose slowly from his chair and began to walk in his direction.

Marquis took several steps back, drawing Ciopori with him.

Vanya tucked her legs beneath her and curled up in her chair.

Even Brooke ducked out of the king's line of fire, and her brilliant blue eyes grew wide with fright.

The king stalked forward like a jaguar, a low, rumbling growl shaking the chandeliers and causing the furniture to shift above the hard wooden surface. When at last he reached his fallen subject, he knelt down gracefully and planted one firm knee directly on Ramsey's chest. "What did you just say to me?" he whispered in a dark, unnatural voice. His feral lips drew back and his fangs showed only a hint of extension, but they were terrifying just the same.

Brooke found her voice. "Napolean...sweetheart... please...*stop.*"

The king didn't respond.

Ramsey tried to croak out an answer, but he couldn't draw a breath. His chest collapsed beneath the pressure of the king's knee, and the sound of it caving in was grisly.

"One soul in the house of Jadon is worth more to me than every soulless bastard born to the entire house of Jaegar." He withdrew his knee, and Ramsey gasped for air, finally taking in some oxygen, but his body continued to writhe in agony. "Including yours, Ramsey Olaru." He bent down so that their noses almost touched, and he met the warrior's horror-stricken eyes with a look of iron resolve. "You are honored by me, Warrior. Your council is welcome; your words are weighed heavily; your objections are noted." He purred like a lion, deep, throaty, and thick with command. "But your direct insubordination will not be tolerated. Not ever." A gathering of foam began to leak out of the corner of Ramsey's mouth, and he began to choke on the spittle.

Dear Gods, what was the king doing?

Was he killing Ramsey from the inside out?

"Now then," Napolean said calmly. "You have five seconds to correct this insanity." With that, he released whatever hold he had over the warrior and waited patiently—so quietly one could have heard a pin drop—while the warrior coughed, swallowed his bile, and struggled to his knees.

Ramsey fell into formal protocol immediately.

He raised one knee so that the other was bent, bowed his head, and crossed his arms over his chest, still sputtering. Once he had finally composed himself fully, he extended his right hand to Napolean and offered him the Crest Ring of the house of Jadon in an act of reverence and contrition. "Forgive me, milord."

Napolean took his hand and kissed the ring. "Speak...*freely.*"

Ramsey drew in a deep breath, trying to find his words. "They will try to kill Saber."

"Of course they will."

"They may try to kill you."

"And which one among them can succeed?" At last, his voice softened. "Rise, warrior."

Ramsey struggled to his feet, and Napolean took a measured step forward. He palmed the back of the warrior's neck, drew him brusquely forward, and kissed the top of his head. Placing a firm hand over Ramsey's heart, he released what looked like a surge of energy, and the sentinel's chest returned to its previous state of health. "Look," Napolean said, speaking as if the entire incident had never happened, "I agree with you and Marquis: I have no love loss or sympathy for our dark cousins, and I am not at all convinced that Saber can—or should—be allowed to live. Still, I believe we need to let this play out. Perhaps the betrayal of those he still believes to be his allies is precisely what our prisoner needs to finally cut those ties; or perhaps his stubborn loyalty to them, in spite of such a betrayal, will grant us the permission we need to allow him to die. Either way, we must let it happen." He stood straight, stretched his back, and turned to face the entire room. "Saber Alexiares has yet to taste his soul, yet the truth of it lies on his tongue. We must allow him to swallow this bitter pill so he can make choices going forward...with all the information." He looked at each vampire present and furrowed his brow. "Now then, the issue we must address next is a logistical one, how to conduct the meeting: How do we meet safely with our dark cousins in a place as open and potentially volatile as the Red Canyons? Who do we choose to bring? And what security measures do we put in place?"

The words wafted to Vanya's ears like smoke from a campfire. They swirled around her head and coated her body like a waiflike scent that was real, and she shuddered.

She had already tasted Saber's soul.

And it was beyond redemption.

103

BLOOD REDEMPTION

While the warriors continued to strategize and plot, making plans for the next night's meeting of delegates in the Red Canyons, Vanya was discreetly interrupted by a smartly dressed human woman with short, neatly layered blond hair: Tiffany Matthews. Apparently, Tiffany had been Brooke's dearest lifelong friend in the human world of business before the capable Ms. Adams had been claimed by the king as his *destiny*. Since Brooke's conversion, the king's consort had taken over all marketing and PR of Dark Moon Vale, Inc., the house of Jadon's considerable and lucrative business holdings in the valley; and Brooke had immediately hired Tiffany as CFO of DMVPrime, the branch of the corporation that focused exclusively on sales, to oversee all of the advertising campaigns, annual budgets, and payroll concerns. It was rumored that in her spare time, *Auntie Tiff* spent a considerable amount of time watching Phoenix, the young prince and future king of the lighter vampire, whenever Brooke and Napolean were tied up with Vampyr business: It was a labor of love that Tiffany didn't mind in the least.

Now, shifting the young prince from one hip to the other, Tiffany bent over to whisper in Vanya's ear. "There is a lady at the door to see you, Saber's mother, Lorna." Apparently, Tiffany was not one to dance around a subject, a trait Vanya deeply appreciated. "I saw her approaching the manse and let her into the foyer before she could ring the bell." She swept her hand around the room, gesturing at the considerable mixed company in the house. "I thought you might prefer some privacy for your visit." She hoisted Phoenix higher on her hip, and the young prince reached up to swat at a dangling earing. "No, no, Phoenix," Tiffany whispered, her voice stern but kind. "You must leave Auntie Tiff's earrings alone, remember?" The little vampire squirmed with disappointment, but soon found another distraction in Tiffany's necklace. "Oh, Lord," Tiffany sighed, sounding only mildly exasperated. "Should I escort Lorna in?"

Vanya held up her hand instinctively. "No, no. Gods forbid she should be thrown into this tank of sharks and subject to her own round of the Vampyr Inquisition." She huffed. "I will meet her in the foyer. Thank you, Tiffany." As quietly as possible, Vanya slipped out of the room, watching as Tiffany made her way back down the hall toward the little prince's rooms.

The king's foyer was a large, magnificent receiving room, surrounded by high, coffered ceilings and several dimly lit, arched niches, each one custom painted in a muted but exquisite pictorial of a Romanian landscape. It opened up on the left to the formal living room, where the warriors were hard at work, and on the right, to the king's private conference room, where as many as sixteen could be seated around an oval mahogany conference table. If one traversed the space vertically, it would lead to the main hall of the manse, which led occupants to the first-floor suite of rooms, the kitchen, laundry, and storage area. Lorna looked distinctly out of place in the grandiose space, swallowed up by the size of the foyer as well as the grandeur.

"Mrs. Dzuna," Vanya said by way of greeting.

To Vanya's surprise, Lorna curtsied in the manner of the Old World. "Princess Vanya." She averted her eyes respectfully.

"Please," Vanya said, not knowing how to react to the visit, especially considering the highly delicate situation that surrounded it. "Just call me Vanya."

Lorna raised her head and nodded politely, her kind brown eyes meeting Vanya's with warmth. "I brought these for you." She held out a magnificent bouquet of cerise lilies, red roses, and light green carnations, all surrounded in vibrant greenery, and extended it forward. "They're from Saber."

Vanya held her tongue out of respect. It would not do to take out her considerable angst—and anger—on this clearly uninformed woman. *What in the name of the gods was the dragon up to now?* Vanya took the flowers and raised them to her nose, deeply inhaling the sweet fragrance of the lilies and then the roses. "They're beautiful. You have exquisite taste."

"Saber wanted you to have them."

Vanya arched her brows. "Again, I repeat: *You* have exquisite taste."

105

Lorna looked away and nodded softly, unwilling to argue the point. And then, appearing to gather her courage, she faced the princess again, this time lifting her jaw in determination. "I spoke with Sabino—*with Saber*—earlier, and he has asked me to invite you on a stroll this evening, perhaps a short walk beneath the canopy of the forest, with a healthy escort of guards, of course. He's considerably drained, and if he has to be chained, I suppose that is okay as well."

Vanya's mouth fell open in disbelief.

She started to say something flippant but thought better of it: By the look on Lorna's face, the sudden deepening of the lines around her eyes and the unmistakable anxiety that stiffened her otherwise delicate features, Vanya knew that the female was *this close* to falling apart. And why wouldn't she be? The situation had to be every mother's worst nightmare. She loved her son, and her hope sprang eternal. What must it be like to have a monster for your progeny?

Despite her compassion, a rush of laughter escaped Vanya's lips. "A stroll? Around the forest? With Saber?" She took a gentle step forward and clasped Lorna's hand in her own. "My dear woman, I...I hardly know what to say. I feel so deeply for you and your husband; I cannot even imagine what this is like, but—"

"If it's all the same," Lorna interrupted, "I would rather not be patronized." She took a deep breath and pushed forward. "I have lived with an ever-present heartache for eight hundred years; and I am no stranger to awful events. I know what Saber is, what he has been all this time. But he is still my son."

"Of course," Vanya said, withdrawing her hand. She linked her fingers together and held them gracefully up to her chin, dropping her head and sighing. "And I appreciate your desire for an honest exchange." She tilted her head back up and brought her linked hands down to her thighs. "In that case, let me be frank: The male is not my long-lost son, and there is no love lost between us. I have neither the goodwill nor the inclination to meet him anywhere, for *any* reason."

Lorna started to wilt in response to Vanya's words, but to her credit, she dug back in. "I understand. He told me of your...history."

Vanya's eyebrows shot up in surprise. "Did he now? He told you—"

"Well, not anything specific, just that there was a history; and it was...not good, to say the least."

Vanya regarded her sideways, frowning. "Unfortunately, Mrs. Dzuna—"

"Lorna."

"*Lorna.* The details are quite...disturbing; and if you did know—"

"Forgive my constant interruptions, Princess," Lorna said, rushing the words. Apparently, she was beginning to feel a bit desperate. "I don't mean to be so rude; I'm just"—she wrung her hands together and shifted her weight from foot to foot— "I'm just so nervous." She licked her dry lips. "You have to understand: There is so much as stake, not just for you and Saber, but for me and his father as well. For the people."

Now that last line hit home.

Her dream.

What really was at stake here?

Vanya lowered her voice to a chilling whisper. "If Saber has told you anything at all about our *history*, then you must know that I find him to be a savage beast, a threat to my well-being, and a blight to the house of Jadon. Frankly, the audacity of this request takes my breath away. Name one good reason why I should meet this male...anywhere."

Lorna nodded her head slowly and took a steady, even breath. "Eight hundred years ago, due to no fault of his own, Saber was lifted from his bassinette as a mere infant. He was ushered into a world of violence and depravity beyond our comprehension, consecrated to the dark lords of the abyss, and raised by a den of...hyenas." Her voice trembled slightly, and her throat constricted as she continued to speak. "He has never known love, kindness, or tenderness. He has *no* frame of reference to draw upon, not one single example of goodness to light his way. And in twenty-eight days, he will be dragged into a cold, sterile chamber to be executed as he has lived: in agony, cruelty, and alone, as a disposable, uncounted being who was never worthy of life to begin with." She dropped her head in her hands and struggled to regain her composure. Finally, looking back up, she continued. "I will have to live with that forever. Our king will have to live with that forever; and yes, Princess, you will have to live with that forever. Will one walk beneath the moon at his side make any difference to you—to us—when it is all said and done? Probably not, but it may very well be the only compassionate gesture he receives in his otherwise pitiless life, the first and only act of mercy he will ever know. Is not love"— she waved her hand in front of her to dismiss the word—"is not *benevolence* a reward unto itself? Saber has never met his conscience. He reacts like an animal, giving vent to every basic urge, acting on every primal instinct. But you and I, those of us raised in a world with celestial gods and goodness, we have been reared with a higher standard, with reason and choice as our guides. Are we not held to a higher standard than the Dark Ones? If we meet savagery with savagery, then what makes us different?"

Before Vanya could respond, the small woman smoothed the hem of her shirt and bent to one knee, genuflecting before the princess as she bowed her head. "Please—"

"Don't," Vanya pleaded as her breath rushed out of her.

Oh, dear gods…

Lorna reached up and grasped Vanya's hand, unrestrained tears rolling down her cheeks in deep tracks of sorrow. "Do not do it for him, milady. Do it for me." She folded her other leg beneath her and descended into a full kneel. "I am begging you as his mother."

Vanya swallowed convulsively, feeling as if she just might faint. As if the entire world was upside down. This was wrong, *so very wrong*, on so many levels. "Please, Lorna, get up." She tugged on the woman's arm.

Lorna lifted her head and met Vanya's gaze, her eyes brimming with sorrow. "What choice do I have left? What pride is greater than my guilt? What act of contrition is too lowly for my son? My only child is going to die a desolate, hideous death, never having known love or goodness. Or the gods. And all of it is partially my responsibility—I let them take him."

Vanya could not bear to hear another word. "No!" she insisted. "You did not. Rafael did not. It happened. It was a tragedy, but no one is to blame."

"Perhaps," Lorna whispered, "yet everyone will pay." She shook her head slowly then. "I don't pretend to believe that one stroll, one moment in the presence of your light, will penetrate a heart so deeply entrenched in darkness that my son will find his way to the light, discover his soul, or emerge redeemed; but I do know that you are perhaps the only person alive who can reach him, should there be any hidden treasure, whatsoever, still buried inside."

Vanya released Lorna's hand and staggered back.

What had the woman just said?

It was her dream…all over again.

"Get up, Lorna. *Please*. I will not continue this conversation with you on your knees." She felt suddenly nauseated, and the room began to spin around her. "I cannot bear it."

Lorna rose slowly and waited in hopeful, deafening silence.

Vanya exhaled slowly, trying to calm her nerves. "Even if I could agree—if I *would* agree—the king would never allow it."

"You're wrong." A deep, husky voice reverberated within the foyer, ringing in Vanya's ears. As the princess spun around to face Napolean Mondragon, her eyes opened wide with surprise, and she inexplicably took a step back.

"Lorna's request is as compelling as it is impassioned," Napolean said tenderly. "I don't believe it will make a difference; but I, too, would like to live my life without regret, without blame, at the end of this Blood Moon." He took a deep breath, and it was obvious by the solemn look on his handsome face that he was forcing himself to make a choice based on conscience rather than conviction. "If you can stand to be in Saber's presence for even a short amount of time, I can arrange for your safety. If you are willing to do this thing, Vanya, I will allow for fifteen minutes. That is all."

Before Vanya could reply, Brooke Adams Mondragon strolled into the room, her signature confident stride preceding her as she stepped to her husband's side, gently wrapped her arms around his waist, and pressed a soft kiss against his broad shoulder. Although Vanya did not possess the supernatural hearing of a vampire, even she could make out Brooke's softly whispered words: "Thank you, my king. This is the right decision."

Napolean placed his hand over Brooke's and nodded almost imperceptibly, and then he turned his attention to Vanya. "Princess?"

Vanya shut her eyes and silently prayed for strength.

For wisdom.

She turned to regard Lorna. "What time would this *outing* take place?"

Lorna shrugged. "He has a terrible fear of the sun—so the later the better—but anytime that works for you would be a gift."

Napolean shifted out of Brooke's grasp and stepped forward then. "It will take a few hours to put an adequate security escort in place. The presence of the sentinels is a must—no one understands safety and its orchestration better than my guards. In addition, I would like the wizard, Nachari, to join you from a reasonable distance: He has developed certain powers that will prove both exacting and expedient should Saber give into some base impulse." Ignoring the look of horror on Lorna's face, he continued: "It goes without saying that I would like to be there, myself. It will be several hours before I can break away, but this condition is not negotiable." He turned to regard Lorna squarely. "You must know, Mrs. Dzuna, that I don't take this request lightly. I am willing to accommodate this…experiment, but should your son make even one threatening move against the princess, I will put him down where he stands, forever. And the whole subject will be finished. No apologies. No regrets."

Lorna stared at Napolean in quiet dismay; her high cheeks flushed a ghostly white. "I understand," she finally murmured.

"Very well," Napolean said. "Will nine o'clock work for you, Vanya?" When he met Vanya's gaze, his eyes were soft with compassion—and perhaps, a bit of remorse.

Vanya nodded confidently, but it was only a disguise.

Dearest goddess Andromeda, what had she gotten herself into?

"Nine o'clock will do just fine."

twelve

Later that night

Vanya waited anxiously with her lethal entourage at the edge of a narrow ATV trail that led into the heart of the Dark Moon Forest. The trail was a well-worn path that snaked through the woods, crossed densely treed meadows, and traversed rocky hills, covering some of the most beautiful territory in Dark Moon Vale. It would offer the pair privacy, provide a clear line of sight for the guards, and leave the princess several options to choose from should she need to run or hide. Not to mention, the warriors would have plenty of room to maneuver should they need to engage in battle. Should they have to take Saber to task.

It was the perfect mixture of seclusion and protection.

Vanya clutched the bunched material of her layered jade skirt impatiently. She had chosen to a wear a loose-fitting top over the long but fluid bottom and a knee-high pair of kick-ass boots just in case: The sharp, pointed toes would come in handy if she needed to protect herself until one of the warriors could step in; and the heels were short and square enough to allow her to run, unhindered, if she had to blaze a trail. She glanced absently at the forest canopy, her eyes narrowing on a dark satin shape perched atop a high tree branch. It was Nachari Silivasi in his newly acquired panther form. The Master Wizard was perilously alert as he crouched low on the tree branch, his glowing emerald eyes fixed on the princess's position. He flexed his powerful haunches lazily, as if merely stretching his muscles, and the cat's body exuded raw, unrestrained power: Nachari would be following the pair from above, ready to pounce at a moment's notice.

Vanya turned away from the awesome sight and cast a

sidelong look at Napolean Mondragon, instead. The formidable king was just as fearsome and alarming as Nachari, despite his far-too-poised, laid-back demeanor. It was clearly a ruse, the calm before a violent storm. The king wore a pair of non-assuming, faded black jeans, a form-fitting cotton shirt, and a pair of heavy steel-toed boots that looked strangely out of place on the regal patriarch. Like Vanya, he had come prepared for confrontation, as if Napolean Mondragon needed an advantage. Sweeping her eyes along his commanding arms and hips, she noticed that he wasn't carrying any weapons. There were no harnesses concealing guns or scabbards encasing swords, no hidden daggers or throwing stars, nothing that said *conflict imminent*, other than the self-assured king's bearing and the iron set of his jaw. Napolean had no fear whatsoever that the situation might get out of hand: Should Saber in any way provoke his wrath, Napolean would simply level a glance in the soldier's direction, and his once-immortal life would come to an end.

Vanya shivered. She was grateful for the support but equally afraid of the consequences. She wasn't even sure what she feared the most, that Saber might be cut down too soon…or not soon enough. She was well aware that her sense of duty was warring with her survival instincts: She was right to give Saber this one last opportunity—to do what?—yet she dreaded coming in such close contact with the lethal predator once again.

What a mix of jumbled emotions!

On one hand, she was his chosen *destiny*, and that meant there was a powerful inborn connection between them, whether she liked it or not. On the other hand, his life had taken a cruel, unforgiving turn, and their differences were likely irreconcilable because of it.

She turned at the distant rumble of a pickup truck, Saxson's GMC Sierra, and stared down the long expanse of dirt road, watching as the oncoming headlights rounded the bend and crept in her direction. Saxson was driving with Santos riding shotgun, and Ramsey was seated in the bed next to a bridled and chained Saber Alexiares.

Vanya cringed in revulsion. Despite her horrific run-in with the dangerous male, she still found it appalling that any being with a soul should be treated so inhumanely. For a moment, she could almost understand his rage.

And then the truck drew nearer, about twenty feet away, before careening to a halt. Santos and Saxson climbed out of the elevated cab and quickly joined Ramsey at the rear of the vehicle to help remove Saber from the elongated bed. They practically dragged the male by his twisted, bound arms, as if forcing him to an execution at the gallows, rather than leading him to the side of the princess for a casual stroll, one which Saber had requested—and Vanya had to exercise incredible patience not to speak out on the prisoner's behalf. For heaven's sake, if they were going to execute him, they should just do it and be done with it, but this ongoing humiliation was a bit much, even for her. And she reviled the male.

Saber appeared to take it all in stride. Either that or he concealed his emotions very, *very* well.

As they slowly removed his bridle and his leg irons, Vanya stole a scrutinizing glance: The male had recently showered, and his thick mane of hair had been thoroughly combed, giving it a clean, groomed appearance, despite the impact of the wind. There was a brilliant sheen illuminating the silken tresses, and they shone like moonlight reflecting off a roiling ocean, deep, dark, and luminescent. His creased black slacks and charcoal gray sweater only added to the effect. Clearly, Lorna had gone shopping for her son, and the results were arresting.

The male looked as handsome as he did deadly.

Vanya watched with unabashed curiosity as Saber shook out his long limbs, now free from their restraints, and held his arms out in front of him, waiting patiently while Ramsey re-shackled his wrists in a more comfortable position. As he took his first step toward her, Vanya's heart sped up. She couldn't help but recall their last encounter, the way he had spoken to her with such calloused authority, pressed his body against hers with such flagrant ownership, taken liberties he had no right to take, and all in such an ill-fated manner.

She couldn't help but recall her dream about the fire-breathing dragon.

She took an unwitting step back, and he froze in his tracks, studying her with far too perceptive eyes. Trying to swallow her fear, she nodded her head, and he started forward once more, covering a great deal of ground with his purposeful strides. Despite his circumstances, his arrogant gait commanded attention, even as his black-and-red hair swayed to his hypnotic motion. When he finally stopped within a couple of feet of her, a shrewd, devious smile curved his lips.

"Good evening, Princess." He drawled the words seductively.

Vanya sucked in air. She tucked a long lock of hair behind her ear and turned to acknowledge Santos and Saxson instead. "Good evening, warriors." It was a purposeful slight to Saber, one meant to take his arrogance down a notch.

Santos declined his head respectfully. "Princess," he said. His crystal blue eyes were ablaze, and he looked like a ticking time bomb.

"How are you, Vanya?" Saxson asked. The warrior's shapely lips were drawn way too thin—reflecting emotions that were wound way too tight. Staring at his harshly serious expression, Vanya couldn't help but think if his skin grew any tighter, he would resemble a human who had just undergone plastic surgery. She tried to *will* him to relax.

"Very well, Warrior. Thank you." She eyed the ground with trepidation, afraid to look at any of the three males before her, lest one of them explode from the slightest provocation. When she had finally regained her equilibrium, she raised her chin and met Saber's eyes. "Saber."

The prisoner seemed unperturbed. "How are you...*really*?" he asked.

Vanya was surprised by the statement. "As well as can be expected...under the circumstances." She would meet an honest question with an honest answer. She turned toward Santos and Saxson then. "If you don't mind, I would appreciate a little bit of distance for our…walk, perhaps five feet or so. I feel a bit like a specimen in a museum. I need some space to breathe."

The sentinels turned their steely gazes to the king, awaiting his instructions, and Napolean nodded slowly. "Saber," the king called, his no-nonsense tone sending shudders down Vanya's spine.

Saber met the king's eyes and waited.

"Say my name," Napolean bit out.

Saber drew back with disdain, and his lip curled up with disgust, but he quickly subdued his reaction and arched an eyebrow instead. "Excuse me?"

The king narrowed his icy gaze.

"Napolean," Saber said evenly.

"Very good," Napolean replied. "It took you three times longer to speak that word than it will take for me to send you to the Valley of Death and Shadows, from any distance, should I choose. Do you understand?"

Saber nodded, his face void of all emotion.

"I didn't hear you."

"Yes."

"Yes, what?" Napolean scolded.

Saber bit his bottom lip, drawing a small trickle of blood. "Yes, milord."

Napolean beckoned Santos and Saxson toward him; waited until the warriors fell into step beside him; and gave Vanya and Saber a nod of consent. "You may walk."

The dark prowling cat, perched high above in the trees, began to bound from one limb to the next while growling deep in his throat.

"Well then," Vanya said, before her voice trailed off. She was at a complete loss for words.

"Nothing says *welcome home* like a leisurely stroll in the moonlight, surrounded by vengeful predators just waiting to rip your throat out," Saber said.

Vanya turned to look Saber squarely in the eyes, and although she felt as if she might just swoon from fear, she pushed it aside, raised her chin, and held his arrogant gaze with one of her own. "You have done little to earn a welcoming party, Dragon. You should be down on your knees thanking all of us for allowing you this indulgence—for being willing to tolerate you for a single moment longer." She immediately regretted her words—where had all that vitriol come from? Okay, well, she knew exactly where it was coming from; but still, it was hardly productive. Saber had requested the meeting, and she needed to let him lead. At least for a while.

The dragon cleared his throat. "I deserve that," he said matter-of-factly. "In fact, when it comes to you, I deserve far worse." He cleared his throat several times as if he just couldn't get past an internal obstruction. "I'm afraid I need to ask for your forgiveness, Vanya." He spoke her name with the practiced expertise of a Lothario, one who had seduced more women than he could count. Dropping his tone to a whisper, he added, "When you came into my cell that night, I was unprepared, caught off guard. I did not expect you to be my *destiny*, and I behaved...badly."

Vanya laughed out loud then. "Badly? You behaved *badly*?" She spun around to face him then, and all the warriors shifted into ready-attack positions. "No, Mr. Alexiares, you did not behave badly. You behaved like a wild gorilla in a zoo, showing your offensive red ass for all the world to see. You behaved abominably."

Saber laughed then, and the sound was almost genuine. "Good analogy."

"Disgusting analogy," she said.

"Okay. No argument from me. Just the same, I would like to—"

"Apology not accepted," Vanya said sharply. "So you might as well change the subject."

Saber walked along in silence for several paces before trying a different tact. "I was hoping we might...start over. Try to find some common ground."

Vanya snorted with derision. "Like what, Dragon?"

He regarded her sideways, then, his heated obsidian eyes staring holes through her own as if he had a doorway to her soul. "Why do you call me dragon?"

Vanya coughed, nearly stuttered. "It's…it's…just how I see you."

"As a scaly, overgrown lizard who breathes fire?"

"Something like that," she said.

"Yet you came tonight," he said.

"So."

"So…thank you."

Vanya eyed him with overt suspicion, careful to step over a large divot in the ground. The smell of pine in the forest was especially strong, and she had to concentrate on her words. "Do not be so cocksure of yourself, Dragon." Despite her recalcitrant tone, she felt more than a little off balance by the Dark One's new approach, his sudden attempt at kindness. His eyes were so intelligent, so keenly aware; and his strong, almost hypnotic presence was unsettling to say the least. "'Tis the same voice that bids you adieu tonight that will bid you farewell at the end of this Blood Moon. *Believe it*," she said cruelly.

He didn't even blink. "I see."

She sighed in frustration. "No, you don't see, but you will. Trust me; it is a much greater motivation than your desire to play games that leads me to endure this time with you, Mr. Alexiares."

Saber sighed in frustration. "Okay, so what *does* motivate you to endure me, Miss Demir?" He held her gaze so steadily that she could hardly look away. "What makes your heart beat so rapidly? Or your lungs draw such shallow breaths?"

Vanya practically growled at him. She was so incensed. So flustered. Did he have no idea, whatsoever, how egregiously he had violated her? "With regard to your inquiry: That is none of your business. With regard to the sentiment behind it: Unfortunately for you, it is hardly that simple."

Saber nodded, offering no challenge to her words. And then, he reached down with his shackled hands and withdrew a single white rose from the waistband of his jeans. He held it out to her. "This is for you."

Vanya looked over her shoulder to acknowledge Napolean— was she allowed to reach out and take it?

The king rolled his eyes in annoyance, but he nodded his head. By the look on his face, perhaps Napolean would kill the dragon before the evening went any further, and she would be relieved of her distress.

Vanya took the flower, studied its perfection, and then callously tossed it aside into the weeds. "This is from Lorna Dzuna, just as the last bouquet of flowers was from your mother. And for the record, that disingenuous gift met the same fate." She frowned. "For what it's worth, Mr. Alexiares, you would do well to remember that I find it rude, unbelievably tactless, and contemptible at the least for a son to manipulate his mother so brazenly. I am not at all impressed."

Saber stared at the discarded rose and sneered. "What do you want?" he whispered softly. His voice was so cool, so measured, that Vanya could not tell if it was a question or a threat.

"What do *I* want?" she repeated, surprised. "You are the one who asked for this meeting."

"In order to try and please you," he said.

Vanya drew her arms to her chest and gripped her shoulders with her hands, feeling suddenly chilled and exposed. "Do you always say whatever comes to your mind?"

"No," he answered plainly.

She ran her fingers through her hair nervously. "Very well…" As she searched for a way to answer his question, her mind raced ahead in a dozen directions. Finally, she settled on the truth: "If you must know what I want, Dragon, I would like you to discard all of your deceits, empty gestures, and false niceties, if only for a moment." She gestured emphatically with her hands. "If you would like to waste this very brief opportunity with gamesmanship, then feel free; but if you would like to use it to your advantage, then you might consider telling the truth while you still can." Saber opened his mouth to speak, but she quickly cut him off. "I am not finished, Dragon. Let us speak candidly to save time: The way I see it, you could have killed me that night in your cell, but you didn't. I imagine that has you perplexed." She shrugged and shook her head. "It shouldn't. You were simply caught off guard, and you had not yet taken the time to weigh the pros and cons of our *situation*, to decide whether or not I might be of any use to you alive, before deciding to dispatch me." Despite herself, she shivered. "Luckily for me, you will not get another chance." She sighed then. "Alas, now you have come to the conclusion that you do need me, after all, to live. That you played your hand entirely wrong, and now, you must make up for it." She rolled her eyes in unconcealed disgust. "I am not a twenty-nine-year-old redhead who is lonely, confused, and easily preyed upon—you will not find a willing pawn in your game this time, Mr. Alexiares." They both knew what she was referring to, the plot Saber had hatched, along with Salvatore Nistor, to go after Kristina Silivasi while Nachari was still stuck in the Abyss. The Dark One had cloaked his appearance to look like Ramsey Olaru, and he had practically seduced—and killed—the unsuspecting female before her brothers caught onto the scheme and stopped him. It was how he had been caught by the sons of Jadon in the first place.

Saber let out a slow, deep breath, but he didn't defend his actions.

Looking him calmly up and down, she continued: "So, as long as that's clear—and we both know what you're doing—the next move is yours. By all means, proceed, Dark One."

Saber's eyes narrowed with astuteness. He looked her up and down in turn, measuring her from the soles of her boots to the roots of her hair, and then he licked his lips. "So, you're not an idiot?"

She gulped. "Pardon me?"

"Knowing exactly what I am, and having disarmed your

protection, you came into my cell in the middle of the night, completely vulnerable and exposed, and you goaded a wild animal—an instinctive predator—into a heightened state of arousal. And then you took great offense when I pounced." He watched her like a circling hawk, as if he could measure the slightest changes in her body rhythms with his eyes. She wondered whether or not he could sense that her breath was shallow; hear that her heart was sputtering; or tell that her palms were sweating as well.

"Even now," he continued, "the thought of it is as deeply stirring to your blood as it is terrifying." He pursed his lips. "I'm just saying that it's good to know you're not an idiot."

Vanya rolled her eyes then, perturbed. "Well, isn't that lovely: You look at me and see... *not an idiot*. I'd hardly call that progress."

The corner of Saber's mouth turned up in a wolfish grin, wild, unrestrained, and hungry. "That's not all I see," he said.

"Oh really?" she asked, measuring him for signs of deceit.

He shrugged. "You are a princess, but not an idiot. I am a monster, but not a blind one. You are a beautiful female, Princess Vanya, and your presence incites my primal nature. That's just a fact."

Vanya flinched. "Does such crude flattery work for you often?"

"No," Saber said bluntly. "I've never needed flattery before: Dark Ones take what they want."

Vanya shrank back this time. "And you've decided that you *want* me? To get you through the Blood Moon?"

"Yes," Saber said, catching her off guard with his candor. "As long as we're telling truths." He held up his shackled hands then. "But that wasn't meant as a threat." He leaned closer to her and spoke in a hushed, conspiratorial tone. "I attacked you in my cell because that's what dragons do when innocent maidens enter their lairs, but now"—he gestured toward the dark blue sky and the hundreds of stars that sparkled above them—"now, we walk side by side as equals in this deadly dance.

I want your submission, but I also want your *permission*." He eyed her appreciatively, and she almost slapped him.

Almost.

She was too afraid of what Napolean, the sentinels, and Nachari might do; and she was equally aware of the thundering curiosity pounding a frantic rhythm in her chest—what would it be like for a princess, a woman who had been raised to know only rigid control, irreproachable honor, and unfailing good manners to give in, just once, to the shadows in her own soul, to be swept away on a wave of unrestrained carnal power, to let herself live, feel, and forget her place, if only for one night?

She checked her reaction.

And then she quickly snapped out of it.

The monster would surely burn her, and then he would kill her, consuming what little light was left in her soul. He would emerge victorious, and she would emerge deeply damaged.

Vanya felt completely disarmed. She had to get the upper hand back. As long as they were telling truths, perhaps she should dig a little deeper into a matter that unsettled Saber. "Tell me of your father."

She had quickly changed the subject, and his face registered his disappointment, but only for a moment. His carefully controlled mask of indifference returned. "Rafael?" he asked, sounding uncertain.

"No, Dragon: We are only speaking truths here tonight. Tell me of Damien."

Saber exhaled so sharply that a high-pitched whistle escaped his lips. "Vanya…" He seemed to be searching for the right words. "There is nothing I could tell you that you would care to hear."

So they were on a first-name basis now? Vanya frowned. "Ah, I see—well, Rafael then." She paused to consider her next words. "Have you seen the Ancient Master Warrior's chest?"

Saber frowned. "Have I seen—"

"Rafael's chest," she repeated.

"No, of course not. How could I? Why?"

BLOOD REDEMPTION

Vanya angled her body to face him, at least partially, as they walked. The ATV trail took a sharp right turn and sloped downward, heading into a heavily treed area that was bordered by a high ridge, with several exposed tree roots protruding out of a nearby hedge on one side, and a steep, ominous ravine on the other. The section of trail was both riveting and haunting, much like the male who walked beside her. "Rafael's chest—his flesh—is very difficult to look at."

Saber eyed her curiously.

"It is so covered in scars and leathered skin that it looks like something one might find on an alligator."

Saber frowned in confusion. "Vampires don't scar. Not as long as we take the time to heal our wounds with venom."

Vanya swallowed hard and nodded. "'Tis true, Dragon, and perhaps that is the point." She looked off into the distance before casting her eyes back on the path before them. "The way Lorna explains it, Rafael blames himself for the night you were taken. He believes he should have sent a sentinel to watch over his wife and son when he left to make the sacrifice. Things were so different then, the way the villages and homes were spread out. They never could have conceived of such a thing occurring." She smoothed her blouse without thinking. "At any rate, every year, on the anniversary of your abduction, the warrior draws a freshly sharpened dagger across his heart in remembrance. Perhaps he seeks to renew the pain—or to atone for his sin—who knows, but he has never healed the wounds. After eight hundred years, his flesh is a veritable wasteland, and his pain is ever present."

Despite his typical poised demeanor, Saber's face registered his shock. His alluring, olive-toned skin turned pale, and his dark piercing eyes grew hazy with shadows. Swallowing his revulsion, he whispered, "What do you hope to accomplish by telling me this?"

Vanya shrugged. "It is simply a fact."

He shook his head. "I don't have those…kinds of emotions, Vanya."

Vanya smiled faintly. "You do, Saber." Before he could argue, she added, "You may not know what to call them, perhaps you can't even connect with them, but you do have them just the same."

Choosing calloused indifference over hurt or empathy, Saber chose a flippant reply: "Well, perhaps my true father and my brothers, Dane and Diablo, will do the same for me when I'm gone."

"Your father cannot," Vanya responded without thinking. "But perhaps your brothers will...if they live."

Saber's head listed to the side then, and his dark eyes flashed with indignation. "What is that supposed to mean?"

Vanya studied him carefully. He didn't appear to be playing games. "Have you not yet been told about the missive—the request sent to the king from the house of Jaegar?"

Saber frowned, all vestiges of game-playing gone. "No...tell me."

"Your father, he's been sentenced to death, the day after tomorrow; and your brothers have yet to stand trial...for treason."

Saber spun around so quickly Vanya never saw him move. Despite his restricting manacles, he reached out and grabbed her by the wrist, clutching the slender bone entirely too hard. Before she could try to wrench her hand free, a muffled groan escaped his lips, and he shot into the air, his legs dangling beneath him, his feet twitching erratically: Napolean Mondragon was standing directly beneath him, his right arm extended upward, his powerful hand clenched around the male's throat, and the king was tightening his fist into a lethal noose.

"Milord!" Vanya exclaimed. She reached up to swipe at Napolean's arm. "Please, stop. I...I startled him. I told him about the missive."

Napolean seemed lost in a red haze as Vanya tried to pry his hand loose from Saber's throat, one finger at a time, to no avail. She prayed the king would not act too hastily, too soon. There was always time for retribution later, and it would be better if the

BLOOD REDEMPTION

Blood claimed its pound of flesh at the end of the moon than if Napolean had to do it, right here and now.

Not for this reason.

Not because the male was about to lose the only father he had ever known.

"Please, milord," she pleaded. "He wasn't trying to hurt me." She glared at Saber, demanding his cooperation with her eyes. "Were you?"

Despite the fact that the male's airway was cut off and his eyes were beginning to bulge out of his head, he gritted his teeth and grunted, "No...I'm...sorry."

Napolean slowly relaxed his hand, but he continued to hold the prisoner in the air above him. Nachari bounded down from the highest branch of a tree and perched just beyond the male's reach, snarling with deadly intent. One nod from Napolean, and Saber was dead.

"For heaven's sake," Vanya cried. "Both of you, stop this at once! *Let him go.*"

Napolean slowly lowered Saber to the ground. And then, in one swift motion, he released Saber's neck, extended his claws, and swiped a wicked gash from Saber's left temple to the corner of his right mouth, leaving a hole so deep that Vanya could see through the fissure to the bone underneath.

"Milord!" she exclaimed, horrified.

Saber winced in pain, but he never cried out. He simply released his own incisors, leaked venom onto his hand, and tried to heal the wound. His venom was too weak. They had been keeping him starved since he got there.

Frantic, Vanya turned to the sentinels for help. "Santos? Saxson? One of you?"

The males stood their ground. They would only take orders from their king.

Napolean shrugged his muscular shoulders and regarded the bloody, shaken prisoner with disdain, his silver-and-onyx eyes flashing a clear, unmistakable warning. "He'll live," he snarled. "And if he doesn't give us further cause to kill him, we'll treat

126

the wound when he returns to his cell." He turned to Saber and spoke in a whisper. "Touch her again. *I dare you.*"

Saber cupped the palms of his shackled hands over his face and slowly stood to his full height. "It was an accident...unintentional." Vanya absently reached up to pull his hands away from the wound, and he jerked away from her touch. He leveled a cautionary glare in her direction. "Stop. It's nothing."

Vanya drew back, admonished. Of course he would think it was nothing. It was a matter of self-respect, of pride. The language of warriors. Saber could not fight back—he could not even heal himself—so this was his defense, remaining unfazed.

In a subsequent act of defiance, Saber turned his full attention on Vanya, and in a remarkably genuine voice, he asked, "Did I hurt you, Princess?"

Vanya took an unwitting step back and swallowed. She looked down at her wrists and rubbed her hands over the bruises. "No, I'm...I'm fine."

"I didn't mean to," Saber said, following the bluish lines on her pale flesh with his eyes. When Vanya shrugged her shoulders, dismissing the statement, he repeated. "*I didn't mean to.*"

For whatever reason, Vanya knew he meant it. The dragon had breathed fire, again, only this time it had burned him back. She nodded. "'Tis not fatal, Dragon."

Saber turned his attention back to Napolean then and frowned. "My father...and my brothers...when were you going to tell me?"

"When I was damn good and ready."

"And when would that be?"

Napolean arched his brows in astonishment. "You have a never-ending death wish, don't you, boy?"

Saber shrugged. "Perhaps." He lowered his tone—as well as his eyes—in reluctant submission. "For now, I just wish to know the truth."

The king let out his breath slowly, regarding the prisoner

with unconcealed disgust. "So be it," he said, and then he gestured at a nearby boulder. "Sit, Saber. Because if you react poorly to this news yet again, I won't be able to restrain myself this time."

Saber took two steps toward the boulder and slowly lowered his body onto the stone. Ignoring the blood that was gushing from his face, he looked up at the king and blinked to clear his vision. "I won't react," he murmured, waiting.

As Napolean explained the details of the missive, the argument that had ensued between the king and his warriors—leaving out those details that would betray personal conflicts within the house of Jadon or overemphasize their low regard for Saber's life—Vanya watched the dragon closely. The male was as still as a statue, as quiet as a mountain pond. He was as cold as a cavern wall, except for his eyes.

And if the eyes were truly the seat of the soul, then in this frozen moment in time, Vanya Demir knew, without question, that Saber Alexiares did, indeed, *have* a soul—because his eyes burned with unspoken anguish; his pupils reflected an overwhelming dread that could not be concealed beneath their blackened depths; and his tear ducts, while they never released a single tear, failed to hide the pressing moisture that threatened to surface as he listened quietly to the news of his father's execution.

As the king's words sank in, Saber struggled to remain calm, cool, and detached. He could not afford to provoke Napolean's wrath again. Not now. Not when he was so close to meeting up with his brothers, to seeing his father, perhaps for the last time.

He couldn't help but wonder about the meeting of delegates, how the whole thing would turn out; for surely, the Dark Ones were up to something. And as the thoughts drifted around in his head, he shifted his gaze to the princess, who was standing off to the side, so unassuming, waiting patiently beneath the branches of an aspen tree, while the males talked of war, strategy, and subterfuge.

Princess Vanya had been born to stand among, within, and at the head of such circles.

She had been reared to foster diplomacy, to consort with kings, and her unique, dusty-rose eyes were as keen with intelligence as they were soft with compassion.

For a moment, Saber couldn't help but wonder about the strange woman: After all, the princess had come to his defense, even against Napolean. She had told him the truth when no one else had bothered; and she had backed off appropriately when he had warned her away. She was an enigma to say the least. A surprising twist in an ever-changing story.

Their eyes met for a brief second, and he refused to look away.

What was she thinking now? he wondered.

She should have been afraid of him—terrified, in fact—yet she faced his blackened soul with courage, defiance, and tenacity. She had even reached out to help him.

It just didn't make any sense.

And for a fleeting moment, he thought he almost *felt* something.

Something he couldn't name.

Perhaps it was respect...or admiration.

thirteen

Salvatore Nistor sat back in the plush, contemporary sofa in the receiving room, just outside the council's chambers. Those who were not on the council were not allowed inside the inner sanctum, but they could come and go in the waiting room as they pleased. He looked around the pristine environment and turned up his nose: Outside of being at the bottom of a cave, it looked like something out of *Interior Décor Magazine*, an opulent display of wealth, power, and intimidation. The place was meant to let all who arrived know they had just entered into the heart of the house of Jaegar.

He shifted lazily, feeling his oats. Indeed, he was one of the most powerful males in the colony. Not only did his sorcery make him an invaluable asset, but his many years serving on the council had given him a certain level of prestige and notoriety. He was just beginning to replay all of his notable accomplishments in his mind when the heavy iron door swung open, and two giant guards entered with Diablo and Dane in tow. Both males were handcuffed and drained of vital life-blood.

He immediately rose to his feet. "Well, it's about time."

Achilles Zahora, a giant of a male who stood to the left of both prisoners, snarled, but not in challenge. It was more of an automatic instinct—one Alpha male responding to the perceived dominance of another. "You said to have the prisoners here at two PM." He eyed the grandfather clock, pressed up against the lacquered cave wall, and snickered. "It's two PM."

Salvatore followed the soldier's eyes, made note of the time, and shrugged. "Ah, well, I suppose it is." He turned to regard the second soldier, Blaise Liska. The male always gave him the willies. To begin with, he was short but stout, maybe five-foot-ten at best, and his cropped, spiked hair stuck up in all directions. In addition to his unruly appearance, his upper chest and arms were so overdeveloped that it almost made his lower body seem slight in comparison. Did the vampire not know one should always seek balance in every endeavor, even weight lifting? He sighed, returning his attention to the matter at hand. "*Prisoners* is such an ugly word. I prefer to think of Dane and Diablo as my honored guests."

Dane yanked his arm free from one of the guards and held his shackled hands out in front of him. "Do you always manacle your guests?" His eyes flashed with heat.

Salvatore smiled apathetically. "Just a precaution, my friend. Just a precaution."

Diablo glared at him with blatant insolence—*this one was not to be toyed with*, Salvatore thought—he was the most volatile of the two, and by the keen look of intelligence in his deep obsidian eyes, it wouldn't take much to set him off.

"Please," Salvatore said, gesturing toward two chic, modern club chairs, each flanking a separate side of the sofa, "have a seat." He turned to eyeball the guards. "The handcuffs are no longer needed. I'm sure my guests will behave appropriately." His eyes bored into Dane's, and then Diablo's, each set in turn. "Won't you?"

They didn't respond, and kudos for that. It would have been weak and subservient at best. "Very well," Salvatore said, waiting as Achilles gruffly unlocked the diamond-embedded handcuffs. "There is much we must talk about before tonight's meeting of delegates, when we rendezvous with our spoiled brothers of light in an attempt to rescue Saber, return him to his rightful house."

Now this got the brothers' attention.

"You mean the house of Jadon actually agreed? The king is willing to meet with us?" Dane took a careless step forward, covering the floor in one long stride, and Salvatore snarled to back him up.

"Sit, boy. We talk...while seated."

Dane looked down at his feet and slowly backed away. "My apologies." He sat in the closest chair, waiting as patiently as possible, and Diablo followed suit.

"Yes," Salvatore finally answered. "The meeting is a go. We shall rendezvous with our mortal enemies just shy of midnight in the Red Canyons."

"How did you pull that off?" Diablo asked, his tone both suspicious and condescending.

"Does it matter?" Salvatore retorted. "We pulled it off—that's all you need to know."

"Okay," Diablo said. His jaw tensed. "So what's the catch?"

Salvatore's smile was much too broad for his face, and it literally hurt his jaw to stretch his skin so tight. An eyeless insect scampered across the floor, not far from Salvatore's feet, and the sorcerer took great pleasure in lighting the creature on fire, using only his eyes to do it. He wriggled his nose. "I love the smell of burning flesh, even when it's bug flesh. If only it could be that easy with our brothers of light."

"So we are going to fight then—wage an offensive?" Diablo asked.

Salvatore rolled his eyes sadly. "No, Diablo, not tonight. Napolean Mondragon will be there…" He shrugged as if to say, *What would be the point*, and then he perked up. "But I do have a foolproof plan if you and your brother would like to be quiet for a moment and listen."

Dane angled his head, only slightly, to regard Diablo, leveling a pointed glance with his peripheral vision. "Please, brother; I'd like to hear what our councilman has to say."

Salvatore nodded with appreciation. Respect was capital. He waited while both brothers got comfortable in their respective chairs, and then he reseated himself in the center of the sofa, where he could watch each male equally and react just as quickly, if need be. Achilles took a strategic position behind Diablo, even as Blaise stood like a hideous gargoyle statue behind Dane. Both guards stared straight ahead, their faces iron masks of indifference. "Now then, my plan centers around Dane gaining access to Saber, and—"

"Why Dane?" Diablo interrupted.

Salvatore cut his eyes at the insolent visitor, his patience growing thin, and Achilles looked down and growled in warning. "Because you, Diablo, will not be there." Before Diablo could speak out of turn, yet again—or worse, object—he added, "You will not attend the delegation. You are needed here."

Diablo sat back in his chair warily, crossed one leg horizontally over the other, and rested a forward elbow on his knee. "Come again, *sir?*"

Salvatore frowned. He would be damned if he was going to explain every detail of his decision—correction, of the council's decision—to the sons of a traitor. He would tell them what he needed to tell them in order to gain their cooperation, and that was all. "Diablo…" He practically purred his name. "You would do well to remember your place." He held up his hand and rubbed his thumb and middle finger back and forth in a taunting manner. "It would take no more than the snap of my fingers to have your head, and your heart, on this coffee table." He took a measured breath. "However, I am trying to exercise at least some measure of decorum and hospitality. Do try *harder* to appease me."

If looks could kill, Salvatore would have been six feet under as Diablo cast daggers at the elder statesman with his devilishly cold eyes. He sat back, plastered a fake—just shy of insolent—smile on his face, and nodded. "By all means, go on, Counselor."

Salvatore returned the smile, wicked grin for wicked grin. "Thank you, Diablo." He turned his full attention on Dane. "Now then, *Dane;* you are the youngest in the Alexiares clan, no?"

Dane nodded cautiously.

"You were born just minutes after Diablo?"

"I was," Dane answered, his eyebrows raised in question.

Salvatore rolled his eyes. "Then that would make you the youngest." He relaxed his shoulders and nodded. "So, it has always been your role to feed your family then, correct?"

"I hunt…yes," Dane said, putting a more virile spin on the subservient custom of feeding one's elders.

"Good." Salvatore clasped both hands together and cracked

his knuckles. "Very good." He leaned forward in his seat. "Because we will be relying upon this *sacred duty* in order to free Saber from the house of Jadon."

Diablo contorted his features in confusion, but to his tribute, he held his tongue.

"You want me to feed Saber? When we meet tonight? Right out in the open—in front of the sons of Jadon?"

Salvatore narrowed his gaze. "My boy, it is *imperative* that you feed Saber tonight, right out in the open, in front of our delegation and the house of Jadon—it is our only chance of rescuing your brother."

Dane frowned, his forehead creasing in consternation. "How would—"

"May I speak?" Salvatore said, failing to conceal the clipped edge in his voice.

"Of course."

Salvatore reached into the pocket of his black silk shirt, retrieved the vial of sterilization serum, and held it up in front of the vampires, preparing to lie with grace and ease. "Do you see this bottle, son? It contains a very potent, mystical substance, one that took a great deal of expertise to prepare, I might add." He raised his chin in a prideful gesture, then set the bottle down on the expensive cocktail table in front of him. "We know that the house of Jadon has not exactly welcomed Saber with open arms; they are keeping him closely guarded, drained of blood, and weakened—"

"Sounds faintly familiar," Diablo growled beneath his breath.

"Pardon me?" Salvatore said.

"Nothing." There went that malevolent smile again.

Yes, well, smile while you can, boy, Salvatore thought. "As I was saying, they are keeping Saber in a weakened state. They are using diamonds to keep him from dematerializing, and Nachari Silivasi has him constantly surrounded with insulation wards and energetic barriers."

"English," Diablo prompted.

Salvatore froze. To kill or not to kill—that was the question.

BLOOD REDEMPTION

Would it be better to just have Achilles slit the boy's throat where he sat? He pondered the pros and cons. Perhaps not. If it was Zarek or Valentine—Dark Lords rest the latter's soul—in the clutches of their enemy, Salvatore would also be on edge. He could make an allowance for temporary insanity. He forced himself to summon more patience. "Yes, well, in *English*: The Wizard is blocking all transmission from coming or going in Saber's presence: He can't dematerialize out of there; we can't speak to him telepathically; and it is impossible to conjure any spells on his behalf." He pointed at the blue vial. "This, however, will level the playing field. One hour after Saber ingests the serum, his body will return to full strength; we will be able to speak to him telepathically, in spite of Nachari's barriers; and he will have a fighting chance of escaping on his own. I, of course, will be able to create a small diversion to assist him, to summon some sort of magic on his behalf." He smacked his lips for emphasis. "It's our best chance—no, it's our only chance—of getting him back safely." He locked his gaze with Dane's and squared his jaw. "Son, you *must* ingest this serum so that it is thick in your own blood, and then you must feed Saber *liberally* so he can absorb it through you. No matter what else occurs this night, the potion is the purpose for the meeting. You will either doom or save your brother. Do you understand?"

Dane nodded slowly as he processed Salvatore's words.

Diablo looked at him suspiciously. Very suspiciously. "You would do that...do this...for Saber?"

Salvatore shrugged languidly. "Why not?"

Diablo looked off into the distance, and something icy and cold glossed over his eyes, darkening his expression. "Did my father really do what he is accused of?"

Salvatore sat up straight. "He did." Slowly licking his lips, he paused to prolong the moment. "Why?"

"Then Saber was truly born to the house of *Jadon*?" Diablo asked.

"He was." Salvatore was practically salivating. Where was this angry male going with this?

136

Tessa Dawn

Diablo shrugged, feigning indifference, but the quiver in his throat betrayed his regret. "Then he can't be allowed to live. Saber, that is. He is our enemy—no matter what."

Salvatore swallowed the sweet secretions in his mouth and shifted erotically in his seat. *Well done, Diablo. Well done,* he thought.

The rebellious male could not possibly have known that the serum was not exactly as Salvatore had described, that in truth, the serum would make Saber infertile for the next thirty to sixty days, rendering him incapable of siring sons and fulfilling the demands of the Blood Curse. He could not possibly have known that, ultimately, the potion would ensure Saber's death at the hands of the Blood. And yet, he had spoken wisely.

Loyally.

Salvatore had no intentions of telling Diablo the truth, not right now.

After all, it would only work if Dane could get it into Saber, and as Salvatore had predicted, Dane was beyond desperate to save his beloved sibling, regardless of the change in Saber's origins. The council could not count on Dane to murder Saber with the serum, so the ruse of transferring the potion as a means of escape, while deceitful at its core, was absolutely necessary. The good of the colony always came first.

Always.

Feeling slightly overwhelmed for the first time, Salvatore held Diablo's pointed stare with an equal amount of intensity, regarding him for the first time with a modicum of respect, and then he continued to lie for Dane's benefit: "Of course I would do this for Saber, Diablo—or any other male in the house of Jaegar." He sought a plausible explanation. "Your brother is innocent; it is your father who has committed treason. As far as I know, Saber has always been loyal to our house; there is no reason to assume that anything has changed."

In truth, they both knew there was *every* reason to assume that *everything* had changed. Saber was a descendant of Jadon, not Jaegar, and despite his loyalty and upbringing, that meant he had the favor of the celestial gods and the potential backing of the all-powerful king, Napolean Mondragon. Saber had a *destiny* now and perhaps a reason to embrace a freer, easier life. He could never fully be trusted again. Not to mention, Saber knew far too much about the colony, its history, government, and ways. Saber Alexiares needed to be extinguished at all costs; and clearly, Diablo understood this, too.

Diablo continued to appear calm, almost too calm, yet his pulse sped up audibly. "Of course."

Tread very carefully, son, and you may yet live, Salvatore said on a private bandwidth, addressing Diablo directly, mind to mind, for the first time.

Diablo winced as understanding slowly began to dawn in his eyes. He swallowed his arrogance and returned Salvatore's honesty with a question of his own: *What is really in the serum, Councilman?*

Salvatore smiled broadly, but he did not answer.

Diablo's head fell forward into his chained hands as if it had suddenly become too heavy to hold up.

To whom do you pledge your loyalty? Salvatore asked him. It was a question from a time long gone, from the fateful day of the Blood Curse, when the men in Romania were asked to choose once and for all, to forever serve one prince or the other: Jadon or Jaegar.

I pledge my undying heart—first, last, and only—to the house of my rebirth, to our royal prince Jaegar, to all his descendants, and to the dark lords who have granted me life.

Salvatore let out a profound sigh of relief.

Diablo looked nauseated, slightly pale, but he was indeed a loyal subject: *Salvatore, please do not ask Dane to do this thing. Even if he initially thinks he is helping Saber, he will eventually learn the truth. Give the serum to me, and I will see to it that Saber ingests it.*

Salvatore shook his head. *Saber is accustomed to feeding from Dane, son. He will suspect something if we send you in your brother's stead. And Dane—*

Must make his own choice. Here and now.

Diablo swallowed hard, realizing for the first time that he was going to lose his father and both of his so-called brothers; his next words were forced out of what sounded like a suddenly dry throat. "Allow me to accompany the delegates this night, Councilman." He spoke out loud for Dane's benefit, trying to sound defiant as usual. "Please don't exclude me from the delegation."

Salvatore chose his words carefully. "Diablo, we have a firm agreement with the house of Jadon; there will be five delegates from each of our respective houses, ten males in total, and this includes Saber." He gestured at the mountain of a guard standing behind Diablo's lavishly upholstered chair. "Achilles is needed for obvious reasons, as am I. Oskar is our head of state, so his presence is imperative. That leaves room for two more: Saber is accustomed to feeding from Dane, so Dane it is. And I'm sure you would not deny your father one final opportunity to say good-bye to his beloved son." He carried on the lie for Dane's sake. "The way I see it, you and Saber will be reunited soon enough if our plan works." His words hung cruelly like phantoms in the air, their meaning abundantly clear: Diablo Alexiares would never see Saber alive again.

Diablo began to tremble in his seat, but in the end, he slowly nodded his head in consent.

Understanding the depth of Diablo's loss, yet still needing to push forward, Salvatore reached for the vial filled with sterilization serum. He broke the top of the bottle on the edge of the cocktail table and slowly extended it to Dane. "There is no time like the present, son. Drink. Every drop."

He watched as Dane lifted the vial to his lips, and his heart felt truly heavy for the first time: Diablo's unexpected reaction had made him optimistic. For the briefest moment, he had hoped that Dane would do the same, refuse to go along with the plan to save and rescue Saber, demonstrate his unyielding fealty to the house of Jaegar through a willingness to kill his own brother, and buy himself a pardon in the process. As Dane sucked down every ounce of the liquid, Salvatore's hope vanished along with the serum: Dane was doomed by virtue of consuming the forbidden potion, but even if the dark lords forgave him, the house of Jaegar would not. He was no longer just the son of a traitor but a traitor himself.

And the penalty for sedition was death.

Dane Alexiares would ultimately be executed along with his father for doing the very thing his council was asking him to do. He just wasn't as sharp as his wicked brother.

Sighing heavily, Salvatore slipped the empty vial into his pocket. If it was any consolation, Diablo had proven himself worthy of life. Salvatore would explain what had happened to the council, and the assembly would surely let the remaining Alexiares boy live. At least the Alexiares line would not be wiped entirely from the earth.

"It is finished then," Salvatore said cryptically. He tried to look at Diablo, but the look of anguish in the male's eyes was too great to bear. Diablo understood exactly what had just happened.

And he was going to let it be.

Survival was one powerful instinct.

"Achilles," Salvatore said, turning to regard the giant soldier instead, "keep Diablo and Dane detained in separate cells until the meeting tonight." There was no point in pushing providence, giving Diablo a chance to have a change of heart...or spill his guts to Dane. As they were all so painfully starting to realize, grief could be a terrible and unpredictable thing.

"As you wish," Achilles bit out in a gruff, no-nonsense tone. He held out Diablo's cuffs, and the male stumbled while trying to stand before submitting once more to the shackles.

Salvatore sauntered over to Diablo and placed a firm hand on his shoulder. "Be strong, son." He spoke quietly in his ear. And then, he strode to Dane's chair and altered the gesture, kissing the male on the opposite cheek—the kiss of Judas. "Tonight, my dear cohort. Everything hinges on what happens *tonight*."

Tessa Dawn

Vanya Demir reached for her journal and tried to quiet her mind. It had always soothed her in the past to put pen to paper, and tonight she was in great need of solace.

Tonight, Saber would be meeting with his dark family in the Red Canyons, and the matter of his life…or death…might be settled once and for all.

The dragon and the treasure.

She recalled the distant, almost foreign look in his penetrating eyes, just one night past in the forest, and shuddered: He had stared at her with such intensity, such scrutiny, such curious…need. It was as if he had seen her in a new light for the first time, and his eyes were trying to adjust to the glare. She bit the end of her pen in consternation, hoping to dismiss the thought—maybe she was just being too cryptic. Maybe she was imagining something that wasn't really there.

Or maybe she had actually felt his…wondering.

His searching for unveiled answers.

His seeking for some sort of clarity.

His feeling something he couldn't name.

For her.

She reached for her journal and began to write: *By all the gods, I am so conflicted…because I know I felt it, too.*

fourteen

The night was filled with shadows—ominous, layered, and threatening in their silhouettes. The temperature was frigid, maybe thirty-two degrees, and a light frost had accumulated along the branches of the native trees, surrounding the large circular clearing in the Red Canyons. The tall evergreens and pines hovered ominously, like soldiers in their own right, come to pay tribute to the uncommon meeting of bitter enemies.

The delegates from both houses materialized in the clearing at the same time: the Dark Ones coming from the west, the house of Jadon from the east. Each group appeared about ten yards away from the other, facing off like warriors of old in two loose semicircles. Ramsey Olaru and Nathaniel Silivasi flanked the sons of Jadon's delegation on the far right and left, respectively, with Napolean Mondragon, Saber Alexiares, and Nachari Silivasi in the center of the circle.

Saber drew in a deep breath, filling his lungs with the cold mountain air and slowing his heartbeat to make his senses more alert for the upcoming encounter.

Tell me what you see, Saber, Napolean commanded telepathically, the moment the Dark Ones came into view. He spoke on the common house of Jadon bandwidth so that all who were present from *their* delegation could hear.

Saber swallowed hard. It was still hard to believe that he was *truly* a son of Jadon, at least by birth, but the fact that he could communicate on the common bandwidth sealed the deal.

He had no intentions of betraying the house of Jaegar—or his father and brother—but if he refused to give the king immediate and truthful answers, the meeting would end before it began. His tongue snaked out to lick his bottom lip nervously. *The three males in the middle are Achilles Zahora, my father Damien, and my brother Dane. The male across from Ramsey, on the outer edge, is the*

BLOOD REDEMPTION

Chief of Council, Oskar Vadovsky, and I believe you know the male on the far left, across from Nathaniel: It's our councilman and sorcerer, Salvatore Nistor.

Napolean's answering growl was barely audible, but Saber heard it just the same. The king looked ready to strike at a moment's notice, his harsh onyx-and-silver eyes flashing an instant, deep crimson red. *Yes…I know of Salvatore.*

What's with the giant's damn tattoo? Ramsey asked, eyeing Saber from the end of the row with his peripheral vision, unwilling to look away from his enemy.

Saber sighed. Ramsey was referring to the larger-than-life black mamba, with jeweled red eyes and daggers crossed along its scales, tattooed around every inch of Achilles's right bicep.

It's the official insignia of the Colony Guard, Saber said. *All who protect the council bear the tattoos around their arms like bands of honor; it simply means that they will live and die in the service of their people.*

So, they're the official bad-asses of the house of Jaegar then? Nathaniel snarled.

Something like that, Saber said. *Achilles has a serious reputation. He's also known as The Executioner.* He swallowed the bile that threatened to rise in his throat. *I think they chose him for effect.*

Indeed, Napolean whispered, his bile rising. *As if I couldn't squash the seven-foot bug with a wink.*

Salvatore Nistor stepped forward slowly, breaking formation with his cohorts. With an eerie, old-world charm, he bowed low and swept a graceful arm outward, encompassing the canyon. "Greetings, house of Jadon," he said to no one in particular, and then his eyes pinned Nachari Silivasi. "And you, wizard. It is nice to meet again, no?" A wicked smile of contempt distorted his features. "How was your time in hell? Painful, I suspect."

Nachari took a bold step forward, the strength of his restrained magick radiating around him like a dark halo, expanding outward and rising upward like a cloud of perilous smoke. "Why don't you ask Valentine; I think he's been there longer."

Salvatore's deceptively handsome face drained of all color,

and all the males in the clearing tensed.

"If you came to taunt and goad," Napolean said, his voice thick with authority, "then this meeting is over. We have neither the time nor inclination to play your petty games."

Oskar Vadovsky stepped forward then. "Very well, Sir Mondragon." He slanted his head in a stately manner. "Perhaps you would do better to address your equal, as opposed to my underlings."

Salvatore noticeably bristled, and his right hand began to tremble slightly, but he held his tongue.

Napolean chuckled, obviously finding the comparison absurd. "So, you're the infamous Chief of Council?"

Oskar raised his chin far too high to be dignified. "I am." He smiled an arrogant grin. "It is good that warriors such as we meet in the struggle of—"

Napolean waved a dismissive hand. "Heard the quote—it's from Ten Bears, a fictional character in a Clint Eastwood movie. Not interested in the plagiarism. We are *meeting* because I am a being of honor, something unequalled in your house. And you are standing"—he waved his arm in a wide arc, indicating all of the Dark Ones in front of him—"*all of you* are still standing, *and still breathing*, because I have chosen not to strike you down out of benevolence. But make no mistake, I have no equal on this field, or any other." He turned to regard Dane Alexiares then. "You are Saber's sibling?"

Dane swallowed a lump in his throat and stepped forward tentatively, leaving the protection of the Dark Ones' formation. "I am." His voice was almost respectful. He raised both hands in front of his body in a gesture of peace and strolled forward cautiously. "Saber is my brother."

Saber felt his heart constrict in his chest, but he didn't make a move. He simply stared ahead, meeting Dane's sharp ebony eyes for the first time in days. *Brother.*

The telepathic communication went through.

Saber.

Thank you for coming.

Dane nodded. *What Father did…we didn't know. I swear—*

"That's enough," Napolean Mondragon said. "Speak out loud or not at all."

Dane cut his eyes at the king, and then quickly turned back to Saber. "You look hungry…starved."

Saber shrugged, indifferent. "I'm fine."

Dane intensified his stare, his eyes narrowing with purpose. "No, you're not. *Feed.*"

Saber drew back, surprised. Dane wanted him to feed, here? Now? He nodded slowly, more of an acknowledgment of his brother's diligent attention to his lifelong duty than an assent to the request.

Dane took it as an invitation, just the same.

Refusing to look to the left or the right of Saber, he held his brother's eyes as he approached him casually and with confidence. When he was, at last, a couple feet away, he spun around in a smooth, graceful motion, turned his back to Saber, and dropped effortlessly to one knee before him, scooping a thick pile of hair away from his neck.

Instinctively, Saber dropped down behind him. It wasn't a conscious decision as much as an automatic reaction, like a baby rooting at his mother's breast. Placing his right hand on Dane's right shoulder, his left palm just above his ear to wrench his head further to the side, he released his canines and struck with swift, agile precision.

"Not so fast, Chief!" Ramsey was there in an instant, his own large palm snaking out just in time to slip between Dane's neck and Saber's fangs. The sound of enamel striking bone was audible across the silent valley, even as the warriors from the house of Jadon drew in sharp intakes of breath, and the soldiers from the house of Jaegar held theirs.

Ramsey drew back his hand and shook it out violently. "Son of a bitch! That's the second time you've bitten me, soldier."

Saber's head snapped to the side, his feral eyes trying to focus on Ramsey. His hunger was severe, his desire to complete what he had started, palpable. Although he tried to speak, explain what had just happened to the irritated warrior, what came out of his mouth was nothing more than a primal grunt.

Nathaniel flanked Saber on the left side and withdrew a razor-sharp stiletto with a hand-crafted grip and a polished silver blade. "Back up." He gave the order to Dane, and by the tone of his voice, not to mention the way he was wielding the stiletto, he wasn't playing. "No contact."

Dane was barely coherent, just this side of feral himself. "Feeding is our custom," he snapped, struggling for the right words. "It is how we greet...communicate... Saber is my brother. You have no right."

Napolean Mondragon seemed to simply appear in the mix, towering over both of them. With one sharp tug, he yanked Saber up from his knees and planted him on his feet. "Breathe," he commanded, watching for signs of sentience—bloodlust was a very real condition, especially for a starving vampire. "Just breathe."

Saber drew in a deep, frantic breath, but his fangs still twitched. He...wanted.

Needed.

By all that was unholy, *he hungered.*

"Shit," Ramsey snarled. He glanced at Napolean, and the king nodded his head in a thin reply.

Too quick to track, Nathaniel tossed his stiletto to Ramsey. Ramsey caught it and sliced his own wrist, and the offering was placed against Saber's mouth.

The vampire devoured the blood like a starving lion being tossed a rare piece of meat: He latched on with ferocity, made a tight, intractable seal, and began to suck in earnest.

Nachari stepped forward and placed an open palm over Saber's throat while chanting some strange Latin combination of words, over and over, softer and softer, until the words faded out.

And so did Saber's unbearable thirst.

For the first time, Saber realized what he was doing, and he shrank back.

BLOOD REDEMPTION

He released Ramsey's wrist, spat on the ground, and wiped the back of his hand over his mouth, utterly disgusted. There was no greater honor in the house of Jaegar than to feed from one's youngest sibling, to perpetuate the cycle of life in such an intimate manner; and there was no greater insult than to refuse a much-needed offering, only to take it from someone else. And a son of Jadon, at that.

Saber felt like he might vomit. "Dane, I'm—"

Dane's stunned expression registered his sentiment. "Forget it," he snarled. "You...you don't have any choice, do you?"

Saber shook his head slowly. "I'm not free here."

Ramsey, Nathaniel, and Nachari stepped back in an awkward attempt to give the brothers some small measure of privacy. "Don't try that again," Ramsey warned, his own deep, gravelly voice registering a measure of disgust.

Saber's lip twitched involuntarily, and he leveled a malevolent glare at the sentinel. "Unless you want to kill me where I stand, don't push it, son of Jadon."

Ramsey raised his wrist to his mouth, dripped a lavish amount of venom over his wound, and sneered. "You're welcome," he bit out, still retreating.

Saber turned back to Dane. "How is Diablo?"

Dane shook his head, his tangled hair swaying along his angular jaw from the motion. "As expected, I guess. This is...things have been crazy."

Saber nodded slowly. "And Father?"

Dane stood up to his full height then and twisted around to point at Damien. "He's here."

"He's been convicted—"

"Of treason, yes."

Saber looked up as Achilles escorted Damien forward. The moment the male came within five feet of Saber, he yanked his arms free from Achilles and shuffled forward frantically, shackles and all. "Saber!"

Saber embraced his father, not caring what the warriors in the house of Jadon might think or do. "*Dark Lords*, Father—

what have you done?"

Damien squeezed him hard, then drew back abruptly and raised his shackled hands to grasp Saber by the chin. "You are my son. You have always been my son. You will always be *my son*."

Achilles snatched Damien by the collar and yanked him away as if tugging on a rag doll. The look in his eyes was one of pure revulsion, and Saber's six-foot-two father stumbled before the guard caught him and steadied him on his feet.

"Tell me you know this," Damien insisted.

Saber worked his throat convulsively, afraid he couldn't speak. "I...I do."

"Well, isn't this just lovely," Salvatore drawled, all at once appearing beside Achilles, behind Damien, and far too close to Saber.

Nachari was back in an instant, responding to the growing threat: "Don't be stupid," he whispered to Salvatore, his eyes reflecting his willingness to strike.

As tensions elevated, Napolean cleared his throat. "Everyone, take five paces back." He never raised his voice. He didn't have to. All of the males complied.

And then, the oddest thing happened.

Achilles flanked Damien on his right side, reaching across to secure his shackled wrists with his right hand, even as his left hand hung loose behind him, and Salvatore flanked Dane on his left side, reaching across to secure Dane's wrists with his left hand, even as his right hand hung loose in a similar position. Then, in the blink of an eye, both males released their claws, drew back their arms, and punctured their respective prisoners with dizzying speed and force, breaking through their backs and penetrating their chest cavities with supernatural ease.

Saber blinked, trying to make sense of what was happening, and just that quick, he recoiled. Achilles and Salvatore were standing side by side like two merchants on a street corner, holding up their wares; only, dangling from their gore-filled hands, were two beating hearts, the dislodged organs severed from their hosts and dripping blood on the ground.

The corpses of Damien and Dane Alexiares slowly slumped to the ground, their deceased mouths still open in shock, their expired knees buckling forward. Before Saber could react or cry out, Achilles drew his sword from its scabbard, slashed deftly through the air, and both of the male's heads toppled forward, decapitated from their bodies.

Saber stood in stunned silence, staring blankly ahead.

Watch your back, son of Jadon! Salvatore snarled at Saber, using the house of Jaegar's private, telepathic bandwidth. *You no longer have a home here.*

And with that, the entire delegation of Dark Ones simply vanished out of view, leaving the dead in their wake.

Time stood still.

The earth stopped spinning on its axis.

Nothing happened.

Nothing mattered.

Nothing *existed*.

Saber took two uneven steps forward and cocked his head to the side in confusion. He looked down at his chest and frowned. Why was he still standing? Still breathing? He stared at his breastbone in bewilderment—where was the gash? Where was the gaping hole in the place where his heart should have been? He didn't see it happen. He didn't *feel* it happen. But Salvatore must have removed his organ too—it was the only explanation that made sense.

The only way to account for the pain.

He absently scanned the ground, fully expecting to gape at the gruesome sight of his own blood and guts, intestines strewn beneath his feet, blending morbidly with the dirt, staining his steel-toed boots. Again, his mind could not connect the dots, make sense of what had just happened; but the pain—*great Dark*

Lords of hell, the agony!—was beyond anything he had experienced in battle before, beyond anything he had ever imagined.

Surely there was nothing left of him but skin and bones.

He looked up then. Staring blankly forward at the headless bodies of his father and his brother.

Damien.

Dane.

And eight hundred years of memories—six hundred years of brotherly antics—flashed through his consciousness in an instant.

They weren't...dead.

They...they...just weren't.

What happened?

He had to go to them. He had to go home. Dane would go hunting soon. He would feed, and Damien, Diablo, and Saber would await his return so they could feed, too.

Yes, he had to go back to the lair.

Saber took another tentative step forward, but for some strange reason, his legs didn't work like they should have: They began to buckle beneath him.

He opened his mouth to say something, and that's when he realized he couldn't breathe.

He hadn't taken a breath for hours.

He exhaled, three times in a row, failing to inhale in exchange. His vision grew blurry, and he started to panic.

Air!

Where was the air!

Why couldn't he draw in breath?

As he continued to pant in desperation, his knees gave way, and he pitched into the dirt. His head fell forward, and he thought he saw his wild hair through his peripheral vision, framing his face in a hideous, matted halo. His hands dug into the earth, and he curled his fingers back, releasing his fangs. Clawing...grasping...trying to hold onto something...so vital.

And then the air came back.

BLOOD REDEMPTION

It rushed into his lungs like a cyclone sweeping across the plains, nearly knocking him off balance, and he gasped. *"Oh Dark Lords."*

He moaned.

His fangs extended from his gums, and he bit into his lips, tearing at them, trying to manage the internal pain.

Blinking several times in rapid succession, Saber Alexiares finally threw back his head and tried to scream, but no sound came out. He simply shouted noiselessly to the empty skies what should have been a deafening roar of defiance, and his body shook.

His chest heaved.

Over and over…and over.

But no sound would come out.

"Saber, uita-te la mine, fiule." *Look at me, son.* Someone was standing next to him, speaking in Romanian. Why in Romanian?

He shouted again; and this time there was sound!

Balls of fire began to fall from the heavens, plummeting to the earth and consuming whatever they touched in a blistering wrath of fury.

"Saber!" A strong, powerful hand on his shoulder.

No! *No.* "Don't touch me!"

The ground shook beneath him, and thunder and lightning eclipsed the sky. It was beautiful. Dangerous. Glorious.

Not enough.

Not nearly enough.

It would never be enough!

As pain racked his body in violent waves, Saber began to sway back and forth, shouting, moaning, pounding the ground, praying for the fires of heaven to consume him where he knelt.

"Son, you have to stop: Your emotion—it's too strong."

That voice. It belonged to Napolean Mondragon. But *son*? Saber Alexiares was no one's son. He had no father…

He had no father.

He—had—no—father.

As a keening wail escaped his lips, renting the air with its ferocity, the soul he never knew buckled beneath a grief beyond his reckoning.

And then his eyes focused on Damien and Dane, their decapitated bodies, and he prayed for death. As the world around him rattled and shook with the fury of a thousand dark angels, he began to grow weak.

Fangs.

Venom.

Something being inserted into his neck.

Ah yes, Napolean Mondragon, the great leader of the house of Jadon was kneeling beside him, curiously injecting venom into Saber's neck. But why?

Why didn't matter.

There was nothing.

Nothing.

And then, in a few interminable seconds, the world went black.

fifteen

Vanya Demir knew better than to pull the same stunt twice, to risk using her magic once more to slip into Saber's cell undetected, and what she intended to do this time was far more difficult, way more complex, and wholly deceitful. Not to mention, she wasn't even sure if she could pull it off.

She had worked feverishly to create an Illusion Spell, an elaborate hoax that created a rift in time, so to speak. If all went well, Saber's guards would see, hear, and sense everything around them as if it were happening right now, in the present moment, when, in truth, they would be experiencing a holographic image from the past, an illusion. Vanya could slip into Saber's cell and interact with him, undetected, while the sentinels would swear he was sleeping soundly, through the night.

She shuddered as she thought about the vast array of spells her female predecessors had conjured—indeed perfected—and the way she was now able to revive it through her work at the University. The males in the house of Jadon had no idea just how powerful their ancient female ancestors had truly been: They were completely unaware of the immense fountain of knowledge that had died with the original women...well, almost died.

Vanya still had access to it.

So did Ciopori.

And when one really thought about it, the Curse still inflicted a great deal of it on an ongoing basis.

Vanya wrinkled her nose and cringed, at both the thought of the awful Curse and the idea of what would happen to her if she got caught. The king would surely throttle her if he knew she was using her magic for personal gain, and that was to say nothing of what Marquis would do if he found out: He would string her up by the highest tree and tan her hide with a prickly branch. Never mind how the highly volatile and totally unpredictable Saber Alexiares was going to react to her entering his cell, once again, unannounced. Even if everything went exactly as planned, she might be in for the fright of her life.

Vanya struggled to dismiss the thought before she lost her courage. After all, she had already weighed the pros and cons: Of course, she knew it was crazy—by all that was holy, it was stark-raving mad, not to mention utterly foolhardy. But what else was she to do? Ciopori had relayed the night's events to her shortly after the warriors had returned from the Red Canyons, and the very idea of what had happened in that clearing had made Vanya sick to her stomach.

Made her want to wretch.

The executions of Damien and Dane were a ghastly abomination she could hardly wrap her mind around, let alone simply dismiss. Despite the fact that they were evil, Dark Ones without souls, Saber Alexiares had cared deeply for them, perhaps even worshipped them, and his sense of betrayal had to be immense.

And the way Ciopori had described his grief?

Great Serpens, even for one as dark as he, it had to be horrific. Irreconcilable. For all his faults—and wasn't that word completely insufficient in light of his sins—he did love his dark family. At least, in whatever approximation of love he was capable of.

According to Ciopori, Napolean had been forced to sedate him just to stop the fallout from his anguish: Saber had unwittingly called down fire from the heavens, and he had been swiftly on his way to causing an earthquake or a tornado. The thought of that arrogant, rebellious male brought to his knees in torment, broken from the weight of his sorrow, kneeling upon the ground in raw, unrelenting pain was even more than she could bear. It was heart wrenching…unimaginable.

Dreadful beyond her imagining.

Yet it was neither Saber nor his pain that drove her to take such a foolish, reckless chance. Plain and simple, it was her dream.

Always...*and still*...her dream.

All she could think of was the nightmare, the dragon, and the treasure.

Her people.

And what was surely about to be lost forever.

Vanya Demir knew that Saber Alexiares was on the edge of a precipice, and if he fell this time, he might never return. And for some unknown reason, she also knew that she was the only soul in the house of Jadon who could truly get through to him, if it was even possible to get through to a soul as lost as his. In this critical, tortured moment, she was his only hope for salvation.

Was it dangerous? *Of course.*

It was beyond dangerous—it was stupid.

Would the ones she loved hold her decision against her? *Absolutely.*

In fact, it might be unforgiveable in the king's eyes. And yet, she could no more turn away from this challenge...*this duty*...than she could turn away from Nikolai or Ciopori if they needed her. Whatever it was that drove her to such desperate lengths, the compulsion was greater than her reservations, the obligation stronger than her common sense.

She drew in a deep breath for courage: This was bigger than a lost vampire and his *destiny*, and she had to see it through.

Staring now at the perfectly constructed Illusion Spell, she watched as Ramsey and Santos peered naively into the cage and saw a troubled, sedated prisoner asleep on his cot—a scene reconstructed from twenty-four hours earlier. They were completely unaware of her presence and totally ignorant of the ruse.

Realizing it was too late to turn back now, she took a cautionary step forward and fixed her eyes on the real crouching tiger in the corner of the cell, the dark vampire, estranged from both the house of Jaegar and the house of Jadon, who was alive, awake, and suffering right before her eyes.

BLOOD REDEMPTION

Saber Alexiares was hunched over like a wounded animal. His heavy shoulders were cloaked by an equally heavy cascade of black-and-red locks that gleamed in the shadowy moonlight as it shone through the tiny window above him; and his hard, sculpted muscles were drawn tight and rigid. For all intents and purposes, he looked like a caged feline, cornered and ready to pounce. He stared absently at the floor; he clawed repetitively at the ground; and he swayed back and forth like a kite caught in a circular wind.

Frankly, he looked more than a little bit insane.

He looked dangerous.

Vanya approached the vampire slowly, careful to stay out of striking distance. The dream-image of a fire-breathing dragon suddenly emerged in her mind, and she quickly shoved the picture aside. "Saber," she whispered softly. "Dragon, are you in there?"

He raised his head slowly—so *very* slowly. His demeanor was eerily calm...yet not. And then his eyes met hers, and her breath caught in her throat: His pupils were vacant yet fixed upon hers. His face was drawn tight yet absent of lines. His expression was empty yet far too aware.

He was a breathing paradox.

Vanya clutched her hand to her heart and whispered a silent prayer to the gods for protection. "Saber," she repeated, adding a little strength to her voice.

The top right corner of his lip turned up, and a wicked glint of fangs flashed in the moonlight. "Princess," he drawled in a mere hiss of a voice. "You come to me...again." His black eyes were so dull and lifeless that it felt like she was staring into the gaze of a shark.

"I...I...yes." She cleared her throat for courage. "I heard what happened. And I came to...to see about you."

He rose so nimbly, so swiftly, and with such lethal ease that her heart almost stopped beating. *Oh great Celestial gods*, she was a dead woman. The dragon was going to kill her right then and there—it was written all over his face: fire, fury, and finality.

She held a steadying hand out in front of her. "Saber...please. Stop, Dragon."

He licked his bottom lip and growled deep in his throat, the warning of a feral predator. "What big eyes you have, Red Riding Hood."

Vanya gulped. "Saber!" She tried to snap him out of it. "This is not a game!"

"Indeed," he replied. "Death never is." The meaning of his words echoed loudly in her mind, ricocheting off her soul, and then he did something completely unexpected: He took two healthy strides forward, sank back onto his knees, and knelt silently before her, dropping his head in resignation. He reached up and clutched her hands in his. "Help me," he whispered in a voice so faint it was nearly inaudible.

Stunned, Vanya bit her bottom lip. She was too afraid to speak, too afraid to move. She had no idea what was about to happen next and could only wait, transfixed by the depth of his emotion.

Seeming to understand, Saber nodded his head in the direction of the watch-room, the space that housed his guards, and the foreboding chamber that sat just beyond the outer walls. "I wish to play no more games," he said softly. "Take me to the chamber of Sacrifice and Atonement, Vanya. Take me beyond the crossbones and open the hatch." His cruel mouth turned up in a smile. "I have had my fill of this incessant torture." He laughed insincerely, the sound rough yet hollow. "I get it. Payback is a bitch, and I had this coming. Still..." His smile turned morose, almost as if he were flashing back and forth between cynicism and sorrow; and his already harsh grip tightened further around her slender fingers. "Still...enough is enough. Isn't this what you, the king, and all the house of Jadon have been waiting for—what my own treasured house of Jaegar has been asking the dark lords for since the moment my true origins were revealed?" Before she could answer, he added, "Just take me to the Death Chamber now, and let the Blood come for me tonight. For the sake of your gods—and your children—let the Blood exact its vengeance and be done with it."

Vanya glanced over her shoulders at the thick, ancient walls made of mud and stone, following his morbid gaze. Even as she wrestled with the meaning of his words, struggling to process exactly what he was asking, she knew…and she understood. Saber wanted to die. He was ready to be taken into the cold, sterile chamber of torture to face his final reckoning. Good or bad, right or wrong, redeemable or evil; he no longer wanted to live. She shook her head slowly. "You know I cannot do that, Saber."

"Why not?" he asked, his voice revealing his angst. "You can put guards to sleep, create magical rifts in time, slink in and out of this cell like an invisible specter. Why can't you take me into that chamber and set me free…in a way your people will both understand and forgive?"

She didn't know how to answer him. There were so many reasons, so many things he hadn't thought of. "It isn't time," she finally said.

He tilted his head to the side and frowned, appearing genuinely confused.

"The Blood," she whispered. "It wouldn't come tonight—not even if we wanted it to." She clenched her eyes shut and moistened her lips. "It is not yet time, Saber. There are still twenty-five days left in your Blood Moon."

Saber laughed unexpectedly, the sound as anguished as it was derisive. He released her hands, made a triangle with his thumbs and forefingers, and pressed the configuration against her lower stomach as if framing her womb. "And so, what? You've come to give me the needed sacrifice then?"

Vanya drew in a quick intake of breath. "No!" She pushed his hands away in revulsion and fought not to squirm. Realizing that a defensive reaction was not going to help the situation —if anything, it would probably make it worse—she purposefully softened her voice and tried for a gentler tone. "No, that is *not* why I've come. I've come to…I've come to…" *Oh heavens*, why had she come?

Suddenly, she felt incredibly stupid.

And more than a little lost.

Whatever had she thought she could do for him?

He suddenly jerked upright and his back grew stiff, almost as if someone had forced a rod through his vertebrae. His eyes flashed a deadly crimson red. "Why are you doing this?" he snarled, clearly escalating.

Vanya shook her head vigorously. "Doing what?"

"This!" he roared, pounding a clenched fist several times against his chest.

She frowned. "I don't understand."

"*This spell.* This vitriol! It doesn't become you, Princess." He looked down at his chest and grimaced, grinding his teeth together as if in terrible agony. "It is something I would expect from someone in the house of *Jaegar.*"

Vanya blanched, her mouth falling open. *What in the world was he talking about?* By the look on his face, one would have sworn she had just thrust a dagger into his sternum and twisted it 360 degrees just for the pleasure of doing so. Had he gone utterly mad?

Saber raised his arms and grasped his hair; he clenched his fists into two tight knots and dropped his head, inadvertently pulling a handful of his mane free. "You've done your worst. You've cast your spell. And my heart bleeds."

It was a statement of such pure vulnerability, Vanya could hardly believe he had uttered it. "I've done no such thing," she insisted. She stared at his chest, half expecting to see blood ooze from a wound, and then she took a careful step backward. She was just about to argue her case when she *felt* the origin of his words. She felt his absolute despair, and she understood the illogical nature of his reasoning. "Oh…gods…" she mumbled, more to herself than him. Gentling her voice, she slowly shook her head. "No, Saber. This is not a spell. No one has cast anything upon you." She blinked several times as her eyes began to moisten. "The pain is called grief, and you are experiencing it…*feeling it*…perhaps for the first time."

BLOOD REDEMPTION

His head snapped up in immediate dissension; his glare was stark with defiance. "No! It is not!" He sounded furious. "You are a sorceress, a celestial being; you know the ancient magic; and you are doing this on purpose." His lips curled back from his fangs, and the visage was terrifying. "And one way or another, you can make it stop."

Vanya swallowed hard, reaching for the right words: What did one say to a wounded animal, a wolf caught in a trap, snarling in desperation to break free from the pain? "Saber, I swear to you"—she glanced briefly toward the heavens—"what you are feeling isn't vengeance, and it isn't magic. It is sorrow, and I cannot take it from you. But I would if I could."

His reaction unsettled her even further as he slowly licked his lips and eyed her with suspicion. "Ah, I see," he murmured, "you are too pure to seek vengeance. And I am too broken to understand. So, what is it, then, dear Princess, that brings you to my cage this night? Is it compassion?" His voice rose in proportion to his torment. "Did you come to offer solace?" His eyes grew dark with mockery. "Or is your visit one of charity and *goodness*, that which is beyond my grasp?" He cocked his head to the side and held her gaze in an unblinking stare. "So now...you are my friend?"

Vanya didn't know whether to strike him or to try and soothe him; and honestly, what was the point of either? "No," she answered matter-of-factly, "I am not your friend." Turning her nose up in defiance, she added, "But I am human."

He smiled then. "Don't you mean celestial?"

She sighed. "Celestial and human. And I do know what it is to suffer."

He shook his head as if dismissing the remark offhand. "So you know what it's like to live for eight hundred years in a familiar world, to strictly adhere to your society's rules, only to see all the rules changed...and to watch the earth shift on its axis?"

Vanya's mouth felt suddenly dry, and she swallowed, trying to gather moisture. "I know what it is to live twenty-one years in

162

a familiar world, to be forced to play by the rules of a cruel and untenable game, only to lose everything in the end. I know what it is to wake up twenty-eight hundred and ten years later to find my entire civilization *gone*."

Although he listened to her words, he didn't seem to *hear* them. It was almost as if something got lost in the translation. "So you know this bitter sting of betrayal?" He stared right through her. "You know what it *feels* like to look into the eyes of someone you have served faithfully, since the time of the Aztec Empire and beyond, only to see abject hatred staring back at you?"

She wondered who he was referring to now: his brother? His father? Salvatore? It really didn't matter. Whoever it was, she understood better than he knew. "Yes, Dragon. I understand more than you know."

His eyelids grew heavy and dense, like he was lost somewhere in the quagmire of his mind, mired in the unrelenting muck of treachery. "Salvatore Nistor is a maggot," he said sharply. "He always has been. Did you know that?" His eyes met hers, and they were unusually focused, considering the fact that the soul beneath them was absent and his stare was ironically vacant.

Vanya hesitated to answer. Of course she knew Salvatore was a bastardly worm. Everyone in the house of Jadon knew this, but how much could she say? Safely? "He is...despicable."

Saber shrugged, taking no obvious offense to her words. He was still so far away, so lost, so absorbed in his pain. "He was never a friend, never a trusted brother, like Diablo and"—his voice faltered, however slightly, as he forced himself to speak his murdered brother's name—"and Dane." He cleared his throat and pushed through it. "But I have been loyal to that son of a bitch—and to the house of Jaegar—all my life. A *long* life, I might add. And now Salvatore wants me dead." The words rolled off his tongue in a derisive manner, and he repeated the sentiment for effect: "*Dead*, Princess. And all because I was born in a place and time—and in a way—I don't even remember. And had nothing to do with."

He was rambling now, and Vanya sighed. "For whatever it is worth, Saber, Prince Jaegar was not some revered councilman or sorcerer, at least not to me, nor was he some elusive paragon of history. He was my *brother*, my own flesh and blood, and he tried to have me killed simply because I was born female. So, believe it or not, I do know how it feels to be bitterly betrayed."

Saber winced at the sound of her words, almost as if he had heard them this time—*was that even possible?* And then his chest tightened, as if he suddenly experienced a sharp stab of pain. "My father is gone."

Vanya let out a slow, deep breath. "So is mine."

"Dane was loyal to me. He wanted to *save* me. And now he's dead."

"Jadon was loyal to me. Ultimately, he did save me. And he is gone as well."

Saber shook his head in resignation. "I can never go back, Princess."

"Neither can I, Dragon."

"I have no home. No people. No life worth living."

She didn't respond this time. How could she possibly make him understand that she also understood that feeling? She was a vestige from the past, living in a new land, a new culture, and a new century, wholly unprepared for any of it.

He lowered his voice and whispered conspiratorially, almost as if he were sharing a shameful secret, "I don't belong in this world." He relaxed his fists and his hands began to tremble before him. "I don't understand this world; and I sure as hell didn't ask for it."

Vanya didn't downplay his words or try to argue with his assessment. She simply nodded with understanding. "Neither did I."

Their eyes met once again, only this time, his pupils were no longer vacant. There was...*something*...there.

A connection?

He stared at her so long it made her uneasy. It was as if he

164

were really seeing her for the first time, not just some idea of an ancient princess or an uncovered relic from a time gone by, and if ever they were going to share a real moment, this was probably it.

Vanya held her breath, unsure of what to do. In her bones, she was too afraid to deepen the connection; yet in her heart, she was equally afraid to break it.

When at last he spoke, his grief was palpable. "Vanya..." He spoke her name humbly. "I can't breathe."

Vanya's heart sank in her chest. The anguish in those three simple words...the honesty. "I know, but it gets easier."

He reached up for her hands once again, but he didn't clasp them in his. Rather, he ran the palms of his own trembling fingers lightly over her forearms in a darkly dangerous caress. "Then even if you did not cast a spell on me, you can. You do know magic—use it."

She wrinkled up her brow. "How, Saber? I—"

"Make it stop." He shut his eyes and held his breath; he clenched his teeth so tightly it looked like his jaw might crack; and then, struggling to maintain his composure, he slowly reopened his eyes and tried once again. "By all the dark lords— or those that are light—just make it stop." His voice was thick with desperation.

"Make what stop, Dragon?" she asked, feeling helpless. Surely, he didn't think she could save him from himself. Stop the pain.

"This," he insisted, sweeping his arm around the cell. "It," he added, placing the palm of his hand over his heart. "*Everything*," he said, gazing at her with such raw emotion that it stunned her.

Vanya took a calculated step back, feeling too confused to think. For the first time since she had met the wayward vampire, Saber Alexiares's expression was no longer blatantly evil. It was no longer a cauldron of pure, unadulterated hatred, and his heart was no longer a paragon of darkness.

He was neither good nor bad, a creature to be explicitly

feared or implicitly trusted.

The moonlight shone hauntingly through the window in a conical spotlight, highlighting his distressed features, and it revealed him for exactly what he was: a wounded, desperate animal, begging for relief. "The pain—the madness—just make it all stop."

"I'm so sorry," Vanya whispered.

"Then help me."

"It just doesn't work that way, Saber."

He nodded, as if accepting her words reluctantly, and then he turned his attention back to the craggy dirt floor and began to claw at the ground, once again, seeming to slip further away into madness.

"Look at me," Vanya insisted. When he didn't look up, she chose to take a great risk: She knelt before him, gently cupped his face in her hands, and tentatively tilted his head to force his gaze. "Look at me, Dragon."

His eyes met hers, and he was so incredibly...lost.

"It doesn't work that way, Saber. You just have to try and live...to try and breathe...one day, one breath, at a time."

"I don't want to breathe," he whispered.

"But you must."

He placed his hands over the backs of hers, the mildness of his touch far more frightening than his cruelty ever could have been, and he stared at her mouth as if memorizing every fine detail. He watched her inhale and exhale in rapt fascination; and then, finally, he issued a new plea: "*Breathe for me.*"

"Oh, Saber..."

"Breathe for me, Princess." His eyes grew cloudy, the pupils narrowed, and the crimson centers faded once again to black; only this time, they were filled with a vivid, unyielding clarity.

"I cannot."

He leaned toward her, stopped just short of covering her mouth with his, and inhaled deeply, as if trying to steal her very breath. "Breathe for me!"

Saber stared at the rose-colored lips in front of him, watching as they gently parted to take in air. The face of the princess seemed divine, otherworldly, cloaked in some kind of radiance that he couldn't name—he had no point of reference. Just the same, her spirit called to his, offering him sanctuary, promising to make the unbearable pain stop.

If only for a moment.

Vanya Demir had the power to vanquish the fire that burned inside of him, like lava flowing through his veins, gathering at his heart. It was scorching him from the inside out, and she could make it stop.

Saber needed.

Like he had never needed before.

Something.

Anything.

Respite.

Just one silent moment in a lifetime of noise—and she could give him that.

"Breathe for me," he pleaded once again, his eyes wandering from her mouth to the golden cascade of hair that blanketed her shoulder. It was velvety soft yet brilliant, like silk spun from flames, and it fell far beyond her shoulders to the bend of her waist, where it rested in thick waves of enchantment. The baby-fine texture of her skin was almost candescent. If he could just...crawl inside...whatever that was...

Wherever she was.

The fire would stop burning.

"Saber, it isn't possible. I—"

"Have you ever been free?" he whispered.

She drew back. "'Tis a strange question."

He shook his head and held her gaze, unblinking. "Have you *ever* been free?"

"Dragon, you ask too personal of a question. I...I am not comfortable with this conversation."

He watched her body language carefully—he might be a heartless bastard, born to a house of darkness, but he wasn't without intelligence. He had lived for eight centuries, and in that time, he had learned to read subtle nuances, what the house of Jadon might call *emotions*; and Vanya was holding onto her self-possession, as well as her royal, celestial dignity, by a thread. She was being everything she was trained to be, and nothing she desired to be.

No, this wouldn't do. She couldn't pull away. Not now.

She must not go away.

In this tragic moment, Vanya Demir was all that was anchoring him to this world, however contemptible his life had become, and he couldn't let her hide behind her safe façade of duty, poise, and purpose—so he pressed her: "In Romania, when Jaegar and Jadon still lived, were you free then?"

Her eyelashes fluttered rapidly, and she unwittingly wrung her hands together. "What does it matter, Dragon? That was so long ago—"

"Don't hide from me, Princess. *Answer.* Growing up...in Romania...were you free?"

She shook her head slowly, at last giving in. "No, of course not. I belonged to my people."

He nodded. "Here. In Dark Moon Vale—are you free now?"

She frowned. "Saber, I don't understand what you're asking."

"Yes, you do." He rushed the words. "I see it in your eyes, Princess. I hear it in your voice. I sense it in your...blood." He reached out to take her hand in his, turned her arm over to expose her wrist, and slowly inhaled her scent. "The way it rushes through your veins with so much force, so much certainty." He stared at her chest, just above her left breast. "The very rhythm of your heart speeds up whenever you're in my presence, and your breaths, they grow so...shallow."

Vanya snatched her arm away and paled, looking suddenly

distressed. "That's because I'm afraid."

"Of me?" he asked.

"Of course!" she exclaimed.

"You should be." He spoke honestly. "But I think it's more than that. You are *alive*."

She averted her gaze, and he gave her a moment to let his words sink in, not fully understanding where this new tact was coming from. Was he playing her like he had done with Kristina? After all, he was evil—not incompetent—and he could manipulate with the best of them, or was there something else driving him?

Something so much more urgent and elemental.

He was just…hurting…so badly.

Needing…so much.

He could no longer bear his own existence, and somehow, he knew this female held the panacea to his anguish, if only for a moment. "You come alive in my presence, Princess," he said. He steeled himself against her expected reaction and reached up to place the palm of his hand brazenly on her heart: It was thundering in her chest. "Don't lie to me, Princess. Not here. Not now. Not to me. Like sees like."

Vanya nearly recoiled at the words, but he didn't care. He was beyond caring. He simply wanted to disappear into the nothingness that had to exist at the center of her being. "Don't lie to me," he repeated. "The truth is, I make you feel alive."

"'Tis not true, Dragon," she argued, sounding almost desperate.

Her words snapped him out of his reverie. "It *is* true," he insisted.

"Gods forgive you for your arrogance," she retorted. "You are a—" She stopped short, either unwilling or unable to complete the thought.

"Monster," he supplied, never missing a beat.

"Evil," she said, averting her misty, rose-colored eyes.

"Yes." He ran the back of his fingers along her gently sloped, angular cheek. The ridges were so high, so pronounced, this enigmatic Romanian female. "I am darkness personified…everything you are not."

"Yes." The word was a whisper, and she trembled. "And you are proud of it."

"No." He shook his head. He was proud—always proud—but not in this moment. Not today. Today, he was only broken. "Breathe for me," he repeated.

Vanya rose to her feet, swallowed convulsively, and tried to step away, but Saber caught her by the hem of her skirt. She brushed his hand away forcefully. "I cannot," she insisted.

He stood, too, then, all at once rising to his full height and unintentionally towering over her dainty frame. He did not mean to intimidate her, only to…to be near her. He hooked his arm around her waist and drew her close, sighing in her ear. "I can't breathe."

"It is not my doing…'tis not my fault." She sounded cornered. Frantic.

"But you can fix it," he said.

"I can't!"

He lowered his mouth to hers and made a seal over her lips—it was so gentle it was nearly undetectable—and then he slowly inhaled, praying for relief. When at last he drew back, he growled the words: "Fire and ice."

She trembled uncontrollably, her eyes misting with very real tears. "What?" She was breathless with fright yet heady with anticipation.

"The life I have lived until now is an inferno, and my soul is on fire. It's killing me. But the life you have lived until now is like ice, frozen in time, barren and cold." He bent his head to her neck and lightly grazed his fangs against her jugular. As far as he knew, it might be blood that he needed, her essence intertwined with his, whatever it was that made her unique. "Give me your ice." He sank his fangs into her neck and drew a quick taste of blood before quickly extracting his canines and sealing the wound. "Take my fire. Use me. I don't care if you consume me or destroy me—just breathe for me."

Vanya pushed against his chest with both hands, although the gesture was weak with uncertainty and failing resolve: Saber knew she was capable of sending him flying across the room, yet there he stood, upright and before her, still in one piece. "Breathe for me, Princess, and feel the life course through your veins, perhaps for the first time in your long existence. Take all that I have, without thought for anyone but yourself. Just once, live for the moment, and we will both be free."

Vanya knew it was wrong.

All of it.

Every word. Every entreaty. The logic was so…flawed.

So selfish.

And yet, it all rang so true.

The vampire's breath scorched her ears; the feel of his skin heated her flesh; and the desperation in his raspy voice seared her soul like an eternal flame, rising from somewhere deep within, threatening to consume her very being. It wasn't passion. It wasn't desire. It was a need as old as time itself, born from countless centuries of feeling alone…remaining untouched.

Unknown.

Despite her very real objections, her wholesale aversion to his touch, her mouth found his and parted. He inhaled and exhaled with her, and the feeling was overpowering. She wanted to run away, to drop the cloaking spell and scream for Ramsey or Santos to break through the magical veil, to stop what was happening in its tracks, before it went too far. But gods help her, she was like a captive bird caught in the vampire's palm.

Entranced.

Intrigued.

Entrapped.

And the need wasn't just his—it was hers. All those years in Romania, afraid for her life, watching the steady demise of her people, never belonging to anything but the aristocracy; all those years buried in the earth, entombed in the ground, while something deep inside of her shut down, it was all rising to the surface.

It was true: She did not remember the Long Sleep or the pain of that existence, but surely the utter sense of seclusion, the overwhelming experience of abandonment—the fact that her repose could have ended up being eternal—had scarred her in ways she could not even fathom. And what had finally saved them? Herself and Ciopori? It had not been her cherished brother Jadon coming to the rescue as he had promised. It had not been some higher calling to a better life, or even an intervention by the gods—she and Ciopori had been saved by Marquis Silivasi, by the fact that someone had deeply and eternally loved *her sister.*

Not her.

She winced at the realization of this fact and the pain she never let herself feel.

Saber couldn't love—she knew this.

Hell, he couldn't even breathe on his own, without needing to take the life force of another, more evolved being, but he was alive and alone. And he belonged to no one.

No one.

Just like her.

The dragon must have sensed her inner conflict because he immediately went in for the kill: He was no longer simply sealing her mouth in order to steal her breath, but kissing her with a passion born of necessity and desperation, in a way that stole her sanity. Saber Alexiares was all around her, all at once. She felt him above her, below her, inside of her head, his hands, as they swept possessively up and down the small of her waist to the flare of her hips; his thumbs as they came to rest just beneath her breasts and began to knead; and his seeking fingers as they molded, grasped, and teased her flesh into growing submission.

She wanted to push back, to fight, to force him away, but she didn't know where to begin.

He enveloped her slight frame like a blanket, wrapping his broad chest around her shoulders like a cloak of masculinity, harsh yet inviting in its pulsating warmth, its scorching fire. He towered over her, however unintentionally, his looming height compelling her back until she was forced to arch to meet his demands, to keep from losing her balance.

Dearest gods, he was like a hurricane, a cyclone enveloping her very soul.

"Saber," she panted, breathless, hoping he would hear and release her from his grasp.

"Vanya," he answered longingly, only tightening his hold. And then just like that, he was lifting her, cradling her in his arms as he carried her across the room in three long strides toward the cot.

No!

Stop!

What was he thinking?

She thought the words, but she didn't speak them.

Her own lips were following his in a lethal, erotic dance of their own, unable to stop responding, tasting, licking. By all that was holy, he was like a drug she could not help but consume. He tasted like fire...and ice...and ecstasy.

She moaned as he laid her down beneath him on the cot, half in protest, and half in desperation. *Where was this going? What was he going to do to her?*

Oh, heavens...help her!

And then her soft, sheer blouse was simply gone. What had he done with it? Did he remove it—there had to be a dozen buttons—or did he rip it? She could hardly wrap her mind around the thought, when a more pressing matter stole her attention: the feel of rough yet passionate fingers finding their way beneath her silk camisole. "Oh, Saber, no!" she cried out as two large hands cupped the fullness of her breasts and began to knead with a mind-numbing skill that wasn't even possible for one such as he—what practice could he possibly have with seduction?

BLOOD REDEMPTION

The tips of his thumbs and forefingers found her nipples, even as that harshly beautiful mouth descended upon the same, each one seeking in turn, to nip, to lave, and to suckle.

"Saber!"

"What?" he growled low in his throat, coming up for air.

"Please…"

He flicked her left nipple with his tongue, teasing it harshly into a rigid state; and then he bit down, the softest of nips on the rose-colored tip, before taking the whole of the crown into his mouth.

She gasped.

He repeated the act on the right side, purring deep within his throat like the primal animal he was.

Tears began to fall from Vanya's eyes. She was so conflicted. So overwhelmed. So uncertain and afraid.

So lost in the dragon's fire.

"Shh, Printesa dulce. Taci. Da-ti drumul. Traieste cu mine." He spoke the words in the purist Romanian tongue she had ever heard, at least since she had awakened, and the beauty of his native accent, so graceful and alluring, sent chills along her skin, burrowing its way into her thundering heart: *Shh, sweet Princess. Be quiet. Let go. Live with me.* The phrase continued to echo in her mind.

"Mi-e foarte teama—*I am so afraid,*" she responded in kind.

He drew back on his arms then, capturing her gaze with a look of such intensity, such hunger, that it stole her breath. His powerful arms nearly glistened in the moonlight, the rippling muscles contracting like two hard globes as he arched above her. "Vanya," he practically purred the word, "I will not harm you this night."

This night?

What did he mean by that?

Before she could respond, he lowered his body to blanket hers; he cupped her jaw in his strong, unyielding hands; and he propped himself up on his elbow in order to kiss her once again, this time, with an urgency she could no longer resist. His passion was tender yet savage, reckless yet controlled. He simply consumed her, and she melted away, becoming one with his desire.

Vanya got lost in the sensations: Saber's moist, warm mouth; his fierce, erotic touch; the play of his fingers against her delicate skin; even the nip of his teeth along her throat, her shoulders, her breasts… Time and time again, he played her like a well-crafted instrument in need of fine-tuning, adjusting his pressure, choosing new erogenous zones, alternately demanding and coaxing submission, all the while building a slow, heated fire in her core.

When he began to grind his sinewy hips between her thighs, her eyes flew open and she studied his face—she was only a heartbeat away from leaping from the cot and bolting—that is, if she could break away from his impassive strength. His eyebrows were creased with tension from the strain of holding back his full ardor; and his jaw was taut with tension as he struggled to remain in control. Yet his harshly beautifully mouth was slack with pleasure, almost as if he couldn't believe the sensations himself. He reached down to loosen the tie on her skirt, and then he slowly rose to his knees in order to ease the garment from her hips.

She was trembling, and, when it was finally revealed, her concave stomach felt like a newly constructed drum: taut, trembling, and heretofore untouched.

Saber sighed, a cross between a long exhale and a deep moan. "Be at ease, sweet Princess, I will not hurt you." And then he removed her panties.

Vanya shivered as he covered her mound with the palm of his hand, meeting the chill and her fear with firm, intoxicating pressure. As he slowly, expertly, began to rotate his hand in dizzying circles, she jackknifed off the bed unexpectedly, her hips rising upward of their own accord. He stared at her brazenly then, his piercing eyes nearly gazing straight through her, as he watched, evaluated, and calculated his every move. As his hand continued to make magic between her thighs—testing, teasing, and finally probing—she held her breath, and he smiled, however faintly.

The dragon smiled.

A tear rolled down Vanya's cheek, and he reached out to swipe it away. And then, he placed it on his tongue and tasted it. The very act of relishing the droplet must have given him an idea because he, all at once, scooted lower on the bed; crouched down before the apex of her thighs; and dipped his head to savor her heat, licking slowly at first and then nuzzling her entirely, while pleasuring her peak with his tongue.

Despite her trepidation, she reacted with abandon.

She drew back her legs, bent each at the knee, and dropped the weight of one thigh against his thick mane of hair, unable to hold it steady for her trembling. He stroked her thigh with avid approval and delved deeper into her core, pushing her ever more closely toward impending release.

When, at last, Vanya felt as if she could take no more—her body was going to come apart and splinter into a thousand pieces—Saber withdrew his mouth from her heat; released his fangs with a slow, easy hiss; and deftly pierced her femoral artery, latching on to the flesh of her inner left thigh.

Vanya jackknifed off the cot.

She cried out from the unexpected pain, and then she simply fractured—completely—lost to the insanity of... *pleasure...* beyond her imagining.

As the orgasm deepened, grew in intensity with every drop the dragon took of her royal blood, Vanya whimpered from the sensations. She was just about to lose her mind, to try and force him to let go so she could stop writhing so erratically, when he released the bite, retracted his fangs, and quickly sealed the wound with his venom. Before she could catch her breath, he lowered his cargo pants from his narrow hips, rose gracefully above her, and nestled his impossibly thick manhood against the seat of her pleasure.

And then he plunged forward.

Without gentleness or restraint.

Tessa Dawn

Breaking through her maiden's barrier with shocking ferocity, while stretching her so impossibly she feared she might just split down the middle.

A sharp cry of agony escaped her lips, and she struggled to claw her way out from beneath him, to free herself from the sharp, scorching spear at her middle. *Dearest gods*, had he not known she was a virgin?

Saber looked all at once startled and confused—inexplicably horrified.

With his body still lodged deeply in hers, he locked their gazes and reached aggressively for her mind. Without hesitation, he burrowed deep inside her psyche and immediately blocked the pain—he simply stole it away as if it never existed, taking the sensations into his own body, instead.

Vanya breathed a sigh of relief; and then she watched in rapt fascination as the conflicting sensations of pain and pleasure— her experience and his, respectively—began to register on the vampire's face. His brow grew heavy with tension as he juggled the overwhelming ecstasy engulfing his manhood with the scorching pain searing her sex. He slowly pulled back. His angular jaw drew taut with indecision as he warred with his desire to force her open and her need to have him withdraw. He rocked instead of plunging. His chest began to quake as he resisted the masculine need for completion in favor of the feminine need for comfort. He slid in and out instead of stabbing.

Saber paused as Vanya stretched.

He felt his way to the right level of pressure until, at last, her body accepted his completely, and a new fire began to build. Then—and only then—he began to release his psychic hold. He transferred Vanya's sensations back into her body, waiting as patiently as he could while she took possession of her own sensations until, at last, she felt her own pleasure—and he could experience his.

The pace picked up, as did the desperation.

As Saber approached the point of no return, his strokes

177

became harsh and unrelenting. Vanya clung to his back, with her hands curled into fists, as she followed him helplessly over a second cliff, spiraling right along with the dragon into a second, even more powerful orgasm.

When at last her heart stopped racing, and his stopped pounding, she cupped his face in her hands, her fingers trembling around his angular jaw. He started to draw back out of impulse and surprise—the moment was obviously far too intimate—but he stopped himself just short of retreating. "Dragon," she whispered softly. "You did something…*kind*."

He shook his head in protest, clearly taken aback by her words, as well as the truth within them.

And this made her smile. "Do not worry," she reassured him. "You are still—"

"A monster," he grunted.

"Yes," she whispered.

"Always," he insisted. "Don't ever forget."

She started to smile, to make an offhanded comment; but he stared her down with a heated gaze, an implicit look of warning, and then he placed an extended finger over her mouth to silence her. "Don't *ever* forget," he repeated.

She nodded, feeling suddenly bereft; for he hadn't really changed. He had only gotten lost in a moment of passion and anguish. He had given in to the desperate need to escape his grief, if only for a moment, but he was still the same fire-breathing dragon. "I won't," she said forlornly.

She would not forget the life he had lived up until now, the brutality he had inflicted upon the house of Jadon, or what had brought him to these circumstances to begin with. And he was right to remind her.

Still, she had new memories to add to her cache now: She would not forget his intelligence or his consideration, either, the keen perception that led him to seduce her with such uncanny insight into her longings, nor his innate responsiveness to her needs. And she would not soon forget the surreal moment when Saber Alexiares, caught up in the throes of passion, realized that he had taken a virgin and chose, instinctively, to carry the full burden of her pain upon his own shoulders—to shield her from discomfort at his own expense.

No, she would not soon forget.

"Do not worry," she repeated. "I will remember *always*, Dragon."

sixteen

Vanya sat at the antique French dressing table in the upstairs guestroom at her sister's house, staring into the exquisitely framed mirror while trying to brush out her long, bountiful hair with a refurbished animal-horn brush she had managed to hold onto from the time before the Long Sleep. Crude as it might be, it was a keepsake that had belonged to her mother, and her mother before that. Using the simple, rudimentary tool always reminded her of her early childhood, before all the insanity, and calmed her nerves.

It had been nearly twelve hours since she had left Saber's cell, and she felt restless to say the least. Placing the palm of her hand flat against her stomach, she tried to quell her nerves. The last thing she needed was to alert Ciopori or her brother-in-law to the events that had transpired the night before. She could hardly believe what had occurred herself.

A soft knock rattled the heavy wooden door, and Vanya took a deep, steadying breath. "Yes?"

"It's me, Vanya. May I come in?" Ciopori's lyrical voice pierced the lingering solitude, and Vanya knew it was time to face the music: She could hardly put her sister off any longer.

"Of course, sister," Vanya replied, trying to speak in a pleasantly dispassionate voice.

Ciopori turned the knob. She pushed the door open and sidled through the narrow opening, her long black hair sashaying as she walked. Truly, she was a rare beauty. "Good evening," she called cheerfully.

Vanya smiled. "Good evening. And how is Marquis this night? Nikolai?"

Ciopori positively beamed at the mention of her favorite males. She rolled her lovely golden eyes and began to chitchat about the latest antics in the Silivasi house, hardly stopping to

181

take a breath, when, all at once, her face went slack, her hands flew up to her cheeks, and her expression turned grave with concern. "Dearest goddess Andromeda!" she exclaimed. She rushed across the room, removed the brush from Vanya's hand, and pulled her up from her seat, nearly causing her to stumble.

"Ciopori!" Vanya chastised, snatching her wrist back from her sister. "Whatever has gotten into you?" Surely, the female was not *that* perceptive. True, Ciopori was not only an original celestial-human being but also a vampire now, with all the powers and enhanced perception that entailed, but taking one look at her little sister and knowing she was no longer a virgin? Impossible.

Ciopori shook her head from side to side, slowly trailing her gaze up and down Vanya's slender body. As her examination grew more discerning, her eyes began to grow misty with pressing tears. "What…" Ciopori whispered, biting her lower lip. She took a deep breath as if she were trying not to hyperventilate. "When…" A tear escaped her eye, and she quickly brushed it away. "How did this happen?"

Vanya was more than a little concerned. She felt her knees weaken, and she wondered if her face wasn't growing pale. *Oh hell*, Ciopori knew. But how?

"It's not what you think," she said, rushing the words like an errant teenager who had just been caught by her mother. Of course, it was exactly what Ciopori was thinking, but surely, Vanya did not have to explain her actions to her older sister. "I can explain," Vanya said, ignoring her own indignation.

"Did he force you?" Ciopori asked. "When!" She turned toward the door in alarm. "Marquis!"

Vanya moved swiftly then. She snatched her sister by her elegant arm, tugged her forward, and thrust a curved hand over her mouth. "Be quiet! I mean it!" She gestured wildly with her hands. "Are you insane?" She eyed the door, listening for Marquis's heavy footsteps pounding down the hall, praying he wouldn't just materialize in the room. "Do you want to get me killed? Do you want to have all hell break loose in this valley?"

She took a calming breath and held her shoulders back, trying to maintain a semblance of dignity. "I mean it, Ciopori. I will not have it. You are my sister—not my mother—and you will not bring Marquis into this."

Just then, the door to the guestroom flew open, and Marquis Silivasi filled the door frame like a velociraptor hovering in an otherwise peaceful sky, his six-foot-two, massive physique consuming the space like a prehistoric menace about to descend on its prey. "What is it?" he demanded, his phantom blue-black eyes flashing an instant crimson-red before returning to their usual threatening hue. He was scenting the room, eyeing the contents, and feeling for errant energy all at the same time—all instinctive reactions for an Ancient Master Warrior in the house of Jadon, a lethal weapon trained to identify the enemy and strike without mercy, all in the space of a single heartbeat. He stepped toward Ciopori, and she quickly sidestepped in front of Vanya to block his line of sight.

"Uh, 'tis nothing, Warrior," Ciopori said with a sheepish smile. "I…overreacted."

"To what!" Marquis growled, the tone of his voice making it abundantly clear that he was not in the mood to play games.

"To…uh…" Ciopori swallowed so hard, her throat convulsed from the effort. "To Vanya mentioning that she would like to see Saber again."

Marquis's intense glare shot from Ciopori to the trembling princess hiding behind her; and Vanya could have sworn that he stared right through his mate to glare at her with x-ray vision. "Over my dead body," he growled.

Vanya struggled not to pass out.

Dear gods, if the Ancient Master Warrior knew what had transpired—

She quickly cut off the thought.

It wasn't even worth the risk of *thinking it* in his presence.

Luckily, Ciopori intervened on Vanya's behalf. "Those were my sentiments exactly." She stepped forward toward her mate, using more than a little feminine charm in the sway of her hips, and his appreciative eyes followed as intended. "But I do believe I've acted too hastily." She placed a soft hand on Marquis's iron-hard chest and pushed against him, failing to budge him an inch. "You should let me talk with my sister." She glanced over her shoulder, and her face grew ashen. "These are matters better discussed between women."

Marquis looked at Ciopori suspiciously, turning his nose up in disapproval. "I'll wait outside the door," he said in a stern *that's-my-final-offer* tone of voice.

Ciopori sighed. "Marquis, that isn't necessary."

He cut his eyes at her in disapproval, although the actual sentiment behind the glare was more of a mixture of undisguised love and concern. "My mate trusts me implicitly. She knows that I would move heaven and earth for her—or her younger sister— yet she stands in our home and lies to me as if I am too foolish to hear the rapid pace of her heart, too dense to note the downward cast of her eyes, or too oblivious to make note of the fact that she has used magic to distort the scents in this room. And Vanya, she hides behind you like a captive bird." He waved his hand in dismissal, letting them both know he wasn't interested in a false explanation. "No, Ciopori. I will wait outside the door for five minutes, while the two of you sort this…whatever it is…out. And then I will enter again like the esteemed male I assume I am to you; and I will expect to hear the truth." With that, he simply shimmered out of view, somehow slamming the door behind him.

Ciopori turned to Vanya and cringed. "Well then!"

Vanya winced. She hadn't meant to get her sister into so much trouble. "Is he going to behead you or something?" She was truly concerned.

Ciopori frowned. "No, he'll calm down. He's just…you know…Marquis. He doesn't get concerned; he gets tyrannical. And when he's tyrannical, he is not an easy vampire to deal with." She held up her hands in exasperation. "We will deal with that in a moment." At that, she reached for Vanya's right hand, held it up in the air in order to expose the trunk of her body, and stared pointedly at her stomach. "By all that is holy, sister"—her voice caught in a sob—"tell me what happened."

Vanya was beyond confounded. *For heaven's sake!* Yes, Saber was a monster, a Dark One as far as everyone in the house of Jadon was concerned, but Vanya was not a child. And this reaction was way over the top. How dare Ciopori stare at her womb, as if pointing out some violation. Not only did it lack respect, but it was completely absent of decency. "To begin with," Vanya said sharply, being careful to keep her voice to a whisper, "I think it bears pointing out that I don't owe you, Marquis, or anyone else an explanation. I am an adult. But for the record, yes—since it's so obvious—I spent the night with Saber." She spat the words out bluntly, knowing that they sounded unnecessarily harsh, but believing it was better to just get it out in the open.

Ciopori practically wilted, her elegant shoulders slouching in defeat. She forced herself to straighten, and she nodded. And then she held her tongue for what seemed like an impossible expanse of time. When at last she chose to speak, her voice was flat and to the point: "Then your conversion? It was...quick...and relatively painless?" She sounded absolutely astonished. "You are yet Vampyr then?" She turned her head to the side, evaluating Vanya from head to toe as if staring at a whole new person for the first time, a changed species.

"Excuse me?" Vanya said, surprised. "Well, no wonder you're so upset. There was no conversion. No commitment."

Ciopori staggered back. She clamped her hands over her heart spontaneously, and her chest visibly shook. "What?"

Vanya frowned. "I...I...spent the night with Saber. I did not agree to be his *destiny* in every way, to fulfill the Curse with him, or to spend the rest of my life with him." She sighed, wishing she could explain it better, even to herself. "I can understand if you're disappointed."

Ciopori let out a short, anguished cry, unable to conceal her mounting emotion. "Disappointed?" she echoed. "*Disappointed?* Oh...gods." She staggered where she stood before slowly reclaiming her balance. "Oh, gods! *No!*"

Vanya felt the very real edge of panic creeping up on her. "I'm fine," she insisted.

Ciopori could barely draw breath. "You are not fine, sister. You are with child!" She clasped a hand over her mouth and pointed at Vanya's stomach.

Vanya looked down.

The words seemed to float around her more than reach her ears, her consciousness, and she had to struggle to comprehend what Ciopori was saying. "What do you mean?" She watched as her stomach gently rolled beneath her skirt, taking note of the protruding midsection where a flat, well-toned stomach had been only hours before; and then she thought about the nausea and lightheadedness she had been experiencing all day. She had thought it was just her nerves, the ever-increasing realization of the events that had taken place the night before. "No," she whispered, "that's not...possible."

Ciopori reached out an arm to steady herself against a nearby bedpost, and then she slowly lowered herself to the mattress in shock. She was virtually speechless.

"Ciopori?" Vanya said, growing increasingly defensive. This wasn't funny at all. "Ciopori!"

Ciopori shook her head slowly from side to side, and then the tears began to stream down her cheeks in uncontrollable tracks of grief.

Vanya took three unwitting steps back, as if she could simply walk away from the truth. "No," she muttered. "That's not possible."

A dim flash of hope crossed Ciopori's eyes. "Then you didn't actually...lie with him?"

Vanya frowned. She was so confused. What was happening? "No...I mean, yes; but he would have had to call it into being, *command* a pregnancy. I never heard him do that."

Ciopori collapsed on the duvet. "He doesn't have to do it out loud. He only needs to wish it, think it...*want* it."

Vanya grew deathly quiet, even as her body stood stock-still.

She didn't move. She didn't breathe. She didn't even feel.

She couldn't.

The moment—the meaning behind her sister's words—was beyond her reckoning.

Saber Alexiares had commanded a pregnancy without converting her first. He had made her with child while she was yet *human*, and that meant only one thing: forty-eight hours from the time of her conception, Vanya Demir would die an absolutely excruciating death as the dragon's unborn sons clawed their way out of her body, taking her mortal life with them as they were born.

Vanya could hardly meet her sister's eyes. *By all the gods, she had been so stupid!*

So naive.

What had she been thinking?

Saber was a monster, a demon from the Valley of Death and Shadows itself, as far as she was concerned, and he had acted true to his nature all along. *May his blackened soul be damned*, he had warned her, hadn't he?

Yet, she hadn't listened.

She had been determined to save the dragon from her dream—to bring something of great consequence and value back to the people—and just like her dream, the dragon had scorched her without mercy.

Vanya slowly made her way to the bed, her trembling arms and legs shuffling absently along the floor as if a puppeteer were working them. Staring blankly ahead, she gently sat down beside her sister on the wrinkled duvet and curled up beside her. She wrapped her arms around Ciopori's trembling shoulders, all the while fighting to hide her own terrible fear, to conceal her mental anguish. There was nothing she could do now. The die had been cast.

The king, and certainly Kagen, would see to it that she didn't suffer unnecessarily, even if they had to euthanize her before that fatal moment. As it was, she had never belonged in this world—this time—or this valley. There was simply no place for one such as her, and now her fate had been decided for her.

She pushed the morbid thoughts away.

They didn't serve her now.

And time was far too precious.

Every moment counted—now, more than ever.

If the gods were merciful—and she hoped that they were—she could comfort Ciopori in her final hours, spend her last moments with Nikolai, and send her dark, dangerous brother-in-law to the cell where they were keeping Saber Alexiares with one final request: *Remove the dragon's head with your bare hands and deliver it to me on a silver platter.*

The biblical character Salome had nothing on Vanya Demir. After all, hell hath no fury like a woman scorned, and in this tragic, barren moment, Vanya knew that she had been scorned beyond imagining.

Saber Alexiares's head, in Marquis's hands, was her last, dying wish.

Saber shot up from his cot into a sitting position, both startled and alert, as Marquis Silivasi stormed into the dimly lit watch room like a Tasmanian devil. The Ancient Master Warrior was wearing a garish, spiked cestus over his right hand, and by the look on his murderous face, he was more than just a little angry.

He was downright furious.

Determined.

Hell-bent.

What in the world?

When Marquis bulldozed past Ramsey and Santos, headed straight for the iron keys to unlock Saber's cell, and neither one of the guards made any attempt to stop him, Saber knew it was time to pay the piper. Marquis's jaw was set in a hard line; his eyes were feral and ablaze; and Ramsey and Santos were only too

willing to stand back and allow the scene to unfold.
Clearly, the males had found out about Vanya.
They knew about the *sex*.
But how?

Saber leapt to his feet and readied himself in a defensive posture, watching warily as the enraged vampire made child's play of the lock, flung open the door, and literally flew into the cell, apparently too angry to walk. "Before I am through with you, Dark One, you will beg me for death!" The vampire's voice reverberated through the tiny space like thunder in a roiling sky, and Saber visibly recoiled.

He shook his bewildered head, trying to dislodge his momentary confusion: *Unholy minions of hell*, he and Vanya had bent a few rules, played fast and furious with their passion, but surely it wasn't *that* serious. She was his *destiny*, after all.

Before Saber could respond to Marquis's threat, the incensed warrior hurled a pulsing stream of fire from the tips of his fingers directly at Saber's scalp, connecting instantly with his wild black-and-red mane. The flame burned so hot that it shone blue in the air before wrapping itself in a conical halo around Saber's skull, and Saber cried out in agony from the searing heat.

"What's your problem!" Saber glowered, panic beginning to set in. He was far too weak from blood loss to defend himself.

Marquis gave him no quarter.

The son of Jadon quickly followed the preternatural flames with an equally dangerous assault: Conjuring two razor-sharp pinpoints of light from his hate-filled eyes, he leveled his gaze at Saber and began to wield the grisly lasers like a macabre scalpel, slicing wickedly across Saber's forehead, just below the hairline, just below the already emblazoned crown. Resolute, he began to carve a gruesome incision around the cranium, outward beyond the brows, downward toward the ears, and angled to the nape of Saber's neck. *Dark lords of hell*, the male brandished the fiery scalpel with the precision of a master surgeon.

He was scalping Saber alive from five feet away!

Saber tried to step out of the line of fire. His hands shot up instinctively to his head and were instantly singed by the blaze. He tried to smother the flames to no avail—*just how far did the warrior intend to take this?*

The question was quickly answered.

As blood seeped beneath the fresh conical incision, Marquis stopped just short of removing Saber's scalp. Rather, he allowed the crimson fluid to pool into a bubbling crown, where it oozed until it began to act like a buffer between the fire and Saber's face, shielding his skin, his brows, and his eyes: Marquis was using Saber's own blood as a natural fire-line. He was preventing the fire from spreading in order to keep it burning longer...hotter...deeper.

Saber tried desperately to extinguish the flames, to gather his wits, but the fire burned way too hot and the assault was far too relentless.

Marquis whispered something beneath his breath, and the flames grew hotter still, shooting even higher in the air. Saber moaned from the pain and felt his reason slipping away into an ever-increasing abyss of horrible agony and shock. His head was burning like the devil, yet the fire wasn't consuming his flesh. He should have been burnt to a crisp by now. At this rate, the damnable thing might just burn forever, until his scalp was nothing more than a bloody heap of blisters, resting beneath charred hair and melted flesh. *Why didn't the warrior just kill him and get it over with?* Did he really intend to scorch him, *indefinitely*, just for the fun of it?

Just for having sex with Vanya?

Did the vampire intend to torture him forever, or would he finally be moved to mercy—or fury—and just kill him already?

Saber panted through the unbearable pain, and then he cringed in horror as realization finally dawned on him: What was it Marquis had said when he had first entered the room? *Before I am through with you, Dark One, you will beg me for death!*

The hot-headed vampire had meant every word.

He wanted Saber to fall on his knees and plead for mercy—mercy the warrior would surely deny him. The son of Jadon was hell-bent on exacting his pound of flesh, and up until this point, Saber had been helpless to deny him his professed due.

Saber Alexiares blinked rapidly, several times in a row, trying to clear his tortured mind, trying to flush the dripping blood from his eyes so he could see his enemy more clearly. He raised both hands to his mouth and blew freezing shards of air over his fingertips until icicles began to form on the ends of the digits; then he massaged his hands rapidly through his hair, hoping like hell that the fire would melt the ice into water instantly. He repeated the process again and again, all the while thinking, *This is like applying some damnable netherworld shampoo*, until at last, the fiery blaze was extinguished.

Marquis laughed, indifferent. "Not going to save you, Dark One."

Knowing the warrior was right, Saber decided to try a different tact. The truth of the matter was this: Marquis was much too strong, and Saber was much too weak. The sentinels had kept him so pitifully drained of blood—deprived of power for so interminably long—that he barely stood a chance in this unprovoked battle. Still, he braced himself against the lingering heat in his scalp, the all-consuming pain, and focused keenly on his enemy. Saber Alexiares had no intention of going down without a fight, regardless of the odds. It was time to change his posture from defensive to offensive.

Without warning, Saber lunged at Marquis for all he was worth; he focused like a laser on the Ancient Master Warrior's neck, his thick jugular vein, and the amount of force it would require to rip it open and tear it to shreds. Their bodies collided with a heavy thud, sending both males flying into the iron bars behind them before they ricocheted off and hit the floor, each laid out prone. Saber sank his fangs deep, grasping, tearing, and shaking his head from side to side like the wild animal he was. It was a desperate attempt at changing the odds, but Marquis kept his cool...and his concentration.

The warrior countered with a brutal uppercut, ramming the full potency of the spiked cestus beneath Saber's jaw; and the maneuver worked beautifully, swiftly dislodging Saber's fangs.

Saber came at him again...and again.

He released his own lethal claws and swiped at the Ancient's eyes rapidly—forcefully—until a tip finally connected, scoring Marquis's cornea. Marquis stiffened ever so slightly and growled deep in his throat, and then he released his own claws and plunged downward with his left hand, tearing what felt like an eight-inch gash in Saber's side.

The two ferocious males traded attacks, punching, stabbing, biting, all the while rolling around on the floor like a furious ball of hate-filled energy; until at last, Saber felt his life force begin to wane at an alarming rate.

He looked down in shock, trying to focus his blurry vision on his body.

He wasn't entirely sure what he was seeing, but his entire lower torso was a bloody pulp, and his insides were slithering onto the ground, escaping from a gaping hole, oozing languidly along the front of his body like lava along the side of a volcano. Stunned, and more than a little confused by the extent of the damage, Saber absently tried to scoop his intestines into his hands and pack them back inside the ruptured cavity, all the while releasing as much venom as he could from his incisors to dress the wound. He had to try and seal his innards back together. And quickly, at that.

He had never felt more helpless, cornered, or *enraged* in his entire life.

Saber Alexiares was a soldier, and a damn good one for that matter. But this fight was completely imbalanced. Untenable. As a starved, wounded prisoner, encased in diamond day after day, night after night, Saber might as well have had both hands tied behind his back, a blindfold placed over his eyes, and diamond shackles manacled to his ankles. Blood was *everything* to a vampire. And he simply didn't have any in reserve. If he hadn't consumed at least a pint or so of Vanya's blood the night before, he would have already been dead.

"You want your revenge?" he snarled at Marquis, hoping to

provoke the warrior's pride. "Then take it fairly." He glared at the son of Jadon in challenge, one combatant male to another. "Let me feed until I'm at full strength, then fight me as an equal. Win or lose based on superior ability—not obscene advantage."

"I'd love to," Marquis growled, still sounding far too confident. "But, unfortunately, time is of the essence. And since all I desire is your suffering and your death, I couldn't give a celestial-damn how easy the pickings are."

Saber realized then that he was about to die.

For real this time.

No games, no taunting, no more reprieves.

Marquis Silivasi had come to deliver him to the Valley of Death and Shadows, and it was only a matter of seconds, maybe minutes, before he succeeded. Saber released his gut, hoping the venom had already begun to work, and threw a lightning-quick punch at Marquis's jaw, connecting with an audible crack. The warrior's head snapped back, and Saber followed the attack with a brutal series of strikes to Marquis's eyes, hoping to blind him once and for all.

Marquis leapt to his feet in an effortless motion and took a leisurely step back. He spit out a mouthful of blood and smiled. *Smiled.*

And then he slowly raised his right fist, the one containing the ancient battle-worn cestus, and peeled it off his hand, cracking his knuckles in anticipation. "You want to do this old school?" he drawled. And then he bowed in a satirical, old-world gesture and snarled like a primordial beast. "By all means, let's dance, devil."

He grasped Saber by the collar of his shirt and yanked him up from the ground. And then he unleashed a furious barrage of punches, jabs, and uppercuts on the weakened prisoner, trading targets at will between Saber's torso, face, and head. Saber felt like he was being lashed by a violent storm: a mad, turbulent, and unrelenting cyclone. There was no mercy. There was no momentary reprieve. There was only Marquis Silivasi and his never-ending fury descending upon Saber with practiced precision and ease. Certain that several of his ribs were broken along with his jaw—at least one lung had collapsed as well— Saber doubled over and, at last, held his hands up in a gesture of surrender.

He wasn't hoping for mercy.

He knew there would be none forthcoming.

Just the same, if he couldn't best his enemy with brawn, then he had better find a way to employ his brains. To use words, if possible.

"Why are you doing this?" he asked through gritted teeth, knowing the question sounded as absurd to Marquis as it did to him. Obviously, there was an endless array of reasons. But what he really meant to ask was...*why now?* "I mean, other than the usual reasons," he added, his tone as flippant as possible considering the overwhelming pain he was in.

Marquis just stared at him with contempt and slowly shook his head. "You are a lot of things, son of Jaegar, but stupid? Not hardly."

Saber was just about to reply when he suddenly felt his legs grow weak beneath him. His kneecaps seemed to rotate, then buckle; and just like that, he sank to the floor, kneeling unintentionally before his enemy and struggling not to topple over completely.

Marquis placed a heavy boot against Saber's chest and shoved him onto his back. He bent over and tugged at his legs, stretching them into their natural prone position, before straddling Saber's broken body, descending to one knee on either side of his soon-to-be corpse, and glaring down at him with lethal intent. Baring a jagged claw, he used the talon to slice through Saber's shirt, ripping it from neckline to hem, exposing the soldier's chest; and then he licked his savage lips. "Know this, *brother*..." He spat the last word with utter contempt. "I will feast on your heart after you are dead and deliver your severed head to Vanya on a silver platter. And you will have all of eternity in hell to contemplate *why*."

Saber felt nothing.

He did...*nothing*.

Marquis Silivasi was a force to be reckoned with, an immovable mountain of strength and resolve. There were no words in the English language, or Romanian, for that matter, that would save Saber from his impending fate; and he would rather just die like a man.

"Then do it," Saber grit out defiantly, locking his gaze with his executioner's.

Marquis winked at him in assent, drew back his powerful arm, and prepared to strike the heart—hopefully, swiftly enough to remove it in one fell swoop.

Saber held his breath.

He refused to shut his eyes or look away.

He would die as he had lived, boldly and without apology.

And then, like a candle flickering in a darkened room, the background of the cell lit up, casting radiant light on the otherwise grisly scene: Flaxen hair; smooth, delicate skin; and vivid rose-colored eyes filled the frame with light, softening even the brutality of murder.

Vanya had entered the cell, and she strode proudly forward until she was standing next to Marquis's kneeling body. Placing a gentle hand on the Ancient Master Warrior's shoulder, she whispered a single command: "*Wait.*"

Her voice was as calm as it was solemn, and the vampire immediately obeyed, even though his bicep twitched from the effort to withhold the final death blow.

Vanya placed her free hand on her belly, pressed against it in a low, firm gesture, almost as if to maintain her balance, and then she bent over to meet Saber's eyes. Her own eyes were glistening with tears. "Before you die," she said, without faltering, "I just want to know one thing."

Saber blinked several times, trying to bring Vanya's regal features into focus. He held her penetrating gaze, fully prepared to answer her question honestly—why the hell not? Clearly, his goose was already cooked.

"Why?" she asked.

BLOOD REDEMPTION

Saber frowned, steeling himself against the pain that racked his body. "Why, what?"

Vanya laughed then, although the sound was hollow and devoid of humor. She rubbed her hand over her belly, indicating the protruding mound beneath her silken blouse. "The pregnancy—*why*? Why would you do such a thing?"

Saber stared for a moment in utter astonishment.

To say he was bewildered would have been an understatement. Indeed, the princess was unmistakably pregnant; and that meant she was carrying his twin sons. He didn't remember commanding it, exactly, although he knew he must have; otherwise, the conception could not have occurred. Still, there was no clear line of delineation in his mind. "I...I don't..." His words trailed off as he searched for an answer.

Saber recalled the aftermath of his passion with the princess vividly. He had been a cauldron of grief, anguish, and desperation when he mated with her, and the entire act, the way he had sought her *ice* and she, his *fire*, was as foreign and surprising to him as it had been to her. He remembered lying beside the princess after they had finished...doing what they had done...feeling lost and out of place. Confused, and even a little bit resentful.

Like what the hell had just happened—and what in the name of the dark lords was he supposed to do next?

Males in the house of Jaegar did not lie in repose with human females, not even half-celestial ones. They did not engage in foreplay or after play, and they didn't make idle conversation or show affection...whatever that was. To say Saber had felt like a fish out of water would've been an understatement. *Fire and ice.* He and Vanya had made a fair trade, and that was that.

Still, one thing had stood out in his mind; it had been too stark not to. For the first time since Damien and Dane had been executed, Saber had not been in pain. It was hard to explain, but it had felt like he had crawled into the eye of a storm and found some sort of—what? *Peace?* He didn't know what to call it. He only knew that one moment, he was floundering in turbulence, lost to darkness and grief, and the next, he was hovering in a space of stillness, almost clarity. And while the storm continued to rage all around him—hell, it continued to rage inside of him—he was apart from the turmoil. Cocooned in the eye of the storm.

Struggling to speak with a broken jaw, Saber tried to put words to what had happened next: "I guess...on some unconscious level, I knew...you were my *destiny*." He groaned from the effort.

Vanya sighed in exasperation, showing her first true hint of emotion. "And that gave you the right to impregnate me without my consent?"

Saber didn't know how to answer that. What did she mean?

The Curse gave all males the right—hell, the ability—to impregnate women without their consent. It was a built-in survival mechanism, and he certainly couldn't justify or condemn such an ancient, incredulous fact; nor was he going to try. Besides, that wasn't exactly what had happened. He hadn't consciously chosen it, done it with any real deliberation. He had just thought it, *remembered it*, and knew it to be what came next.

She was his *destiny*.

They were bound by the Serpens Blood Moon.

And now she would carry his sons and save him from the ultimate vengeance of the Curse.

The pregnancy had come as much from his DNA as his mind. It had been an *instinct*—not a plot—an ingrained impulse that had a life of its own: Somehow, somewhere, in a place he didn't even know how to reach, let alone name, he had acted to sustain his existence, to seal the cocoon and remain pain-free for just a little while longer. Saber had sought to remain in the eye of the storm for as long as possible, the only way he knew how; and in truth, he was absolutely stunned to see Vanya standing before him now, growing heavy with child. All of this...it was so new to him. He hardly understood it himself.

"I don't know," he finally answered honestly. "I just...did it...somehow." It was a weak explanation, but it was the only one he had.

Vanya exhaled so sharply that the air in her lungs rushed out in a whistle. "You just...*did it*?" she repeated.

Saber stared at her blankly. What point was there in hashing this out? As far as she was concerned—as far as any of them were concerned—he was beyond logical thinking or basic moral reasoning; and perhaps it was true. Even as they sought to convince him that he was born into the house of Jadon, as opposed to the house of Jaegar, Saber was not expected to have the thoughts, instincts, or desires of any other male: He wasn't supposed to claim his *destiny*, to desire her conception, to react with the same primordial nature as any other vampire.

He was simply supposed to wait to die at the end of the Blood Moon, as if his eight hundred years on earth were *nothing*.

Less than nothing.

So be it.

"I wanted to live," he said defensively. "And that is all." When her expression flashed from confusion to disgust, he knew whatever momentary connection they may have shared in that rare interlude of passion, however misguided or ill-conceived, was indelibly gone. As dead as his father and his brother. He had been a fool to think that something tangible, albeit impossible to name or pin down, may have passed between them in the desperation of night; and she had been a fool to enter the lair of her enemy, to ever trust a son of Jaegar.

Fire and ice: an inevitable conclusion.

And now they would both pay for their stupidity.

Vanya seemed utterly appalled by his words, indeed, wholly repulsed by his existence. She visibly cringed, curled both dainty hands into unconscious fists, and slowly nodded her head in antipathy. "Foolish male," she whispered, almost robotically. "You foolish, *foolish* male."

Saber didn't respond. He just lay there silently, awaiting her condemnation, or perhaps his death, whichever came first.

She ground her teeth together and locked her jaw. "Then it was *survival*?"

Saber tried to shrug, but his shoulders hurt too badly. Not to mention, Marquis was pinning his arms to the ground. *What did she expect him to say?* "Yes."

"And everything we shared—all that passed between us—that, too, was survival? Never affection?" Her voice grew soft with resignation. "Never...*love?*" She sounded so weak and pitiable, so unlike the spitfire female he had come to know over their few, brief encounters—not at all like herself—and the question, frankly, stunned him.

Love?

What the hell did Saber Alexiares know of love?

He studied her eyes, wishing he could grasp what was happening, what she was getting at, if only to prolong his survival. He was moments away from his mortal end, consumed in unspeakable physical pain, which he was trying desperately to conceal, and at a complete loss for words...

About a subject he could barely comprehend.

"What the hell are you asking me, Princess?" His eyes bored into hers as if there were no one else in the room. "What do you want me to say?"

Vanya finally lost her composure. Her angst turned to tears, and her searching gave way to defeat. "Nothing," she uttered desolately. "*Nothing.* I just...I just want you to understand that I am yet human."

Saber was positively dumbfounded. "So?"

Now this sparked her anger. "So perhaps in the house of Jaegar, the males rape women at random, force their seed into their bellies, then wait with glee while the wretched victims die, but that is not how it is done in the house of Jadon!"

Saber visibly recoiled at the word *rape*, and Marquis bristled from his head to his toes. "You raped her?" the angry warrior snarled.

Saber kept his attention focused on Vanya. *What are you saying, Princess?* He spoke telepathically.

Marquis reacted instinctively, grasping Saber by the throat and tightening his fist like an iron vise. His fingers trembled with rage, and Ramsey and Santos took several steps forward toward the bars. The sentinels had been watching the whole scene play out from the moment Marquis had entered Saber's cell, but they had been unable, or unwilling, to interfere.

Until now.

Perhaps they now wanted to kill him themselves.

"Release his throat, Marquis," Vanya said, her tone brooking no argument. "He will die soon enough." She raised her chin in an unusual show of defiance, as well as a halfhearted attempt at dignity, and then she regarded all the males in the room as one. "The monster did not rape me. I was a willing...fool." She shuffled closer to Saber and bent over to meet his eyes in an unbroken stare. "In thirty-four hours, I will die a horrible death." She made a tent with her fingers around her stomach, as if framing the pregnancy for effect. "These children—your offspring—would not have ensured your survival. As it stands, they will claw their way out of my body, break my spine, rip out my intestines, and kill me as they emerge into the world. Only a vampire can bear the children of a vampire, Saber! *I am yet human.*"

Despite Marquis's continued pressure on his larynx, Saber gasped audibly, causing his collapsed lung to spasm with unearthly pain. He smacked Marquis's arm away from his neck in a reflex and almost sat up straight, until the pain brought him up short. That, and the 200-pound warrior sitting on his broken ribs. Still, he was too stunned by Vanya's words to register anything other than what she had just said.

The pregnancy was going to kill her.

And soon.

He was too flabbergasted to reply.

While it was true, the children of Dark Ones, those conceived in brutality with males from the house of Jaegar, tormented and destroyed their hosts upon emergence into this world, nothing could have been further from the truth when it came to the children in the house of Jadon. The children of the light Vampyr were conceived beneath the providence of a Blood

Moon, protected by the *four mercies* bestowed on Prince Jadon—at least the one born of light was protected.

At any rate, it wasn't supposed to be this way!

Saber might hate what had befallen him. Hell, he would likely resent it until time was no more, but he had come to believe it—*he was the birth-child of Rafael and Lorna Dzuna*—how could *his* offspring destroy their mother?

His mind was spinning—whether from loss of blood, delusion brought on by pain, or the sudden, inexplicable turn of events, he wasn't certain. All that he knew was this was wrong.

Completely.

Wrong!

By all that was dark and unholy, he had not acted in a way to destroy the princess.

Yes, he was a dark soul. Perhaps he was even a scourge in the otherwise noble house of Jadon, an imposter in a world that revolved around justice and honor, but to do this? To murder Vanya so heinously? Such a thing went even beyond his purview.

Vanya Demir was the only being in this gods-forsaken valley that he didn't detest all the way down to his blackened soul. She was the only person he would actually hesitate to kill.

"I...I don't understand." He struggled to speak beneath a growing influx of fluid pooling in his lungs.

Vanya glowered at him. "Do not act as if you did not know: Conversion must always come first!"

The words rang out in Saber's mind like a tiny metal ball in a pinball machine, the carbon-steel pinging around from side to side, bouncing from chamber to chamber, as he fought to process what Vanya had just said. His gut clenched beneath the weight of her words, as well as Marquis on his broken ribs, and he felt at once like he might just heave. He had no idea where the sensations were coming from, but the world seemed to simply drop out from beneath him.

He struggled once again to sit up, only to meet Marquis's impassive resistance, slamming him back to the ground. As what little air he had rushed out of him in a whoosh, he reached for

Vanya's mind. *Then I will still convert you.* He said it telepathically.

Directly.

Sincerely.

"It is too late," Vanya whispered.

Saber's eyes shot wildly around the room. Ramsey and Santos were now standing inside the entrance of the cell, their collective expressions displaying a harsh mixture of mortification, rage, and unfathomable sorrow. He turned to Marquis, uncaring that the male was his enemy. "Warrior, is this true?"

Marquis shifted his weight more fully onto his knees and leaned forward over Saber's body. "As true and as certain as your death," he replied. With that, he drew back his powerful arm, plunged forward with all of his might, and burrowed deep into the chest cavity, where he grasped the Dark One's heart.

seventeen

"Easy now, Warrior."

Napolean Mondragon's powerful voice reverberated in the cell, even as his noble hand tightened deftly around Marquis's fist, which was still lodged in Saber's chest. The wise king bore down with a gentle but exacting pressure, holding both Marquis's hand and the fragile organ tenuously in place. "Let's not act too hastily," he crooned, as if to a small child.

The king had appeared out of thin air, and Marquis looked up at him in astonishment, even as Saber fought not to writhe in torment, lest he dislodge his own beating heart.

While Saber panted in agony, the Ancient One calmly turned his head to regard the sentinels. "Ramsey." He spoke quietly, deliberately, as if he weren't actually holding the lives of several people in his hands, literally balancing life and death in his cautious, all-powerful fingers. "Get Vanya out of here. Take her to Kagen's clinic, *now.*" He gestured toward a pair of diamond-encrusted shackles hanging on the guard-room wall, and inclined his head toward Santos. "Warrior, bring those for the prisoner....then depart."

The sentinels obeyed immediately. Ramsey stepped to Vanya, wrapped one powerful arm around her back, the other beneath her legs, and lifted her effortlessly to his chest, strolling out of the cell as if she weighed no more than a feather, even in her condition. Santos followed suit: He quickly removed the manacles from their peg and laid them noiselessly on the ground beside the king. And then, with a graceful nod of his head, he simply dematerialized.

Napolean locked gazes with Marquis next. He transferred a visible light from his own silver-lined pupils into the Ancient Master Warrior's blue-black orbs, and spoke in a dark, velvety voice, deeply laced with coercion: "Marquis...*release his heart.*

Slowly." His eyes never left the warrior's.

Marquis's fist opened of its own accord, and the huge warrior rose from the ground and floated backward through the air like a ghostly apparition, transplanted several feet away. The king had taken absolute control of Marquis's body with his mind. He had broken his hold, levitated the giant vampire backward, and removed him from the volatile situation as if the ferocious warrior were nothing more than an afterthought. By the look on Marquis's face, the ancient son of Jadon was as surprised by the sudden turn of events as Saber.

"Leave us now," Napolean said to Marquis. His tone was no-nonsense. Softening it a bit, he added, "Go take a walk. Clear your head. *Feed*."

Marquis grunted his disapproval, perhaps disorientation, and then he slowly shook out the cobwebs and strolled out the guard-room door.

Saber groaned. Not only was he in insufferable pain, but he was now alone with the most formidable being on the planet. His eyes moistened with pain-filled tears as he fought for breath that just wouldn't come. He half wondered if he wasn't already dead, half wished that he was, just to escape the agony.

It was unbearable.

Beyond anything he had ever endured before.

"Shh…breathe," Napolean whispered, turning his full attention on Saber. He blew a soft, breath toward Saber's scalp, effortless and calm, and the pain from the burns cooled instantly.

At least it was something.

Raising his free hand to his mouth, Napolean extracted several drops of venom onto the pad of his forefinger, drew a line along the deep circular incision beneath Saber's hairline, and watched as the wound closed up as if it had never been. He repeated the process, healing the wicked gash in Saber's side. He then stared fixedly at Saber's open chest cavity and ever so slowly, carefully, began to massage the serrated organ back into place. He raised his free hand to his mouth once more and fully released his incisors in order to discharge more venom.

A lot more venom.

He gathered the healing fluid in his palm, lavishly coated each of his fingers with the viscous substance, and then he bent forward to insert a second hand into the gaping wound, where he continued to knead the heart.

Saber jackknifed off the ground.

His back contorted in a terrible arc of pain, and he began to curse uncontrollably in Romanian—perhaps interspersing a bit of Farsi and Japanese, who knew—while sucking in air like a vacuum. His collapsed lung began to slowly inflate, even as his heart knit back together, and the air gradually returned to his body.

"You think this is pain?" Napolean whispered hauntingly. "This is nothing." He shifted his gaze from Saber's chest to his face, and continued speaking coolly: "If Vanya dies, I will play in your heart for hours, shredding it, then healing it, slashing your aorta to pieces only to repair it, until I finally tire of the game—which I suspect could take weeks, perhaps months." His resolve was as savage as his tone, despite the calm, cool expression on his face.

Saber swallowed his fear. He had no doubt that the ancient king meant every word he had spoken. He breathed a sigh of relief as the pain began to ebb; and then he locked his gaze with the king's as cautiously as he could. "Let me try and convert her," he said, knowing it was a long shot. Feeling as if he owed himself, if not the Ancient One before him, at least some explanation, he added, "I didn't know." He repeated the words with surprising sincerity. "I swear, *I didn't know.*"

Napolean eyed him sideways. "What didn't you know, Saber? That you were impregnating her, or that she had to be converted first?"

Saber glanced away—but only momentarily. Now was not the time to lie to this king, and he was trying to gather his thoughts. "Either...both."

Napolean's eyes flashed crimson, and a low, almost

indiscernible growl rumbled in his throat. "Explain yourself, son. *Now*."

Saber recoiled at the command. He resented this male almost as much as Salvatore, but now was not the time…

He inhaled deeply and tried to answer the question in as civil a tone as possible. "I don't deny that I knew…something…that I was aware she was my *destiny*, and that the whole purpose behind the Blood Moon was to fulfill the demands of the Curse. But it was more like I felt it, remembered it. I didn't consciously will it. At least I don't think I did. I just wanted to…exist…without pain; and somehow, that must have transferred into intention."

Napolean took Saber's full measure, those severe, mystical eyes boring so deep into his that it felt like the Ancient One was probing his mind. But he wasn't. He didn't have to. He simply assessed him carefully and nodded calmly. "Go on."

Saber took another deep breath, knowing that his next words would seal his fate. "As far as conversion, the fact that she isn't Vampyr…" His voice trailed off, and he sighed. "You have to understand, as a soldier born into the house of Jaegar"—he caught the slip and sought to rectify it—"*brought* into the house of Jaegar"—*damn, the admission was killing him!*— "we never talked about the Blood Moon, not in that way. How could I have known? I mean, who was there to teach me…about the Curse…the way it worked in the house of Jadon? Damien? *Salvatore?* There were no circumstances under which I would have ever considered the thirty days following a Blood Moon or what it really entailed. In truth, it never occurred to me that she had to be converted first." He held his tongue then, letting his words linger, knowing that the king had never heard him speak a sincere, uncorrupted word since that fateful day in the valley when his body didn't burn. Truth be told, the Ancient One probably didn't even realize a Dark One was capable of candor…that *Saber* was capable of honesty.

He was.

He just didn't choose it that often: Outside of his

interactions with Damien, Diablo, and Dane, it wasn't usually the best tactic.

But this was different.

This was about earning the opportunity to try and save Vanya, to try and save his unborn son. While wanting to save the latter was an obvious motivation—his son would be his own flesh and blood, independent of what house he was born into—the desire to save Vanya was more of a mystery to him: He hadn't been raised to care about females or citizens outside of the house of Jaegar. And maybe *care* was too alien of a word. Too strong? *Too different.* But just the same, he desperately wanted to try.

There was something so inherently wrong with what had happened: He and Vanya had made a trade, an even exchange.

She had come to him without an agenda, save only to try and lessen his pain, however ill-conceived her compassion might have been. And he had taken her up on the bargain. Hell, he had taken her virginity and allowed her body to give him momentary sanctuary...however it had occurred. And that meant something to Saber. His word—dark as it may be—was still *his* word. Could he kill an innocent as prey? Yes, without hesitation. Could he plot and scheme and callously use his enemy to achieve his own ends? Been there; done that; tossed the tee-shirt. But could he lure Vanya to his bed in a moment of raw, uninhibited need; convince her to step outside the boundaries of both their worlds; and then murder her for consenting so loyally?

Not in this life or the next.

He may not have a soul, but such a thing went against the very fiber of his being. Whatever that was.

Napolean shook his head slowly, bringing Saber back into the present moment. He seemed to consider his next words carefully, before clearing his throat. "And it also never occurred to you that Vanya was a cherished female, *an original princess*, when you stole her innocence and took her body so selfishly...in this filthy cell, I might add." It was more of a statement than a question.

BLOOD REDEMPTION

Saber was not about to respond rashly. He had to control his anger, keep a handle on his defiance. After all, he had his own agenda. Still, who the hell were these males to constantly demean his motivations, to treat him like he wasn't a grown-ass male, capable of handling his own *destiny*? Respect, he didn't expect. But recognition? He felt it was his due. Dark Ones may have been soulless, a separate species in their own right, but they were still soldiers, males—*vampires*—and they had come from the same legacy of celestial gods and humans as the sons of Jadon. "She came to me," Saber whispered, hoping not to provoke Napolean's wrath but determined to stand his ground.

"Excuse me?" Napolean said. His voice was laced with warning.

"Vanya," Saber reiterated. "She came to me…on more than one occasion. The fact that I was in a filthy cell—that wasn't my call."

Napolean chuckled, slowly, deeply. And the sound was akin to a set of brass claws being raked across a blackboard, chilling in its dissonance. "You're right; it wasn't your call. Your call was to go after Kristina Silivasi, to attack Nachari's *destiny*, to act in a way that guaranteed your death and execution, *by me*." He rocked back on his heels and glared at Saber in challenge, all the while continuing to make repairs in his heart as if the two motivations were wholly separate. "*My call*," he continued malevolently, "was to let you live…while we watched you…see if there was anything worth saving in your blackened heart." He narrowed his gaze, and his piercing eyes contracted into two tiny slits, the silver centers glowing with barely restrained wrath, even as he tightened his grip on Saber's heart. "Tell me I was wrong, and I will rectify it now."

Saber swallowed a buildup of saliva. He swallowed his retort, and he swallowed his pride. "I don't know," he said evenly, "if there's anything but blackness in my heart." It was the frankest admission he had made yet. "But last night, it wasn't about that…hatred…*or* what you call love."

"What was it about then?" Napolean murmured.

208

Saber looked away, glancing off into the distance at a spot on the wall. "It was about a son who had just watched his father get executed." His eyes met Napolean's once more in the briefest of contact; but the intensity was too much to withstand so he looked away again. "And a brother who had just watched"—he bit his lip and swallowed a droplet of blood—"just watched his ally, his friend and brother, get slaughtered." He winced. "It was about falling...hell, spinning." He tilted his head to the side swiftly, cracking his neck as if he could snap the pain away. "Reeling." His shoulders stiffened. "And it was about a woman who, for whatever reason, had the power to make it all go away. For a minute. Just one minute." He closed his eyes in shame, hating that Napolean had witnessed his grief so intimately in the Red Canyons, despising that he was surely witnessing it now.

When Napolean didn't speak—not a single word—Saber began to feel cornered, exposed, inexplicably pressured. He forced himself to regard the fearsome leader of the house of Jadon straight on, while he let his next words fly. "You are the king of the house of Jadon, right? Hell, king of the whole freakin' world. You've always known about the Curse, about *destinies*, and protocol...and honor. Yet, even possessing all that wisdom, can you tell me you never crossed a line, played hard and fast with the rules?" He continued to stare directly at him, refusing to blink or look away. "Can you tell me you never felt the weight of the world on your shoulders and wanted to ease the pain in the wrong set of arms? In *Vanya's* arms?"

Napolean jolted.

And then he froze.

Not a single muscle twitched. Not a hair on his head rustled. He simply stared back at Saber with a look of fierce incredulity on his face, his jaw set in a hard line. "You've glimpsed her memories?"

Saber shrugged.

"Does she know?"

Saber was not about to go there. "Either my words are true...or they aren't."

BLOOD REDEMPTION

Napolean scowled. "What do you know about truth, Mr. Vampire-Soldier-*Dark One*? So far, you haven't been man enough to face any of the truths presented to you. You would rather plot and scheme, lash out at the whole free world, and feel sorry for yourself." He leveled a cautionary gaze at the stricken vampire before continuing, a clear warning not to interrupt. "What happened between me and Vanya is none of your damn business. Not only was it a long time ago, but it was an entirely different situation."

"Why?" Saber retorted, feeling suddenly emboldened. "Because you're the great Napolean Mondragon?" His next words came out in an uncensored rush. "The gods gave her *to me*, milord."

"What did you just say?"

"The—gods—gave—her—to—me, *milord.*"

Napolean withdrew his hand from Saber's chest as if the cavity had suddenly burned him. He rose from the ground in absolute silence, took a calculated step away, and spun back to face the defiant prisoner. "I heard you the first time."

"Then why did you—"

Napolean waved his hand in harsh dismissal. "*Stop talking*, you fool!"

"Why? Because the truth—"

"Because you are dead if you don't! Even I have limitations!" His enormous body shook where he stood, and it took him no less than a minute to fully calm down. "And such a thing won't serve Vanya right now—which is the *only* thing I care about."

Saber struggled to stand upright. He paused to test his broken body and assess his rapidly healing wounds before daring to place his full weight on his feet. Once he was steady, he turned to face his accuser and finish the conversation the way he had started it: with brutal honesty. "What the hell do you want from me, *milord?*"

Napolean took several steps back, crossed his arms over his powerful chest, and leaned casually against the diamond-encrusted bars, staring at Saber as if he suddenly didn't have a care in the world. And truth be told, he probably didn't. His easy demeanor, as well as the contrived look of indifference on his face, said it all: *I can take your life in a heartbeat; you are nothing before me.* "Speak freely, male, or forever hold your peace." Napolean's voice was a mere whisper. "This is the only opportunity I will ever give you."

Saber gawked at the cocky display before him and raised his hands in a mock gesture of surrender. "*Seriously?* What do you want me to say?"

Napolean smiled then, laughing almost softly, although there was certainly no humor in his voice. He shrugged. "That's up to you. Why not start by facing the truth."

"The truth?" Saber snickered. "As you see it or as I see it? Because trust me, *Your Grace*, there's more than one truth here."

"How about the truth of your position."

"My position?"

"Your position."

"Yeah...my *position*," Saber parroted. "Like I don't know where I stand."

Napolean raised his eyebrows in question. "You don't seem to know much of anything—who you are, who *I am*."

Saber laughed blatantly then. "You think I don't know who you are, Napolean?" He waited to see if the ancient king would strike him dead just for using his name so casually. When it appeared as if he were still breathing, he continued: "Because I'm too dark, too stupid, and too defiant to recognize *power* when I see it—is that it?"

"You tell me."

"Your ego is astonishing, milord."

Napolean shrugged. "Perhaps. But yours, it's just pathetic...obvious...*tiresome*."

Saber's fangs shot out from his mouth involuntarily, but Napolean didn't seem to notice, or maybe he just didn't care. "As I said, you aren't even man enough to face the—"

"You are Napolean freakin' Mondragon! Son of Sebastian and Katalina. Born to the house of Andromeda. You weren't born to the Curse; you were *made* by the Blood itself—an original vampire. If you say that day should be night and night should be day, the sky itself bows down to make it happen. Yeah, I know who the hell you are."

"Then you know that my word is my bond."

"So?"

"So, why are you holding back, Saber? I said, *speak freely.*"

"As if it's going to make any difference."

"Probably not."

"Yeah…probably not: I get the game, milord."

"Do you?"

Saber snarled in frustration. "What the hell are you trying to accomplish?"

Napolean held up both hands, clearly undaunted. "I thought you got the game."

"You know what I get?" Saber asked, not bothering to wait for a reply. "I get that you loathe my existence. I get that you're accustomed to having absolute power, and you can't stand the fact that my allegiance was to another house—*is* to another house. You can break me; you can torture me; hell, you can even execute me with a glance; but what you can't do is change me. No matter how hard you press down on my neck, you can't make me have a soul or a conscience. And that's really what this all comes down to, isn't it? I'm not worthy in your lofty eyes, yet the gods still saw fit to give Vanya to me. And *Vanya* still saw fit to give *herself* to me."

Saber expected an instant rise out of the ancient monarch, but he didn't get one. "And who are *you?*" Napolean asked. "Why do you think the gods would have given someone as precious as Vanya to a being as lost and worthless as you?"

Saber shook his head in insolence. "Maybe they didn't know I would end up batting for the wrong team—growing up in a house of darkness?"

"So you acknowledge that you *were* born here, into the house of Jadon?"

"That's not what I said."

"That *is* what you said."

"I said—"

"You were batting for the *wrong* team." He waved his hand in dismissal. "But never mind that. So you're saying you prefer to belong to the house of Jaegar then? With all its obvious loyalty and affection toward you?"

"Cute," Saber replied. "What the hell does it matter? I don't know where I was born, who I belong to. I don't even know who I am for that matter. Does that make you happy?"

"Me?" Napolean raised his brows and shook his head. "No." He seemed to choose his next words purposefully. "Apparently, it doesn't make Salvatore happy anymore, either. Or that other soldier—what was his name?—Achilles."

"Watch yourself," Saber warned.

"Or what?" Napolean asked. "You're no threat to me. And from what I can see, you've got no ties to either house. Perhaps you've never genuinely cared about anything...or anyone."

Saber felt his chest begin to tighten, his legs begin to shake. This was bullshit, and Napolean knew it. The king had stood right there and witnessed Saber's breakdown, his overwhelming grief at the loss of his father and brother, and now he was throwing the whole thing back in his face as if Saber would not have rather died than fall apart in front of his enemy. "And I'm supposed to be the Dark One," Saber bit out. "You wear it well, milord, much better than you think."

"Wear what well?" Napolean queried.

"You know damn well how I felt about my father and my brother, that I just lost *everything* that mattered. And yes, Napolean," he continued, his voice rising in intensity, "my dark, soulless family mattered! I bet that really turns your stomach, the fact that the house of Jaegar actually matters to me! That my one remaining brother, Diablo, matters more than anything or anyone else on this earth, including my life...or you." The more he spoke, the angrier he became. "And isn't that just the rub?"

"Meaning?"

"Meaning that the eight hundred years I spent on this earth, while utterly repugnant and worthless in your eyes, actually mattered to me. Matter to me, still."

Napolean exhaled slowly. He rolled his head on his broad shoulders as if to release some tension. "And what about the princess—what about Vanya? Does she matter, Saber?"

Saber frowned. "I already told you: I never meant to hurt her. I certainly didn't try to kill her. Not last night. Not the first time she came to my cell."

Napolean looked momentarily perplexed, and more than just a little bit concerned, but to his credit, he let the statement go. "You just took what was presented to you when it was presented?"

"Yes."

"And you're not sorry."

"I don't *know sorry*."

"And you don't love her?"

"I don't *know love*."

"Then why try to convert her? Why not just let her die and be done with it? Present yourself to the Blood in twenty-five days and call this whole miserable experiment quits?"

"Because I can't do that."

"Why not?"

"Just can't."

"*Why not?*"

"I owe her, Napolean. At least that much." He rubbed his brow in frustration. "You wouldn't understand."

Napolean nodded then, weighing all of Saber's words carefully. When at last he moved to speak, his words rang out like distant thunder. "Let me tell you what I understand, Mr. Alexiares."

Saber met the king's gaze boldly, but he didn't offer a flippant reply. And he didn't interrupt.

"I understand that you *loved* your dark family, that love comes from the soul, which you do have, and I understand that you will *always* love your family because of it. I understand that your life has value to you, even if the only thing that sustains it right now is nursing your hatred toward us. I understand that you did not grow up dreaming of your *destiny*, imagining her voice, or waiting for the day when she would finally be revealed to you beneath the Blood Moon, that you have no reference for that type of emotion and no reason to suddenly feel it, simply because the sky and the moon change, and you are suddenly faced with the gift of a beautiful woman. And I even understand why you gave into your desire the other night with that same beautiful woman, although the thought sickens me to my core. But most of all, I understand why you need to try and save her…and your unborn son. Because if you value nothing else in that gods-forsaken hell of an existence you live in, you value loyalty, the very thing that Salvatore obliterated the other night in the Red Canyons, and make no mistake, the house of Jadon may not be the team you care to bat for, but the house of Jaegar will *never* be your home-base again. The bottom line is Vanya showed you loyalty. I get it. I get all of it." He stepped away from the bars and uncrossed his arms. "But there are a couple of things that you need to get, maybe not right now, but eventually, if you even have a prayer of existing in any state other than agony, whether in this world or the next."

Saber didn't want to listen—what did Napolean care about his eternal state of existence?—but he couldn't quite tune him out. He couldn't quite forget the day Nachari Silivasi had sauntered into his cell and burned his own hellacious memories into Saber's brain, replaying each scene from the wizard's captivity in the Valley of Death and Shadows, moment by moment, detail by detail, until Saber had cried out from the horror of it all. Despite his defiance, Saber would have to be a fool to want to go there, to exist there…forever.

"We're not all puritans in this valley, Saber," Napolean continued. "And if you could pause for just one second, stop hating everyone and everything around you long enough to use that keen intelligence for something other than plotting evil and exacting revenge, you might just recognize that none of us asked for this Curse, this legacy, any more than you did. And maybe, just maybe, there are some things you can respect, even value, right here in the house of Jadon: like courage, strength, and even loyalty. Perhaps they even exist here in a way they could never exist in the house of Jaegar."

Saber looked away in an act of dismissal, pretending the king's words fell on deaf ears.

"Look at me, son," Napolean demanded, refusing to be dismissed. "*Look at me.*"

Saber met his eyes halfheartedly.

"You have taken cruel advantage of every olive branch we have offered you; you have pushed every warrior in this house beyond his endurance; and ultimately, you may have already destroyed the one and only soul in Dark Moon Vale that you did not wish to destroy. Your anger might be justified in your own mind—your hatred, a living, breathing entity—but your actions are reckless and indiscriminate. And even you can't abide by the havoc you have wreaked at this juncture, potentially destroying Vanya and your own unborn son. So tell me, Angry One, when does it end?"

Saber didn't reply.

"Does it...*ever*...end?"

Saber shrugged his shoulders; he was beginning to feel nauseated. "What do you want me to say?" he whispered.

"I want you to say that *you* get it. What you've done. Who you are. What you're facing—and what Vanya is facing—because of you." Saber started to speak, but Napolean held up his hand to silence him. "I do not know if we can save the princess at this stage—conversion during a pregnancy has never been attempted before—and even if Vanya survives, the babies will likely perish, both of them. Should they start to ascend before she is fully Vampyr, we will have to act quickly to euthanize her, spare her the agony of such a brutal death. Can you at least acknowledge that we can't have an enemy combatant, *an embittered wildcard*, in the room, while this unfolds? That even if we can't trust each other—even if we despise each other—we still have to rely on each other...to try and fix what

216

you broke?"

Despite his unease, Saber was listening carefully now. He was no longer rolling his eyes or shrugging his shoulders. Whether Napolean realized it or not, Saber got the seriousness of the situation. In fact, the full breadth of it, the weight it placed on his exiled shoulders, was as foreign as it was revolting. To say he was a fish out of water would have been the understatement of the century. Saber was a vampire without a lair. A son without a father. A brother without a sibling.

He was a soldier without an army and a soul without a clue.

"I believe we have to try," Napolean continued, bringing Saber back into the present moment, "and that is the *only* reason I healed your wounds and stopped Marquis from sending you to the afterlife. But you have to be willing to take direction. To stop lashing out long enough to do some good."

Saber clasped his hands together and rested his forehead on his thumbs. He closed his eyes and simply concentrated on breathing. After a long moment of silence had passed, he nodded. "I do get it."

"Say it again."

"I *do* get it."

"Louder, Saber!"

"I get it, Napolean: *I get it.*"

Napolean exhaled slowly. "Then I think we understand one another."

eighteen

Saber kept his eyes cast downward, his vision focused like a laser, dead ahead, as he and Napolean made their way through the front door of the clinic. They walked, side by side, past the waiting room where Marquis, Ciopori, Nachari, and Ramsey paced fitfully back and forth, casting blatant, hate-filled glances in Saber's direction, and down the long hallway to Exam Room Three, where Vanya awaited with Kagen for the conversion.

Napolean had spent the last hour and a half with Saber, coaching him on the dangerous procedure to come, going over every single aspect of what he had to do, every subtle nuance of what he could expect, and Saber had listened and learned with keen attention to detail. He had asked questions, envisioned various scenarios, and tried as best he could to prepare himself for every eventuality.

Yet, he knew he wasn't ready.

This could either go fairly well—which would still be defined as pain, torture, agony, and a very close call—or this could go horrifically wrong. The fact that Marquis, Nachari, and Ramsey would be waiting just outside the exam room to rip his throat out should the conversion fail was hardly lost on him. The fact that Ciopori was being kept out of the room for fear of her emotional reactions and consequent volatility only made matters more dubious. The fact that Napolean had instructed all others in the house of Jadon to stay away from the clinic, despite their intense emotional and spiritual investment in the outcome, was at least a relief of sorts: Saber would not have an audience for the conversion, and there would be nothing to distract him from concentrating fully on the critical matter at hand—saving Vanya at all costs.

Saving his unborn child, if still possible.

Saber stopped short outside of the exam room and tapped

BLOOD REDEMPTION

his foot nervously on the floor, trying to maintain his cool. He felt like the ground was shifting beneath him, and his body just might begin to sway or, worse, topple over. He took a deep breath and drew on his resolve.

"Are you ready?" Napolean asked him, placing a steadying hand ever so briefly on his tense shoulder.

Saber shrugged it off instinctively—old habits were hard to break, and this was only a momentary truce. He swallowed hard. "I think so."

"Not good enough," Napolean said.

"Yes," Saber replied. "*Yes.*"

"Very well." Napolean turned the handle and gently opened the door, extending his other arm to usher Saber in first.

Oh, hell, Saber thought as he took that first step and his gaze immediately locked with Kagen Silivasi's. The Ancient Master Healer was waiting just outside of a drawn curtain, his arms crossed snug against his chest; his jaw locked down so tight if he bit down any harder, his teeth might just crumble to dust; and his brow so furrowed, the lines could provide Saber with a roadmap: straight to hell.

Saber swallowed his pride and attempted a nod. "Kagen."

The healer's dark brown eyes flashed crimson, only for a moment, and then they returned to their rich, chocolate brown. "Saber." *At least he hadn't said Dark One—that was a start.*

Saber turned his attention to the drawn curtain and the pregnant female lying just beyond its veil. "Is she—"

Ready? Kagen interrupted telepathically, clearly unwilling to expose Vanya to any part of their conversation. *To suffer? To die? To see the likes of you as it happens? Doubtful.*

Kagen! Napolean's censor was immediate and absolute. *There will be none of that! Not right now. Take caution: I will not admonish you twice.*

Kagen turned his attention to Napolean and nodded in assent. "Milord." He spoke his acquiescence out loud, and the matter was closed.

"Is he here?" A faint female voice echoed from behind the

curtain; and Saber's heart skipped an unexpected beat—*what was that all about, anyway?* Vanya was clearly nervous, in a lot of distress, and by the quivering tone of her voice, she was also in a lot of discomfort.

Already.

Most likely from the rapidly progressing pregnancy.

"Yes, Princess," Napolean answered immediately. And then, as if the other two were not in the room, he strolled behind the curtain and began to speak to her in soft, comforting tones. "I understand that Kagen has kept you at least somewhat comfortable with a sedative for the last hour or so?"

"Of course," Vanya responded, sounding regal as always. "'Tis not the last hour I'm concerned about."

Saber heard the soft rustle of a sheet, then the soft clasp of skin against skin, and he knew that Napolean had taken her hand. "I know," Napolean answered softly. "And I'm sorry that you cannot remain sedated for the entire…procedure."

Vanya chuckled softly then. Insincerely. "Procedure? Is that what we're calling it now?"

"Conversion," Napolean corrected.

"*Attempted conversion*," Vanya amended, her voice wavering with the onset of tears.

"Shh, now. None of that." *Was he stroking her hair?* It almost sounded like he was, but Saber couldn't tell.

"I need only honesty between us right now, milord," Vanya said. "I don't think I can bear it otherwise."

"Of course," Napolean answered. "Do you still have questions Kagen hasn't answered?"

Vanya sighed loudly. "Just…just…if it's not working…if you know…you see that it's not…" Her voice trailed off, and she had to struggle to collect herself. "Then don't wait too late. Bring Ciopori in, so she can say good-bye. She will…need that."

Saber clenched and unclenched his fists.

Three times.

Trying to contain the errant energy swirling like a crosswind through his body. This was madness. Insane.

Surreal.

"I give you my word as your king," Napolean answered.

Vanya choked back a sob. "Very well then. Is…is the dragon with you?"

Napolean sighed. "You know that he is; and I believe he is truly going to try on your behalf."

Saber could not take another moment of this. Driven by sheer grit, he took three giant strides toward the curtain, swiftly pulled it back, and stepped to Vanya's side. "I'm here, and I am going to make this work. Or die trying."

Vanya's dusty rose eyes grew large, and her mouth fell open. Once she had recovered from his hasty entrance, his sudden presence behind the curtain, she bit down on her lower lip and murmured, "Perhaps. Perhaps not."

"No," Saber argued. "Not *perhaps not*. You know as well as I do that your focus, your belief, is as critical to this conversion as your body's compliance. *It will be so.* That is the only acceptable outcome; and that is the only thought you will allow in your head."

"I don't—"

"It will be so. Nothing else." He locked his gaze with hers in an indomitable battle of wills. "*Nothing else.*"

Vanya drew in a sharp intake of breath. "Forgive me, Dragon, but am I to believe that you suddenly care?" Before he could answer, she placed an absent hand over her belly and smirked. "Ah, but of course; I'm carrying your unborn son."

Saber felt the impact of her words like a knife in the back, exactly as they were intended. *Good, she would need that grit and fire to survive.* "Exactly," he said, "and as you're well aware, even a jackal will fight for its young." He leaned over the gurney then, so she could see the heat in his eyes. "I am all that you believe and more, sweet Princess: heartless, cruel, and reared by the devil himself. So be it. Then you know that I will try to save the offspring in your belly; you know that I will fight like a thousand spawns of hell for what is mine; and you know that I will not give Salvatore Nistor the satisfaction of achieving his greatest

Tessa Dawn

desire, the victory of destroying an original princess. Not when he murdered my father and my brother. Not when the desire for revenge is still so sweet on my tongue. You know better than to trust my love...so trust my hate then. Trust what you know."

Napolean cleared his throat and took an uneasy step back. Clearly, the ancient king was less than enamored with Saber's approach, concerned that such a harsh tactic might cause more harm than good; but he took one hard look into Saber's eyes and let the diatribe go. Perhaps the ancient monarch understood, or at least accepted, that Saber was trying desperately to harness the only passion he knew how to work with, the one thing that had fueled his life from the day Damien had first called him son: flagrant defiance against anything that opposed him.

The king looked at Vanya, regarded her warily, but he didn't speak up or interfere.

"Let us be done with this," she said. "One way or the other. Let's just do it."

Now, this was something Saber understood. Standing upright, he rounded the gurney and carefully lifted the princess into a seated position. Kagen ducked instinctively beneath the curtain, and Napolean almost leapt toward him in reaction, but both males quickly restrained their reactions.

Saber paid no notice.

He straddled the narrow cot in one smooth motion and drew the princess back against his chest, locking his iron arms around her shoulders to hold her in place and...*comfort her?*

Lean into me, Vanya, he whispered telepathically on a private bandwidth. Ever since he had taken her blood, it was an easy feat. *Try if you can to relax, or at least not to fight.* He followed her breathing with his own, matching her every inhale and exhale breath for breath, until he was at last leading the rhythm with a deep, hypnotic cadence of his own.

And then he did something unexpected, even to himself.

He nuzzled her neck with his mouth, stroking back and forth against her delicate skin with exquisite—unexpected—gentleness. His lips, then his jaw, then the smooth ivory tips of his elongating fangs all caressed her jugular in turn, while he chanted softly, almost indiscriminately, in her ear, speaking intuitively in the one ancient language they both would understand: a single primordial song that would swell within their...souls.

"Fi linistita, micuta. Vino departe cu mine. Asculta vocea mea. Pluteste...pluteste... departe. Totul este bine...*totul este bine*...totul va fi facut sa fie bine."

Be still, little one. Come away with me. Listen to my voice. Float...float...away. All is well... all is well...all will be made well.

Vanya drifted slowly away.

Sinking ever more deeply into the burgeoning warmth enfolding her neck.

A dragon's fire.

Only this time, it wasn't scorching her. It was enveloping her, soothing her, beckoning her deeper and deeper into the apex of his lair. She felt her resistance waning, her fear dissipating, her confusion fading. It was like her mind was suddenly hazy, filled with soft, albeit grayish, clouds, and they simply overcame her distress with their power.

Power?

By all the celestial gods, where had Saber Alexiares acquired such power? When had a male from the Dark Ones' Colony learned such focus, attained such skill? Vanya shuddered at the thought; he was powerful beyond measure.

And dangerous.

Yes, of course, he was so very dangerous.

After all, isn't this what he had done the night they had made love—*had sex*—in his cell? Overcame her will with his own? He had drawn her inexplicably, irrefutably, into the turbulence of his soul, exacted the strength of his desire over her own until she could no longer resist him.

Until she no longer wanted to resist him.

Until she had wanted to accept him.

Completely.

Her eyelids drifted down, growing increasingly heavy. She was so sleepy. She was so...content. And then his incisors pierced her skin, sinking deeply into her jugular like a knife slicing through warm butter. Effortless yet exacting.

He was so...in control.

And then the venom began to pump from his fangs, slowly at first, a sharp twinge, like that from a syringe, stinging inside of her veins, burning, then searing.

She fought to sit upright, almost jolted out of her trance, but his arms tightened around her, and his chest stiffened. He held her in an iron grasp, as unyielding as it was unforgiving.

"Saber," she cried out, beginning to feel the first perilous edge of panic.

Shh, little one, he whispered telepathically. And then he continued to chant.

Vanya knew that soon the pain would grow unbearable. Soon it would travel to her heart, and Saber would be unable to keep up the communication throughout the conversion. She would be on her own to endure...and survive...if the gods willed it. She tried to settle in, to let go. To give her body, mind, and soul over to the dragon that held her in his fiery clutches, but the pain was simply growing too intense.

The noise in her belly, for a lack of a better word, was beginning to grow more dissonant as the unborn vampires began to respond to their father's venom, to the assault of conversion, and the upheaval of their rest.

The venom was traveling quickly now.

Too quickly.

And it was scorching, like acid, almost as if the will and the fire of the male who wielded it had set it on a course of absolute and utter destruction. And, of course, that was precisely what he was doing, destroying Vanya's humanity one cell, one atom, and one nucleus at a time, in order to remake her—to remake them all—as he was: Vampyr.

Dark.

Soulless.

No! Vanya cried out within her soul, although no sound escaped her lips. Her teeth were simply clamped down too hard to speak, her breath too shallow to feed oxygen to the words. But she couldn't let this happen. She couldn't let this powerful...dark...dangerous...deadly male infuse her with his very essence; yet she was powerless to stop him.

As the venom entered her heart, filling all four chambers in quick succession, she began to writhe beneath him. *Great Cygnus*, this was beyond her endurance!

The pain.

The agony.

The power.

"Saber, please! Oh, please...stop!"

Saber wiped a bead of sweat from his brow, quick to replace his arm around Vanya, to clamp down once again with unyielding force. Vanya had stopped struggling in earnest hours ago. Now, she only whimpered and cried out a few times each minute; but she was exhausted. Beyond exhausted, really. She was depleted, laid bare, devastated by the suffering.

Saber glanced at the clock: It was seven AM, and they had been at it for over ten hours. His gaze moved from the time to the healer, who was now standing anxiously beside the gurney, checking the electronic fetal monitors for the umpteenth time. Saber couldn't speak. He couldn't even reach out telepathically. The conversion was simply commanding every ounce of his attention, his absolute concentration and focus.

Luckily, Kagen understood the question in Saber's eyes. "I can't make heads or tails out of this," he snapped in irritation, reaching for the printed chart to take a closer look. He stared at the graph, the erratic lines and waves, in abject frustration before crumpling it up in his hand, throwing it to the ground, and rapidly removing the elastic belts securing the fetal sensors from Vanya's belly. He reached for his fetoscope instead. "Quiet!" he barked out to everyone, and no one, in particular.

It wasn't as if anyone was speaking or making noise.

Not unless sweat made a sound.

Kagen moved the horn several times around Vanya's exposed belly, listening intently with his hyper-acute, vampiric hearing. "Son of a rattlesnake," he swore beneath his breath.

"What is it?" Napolean demanded, taking a measured step toward the Master Healer.

"It's just..." He bent over to listen again. "It's way too erratic."

"What do you mean by erratic?" Napolean asked.

"The heartbeats. They're beyond erratic...they're stressed...almost frenetic."

"Speak plainly," Napolean barked, unable to restrain his anxiety.

"Something's happening that doesn't make sense," Kagen insisted. "It's like there's a sudden surge of exertion...as if...the babies are moving."

"Isn't that good?" Napolean asked, his brow furrowed in confusion. "I mean, it tells us they're alive. We weren't expecting them to last this—"

"No," Kagen argued, shaking his head vigorously. "It's not...normal movement. They're—"

Vanya's sudden, ear-piercing scream cut the healer off mid-sentence.

"No!" Kagen shouted. He jumped back, dropping the fetoscope on the floor.

"What?" Napolean demanded.

"Her ribs!"

Saber watched in horror as the apex of Vanya's stomach began to bulge unnaturally, and he couldn't help but jerk when one of her ribs cracked audibly, puncturing through her skin.

"Sweet Andromeda," Napolean cried, his tired, bronzed face suddenly turning ashen in color. "Oh…gods…" He hung his head.

Saber was so confused. Beyond confused. He was disoriented and *angry*. Ten hours! They had been at this for ten hours, and he didn't dare stop now: Vanya's system could not take a sudden withdrawal of venom. Her failing human cells could no longer maintain her life at this juncture; and her newly formed Vampyr organs were not yet strong enough to stand alone without the venom. This was no longer about Saber's origin, whether he was dark or light. As a male born in the house of Jadon, if Vanya was Vampyr, the babies would be born in a normal fashion, dematerializing from her womb at their father's command; but if she was still human, they would continue to claw their way out. As it stood, she was on the edge of both, yet in the cradle of neither; and the infants were in a full-fledged panic, desperate to get away from the pain of conversion.

Yet she was so close.

So close!

She just needed a little more time…

He bore down with everything he had, sending his venom into her bloodstream at double the rate and intensity; but this only sent the unborn vampires into frenzy.

Another rib cracked, and the princess nearly shot off the gurney, momentarily breaking Saber's hold.

Napolean took over.

He rushed to the side of gurney, shoved Saber aside with one powerful thrust of his hand, instantly dislodging his fangs from Vanya's throat in a manner that caused a brutal tear, and turned to regard Kagen, even as he began to gently lift the princess's head into his hands. "Get Ciopori!"

Saber stumbled backward, stunned that the king had stopped the conversion. "There's still time," he argued, incredulous. "There's…there's still twenty-one hours left in the pregnancy; the babies can't be coming now." He shot his own heated glare at Kagen. "Heal her ribs with your venom while I—"

"Saber!" Napolean's voice struck him like a physical object, the weight and intensity of it bringing him up short. "We talked about this. We knew it might happen. These children are going to claw their way out of her belly in minutes if we don't stop it. It's too late." He turned back toward Kagen. "Get Ciopori! *I promised.*"

Kagen threw both hands up in the air and took a stunned step backward. The look on his face said it all: Why? When? How had this happened?

So quickly?

He gathered his composure and dematerialized out of the room.

Saber spun around, almost in a fury. "No!" he shouted as Napolean lifted Vanya's head to his mouth and began to release his fangs, the fangs he would use to drain her body of blood as swiftly as he could.

To euthanize her.

Kill her.

"Are you crazy!" Saber shouted. Something deep within him, something he couldn't even name, rose up in utter, uncompromising defiance. Vanya was not Napolean's to take! She was his!

Saber's!

His *destiny.*

And she wasn't going to die.

"Hurry!" Vanya shouted, grasping at Napolean's forearms with such ferocity that her nails scored his skin, drawing blood. "By all the gods, make this stop!"

Saber reeled backward on the floor, propelling his body as far away from the morbid scene as he could. It was happening too quickly. Too suddenly to comprehend.

Napolean sank his lethal fangs into the princess's neck at the exact same moment that Ciopori materialized in the room. He was sucking her blood, and Ciopori was weeping.

No—she was wailing.

She rushed to Vanya's side and took her hand.

"Sister...*sister*...I'm here. *I'm here.*"

Vanya looked panic-stricken.

Pale.

Feral.

She grasped wildly for Ciopori's hands and clutched them in an inexorable grip.

"Don't fight it," Ciopori implored, her chest heaving beneath the weight of her sobs. "Go peacefully, sister. Jadon will be there to meet you; and I'll be there soon. Just...just...go."

Son of a bitch! The words faded into the background even as the entire scene metamorphosed into a distant but tangible nightmare.

This was not happening.

It. Just. Wasn't. Happening.

Saber looked up toward the ceiling in utter hopelessness. This didn't make any sense. It just wasn't right. By all that was unholy, Vanya was an original celestial being, born before the Curse, born outside of the Curse! She was a good soul. A pure heart. She was light and kindness and all that remained untainted in this gods-forsaken world. There was nothing in her like the darkness that dwelled in him, no remnants of a being like Salvatore, no vengeance like that embraced by her sisters of old...by the Blood. There was nothing but flowing flaxen hair; soft, rose-colored eyes; and a regal, delicate jaw. There was nothing but hope and love and charity—and all that shit Saber would rather choke on than become.

But this wasn't about him.

It was about her.

Where were her gods?

Where was Napolean's justice?

Where was...where was...Serpens! The light god of his birth.

Saber raged at the injustice of it all as his soul interrogated his god—and not S'nepres, not the dark twins, not the demons of his childhood—where was the god who had seen fit to give him life so long ago, before Damien Alexiares had chosen to change it?

"Where are you!" he shouted to the heavens, not caring who heard. "Where the hell are you, and how can you do this!"

Without even realizing it, he scrambled to his knees on the floor and banged his head against the heavy tile, hoping to put himself out of his misery. "Serpens," he prayed—or cursed— whatever it was. "Don't do this to her! *Not to her.* I'm the dark soul. I'm the dragon. Take me instead. My soul for hers. My life for theirs." He grasped at his wild black-and-red hair and tugged in anguish. "I'll go wherever I belong, to the Valley of Death and Shadows, to the Chamber of Sacrifice, whatever it is you want! Just tell me. Don't punish *her* because I never worshipped *you.*" Blinking to press back angry tears, he grit his teeth together. "What do you want from me? *Tell me what you want!*" Snarling, he added, "Fine. I acknowledge that you are the god of my birth— you, not your dark twin—that you gave me life, Serpens!" He pounded his fists against the floor. "I'm kneeling before you now like a child, *begging*, when you know damn well I've never knelt before anyone or begged for anything in my life...*ever.* Save her!"

The entire room seemed to disappear as Saber pounded his fists into so much blood and pulp against the cold, unforgiving floor. As his barren heart wept beneath the loss of his unborn child and the female who had done nothing to deserve his wrath.

As he finally understood the full measure of his sin.

Yet remained helpless to do anything about it.

nineteen

"Saber."

"No!"

"*Saber.*"

"Leave me alone." Saber swiped at the hand in front of him, wishing he had the strength to crush it, but knowing he did not. He just wanted everyone to leave him alone. *Hell's bells*, they could execute him later—or now, while he wasn't looking—whatever. Just leave him out of it.

"Son, are you that blind?"

Saber felt utterly exhausted. Depleted. "Just leave me alone."

Napolean squatted in front of him. "Look," he demanded, reaching out to grasp the stubborn soldier by the jaw. "*Just look.*"

Saber slowly raised his head and stared at the king. "What?" he asked. "What more do you want from me?"

Napolean shook his head. "Over there." He pointed across the exam room toward the gurney, toward the all-too-recent scene of the unholy nightmare, and—

And Vanya was drinking some kind of fluid from a flask.

The princess was propped up on a pillow, and Kagen was giving her a vial of blood, even as Ciopori wiped her brow with a damp washcloth.

Saber stared more intently: Vanya was slowly, gently...*breathing.*

She was still alive.

Saber sat upright. He looked at Napolean, looked back at Vanya, and then looked at Napolean again. "What happened?"

Napolean sighed and slowly shook his head. "I think *Serpens* happened."

"What?" Saber asked.

"You may have just had a run-in with your soul, Mr.

233

Alexiares."

Saber could hardly believe his eyes. He stood gingerly and took a tentative step in Vanya's direction. "Princess?"

Vanya rolled her glorious eyes. "What, Dragon?" she snapped in annoyance.

Saber laughed out loud. He actually *laughed*. "Are you kidding me?"

Ciopori shot him a murderous glare. "Does anyone in this room seem to be kidding, or laughing, other than you?" Her words were sharp and surprisingly *welcome*.

"No," he said, as the realization finally sank in. Vanya—was—alive. Serpens had actually heard his prayer, or rant—whatever—and he had somehow spared her life. "The conversion?" he asked, finally coming back to his senses.

"She's through it," Kagen said.

"Through it?"

"Vampyr," Kagen clarified. "The conversion is complete."

"And...and our son?"

Vanya raised herself to one elbow. "The pregnancy is still viable, Saber. And Kagen assures me that, while there are still twenty hours left to go, the children will be born in the usual way...once they're ready."

"The usual way?" Saber repeated, certain that he was beginning to sound like a ninny. It didn't matter. He wanted to be sure that he understood.

"You will call them from her womb when they are ready," Ciopori chimed in. "And then you will fulfill the demands of the Curse as required." Her voice was still clipped with anger.

Saber nodded solemnly. "Of course." He took a few more steps forward, daring to approach the gurney once more. "And you, Princess—your pain?"

"I am no longer suffering, Dragon," Vanya said matter-of-factly. "And Kagen has healed my wounds."

Saber met the Master Healer's gaze then, studying the deep reflective centers of his otherwise dark brown eyes. He didn't have a vocabulary for *thank you* any more than he had an understanding of the true sentiment, but he hoped his expression conveyed at least something of his relief.

Vanya cleared her throat then. She struggled to sit up beneath a massively protruding belly and regarded Saber with a sidelong glance. "I trust you will see me through the rest of this ordeal?"

"Of course," Saber said, not sure if he understood where she was going with this.

"You need to block her pain and keep the discomfort at bay, vampire," Ciopori said crossly.

Saber nodded at the prickly princess. *That* he could do. "And when our son is born, I'll take care of the...sacrifice." He eyed Napolean for confirmation. At this point, he wasn't quite sure if the god Serpens had accepted his trade or not: if he needed to trade his life for Vanya's, turn himself over to the Blood, or butcher a dozen cows, perhaps perform a pagan ritual...or two. Again, he just wanted clarification.

"I will walk you through the sacrifice," Napolean said.

Saber reached out to place his hand on Vanya's belly—he was ready to move forward with the process, to begin blocking her pain, and *gods be merciful*, hopefully, get it all over with without further incident, when Vanya grasped him by the wrist to stop him. "Wait," she said resolutely.

He met her gaze.

"You need to understand something first."

He nodded, waiting.

"You keep saying *our son*..." She looked away as if to gather her courage. "Dragon, when this is all said and done, I plan to raise *my* son in peace." She sighed, and her eyes betrayed the slightest hint of regret, although the set of her jaw reinforced her resolve. "The gods spared me today from my own foolishness, and I am grateful to you for pleading so mightily on my behalf, *our behalf*, but I cannot forget or forgive the suffering I have endured these last twelve hours. Every time I come near you, I get burned by your fire. I am wise enough to know when enough is enough. I cannot save you, Saber; nor do I wish to try. Please know that I wish you no harm, but when this is finally over, you will not see us again. And I need you to respect that. To leave us alone."

Saber pulled away from her grasp. He wrapped his right fist in his left palm, and held both to his chin as he struggled to process all he had heard.

He didn't speak.

He didn't lash out.

And he didn't argue.

Hell, less than one week ago, perhaps just one day ago, he would've tried to murder everyone in the room, taking Vanya out as a mere casualty of war. But he didn't have the strength to fight the world right now.

He didn't possess the resolve.

There was no place in this valley for him—dark or light— and that was simply the way it was: If Napolean let him live, and that was still to be determined, perhaps he could find a place of his own. Perhaps he could still reach Diablo.

It didn't matter.

Eternity was a very long time, and his immortality was looming very large at the moment. He knew better than to make any decisions right then, whether to submit, strike back, or disappear. For now, he would get through the pregnancy and the sacrifice, and live to decide another day.

"I *don't* respect that," he finally said, coldly. "But I won't challenge it, either. At least not today."

twenty

Saber pressed both palms flat against the rough mosaic tiles in front of him. He shifted his weight onto his rear leg, arched his back, tilted his head, and closed his eyes, as the warm water rained down on him, the large, circular showerhead providing a steady stream from above. It had been seventeen hours since his son was born, sixteen since he had made the required sacrifice, and this was the first chance he had had to reflect on the day's events. The water felt incredible, better than anything he had experienced in a long time. Blinking several times to rinse the soap from his eyes, he watched as foamy gobs of shampoo and body-wash rolled off his chest, fell to the shower floor, and snaked in haphazard streams down the spherical drain.

What in the world was he supposed to do now?

He let his head fall forward, allowing the water to wash away his stress, if only for a moment, while he replayed the sequence of events in his mind.

Vanya's pregnancy had proceeded in a normal, uneventful manner, at least as far as pregnancies in the house of Jadon were concerned. She had chosen to remain asleep for the duration of the ordeal—perhaps it was a reaction to the conversion, or perhaps she couldn't bear to spend one more moment than necessary with the fire-breathing dragon she had come to despise.

Saber.

Saber took in a mouthful of water, rinsed the remaining residue of toothpaste out of his mouth, and spit it on the shower floor. What did it matter why she had chosen to remain unconscious for the birth of their son? The outcome was the same. Saber had sat alone in the dark, beside the princess, as she slept on the gurney. He had kept one hand firmly on her belly in order to block the discomfort of her pregnancy, hold it in his

237

own body, instead, while she had remained unconscious, no doubt, dreaming of better days.

Days without Saber.

As if that had not been degrading enough, Napolean Mondragon had coached him telepathically throughout the entire process; and while the king was at least judicious enough to wait outside the curtain, allow them some small measure of privacy, his overwhelming presence had felt like an iron fetter around Saber's neck.

He had not even been allowed to catch his own son as he materialized.

Kagen had done it for him.

Saber shifted his weight from his left leg to his right, stretching the opposite calf. *Kagen Silivasi had cradled Saber's newborn son in his arms*, while Napolean Mondragon had stepped beyond the curtain to receive the Dark One, keeping him securely tucked in his ancient arms. Saber had followed behind like a servant, accompanying the implacable king to the Chamber of Sacrifice and Atonement in order to relinquish the child to the Blood. In order to recite the required supplication.

He didn't even know if Vanya had named the Light One.

He ran his hands through his hair, combing it out with his fingers, his thumb and forefinger working through a particularly thick mass of black-and-red tangles. Had Vanya been excited when *Kagen* awakened her? Had she reached out for the babe, or turned away in disgust?

Saber had no idea.

He only knew that he had left the room like a banished specter, cast out into the night, with the unwanted, unnamed one to fulfill the demands of the Curse. And wasn't that just the most contrary, offensive experience of his life.

Saber had been raised in the house of Jaegar—not the house of Jadon. His whole life, he had expected to see two dark sons emerge from a tortured soul, a human woman who would be no more than an incubator for his future, should he have ever chosen to pursue that eventuality. He had simply accepted that the demands of the Curse were inevitable: The firstborn child would be relinquished to the Blood, while the second born would return with him to the colony, to be raised as his own cherished offspring. Never, in eight hundred years, had he expected to see two distinctly opposite twins: one born with coal black hair, absent of even the hint of red tendrils; the other bearing the signature *crown of the cobra*, a brand identifying him as dark, soulless, and damned. It had seemed impossible, wrong, and foreign to every cell in his body to take that child of the Curse to a platform, exalting a granite altar, and place him in a smooth, rounded basin while a dark, inky fog swirled eerily around him. To watch as the Blood shrieked, gloated, and claimed the evil offspring...until the child was no more.

For a moment, Saber had struggled against his own impulse to oppose Napolean and the whole damn Curse, to snatch the child from the basin, return him to his rightful home in the Dark Ones' colony, and to go back to life as it was supposed to be. As he had been raised to believe it one day would be. But for the first time, he had known that he had to submit, allow fate to unfold against his will, acquiesce to the vilest of revengeful omens.

After all, the truth was no longer deniable: Saber Alexiares had been born to Rafael and Lorna Dzuna, into the *house of Jadon*. He was ruled by a celestial deity—not a dark lord—*Serpens*, the god of transformation, to be exact. And that same god had heard his plea for mercy in a moment of absolute confusion and desperation. He had spared Vanya and his rightful son.

Saber shook his head briskly, wishing he could just wash it all away. Wake up from what surely had to be a never-ending nightmare.

But it wasn't.

And he couldn't.

He reached forward to turn up the hot water, aggressively adjusting the spray until it was nearly scalding his skin. The heat felt stimulating on his back, cleansing, somehow purging in light of all the recent events.

BLOOD REDEMPTION

Saber could not have saved that child without condemning himself to die.

Not only would the Blood have come for him at the end of the thirty-day Serpens Moon; but after his agonizing and vengeful death, he would have spent all of eternity in the Valley of Death and Shadows, having forfeited his immortal soul. A soul he didn't even know he had a month ago.

And beyond that inescapable truth, the dark offspring would have been like him, a son without a home, a being without a people. Even if the house of Jadon had let the creature live, which was doubtful, what would he have grown up to be? A murderer? A rapist? A dark cauldron of hatred and base instincts who sought only to destroy and procreate? Would he have turned out like Salvatore Nistor?

Saber slammed two fists against the tile wall, immediately checking to see if he had broken any bones. He then scanned the mosaic to see if he had damaged any of Napolean's rare, expensive tiles. Nope, they were still in place: *Thank the lords for little favors*. It was just that he couldn't wrap his head around all this darkness and light. Saber believed that his sons, both of them, deserved to have life; but that was because he was viewing the world through the lens of his own existence. As much as it pained him to admit it, he had always had a soul; and that meant that even in his darkest hour, he had seen the world differently than the other males around him. There had been something, however small, redeemable in his heart. How could he understand, then, the type of monster his dark son would grow up to be? Sure, he had lived with them—in the case of Damien, Dane, and Diablo, he had even cared deeply for them. Loved them. But that was because in his own demented way *he could love*.

"Shit," he whispered beneath his breath. It was all just too much to consider.

And it was all water under the bridge anyhow, too late to go back and change things.

Saber bit his bottom lip so hard that he drew a trickle of

blood, wishing he could call on his father—on Damien, that is—and just talk to the male. Try to understand why he had done what he had.

Ask him for advice…

Punch him right between the eyes and pummel his smug face until his jaw caved in.

And wasn't that really the crux of it?

Damien had made the most selfish, destructive choice imaginable when he had taken Saber from Rafael and Lorna, and what the hell had he been thinking, anyway? Did he really believe it would never come out…be discovered? That the two distinctly different fates, those awaiting the males in the house of Jaegar versus those awaiting the males in the house of Jadon, would never rear their inevitable heads?

Gods…Dark Lords—whatever the heck he was supposed to pray to now—*what had the fool been thinking?*

As the water began to turn cold—he had been in the shower so long his skin was beginning to shrivel up—Saber couldn't help but wonder *what if.* What if Damien had never made that ill-fated choice? What if he had left him in the house of Jadon? Sure, he would've grown up surrounded by a bunch of arrogant, sanctimonious, jackasses; and he would've probably been sporting some ridiculous title like Master Wizard or Master Warrior about now—although he had to admit, both Nachari and Marquis Silivasi were a couple of bad-ass vampires—but at least he would have been prepared for his Blood Moon. He would have known what it meant; and he might have approached Vanya differently.

He might still have his son.

As it stood, what did he have now? He had lost the house of Jaegar, his father, and his brother.

And he had lost his child. And the princess.

He winced at the realization: What did that mean, anyhow? Saber knew about as much concerning relationships and love as a fish knew about a bicycle. The two articles were simply diametrically opposed: Saber and love. Still, he did know something about family...and loyalty. He knew how to hold onto what was his and how to fight for his tribe.

He knew...something.

He knew...nothing.

Not a damn thing.

Unable to withstand the cold, frigid water that was now pouring out of the spigot, he turned off the spray, reached for a large white towel, wrapped it around his waist, and stepped out of the shower. He had to stop *thinking*. His head was going to explode.

He regarded a pile of fresh new clothes, stacked neatly on a knee-high, folding table beside the bathroom door, and almost smiled. *Almost*. It would take a heck of a lot more than some fresh duds to raise his spirits at this juncture; but still, the idea of a fresh pair of Jockey shorts, some clean cotton socks, and a new pair of smooth black jeans to cover his neglected body with, at this point, sounded pretty good. The crisp red shirt and the sturdy Timberline boots were a welcome sight for sore eyes in their own right.

He dressed quickly, ran his fingers through his hair one last time to remove any remaining tangles—at least push it away from his face—and then he stepped outside the door into the clean, night air.

Napolean was waiting as expected. "Saber," the monarch said, taking Saber's full measure with a subtle, almost indiscernible, sweep of his eyes.

How was he supposed to address him now? Saber wondered. *Ah, hell...* "Milord," Saber replied. The word would never fit nicely on his tongue, but Saber was just too tired, too emotionally exhausted, to fight the whole free world this night.

Maybe tomorrow.

"You look better," Napolean commented halfheartedly.

Saber smirked. "Yeah."

To Napolean's credit, the king did not try to fill the silence with words. He simply stared off into the distance at a large grouping of pine trees, and Saber followed his gaze. The night was quiet, peaceful. The sky was a deep, midnight blue, and there were stars shining as far as the eye could see. *How ironic*, Saber thought absently. He watched as a blazing torch shot across the darkened canvas at dizzying speed, a shooting star, a meteor, burning out in the earth's atmosphere in real time, maybe milliseconds, after possibly existing in the cosmos for millions of years…or more.

Saber couldn't help but find the omen appropriate. "So what now?" he finally asked.

Napolean shrugged. "Indeed, that is the question."

Saber restrained a smart-mouthed retort. He wasn't in the mood for posturing. "So am I free then?"

Napolean shook his head slowly, his deep, dark eyes, always brimming with silver light in the centers, growing even darker with intensity. "Are you?"

Saber sighed in frustration. "No riddles, Napolean." He caught the disrespect and tried to rectify it. "Please, milord, not tonight."

"No riddles," Napolean agreed. "Only truth."

Saber waited, not entirely sure if he was ready to hear this new *truth*.

"If you're asking, are you going to be restrained, taken back to the cell? Then the answer is no. So, I guess, in that sense, you are free," Napolean said. "But no one is going to hold your hand, or try and lead you back to the light, either."

Saber squared his shoulders, facing the powerful monarch directly. "You trust me? To move freely through Dark Moon Vale?"

Napolean chuckled then, the sound utterly absent of humor. "Trust you? No. I don't think you even trust yourself at this juncture." He brushed a seeking mosquito off his arm. "But the thing is: I don't have to trust you, Saber. I took your blood. I can feel you, sense you, no matter where you are. And unlike any other vampire walking this earth, I possess a unique ability."

When the king did not elaborate on the statement, Saber decided to just bite the bullet and ask: "And that is?"

"I can kill from a distance."

Despite himself, Saber shuddered. Although his curious mind wanted to inquire *how*, he thought better of it and simply nodded instead. "So if I mess up, I'll just, what? Drop dead?"

"Pretty much," Napolean said, his tone betraying no humor. "Only it won't be quite that pleasant."

Saber chose to ignore the last half of that statement. "And by mess up, that means—"

"That means if you take the life of an innocent while feeding. If you threaten, or in any way harm, any member of the house of Jadon or the surrounding human population. If you commit any act of treason by consorting with the enemy, the house of Jaegar."

"So, I can't contact my only remaining brother, Diablo?"

"To what end?" Napolean asked. Before Saber could reply, he added, "Again, vampire; it's as I said—I can feel you. I will know your motivations. So I suggest you proceed with caution."

"And Vanya? My son?" Saber asked, not really wanting to hear the answer.

Napolean sighed deeply then. "I'm not your father, Saber. I'm not your conscience or your god. I can't tell you how to go forward with regard to the personal matters of your life; and contrary to what you might believe, I don't police the sons of Jadon. They aren't perfect. They make choices; they make mistakes. And I let them. But in terms of the princess, I will say this: She has asked you to respect her will, her choice, and she has agreed to let you live your life, such as it may be. You will...honor her...as the priceless gift to the house of Jadon that she is. To me, that means *respect*. The how of it? That's beyond my reach or my responsibility. You're a grown male."

Saber stared deep into the king's eyes, searching for signs of what, he didn't know, just wanting to somehow categorize this enigmatic vampire into a neat box that he could deal with: friend, enemy, oppressor...opportunity? The world was so mystifying now. So hard to understand and predict.

To navigate.

"All right," Saber finally replied, not knowing what else there was to say. "I guess we'll see what happens then." With that, he took a deep breath, turned on his heel, and began to stroll out into the endless night.

"Saber," the king called after him.

Saber took a deep breath and slowly turned around. "Yeah?"

"Here." The king tossed two small leather objects in Saber's direction, and catching them both easily, Saber glanced down to survey the articles. The first was a beige leather wallet. Opening it, he thumbed through a host of crisp one-hundred-dollar bills, the sum appearing at first glance to be about two thousand dollars. Beneath the bills, tucked into the stiff, horizontal pouches, were two remaining items: a driver's license and a business card, the latter bearing information about the Dark Moon Vale Bank.

"The cash should be enough to get you started," Napolean explained. "As for the license, I assume you can drive?"

Saber smirked. "Yeah, I can drive." He smiled despite himself then. "But I didn't think you guys would be into the fake ID business."

Napolean waved his hand in frank dismissal, if not slight derision. "Human customs grow tedious, but we do live among them. So yes, we do what we must to remain concealed and placate the locals. As for the bank," he added, "it's a similar front. It's owned, at least on paper, by one of our loyal human families. They know who we are...and what we are...and they would never betray us. Once you are on your feet, anything you need may be taken care of there: credit cards, various accounts, whatever you feel like you need."

Saber rubbed his brow with his thumb and forefinger. He had no idea what this meant—was he expected to get a *human* job? To take out a loan when the cash was gone? It made no difference: In eight hundred years, Saber had mastered more trades and skills than he could count. If all else failed, he could always create gemstones by harnessing his emotions and infusing them into the local rocks. A handful of diamonds produced a lot of human cash. "Cool," Saber replied casually, "and this?" He held up the small leather pouch, bound at the tip with what appeared to be a very old, if not ancient, leather strap.

Napolean took an intimidating step forward then, his long, black-and-silver hair swaying in what was almost an otherworldly radiance behind him. Without aplomb, he placed both hands on Saber's biceps, each one, just below the vampire's shoulders. "If you had remained in the house of Jadon, your father would have brought you before me for your naming ceremony. At that time, I would have accepted your name before the gods, acknowledged Serpens as your deity, recorded your ties in the annals of our people, and welcomed you into the house of Jadon. I would have also taken your blood in a more—how shall I say?—ceremonial fashion than the way it was done in that cell. However, none of that had a chance to occur; and I make no false assumptions that you have any desire to take your once-rightful place among us now." He sighed regretfully. "Or that you actually *have* a *rightful* place among us now. Much of that remains to be seen. However, I would have also given that pouch to your father in private, and upon turning twenty-one years old, graduating from the local academy, your father would have given it back to you at your formal induction ceremony. That opportunity is seven hundred and eighty years overdue."

Saber looked down at the age-worn pouch, not at all sure that he wanted to view its contents. "What's in it?"

Napolean's eyes narrowed, and his jaw turned paradoxically soft yet stern at the same time. "It contains the signet ring bearing the crest of the house of Jadon on it, the one our males wear on the fourth finger of their right hands."

Saber practically recoiled.

He took an involuntary step back as if the king had suddenly burned him, and simply glared at the being in front of him. He opened his mouth to protest, then just as quickly closed it, at a complete loss for words. "*Why...*" he finally uttered.

Napolean appeared undaunted, as if he had expected the reaction. "Because it is—or at least it once was—your birthright." He held up his hand to halt any further protest. "But don't get it twisted, son; it isn't a gift. When our males slip the Crest Ring on their fingers, they also kneel before the whole of the house of Jadon; they slice their left wrist in a symbolic gesture, offering their blood as a sacrifice to the people; and they pledge their loyalty, protection, and service to not only their Sovereign but to our continued existence as a species. It a great honor, but an even larger responsibility."

Saber didn't know what to say. He felt the right corner of his lip turn up in his signature scowl, but he couldn't contain it. *Was the king kidding?*

"I didn't give you that pouch, that ring, so you could casually slip it on your finger when or if it suits you." His set his jaw in a stern line. "I gave it to you to carry around, to feel the weight of it both literally and figuratively. To know that it is there, at least in potential, should you one day choose to be more than you are today."

Saber thought about the sacred customs of the house of Jaegar, the house he had grown up in, the formal induction ceremony where the males ultimately pledged their undying hearts—first, last, and only—to the house of their rebirth, to the royal Prince Jaegar, to all his descendants, and to the dark lords who granted them life. Saber had made that pledge a very long time ago, and he felt like he was going to be sick. His head was spinning. The ground was shifting subtly beneath him, making him dizzy. It was all too much to take in, to even comprehend, let alone consider.

Not sure whether he should toss the pouch to the ground and risk the king's wrath or offer some poignant words of recognition, he slipped the pouch into his jeans' front pocket, instead, not bothering to even look at it.

At least not then.

Napolean nodded, and then he stretched out his right hand, indicating the wooded expanse before them, as if he were Moses himself signifying the Red Sea. "Your future awaits you, Saber. You may choose to live or die as you will. And as long as you keep our laws, I will not interfere by making that choice for you." He bowed his head in silent reflection then. "I hope you find peace."

Saber looked off into the endless distance, at the rocky crevices and looming mountain peaks of the Dark Moon Forest, the endless groupings of junipers and pines, standing in utter indifference as they dotted the landscape. He glanced toward the rising hills and hidden caverns that were well beyond his sight: So, this was it then.

His future.

Bowing his head in a gesture of retreat more than respect, he slipped away into the night.

twenty-one

Six weeks later

Vanya Demir pushed the sleek, ultra-modern stroller under the shade of a narrow-leaf cottonwood tree, applied the foot brake, and closed the sun shade to provide the infant with some protection from the ever-seeking rays of the sun. "Now stay put," she whispered lovingly to the cooing, wriggling child lying inside the mesh cradle.

"And just where do you think he might go?" Ciopori asked, laughing. She set her own seven-month-old son down on a large, quilted blanket beneath the shade of the same tree, laid out a bright assortment of toys for him to play with, and peered inside the stroller. "My gosh, he is a handsome somebody, is he not?"

Vanya smiled proudly. "Handsome and very alert already. I think he wants to see the entire world in a day."

Ciopori positively beamed. She bent over and placed a gushing kiss on her nephew's forehead, then found a place on the blanket where she stretched out her legs and kicked off her sandals. "Warm weather for April," she commented, sighing.

"It is," Vanya agreed. "We were lucky to be gifted with such a beautiful day to spend outside."

"Indeed," Ciopori said. "It's rare this early in spring."

Finding her own place on the blanket beside Ciopori, Vanya threw back her head and stared at the glorious blue sky, soaking up the luxurious rays of the Colorado sunshine. "Ahh," she exhaled, "heavenly." Without realizing she was doing it, she scanned her surroundings, surveying the landscape to the left and then the right, peering beyond a thick, nearby grove of fir trees, casting an eye over the peaks of neighboring hilltops, and checking beside each adjacent boulder, before settling into a more comfortable position.

Ciopori was perceptive as always. "What are you looking for, sister?"

"Hmm?" Vanya asked.

"You check your surroundings so diligently. Are you still afraid you might run into...a certain male vampire?"

Vanya frowned. She tucked an errant lock of hair, one that had somehow come loose from her thick, uniform braid, behind her ear and shrugged. "Oh, I don't know." She groaned. "I swear, sometimes I feel like he's watching me, like he's lurking beyond every bush and tree, just waiting to pounce. I don't know. I must be paranoid."

"So, you have heard nothing at all from him then?"

"Nothing," Vanya said insistently. "He has honored my request so far...faithfully."

"That's good," Ciopori said. When Vanya didn't respond immediately, her voice rose in question. "That *is* good, right, sister?"

Vanya gave Ciopori a sideways glance. "Of course. *Of course.* I'm just a little surprised, that's all."

Just then, Nikolai reached beyond the outer edge of the blanket, scooped up a large pine cone along with a fistful of dirt, and was just about to stuff it in his mouth when Ciopori snatched it away and tossed it aside. "No, Niko. We do not eat pine cones. Or dirt." She brushed off his hands and handed him an intricate, brightly colored block-puzzle instead, and the child immediately set about the task of putting the pieces together. "Well, I for one am relieved. Like you, I didn't expect him to honor your request, but I must say that I'm grateful he has." She leaned forward and tapped on the broad trunk of the nearest tree. "Knock on wood."

Vanya nodded. "Yes, knock on wood." She saw a large black ant crawling on the blanket, making its way swiftly toward Nikolai, and she gently flicked it away. "You know..." She spoke in a whisper, not at all certain why she felt the need to lower her voice. "I hear he's living in a cave...like an animal."

Ciopori frowned. "You *hear*? From whom?"

Vanya shrugged. "Nachari may have mentioned something, once or twice, maybe Ramsey."

Ciopori shook her head in dismay, her long raven hair swaying from the motion. "Honestly, I wish they would just keep these things to themselves. You don't need to hear about…that vampire." She breathed a heavy sigh. "You know what I'll do? I'll speak to Marquis about it. I'm sure, after a word from him, they will stop telling you—"

"No," Vanya interrupted in a rush. "That's not necessary."

"Excuse me?"

"It's truly not necessary, sister. I mean, they don't bring me information that often, and in reality it's…well, they only tell me when I ask."

Ciopori looked away. "Oh…"

Vanya raised her eyebrows. "What is that supposed to mean?"

"What?"

"Oh."

Ciopori frowned defensively. "I don't know, just *oh*. Oh, I didn't realize you still inquired about him, that's all."

Vanya spun around to face her sister. "Well, of course I inquire!" Catching the rising ire in her voice, she sought to soften her tone. "I mean, not about Saber, but about…his whereabouts and such. I…I don't want to be caught off guard by him again. That's all. It certainly isn't as if I care. About him." She huffed with annoyance. "Most certainly not."

Ciopori sat forward, cocked her head to the side, and stared at her younger sister like she had pie on her face.

"What are you looking at?" Vanya asked.

Ciopori's nose twitched almost imperceptibly. "I'm not sure. You tell me."

Vanya rolled her eyes playfully, or at least she hoped it appeared playful. "Tell you what, sister?"

"Tell me what you're thinking, *really thinking*, about Saber."

"I'm not *really thinking* anything." She glanced at the stroller and listened for any sign that Lucien was growing fitful. Satisfied that he was still resting peacefully, perhaps staring at his mobile, perhaps even falling asleep, she said, "Perchance I'm just thinking that it's going to be quite a challenge to raise this little one properly on my own; you know, without a male influence. Or a father."

Cioporri scrunched up her regal face. "You have Marquis, Nathaniel, Nachari, *and* Kagen. Heck, you have Napolean if you want his assistance...plus Ramsey, Santos, Saxson, and Julien...not to mention Rafael, his—"

"Dear lords," Vanya interrupted. "Please tell me you do not intend to name every male in the house of Jadon."

"I will if I must," Cioporri countered.

Vanya rolled her eyes blatantly then. "I know, sister. I do. I just meant that the whole situation is so...unusual. Unprecedented."

"Agreed." Cioporri patted Vanya's hand to reassure her. "But you will get through it. You will."

Vanya nodded. "Of course, I will." She looked off into the distance. "It's just surprising that Saber hasn't...tried at all...don't you think?"

Cioporri sat upright then. "Are you hoping that he will?"

"No!" Vanya waved her hand in emphasis. "*No.* I meant what I said, and that was my final word. Besides, who would want a fire-breathing dragon for a mate? Saber? Alexiares? The king of mean?" She shuddered. "He's terrifying. *Awful*, really. Dear goddess of light, what that monster put me through..."

"Precisely," Cioporri echoed.

"Yet..."

"Yet?"

"*Yet* things are not always so neatly black and white...in the universe, I mean."

Cioporri held her tongue, but the expression on her face said it all: *What are you talking about? And what part of this is gray?*

Vanya searched for the right words. "I'm just pointing out that there are, there *were*, oddities, that's all."

"What sort of oddities?" Cioporri said, giving Vanya her full, undivided attention.

Vanya stared at the complex patterns in the quilt and absently traced the lines of one particularly beautiful design with her forefinger. "Well, it was more than just a little odd, the way he had such a complete meltdown that morning in Kagen's clinic, during the conversion." Her voice became thoughtful. "Quite odd, indeed."

Ciopori shook her head, not exactly in dismissal, but not in agreement either. "You mean the morning following that horrific, *agonizing* night of your conversion? A conversion he was forced to attempt, I might add, only because he had previously gotten you pregnant against your will?" Despite her best attempt at diplomacy, she fumed. "Do you mean the morning he almost killed you, broke several of your ribs, and caused everyone who loves you to suffer unspeakably, believing you were as good as dead? Is that the oddity you speak of?"

Vanya bristled. "Well, technically, Saber didn't actually break my ribs. The babies—"

"Panicked in reaction to their own pain and suffering! Tried to escape an unholy infusion of venom they were never prepared to withstand to begin with, and nearly clawed their way out of your body in a desperate attempt to escape. And yes, Saber was the cause of it all."

"Of course he was," Vanya said in frustration. "I just meant that it was strange, odd, the way he fell apart, the way he called on Serpens, as opposed to the deity's dark twin, to save us. The way he offered to trade his life for ours…without hesitation." She sat up straight then. "For a male who has never given a second thought to anyone's well-being other than his own, it was quite an unexpected leap…don't you think?"

"You were carrying his son," Ciopori offered.

"Of course," Vanya bit back. "And I was, what? Nothing more than a receptacle to house his offspring?"

Ciopori bit her bottom lip. "You said it—I didn't."

Vanya sighed. She needed to find a way to steer the conversation back to something light before it became any more contentious. "By the way,"—she smiled halfheartedly, trying to force some humor into her voice—"did I ever mention that Napolean's fangs are positively brutal?" She rolled her eyes for effect. "Honestly, for a male who was trying to protect me, euthanize me, if one must be frank and speak the word, in a dire moment of desperation...*Great Cygnus*, I would rather take the broken ribs and agony, thank you."

"Do not try to make light of this, Vanya," Ciopori said, incredulous. "I'm sorry, but there isn't a humorous thing about it."

"Fine," Vanya replied. What else could she say?

Ciopori shook her head and tried to gather her own wits about her. "It is true: Saber's reaction, calling on Serpens the way that he did, was so..." She paused, as if searching for the right word.

"Raw? Vulnerable? Astonishing?" Vanya supplied. "Especially for a Dark One."

Ciopori nodded. "I believe he had a rare, unadulterated moment. And thank the gods he did. But it certainly doesn't make him a saint or erase all of the unforgivable, destructive moments that came before."

Vanya threw her hands up in exasperation then. "Why are you being so preachy and condescending, sister?" She squared her jaw and narrowed her eyes. "Do you think I'm truly unaware of this? That I, of all people, cannot enumerate Saber's infinite faults and shortcomings in brutal detail? For heaven's sake, I'm not defending the male. I'm simply saying that life is not that simple: *Souls* are not that simple. You asked me what I meant, and I was trying to answer you."

Nikolai squirmed in distress, and his unique amber eyes, with their deep centers of blue, began to cloud with tears. "Shh, vampire," Ciopori whispered, gently rubbing his back. "It's okay." She lowered her voice then. "Perhaps I'm overreacting because I think there might be something else going on here."

Vanya reached for Nikolai's favorite stuffed tiger and wiggled it up and down in front of him until he finally reached

Tessa Dawn

out to take it. "Like what?"

Ciopori looked positively afflicted. "Like ... perhaps ... *feelings*."

Vanya shook her head adamantly. "Rest assured, Ciopori, I feel nothing for the spawn of the underworld. While I may have seen sides of him you have not—the loyalty he felt for his family, the skills he has honed as a soldier and a vampire, even the sharp intelligence that is overshadowed by all that duplicity and rage—I also know him to be reckless, bitter, *broken*, and utterly unreachable. Believe me, I know who *and what* he is."

Ciopori sat back, seemingly satisfied, and Vanya let the subject rest.

For a moment.

"You must admit, however, he is sexier than Adonis when he wants to be," she whispered distractedly. She had no idea where the words had come from, or why they kept coming. "His eyes...his mouth...all that wild hair. Even his attitude has an air of carnal mystery about it."

Ciopori looked positively stricken. "Carnal mystery?"

"Yes, sister, *carnal mystery*."

"I guess," Ciopori said, clearly aghast. "I suppose if a female looked hard enough, she might find him appealing in some global terrorist, serial-killer kind of way—sexy until the pick-axe comes out."

Vanya grew intensely quiet then. She nodded in agreement, forced an insincere smile, and looked back up at the sky. When her eyes drifted shut, her smile gave way to a frown, and her lips began to quiver, ever so slightly. Ciopori froze.

"*Oh, gods...*" Ciopori whispered. She shifted onto her knees, shuffled over to Vanya, and wrapped her elegant arms around her shoulders. "Oh Vanya," she crooned. "Forgive me."

"For what?" Vanya said, trying to keep her voice steady.

Ciopori strengthened her embrace. "For being so stupid. So single-minded." She bowed her head and rested her chin in a soft patch of Vanya's hair. "You are his *destiny*, aren't you? Chosen by the gods. Of course there are feelings."

Vanya swallowed a lump in her throat, but she didn't reply.

"How long have you been hiding this?"

Vanya didn't answer.

"Are you hurting...deeply?"

Vanya blinked rapidly, holding back a reservoir of approaching tears. "Not so badly," she murmured.

"And you've had no one to talk to—because we all despise him so intensely?"

Vanya tried to shrug it off. "That's okay."

"No," Ciopori argued. "It isn't. It truly isn't. I feel like a complete...*ass*."

"Mm...maybe just a little bit," Vanya said.

Ciopori chuckled softly, but the compassion in her voice betrayed her regret. "Tell me," she coaxed. "Your thoughts."

Vanya dropped her head into her hands and simply shook her head. "He's living in a cave," she whispered. "Just like in my dream." She raised her eyes in order to meet Ciopori's searching gaze. "Napolean gave him money, but we all know he hates the sun, more than most of us can fathom. And I imagine growing up in the colony, underground in a lair, there's probably some strange comfort in burrowing deep into a mountain..." Her voice trailed off. What was the use? *Gods be merciful; he was living in a cave.*

Ciopori stroked Vanya's hair softly. "I know, sweetie. And I'm so sorry."

Vanya nodded absently. "Sometimes I think my cell is going to ring, or there's going to be a knock on the door, and it's going to be Napolean calling to tell me that it's finally over. That Saber gave into some dark impulse or another, perhaps he killed a human or lashed out at someone in the house of Jadon, and the king has finally...put him down." She cringed. "And the worst part is: I would almost be relieved, thankful to hear it, because waiting for it, never knowing when it's going to come, is torture." She stirred restlessly then. "During the conversion, in the very beginning, he was chanting, almost singing to me in Romanian, which was so *intimate* and powerful. Surprisingly gentle. It was so beautiful, Ciopori. And how could something so beautiful come from someone so dark?"

Ciopori exhaled slowly. "Can you tell me what he said?"

Vanya smiled. "He said, 'Fi linistita, Micuta. Vino departe cu mine. Asculta vocea mea. Pluteste...pluteste...departe. Totul este bine, *totul este bine*, totul va fi facut sa fie bine.'"

Ciopori drew back. "Be still, little one. Come away with me. Listen to my voice. Float...float...away. All is well, *all is well*, all will be made well."

"Yes," Vanya said. "He knew I was in a place so *elemental* that I couldn't hear in English. He just instinctively knew that I needed to hear him speak in my native tongue." She paused briefly. "And it wasn't the first time—he did it once before."

Ciopori placed a soft kiss on the crown of Vanya's head. "I see." When Nikolai set his stuffed tiger aside, crawled into Vanya's lap, and reached up to give his aunt a big, slobbery kiss of his own, both females chuckled.

"Thank you, Niko," Vanya said. She scooped the child into her arms, in order to hold him close, and then she paused to select her next words carefully. "He never had a chance, you know. Saber, I mean. And I don't mean from us, the house of Jadon, I mean in life, from the day he was born. Ultimately, he's still responsible for every choice he's made—every soul alive is—but still..."

"Still?"

"It's just so unfair."

"On that point, we truly agree, sister," Ciopori said.

Vanya stiffened. "And gods forgive me for saying it—because I know Saber never would—but wherever Damien Alexiares is, I hope he is suffering. *Immensely*."

Ciopori smiled. "Me, too."

Vanya pressed the heels of her hands against her eyes, struggling to contain her emotions; she refused to shed unwanted tears over the likes of Saber Alexiares, *destiny* or not. "Nachari says he hasn't fed—not in weeks—maybe not since the night of my conversion when Napolean gave him blood to help him...so he could help me. It's been six weeks."

Ciopori squeezed her shoulder. "He won't starve, sister. He's a survivor. He'll feed eventually."

"Without killing his prey?" Vanya said.

Ciopori wisely avoided the question. "Your heart isn't just hurting, is it?" she asked. "It's breaking."

Vanya shook her head slowly then. "No, I have Lucien, our son, and a bright future ahead." She cleared her throat and steadied her resolve. "Once Lucien is old enough to travel, probably around three months, we'll return to Romania. It should be easier then, with some distance. It's not like I want to undo anything, change it. Saber is who he is. And honestly, I don't think he can change, not even if he wanted to. It's just...difficult. That's all." She took a deep breath and held it in a few seconds longer than was natural. "And as for my heart? It is...painful...at times—sometimes it actually feels as if it's bleeding—but it's also healing. Truly." She handed Nikolai to his mother, stood up, and made her way to the stroller, where she lifted her own newborn son out of the cradle and held him to her heart, needing to feel the sweet warmth and promise of her future. "We are survivors, too, you know."

Ciopori balanced Nikolai on her hip, rose to her feet, and nodded with compassion. "I know, sister. I know. So let us pray then that your healing is swift and complete."

Saber dusted a scattering of sandy earth off his jeans and wiped his brow. With a lack of anything better to do, he had spent the last six weeks pouring his energy into mindless work: excavating a large, hidden cave he had discovered at the outskirts of the Red Canyons and renovating the inside to reflect a modern, architectural wonder. He had called upon many of the skills he had learned over the long centuries of his life: basic carpentry as well as artistic woodworking; the ability to sculpt clay and stone in his powerful hands; his innate understanding of color, contrast, and harmony in order to paint, tile, and mold each crevice, each rocky ledge, into an original work of art, even as each remained a naturally occurring phenomenon. He chewed on his bottom lip as he stepped back to survey the entrance to his dwelling.

He had carved a sophisticated arch into the apex of the opening, supporting it with two large wooden beams, shaped roughly like Roman pillars, only far more rustic and reflective of the native landscape and surroundings. He studied the carved images of an eagle, a mountain lion, and a bear he had whittled into the wood by torchlight, searching for minor imperfections, unfinished slopes, and angles that were not yet perfected, before he set about the task of staining the individual totems in the likeness of their woodland counterparts.

The whole thing was ludicrous, really. What difference did it make if he hunkered down in a cavern fit for a king, or a muddy hole in the ground, like a rodent? Either way, his life had no meaning anymore. It was tedious, monotonous, and without purpose. And trying to stay three steps ahead of this reality with grueling, mind-numbing work didn't quite cut it. His impulses nagged at him constantly. He wanted to fight, to hunt, to *kill* something, anything, just to feel alive again. He wanted to break the laws and provoke Napolean's wrath.

He wanted to see his son—at least to know his name.

He wanted to scream and shout and unleash his rage on the whole unsuspecting valley, prove once and for all that he was a demon, a vampire, a soul drowning in the abyss of his existence.

But he could hardly stand upright without swaying.

Saber Alexiares was hungry. Starving, really.

He was dying.

And that suited him just fine.

He reached into the leather belt firmly attached to his hips and withdrew a chisel in order to work on the eagle's beak, and then he stumbled sideways and had to catch himself on a nearby pillar. "Son of a jackal!" he swore, feeling his head swim beneath the dizziness, his vision go blurry before him.

He slowly slumped to the ground and rested his arms on his knees, waiting for the vertigo to pass. He let his head fall back until it rested against the stone behind him, and stared up at the sky. At least the night was littered with lots of stars, and the moon was bright, offering him plenty of natural light. It was ridiculous that, even after all this time, he still had to wait to work after dusk—that he still preferred to avoid the sun. "I can't do this anymore," he mumbled angrily. "*I have to feed.*" But where could he go? He doubted he even possessed the strength to exert mind-control over a human, and the blood of an animal would never sustain him. Not hardly.

So, where did that leave him?

In order to drink his fill, Saber would have to hunt like an animal. Stalk, attack, and devour his prey. And then Napolean would kill him.

But if he didn't hunt, he would die of starvation anyway: Either way, he was truly and summarily screwed.

As his vision grew even dimmer, he felt his heart begin to slow, to beat at a pitiful, lethargic pace, and for a moment, he almost welcomed what was coming next.

Death.

Final, inevitable, and longed for.

And then his survival instincts took over: *Diablo...*

He sent the telepathic communication out into the cosmos on a private, familiar bandwidth, not caring if Napolean intercepted it before it had a chance to be heard. If there was one being on the face of the planet who would still welcome his communication, feed him if he could, and if not, soften the blow of his final moments on earth, it was his last remaining brother. *Diablo!* He made the plea more insistent. *Can you still hear me?*

Brother? The answering reply swept swiftly into his mind. *Where are you?*

Saber sighed with relief. *Just on the edge of the Red Canyons, on the southwestern corner of the gorge, before the valley merges into the thick of the forest.*

Tessa Dawn

And you're alone? Diablo sounded incredulous.

Yes, they set me free.

When! Diablo demanded.

I don't know, Saber mumbled, feeling his life-force wane even further. *Weeks ago.*

And you're just now calling me?

Diablo, Saber whispered. *I'm dying.*

The connection became silent for what seemed like an eternity. *How?*

I need to feed.

What the hell are you doing, Saber! What the hell has happened to you? As always, Diablo led with anger first. *Come to the colony—now!*

Can't, Saber said. His heart stopped for a series of two beats before beginning again, and his stomach began to turn over in growing waves of nausea. When he didn't get a reply, he began to get concerned.

Diablo?

Still nothing.

Diablo!

Be quiet! Diablo demanded. *I'm trying to listen...to hone in...to track the vibration of your blood.*

Hurry, Saber said. *I don't have a whole lot of time...or a whole lot of blood left to track.*

Shh, Diablo repeated.

Then just like that, the air began to shift into subtle colors in front of him. At first, Saber wasn't sure if he was seeing a mirage, if his vision wasn't, at last, fading into blindness; but soon enough, the outline of a tall, muscular male with deep, piercing eyes and red-and-black banded hair began to take form in front of him.

Saber's mouth turned up in a half sneer, half smile as his brother fully emerged at the cave's entrance. "Diablo."

Diablo smiled in return. "What's up, son of Jadon."

At first, Saber didn't catch the slur. Everything was still so hazy. But when Diablo took a swift step forward, wielding a

261

deadly, sharpened scythe in his left hand, Saber was sentient enough to understand that the weapon had no place in feeding. To his own surprise, he didn't react. After all, wasn't that just the proverbial cherry on top of the never-ending, jacked-up Sunday he had been scarfing down ever since the day of his intended execution? So Diablo wasn't there to feed him—he was there to kill him.

"*Damn*," Saber swore, pressing his palm against his stomach, trying to quell his nausea at least long enough to talk some shit before he died. "So it's like that?"

"Yeah," Diablo snarled. "It's just like that." He bared his fangs and began to walk in slow, predatory circles around Saber. "My twin is gone. My brother lives with the enemy. And my father was executed for treason, all because he cared more about some illegitimate, privileged son of Jadon than he did his own kind."

Saber shook his head, trying to clear his vision. He wanted to see Diablo's eyes. "I never turned on you, Diablo. I never committed any treason."

Diablo squatted down in front of Saber and brandished the scythe, turning it over, then swiftly back and forth, in his iron fist, before pressing the blade taut against Saber's neck. "You're one of them," he whispered, his voice completely absent of affection or compassion, almost as if it had never existed in the first place. "*You're one of them, Saber.*"

Saber held up both hands in a gesture of surrender, and forced his head to nod toward the cave. "Yeah, as you can see, the whole house of Jadon is out here with me. I'm definitely in the inner circle."

With a lightning-quick flick of the wrist, Diablo nicked Saber's artery, stained the scythe with his brother's blood, and brought it up to his wicked lips to taste it. As his tongue swept over the blade, he growled. "Tastes like the blood of a traitor to me."

Saber drew in a deep breath, and then he ran his fingers through his hair. His eyes were stinging—and not from hunger and disorientation—but from pain.

And betrayal.

As much as he told himself it didn't matter—what else could possibly happen?—he could no longer maintain that nothing other than an organ beat in his chest.

Because this hurt.

It hurt somewhere he didn't even know he had.

Diablo took a step back and laughed. "Damn, you really are one of them, aren't you?"

Saber struggled to shift his weight onto his knees, first the right, and then the left. "You know," he bit out beneath the grueling effort, "until this very moment, I would have argued that point with my dying breath." He laughed then, not knowing where he found the energy for sarcasm. "No pun intended." He steadied both hands against the ground to keep from toppling over. "Because until now, I never understood all this talk about souls, how some vampires have them, why others don't, what difference it makes anyway." In an act of total submission, he bowed his head as a sacrificial offering. "But now...now I think I get it."

Diablo regarded him suspiciously, raising the scythe in both a defensive as well as threatening motion. "And what the hell is that supposed to mean?"

"It means," Saber said forlornly, "that the only reason I'm not going to draw on every ounce of strength I have left in order to come off this ground and take you into the afterlife with me is because I have a soul." He paused to consider the utter absurdity of it all. "And the reason you're going to wield that scythe like the monster you are—and take my life without consideration—is because you don't. You were my brother," he whispered in resignation. "But I was never yours."

Diablo stood like a granite statue: cold, hard, and unfeeling. "I feel sorry for you, *brother.* Maybe the next life will be better to you than this one." With that, he raised the scythe above his head and brought it down in one clean motion.

Saber shut his eyes, waiting for the final blow.

Waiting to feel the cold bite of the iron blade that would slice his throat and end his life.

Waiting for the immediate numbness that would follow.

Diablo was a wizard with a scythe. The execution would be swift, clean, and instant. Absent of suffering.

When nothing happened—the momentary pain never came—he blinked in surprise and opened his eyes, half wondering if Diablo hadn't experienced a change of heart after all.

The look on Diablo's face said something altogether different: There was shock, horror, even agony, but not second-guessing or some newfound loyalty.

Ramsey Olaru rotated a thin pine needle between his teeth before spitting it out on the ground. He held up a still-beating heart; juggled it up and down, perversely, with his right hand, before tossing it aside; and took a judicious step back, in order to avoid the falling body of the slain vampire. Of Diablo Alexiares. "Not today, Dark One," he growled, sounding almost nonchalant. "Not on my watch." He turned to regard Saber. "Look, I get the whole loyalty, I-can't-kill-my-own-brother thing. Fortunately, I don't have that problem."

Saber just stared at him in stunned silence.

"Turn around," Ramsey ordered next.

"What?" Saber asked, still in shock.

"Look," Ramsey said. "I'm trying to be delicate here, since you obviously had some kind of connection with this...trash." He kicked the heap of bloody garbage at his feet. "Turn around, so I can incinerate the body." Before Saber could reply—or protest—Ramsey shrugged. "All right, have it your way." With that, he narrowed his devilish, hazel eyes; leveled his gaze at Diablo's scalp, all the while building an intense heat with his glare, until two fiery red beams of light shot out of the focused orbs; and in a manner of seconds, set the Dark One's scalp ablaze. The unearthly beams of light turned from red to blue as Ramsey focused them up and down the torso next, drawing on ever more intense heat, until the entire body began to smolder, burn, and turn to ash. When he took something out of his pants—an appendage Saber was never meant to see—and began to focus an ice-cold stream on the blaze in order to extinguish the fire, Saber's jaw literally dropped open. "You really are one gnarly son of a bitch, Ramsey," he said.

Ramsey shrugged, tucked himself back inside his pants, and snickered. "You're not exactly smooth around the edges yourself, Chief."

Saber was just about to make a smart-ass comment, something along the lines of *maybe my upbringing had something to do with it*, when, all at once, he noticed the outlines of two rage-filled soldiers shimmering into view behind Ramsey Olaru: It was Blaise Liska and Achilles Zahora, two of the strongest fighters in the house of Jaegar. "Ramsey!" Saber shouted in warning. "Behind you!"

Ramsey spun around like an overgrown ninja, nimble, quick, and deadly, dropping instantly into a defensive fighting stance. "Well, look what we have here. The hyenas have come to Pride Rock to play with the lions."

Saber tried to leap to his feet but stumbled over sideways instead. "Call for back-up," he panted, quickly realizing that he didn't even know the common bandwidth for the warriors in the house of Jadon. And by all the jackals of the underworld, he knew he wouldn't be any help to the sentinel in his current condition, not even if he wanted to be.

"Just drink this and stay out of the way until you can stand on your own two feet," Nachari Silivasi said.

And just where had he come from?

Nachari dropped several fresh vials of blood at Saber's feet and nodded at the contents. "It's Marquis's."

"*Blood?*" Saber asked, stunned by the admission. It really

didn't matter at the moment, although he found it impossible to believe Marquis would have offered his blood to help Saber. Just the same, he popped the red tops with amazing speed and began to guzzle the contents, even as Nachari spun around to take his place at Ramsey's side.

The Master Wizard drew a polished, ancient sword from a time-worn scabbard at his side and tested the weight in his right hand, deftly.

"A sword?" Saber asked, incredulous. *"For a wizard?"*

Nachari smiled broadly, his absolute arrogance shining like the noonday son. "Yeah," he answered, holding it up with pride. "Nice, huh? I got this from my father in like"—he eyed Ramsey sideways—"what year was that, Ramsey?"

Ramsey wrinkled his brow. "I think it was around fifteen twenty-six...or twenty-seven."

Achilles Zahora roared in defiance, the frightful giant clearly unaccustomed to being ignored.

"Damn," Nachari said, "need attention much?"

The angry soldier lunged at Nachari, but Nachari leapt adroitly into the air and summersaulted above his head. Landing behind the massive Dark One, he slashed at his vital organs with the sword.

Achilles caught the blade in the palm of his hand. He was just about to tighten his fist, try to crush the heavy steel, when Nachari drew it back, slicing deep into his palm. "I know you weren't trying to break a priceless relic," he snarled.

Achilles licked the blood from his palm, dripping venom in the wake of his tongue, and snarled as he eyed the instantly healed limb. Without hesitation, he sent ten streams of fire sizzling from his fingertips, all aimed at Nachari's heart.

The wizard caught them in his own palms and sent them right back, creating an even greater conflagration, with a much hotter flame.

As Achilles braced himself against the assault, tried to put the fire out, Blaise tossed a series of shuriken at Nachari's head, one deadly, razor-sharp blade after another, hurling the objects faster than they could be seen. Nachari used his hearing to detect each one, in turn, and his telekinesis to send them splintering into the nearest tree. "I'm afraid you'll have to do better than that," he taunted.

Achilles puffed up like a blowfish. He reached into his waistband and pulled out two ten-inch daggers, wielding each one in a circular motion, both hands working together in mortal synchronicity. And then, the whole scene shifted into overdrive.

Achilles lunged at the Master Wizard, slicing upward then down, across then back, in then out, in a fluid series of motions almost too proficient to combat. Just the same, Nachari anticipated each move with uncanny stealth and grace—he was obviously using some sort of sixth sense to react to the unpredictable attacks. He blocked, dipped, shifted, and countered like a partner in a lethal dance, two vampires performing a deadly tango on an earthen stage. All the while, Blaise and Ramsey went at it like two heavyweight fighters locked in a prized title ring: fist to fist, jab to uppercut, cross to hook.

Saber watched in morbid fascination, his eyes darting back and forth between the warring sets of vampires, trying to make sense of the attacks and counterattacks that appeared as only a series of blurs, even as he waited for his own body to rejuvenate, to give him just enough strength to join the fight.

And then he heard the *umpf.* The sound of blade piercing skin, or an organ being serrated, of Achilles finally making contact with his lethal dagger. Nachari sucked in wind and coughed, his body reacting to the pure physics of the blow. He reached down to grab the hilt of the blade, to prevent Achilles from twisting it further, from plunging it deeper.

And then he simply *shape shifted.*

Out of the body of a man and into the body of a panther.

The giant cat came up screaming, howling, and grunting—whatever it was that panthers did when they were *really* ticked off, Nachari Silivasi was doing it. The dagger broke loose from the vital organ as the cat twisted, turned, and flexed its incredibly nubile body in more dexterous ways than it could have ever been meant to go. Roaring in fury and pain, the cat leapt from its haunches; flew through the air, its open jaw exposing a vicious set of teeth; and latched onto Achilles's throat. Nachari tore at the esophagus with a fury, whipping his enormous head back and forth to the side, ripping out skin and cartilage and tissue as he vented his wrath.

Saber was so captivated by the magical movements of the cat that he almost missed what was happening with Ramsey: The tough-as-nails sentinel had just struck a wicked blow with his elbow, connecting squarely with Blaise's throat, and he had followed through with the heel of his hand, a hard thrust right against the soldier's nose, shoving the bones back into his brain. Blaise had fallen instantly to the ground and was grappling to find his equilibrium, struggling to put the bones back in place before Ramsey finished him off. As Blaise groveled on the ground, Ramsey bent over to pick up Diablo's scythe—no doubt, he intended to remove Blaise's head and heart, end it before his enemy could recover and come at him again. But he never got the chance.

Blaise got to the scythe first, and in one swift, determined motion, he swiped at Ramsey's Achilles tendons, first the left, then the right, slicing clear through the meat to the bones, before Ramsey could move away. The warrior's legs twisted in an unnatural position, his massive body toppled backward, and he arched his back in an effort to get back up, to use something other than his feet to propel him.

As Blaise released his wings and rose from the ground, Ramsey was now a sitting duck. The dark soldier straddled Ramsey with unparalleled ease, and then, he drew the scythe upward and began to slash down, in hopes of removing his enemy's head in one final score.

Saber leapt from ten feet away.

He landed on the soldier's back and reached for the scythe; he tore into Blaise's throat with his canines and bit down until he felt the clavicle snap; and then he released his own lethal claws and punctured Blaise through the back, tunneling for all he was worth with one, and only one, objective: Get to the heart.

Saber was like a rabid animal.

All of his rage and helplessness and betrayal unleashed in one furious moment.

Blaise's heart felt like a golden conquest beneath his fingers, the rarest jewel he had ever held, and when he wrenched back to dislodge the organ, he yanked with so much fury that he took the lungs and liver with it.

And still it was not enough.

More was required.

He tossed the heart across the valley floor and dug into the soldier's neck with his claws until he felt the spine beneath his grasp, like a pliant switch within his hand. He tugged with the same lethal force, until the entire spinal cord was simply dangling in the palm of his hand, dislodged in one fierce tug, and yet he wanted more.

Snapping the cord like a pharaoh's lash, high in the air above him, he headed toward Nachari and Achilles—the male who had killed his father. He brought it back and slung it forward, catching the dying vampire in the forehead and, unfortunately, the wounded panther in the corner of one eye. The nubile cat leapt straight into the air and shifted directions in mid-leap, morphing instantly back into a vampire as he landed on his feet.

Nachari Silivasi rotated both arms in a circular motion, almost as if he were spinning his aura, and then he shoved both palms forward, outward, sending a mystical energy into Saber's chest. The glowing, supernatural force lit up Saber's body like a Christmas tree, and he immediately felt like he was burning from the inside out, exploding, about to be incinerated. When the wizard's eyes turned an eerie shade of orange, rather than the normal, vampiric red, Saber backpedaled wildly. He held up both hands and continued to retreat even as Nachari strolled lethally forward, his face ablaze with power and rage.

"Whoa!" Saber shouted. "*Whoa.*"

What the hell?

BLOOD REDEMPTION

He knew Nachari had it in for him, that he had always had it in for him—and he had every right, really, considering what Saber had done to Deanna—but what had all this been about? Surely Ramsey and Nachari had not fought so fiercely, at the risk of losing their own lives, just to savor the privilege of killing Saber themselves.

Or had they?

After all, Saber had reached out to Diablo, despite Napolean's earlier warning.

Saber was just about to lunge at Nachari, make whatever pitiful effort he could to save his own life, when the wizard's eyes flashed three times, *turning* from orange to amber; from amber to red; and finally, from red to deep forest green. The wizard stopped advancing. "Saber?" he said, almost absently.

Saber struggled to find words beneath the scorching heat that was still simmering in his body. *Damn, what was with these sons of Jadon and fire?* Didn't anybody fight with regular weapons anymore? He nodded the best he could. "Yeah."

Nachari rocked back on his heels. "Oh…*shit*. My bad. *My bad*…it was the hair."

"What?" Saber said, incredulous.

"The hair," Nachari repeated. He raised his right hand, like a kid in a kindergarten class who wanted nothing more than for the teacher to call on him next; drew two or three intricate designs in the air; and spoke a series of cryptic words in Latin. And just like that, the fire inside of Saber's body cooled, then disappeared. Nachari reached up, grabbed a lock of his own wavy hair, and held it out in a demonstrative gesture. "You really need to get that fixed, Saber. Try some Clairol or something. Maybe work with some henna. *Something*."

Saber sneered. He looked down at his body; patted his chest, arms, and thighs, just to be sure the metaphysical assault was really over; and snarled in defiance. "Yeah, or maybe you just better learn to get used to it."

Ramsey snorted in the distance then. "When you girls are done comparing beauty notes, could I possibly get some venom

270

over here?" He was lying on his back with his knees pulled up to his chest, holding his calves in his powerful arms, and his face was drawn tight with pain. "That son of a jackal cut my freakin' ankles."

Nachari sauntered over to Ramsey, squatted down, and began to apply copious amounts of venom to the backs of his heels. He glanced over his shoulder to regard the headless, heartless pile of spineless mush that was now Blaise Liska. "Looks good and dead though."

Ramsey nodded. "Yeah, I think your boy over there had a cathartic moment." He glanced across the meadow. "What about Achilles? Where is he?"

Nachari spun around as if he had almost forgotten the second dark soldier and frowned.

Achilles Zahora was gone—and just how was that possible, anyhow? The male had been one breath away from the spirit world when Saber lashed him with Blaise's spine. "Damn," Nachari whispered. "That's one tough SOB."

Saber made his way over to the two males, not exactly sure what to say or how to act. The whole afternoon had been so bizarre: first, his hunger getting the best of him; then, Diablo coming, not to feed him but to kill him; and last, the fight with the Dark Ones—the ones he used to call friends.

Family.

He kept a healthy distance from Nachari and Ramsey out of some peculiar sense of protocol…or, perhaps, respect. Sure, they had fought together like brothers, but that didn't make them friends. Not by a long shot.

When, at last, it looked like Ramsey's wounds were almost healed, and the ill-tempered sentinel could take it from there, Nachari turned around to eye Saber. "So, what was all this about, anyhow?"

"Excuse me?" Saber asked, all at once becoming defensive.

"This." He waved his hand around the valley floor, indicating the battle, the Dark Ones, and the whole grisly scene. "All this…because you refuse to *feed*?"

Saber shook his head. "That's none of your business, Nachari."

Nachari excreted some venom onto his own hand and placed it on the tear just above his pelvis, where Achilles had sliced his small intestines. Breathing a sigh of relief, he said, "I think you just made it my business."

Saber glared at him. "If you're waiting for me to say thank you, then fine. Thanks, all right? I am not—"

"*You*—are being an ass," Nachari offered matter-of-factly.

Saber flinched, but he didn't say anything.

"You wanna live out here in a cave? That's your business. But when you grow so weak that our enemies think they can confront one of us out in the open, this close to Dark Moon Vale? That's everybody's business."

"I let it go too far," Saber said by way of explanation—it was the only one Nachari Silivasi was going to get.

"Starvation?" Nachari asked.

Saber shrugged, refusing to say any more.

Nachari frowned. "Look, it might not be my place, but somebody's got to say something: You never killed before while feeding, so why do you think it's gonna happen now?"

Saber was momentarily stunned by the vampire's words. "What makes you assume I never—"

"Give me a break," Nachari said. "What am I?"

Saber blanched. "I don't know what the hell you are." He looked him up and down suspiciously. "Vampire...panther...King freakin' Arthur with his beloved Excalibur—you tell me."

Nachari smiled faintly then. "Yeah, it is one bad-ass sword, isn't it?" He patted his scabbard absently. "Seriously though, I'm a wizard; and you've never killed while feeding."

Saber stiffened. "I never had to, *Wizard*. In the house of Jaegar, the youngest brother feeds his family; and trust me, Dane killed."

"Not your karma," Nachari said. "Besides, what about the two hundred years you spent on this earth before Dane and

Diablo were born? You hunted, you drank, but you did not kill your prey."

Saber looked at him in amazement, feeling more than just a little bit exposed. He had never really thought about it: As far as he was concerned, times were different then; populations were sparser; it wasn't wise to leave entire villages dead in your wake—vampires didn't know when they might run into another viable food source. "Wasn't prudent," he said brusquely.

Nachari reached out a hand to help Ramsey up, watching as the stalwart warrior tested his weight on both legs and nodded. Turning his attention back to Saber, he said, "Look, you already know what I went through in the Valley of Death and Shadows, and I would say you have a pretty good idea of what I brought out of the experience." Both vampires knew Nachari was alluding to his advanced wizardry skills and his ability to shape-shift into the panther. "The thing is...what you might not understand...is the lesson behind it all." He breathed a heavy sigh. "Sometimes it's just easier to embrace what you are than to expend so much energy trying to deny it." He caught the look of confusion on Saber's face and added, "You're a lot of ugly things, Saber; but you've never killed your prey while feeding. Just go with it."

Saber took the wizard's words and filed them away in his to-be-processed-later compartment. Eyeing Ramsey warily, he tried to come up with something appropriate to say. Maybe something akin to *thank you*. "You killed my brother," he barked. Okay, so that didn't come out quite like he intended.

Ramsey snorted. "I killed your enemy, Dark One."

Saber nodded. "Yeah..." And then he smiled in his own fiendish kind of way. "So if they're all Dark Ones, and you're still calling me *Dark One*, then what were you doing in this valley fighting this night?"

"Oh, you're one dark son of a demon, all right," Ramsey said, plucking a needle off a pine tree and shoving it between his teeth. "But you're still a descendant of *Jadon*."

Nachari nodded in absolute solidarity. "This is *our house*,

Saber. And nobody comes into our house, attacks one of our own, and expects to walk out unscathed." He winked then. "You, of all vampires, should know that by now."

twenty~two

Saber knew Nachari was right. It was time to feed, and the little bit of blood the wizard had brought him in the three vials was not going to last him long, no matter how powerful Marquis Silivasi might be as an Ancient. But first, he had to make a pit stop.

Staring at the large wooden door in front of him, the quaint cottage home on the edge of Dark Moon Vale, just south of the eastern cliffs, he tried to gather his courage. This could either go very well...or very badly: The prodigal son returned.

Not exactly the traditional Sunday-school story.

He plucked an errant piece of cotton off his crimson-red shirt and knocked crisply on the door four times.

When Lorna opened it and saw him, she practically fainted. She glanced surreptitiously over her shoulder, as if to check for Rafael, grabbed a shawl off a nearby hook, and quickly stepped outside. "Saber," she said softly. "I'm so surprised." She placed her hand absently over her heart. "So happy to see you."

Saber read between the lines: Lorna was thrilled to see him. Rafael? Not so much. And judging by the swift drop in the outside temperature, coupled with the way the female had hurried out in spite of it, the adopted son of Damien Alexiares was not welcome in Rafael Dzuna's home.

That was cool.

Saber stepped back from the porch, suddenly feeling horribly out of place and more than just a little awkward.

Lorna sought to bridge the silence for him. "So, what are you doing here?" She quickly retracted the question. "Not that I'm complaining."

Saber nodded. "It's okay. I just..." He checked his watch: ten o'clock PM. *Great, just great.* "I was hoping..." He fidgeted and sighed. "Have you seen my son yet?"

Lorna's face lit up with adoration. "Oh yes, he's so beautiful."

"Handsome?" Saber asked, hopeful.

"Yes. Yes, of course. *Handsome.*"

Saber nodded and forced a civil smile. "Then he's well?"

"Oh, yes—growing like a weed."

"And Vanya, the princess?"

Lorna smiled tenderly. "She, too, is well."

He sighed heavily and forced himself to ask his next question. "What's my son's name?"

Lorna froze. Her body tensed, and she frowned. "Oh, Saber—"

"Please," Saber said, waving his hand to halt her sympathy—that was the last thing he wanted or needed. "Just—"

"His name is Lucien," Lorna said. "Lucien *Sabino* Alexiares."

Saber blinked in surprise. So, Vanya had named the child after him, *sort of,* by using the name his parents had given him at birth? Maybe she had done it out of deference to Lorna and Rafael. But she had also given him Saber's surname: a Dark One's surname, Alexiares. Now this truly surprised him.

"You look surprised," Lorna commented, as if she had read his thoughts.

"Little bit," Saber said honestly.

"I don't think it's that unusual," Lorna said. "I mean, not when you really think about it: Vanya is the sister of both Jadon and Jaegar, both light and dark. And Alexiares is a name from her *brother's* house. Perhaps this is her way of acknowledging all of who she is, all of who Lucien is." She paused then. "All of who you are."

Saber studied her face, the subtle lines at the corners of her eyes, the full arched brows that framed her knowing, compassionate eyes. "I think I owe you an apology, Lorna, for being so...so obstinate...so cruel to you."

"No, it is I who owe you an apology."

"For what?" Saber asked, astonished.

"For not truly understanding that you are...*all* of who you are...from Jadon's house, yes. But also from Jaegar's house. We truly didn't accept that before, acknowledge just what all that meant *to you*; and for that, I am sorry."

"Lorna," Saber said pointedly. "I gotta tell you, lady. You are *way* too nice. You need to get that fixed before someone seriously takes advantage of you."

Lorna chuckled fondly. "Oh...thank you."

"Yeah, see; that's exactly what I mean." He ran his hands through his hair and simply shook his head. "So..." He truly didn't know what he was doing there. It wasn't like they had a relationship to speak of; and apparently, he didn't have any words, either. "How are you?"

"Oh, I'm okay. I've been worried about you, though."

He raised his hand again.

"Too nice?" she said.

"Way too..." he replied.

"Okay." She rocked back and forth on her heels nervously. "Are you eating...staying warm?"

Saber laughed so loud the sound startled him. "Oh, man." He met her eyes and smirked. "I can't do this, Lorna. I'm sorry; I thought I could."

Before she could answer, Rafael rounded the corner, approaching the wraparound porch from the backyard. "Of course you can't," he said derisively. "So, why did you come here then? Don't you think your mother has been through enough?"

Saber was just about to face off with the bitter warrior, challenge him male to male, when he noticed for the first time that Rafael was not wearing a shirt. And his chest, *great lords of the spirit world—dark or light—*it was a virtual wasteland, littered from armpit to armpit with crisscrossed lines, his pectoral muscles a savage map of suffering.

Saber flashed an undignified scowl. Despite himself, all he could do was gape. Was this the pain...the suffering...the physical expression of the mental anguish this male had felt for so many years? The outward expression of his inward guilt? "You need to let that go," Saber finally said, inclining his head at the scars.

Rafael scowled. He strolled up to the front door, turned the knob, and stepped inside. Before he shut the door in Saber's face, he called back: "I have let it go."

Saber looked down at the ground. It was better than watching the appalled look on Lorna's face—talk about a tale of two parents. "All right then," he mumbled. "Thanks for telling me about Lucien…I should probably get going."

Lorna sighed, clearly not knowing what to say or do. "Will you come back soon?"

Saber shook his head. "Probably not. It was a bad idea."

No," she argued, "it was not a bad idea. It was a wonderful idea, and I'm glad you did it." She stopped herself short and placed both hands neatly on her thighs. "Way too nice," she mumbled.

Saber licked his lips and inclined his head; and then something crossed his mind—*his heart?*—unbidden. Something he had never planned to say but now knew that he had to. And not for himself, but for the embittered man who had retreated inside the house. "Will you do me a favor?"

"Of course," Lorna said. "Just name it."

"How did I know you were going to say that?" he teased, winking before she could apologize.

Lorna seemed positively giddy, not just by the request, but by the banter. "Name it," she repeated.

Saber inhaled deeply before looking off into the distance. "For whatever it's worth, tell Rafael that I never raped a woman or killed a child."

Lorna gasped audibly.

And then the front door opened and Rafael stepped outside. Apparently, he had been listening all along. "Why not?" he asked, his own face showing the faintest hint of hope.

Saber shrugged. "Don't know. I guess I didn't like the taste of kids' blood—and didn't want to have to kill my own unborn offspring…or to be a father." Searching for a better explanation, he added, "In the house of Jaegar, we don't really command pregnancies. The moment we—the moment *they*—release their seed, the female is pregnant. If you don't want sons, you either have to kill the victim, refrain from…finishing, or make it so she can't get pregnant before you violate her. Just seemed like a lot of hassle." Rafael stared at him blankly, and Saber's demeanor grew impassive. "I wish, for your sake, it was something deeper than that, nobler than that. But, that's really the long and short of it."

Rafael seemed to exhale as if he had been holding his breath his entire life. The tightness in his chest relaxed, and his harsh, unforgiving expression softened. "Maybe, just maybe," he whispered, "it's time for you to entertain the possibility that you did it because you have a heart as well as a soul—maybe you've always had both."

Saber's lip turned up in a half smile, half scowl. "Nah; it wasn't that deep. Besides, what does it matter now?"

"It matters," Rafael said, "because it means that in time, and with healing, you might still be able to love."

Saber looked away. "I don't…I don't know what words like that mean."

"You do know," Rafael argued. "You just haven't made the connection—between the emotion and the word."

"Yeah," Saber retorted sarcastically, "*love*, whatever that is."

Rafael stiffened like someone had punched him in the gut. He grit his teeth and placed an implacable fist over his chest. "This," he snarled, indicating the brutal scars that he carried in his own harshly masculine way. "*This is love.*"

Saber turned on his heel and stormed off into the night. *Enraged.*

He paced no less than twenty yards away before turning and stomping back. "What the hell is wrong with you?" he growled.

Rafael stepped off the porch and met him in the yard. He reached out a firm hand and placed it on Saber's shoulder. "Son—"

"Don't you say that to me!" Saber fumed, slapping Rafael's hand away angrily. "Don't you ever say that word to me." His fangs shot out of his mouth, and he had to struggle not to bite something, destroy something, kill something.

Anything.

Love? What the hell was this word they kept tossing around like a ball in the park? *Love* should have stayed Diablo's hand when he came to kill him earlier. *Love* should have stopped the house of Jaegar from executing Damien and Dane. *Love* should have brought Vanya to the cave the moment she found out what had happened with the Dark Ones!

Love!

There was no such thing as love.

"You've got to reach past that rage, Saber," Rafael said. "You've got to tap into what's beneath."

Saber swallowed a curse. "What's beneath? There's *nothing* beneath. Don't you get it? There's nothing else here!"

"Then why are you so angry?"

"Why am I so angry?"

"Yes, why are you so *angry?*"

Saber's nostrils flared. "I don't know. I don't know!"

"Maybe because in eight hundred years, no one has ever loved you back. Until now."

Saber clenched his fists. "Shut up, old man. Or I swear to the gods I'm going to hurt you." Rafael stepped back then, but he didn't retreat. He simply shook his head slowly and tapped his chest. "Worse than this?" he asked. "You can't possibly hurt me worse than this."

Saber dropped his head in his hands. "Look, I'm sorry someone stole your son, that—"

"Someone stole *you*," Rafael said forcefully. "*You* are my son."

Saber shook his head. His eyes darted back and forth, scanning everything around them *except* Rafael's anguished face. "No, it wasn't me. I was never that kid."

"You were that kid. And you were full of life and curiosity, alert and observant, just like Lucien is now."

Saber looked up at him and scowled. "Then why..." he

whispered, unable to complete the sentence.

"Why what?" Rafael asked.

"Why didn't you search for me?"

Rafael stepped back, reacting as if he had just been burned. "By all the gods, Sabino...*Saber*...we looked for decades."

Saber felt depleted. "Then why didn't you...just know?"

"Just know what? Where you were? That the Dark Ones had you? How could we? It never even occurred to us. We just...didn't...that's all. And I am so, so sorry."

Saber swallowed his rage. He cleared his throat and nodded, finally bringing his emotions under control. "Yeah..." He blew out a long breath. "Yeah, well, it's all in the past."

"True," Rafael said, "but you're here now."

"I'm not *here*," Saber argued, gesturing emphatically at the cottage and the forest around them. "Not like that. I just wanted to come by and ask about Vanya...my son."

"Okay," Rafael said. "So maybe that's a start."

Beginning, middle, and end, Saber thought, but he didn't speak it aloud. He looked down at the ground, too tired to argue or provoke Rafael further. "Yeah, maybe," he conceded. "I've gotta go."

Lorna joined them in the yard then. "Where will you go?" she asked. "What will you do? How will you live?"

"Too much, Lorna," Saber said. "This is all...way too much."

Lorna folded her hands together as if she could capture her words between her fingers, trying to be stoic. "I'm sorry," she whispered.

"Damnit," Saber barked. "Stop apologizing. *Please.*"

Lorna clasped her hand over her mouth in an increased effort not to speak, and then she began to cry uncontrollably.

Saber stepped back.

He had to get out of there.

Talk about your world's worst ideas.

He was just about to turn and leave when something brought him up short. Maybe it was the sound of Lorna's tears, maybe it was just the pitiful nature of the whole damn scenario; but he couldn't leave things like this. He couldn't leave *her* like this. Forcing himself to step toward the weeping woman, he reached out and cupped her face in his hands. "No tears, Lorna. Not for me."

She did her best to stifle her sobs, and after taking several deep breaths, she finally grew quiet. "If you are ever in need, please…come home," she whispered.

Home.

Now that was another million-dollar word.

He wasn't about to touch that one with a ten-foot pole.

Instead, he took her small hands in his considerably larger ones and held them firmly. "Thank you, Lorna," he said. It was the best he could do.

"You're welcome," she replied, and then she forced herself to remove her hands from his. Raising her chin, she bid him adieu in the formal protocol. "Be well, *my son*." Despite her obvious attempt at courage, she was hardly able to get the words out. And in that singular, vulnerable moment, Saber truly saw the woman that she was, perhaps for the first time, the undeniable *love* she felt for him, even if he couldn't comprehend it.

He placed both hands lightly on her arms and kissed her softly on the forehead. "Be well," he offered in response. Then he did the most unexpected thing imaginable: He dropped his head, nuzzled the side of her cheek, and deeply inhaled her maternal scent. Pressing his lips to her ear, he repeated the formal refrain, adding a single word:

"Be well, *Mother*."

twenty~three

Saber stood outside of the country-western bar, trying to gather the courage to go inside. It wasn't that he had any fear of humans—far from it—but he knew that Napolean would be watching, sensing, whatever it was the ancient king did from his mansion in the vale. And all Saber wanted to do was feed, get in and get out, before something went wrong.

He checked his attire, hoping it was suitable for blending in: a pair of black, low-rise jeans falling over a custom set of steel-tipped, black-and-red cowboy boots, and a similar, form-fitting red shirt. After all, country-western wasn't exactly his gig, but what else was open in a small mountain town on a Sunday night?

He tried to turn down his *mojo*, whatever that unspoken vibration was that screamed *predator—run!* at human males, causing them to act skittish at the least, and *pure unadulterated sex* at human females, causing them to act recklessly at best; and then he opened the front door of the Black Bear Tavern and strolled in.

A tall, lanky brunette, wearing way too few clothes, caught his eye immediately from across the smoky room. She was sidled up to the bar, nursing what smelled like a whiskey sour, and she immediately batted her dark gray eyes at him, unwittingly licking her lips.

Saber turned on the charm and smiled, not too brazenly, but just enough.

She had a generous, overexposed chest and a long, graceful neck, which meant easy access for him, a quick, clean bite. And she was definitely willing. Oh, was she ever willing.

He began to make his way across the bar.

It was time to stalk his prey.

BLOOD REDEMPTION

Vanya pulled the quaint brass arm on the vintage slot machine for the umpteenth time, waiting to see what images would pop up on the pay line, another mismatched set of pine cones, wolves, and gold nuggets or a winning combination?

They had been at it for hours—Vanya, Ciopori, and Kristina Silivasi—making their way through the Dark Moon Casino, trying their hand at craps, poker, and the slots. It had started out as a sisters' night out, Ciopori's sympathetic idea to spend more time with Vanya, to try and keep her mind off her troubles; but it had ended up as a threesome when they ran into Kristina Riley-Silivasi at the casino door. Not only did the rambunctious redhead live nearby, on the top floor of the Dark Moon Lodge, but she used to be a cocktail waitress for the casino before Marquis had mistakenly claimed her as his *destiny*; and she swore she knew every hot spot on the floor, exactly what to play to strike it rich.

Judging by the losing line-up that appeared on the screen, Vanya was no longer convinced that Kristina knew anything at all, let alone what she had promised. She was just about to give the arm another crank when the screen turned gray, the woodland images disappeared, and a milky scene of a smoke-filled bar appeared in place of the icons. What in the world? Was her vision playing tricks on her?

She leaned in closer to view the image more carefully. There was an old saloon feel to the tavern; the floors were covered in wide plank oak, most of the slats littered with the remnants of shelled peanuts; and some ghastly rendition of "Back in the Saddle Again" was playing in the background, as lonely, inebriated humans milled about, drinking, dancing, and talking.

And Saber was standing right in the midst of the scene, talking to a tall, scrawny brunette by a bar. Vanya gasped, and then she narrowed her focus. The female was dressed like a lady of the night, her garish lime-green top appearing more like a string-bikini than a cropped vest, and if her miniskirt grew any more...*mini*...she would be sharing her secrets with the world. And Saber? The male was leaning into her like a jungle cat about to climb a tree, smiling that wicked, way-too-sexy grin and whispering something in her ear!

Vanya drew back in disbelief.

Her mouth fell open and her body grew tense.

And then she leaned in once more to take a closer look. The picture was coming into much clearer focus now, and she could see every movement, every nuance and impropriety, in great detail.

Saber was...laughing now.

Laughing!

As if the dragon possessed anything resembling a sense of humor in his wicked repertoire.

Vanya set down her own cocktail, a small tasteful glass of Kahlua and cream, and practically pressed her nose to the screen. Saber brushed his hand against the woman's bare hip, tightened his fingers at the small of her back, and whispered something else in her ear.

What had he said?

Vanya didn't know, but by the look of mounting interest on the female's face, it had traveled right down her spine and anchored in her solicitous toes. No doubt, the vampire was using coercion, but to what end?

To seduce her?

Vanya could hardly believe her eyes; and then she all at once connected the dots: Saber was there to feed. And he had chosen this awful, *awful* woman as his prey. Were there no acceptable alternatives around? Perhaps a much larger human male; a couch potato; or a construction worker? Surely, the blood of a male would be more satisfying...more nutritious.

She sat back, not knowing what to do. *How could he!* she thought.

Just then, Ciopori rounded Vanya's chair, placed an elegant

hand on the back of her stool, and leaned over to view the screen. "Are you having fun, sister?" she asked, clearly oblivious to the scene Vanya was viewing.

"Don't you see it?" Vanya asked.

"See what?" Ciopori stared more intently at the screen and shrugged. "I see that you are not very lucky at slots." She patted her on the back. "Keep at it. You have to win something eventually."

Vanya panted, almost unable to breathe. Saber was leaning further into the female now, his broad muscular chest brushing ever so slightly against the woman's flagrantly overexposed chest; and he was dipping to her neck to…kiss her. Not to bite her, *but to kiss her.*

Vanya bounded from the stool, stunned. And angry. Why in the world was kissing necessary—in order to feed? She hardly thought so. As she continued to watch in morbid fascination, and more than just a little horror, Saber reached for the human's hand, pulled her up from the seat, and began to lead her out of the bar.

Well, this was just…unacceptable.

Vulgar.

Hardly fitting of a male who had a six-week infant with another female, less than fifteen miles away.

"What is it?" Ciopori said, clearly picking up on the fact that Vanya was troubled.

"Where is Kristina?" Vanya said brusquely.

Ciopori frowned. "I don't know. She was standing by the roulette wheel, last I saw her. I think—"

"What's up, V?" Kristina said cheerfully, strolling casually up to the chair. "Looking for me?" Her bright blue eyes were alight with mischief.

"Indeed," Vanya responded testily. "Do you have your Corvette nearby?"

Kristina looked mildly surprised. "Uh…yeah, I mean it's in my garage. I don't keep it in the parking lot; but yeah, I have it. Why?"

"Are you too afraid of Saber to go anywhere near him?"

Kristina blanched, her pale skin growing even paler. She was clearly remembering the horrific ordeal Saber had put her through not all that long ago. "Not sure," she answered honestly. "What do you mean by *near him?*"

"Would you take me to him?" Vanya asked directly.

Ciopori spoke up sharply then. "What in the world is going on, Vanya? Whatever are you talking about?"

"I'm talking about taking a little drive to Silverton Creek, to the Black Bear Tavern."

"The Black Bear *what?*"

"*The Black Bear Tavern,*" Vanya repeated, her blood beginning to boil.

Kristina drove like the wild, newly made vampire she was, while Ciopori sat in the backseat, staring out the window with unconcealed dread on her face; and Vanya stirred restlessly in the passenger seat, trying uselessly to get hold of her emotions.

Why was she doing this?

Was she insane?

Absolutely certifiable?

What difference did it make to her if Saber kissed the woman, bit the woman, and danced her into the sunset?

She shook her head, tossing her long blond locks behind her shoulder in an effort to clear her mind. Nothing made sense anymore. None of it. She had no idea what she was doing, why she was doing it, or what she possibly hoped to get out of it, other than to grab a tiger by the tail. She only knew that every living, breathing cell in her body was rebelling *violently* against what she had seen on that screen, and she could no more deny the impulse, or to try and stop it, than she could ignore Lucien when he cried at night, or Nikolai when he reached for her arms.

The seconds seemed like minutes. The minutes seemed like

hours. The miles seemed eternal as Kristina expertly steered the Corvette through one s-turn after another, heading up the steep pass toward the quaint mountain town. Would they never get there? And what if they were too late?

Gods be merciful—too late for what?

Vanya wrung her hands together and forced herself to stare out the window the rest of the way. She was physically relieved when they finally pulled into the gravel drive, and the large iron sign, a black bear standing on his haunches, holding a mug of beer, finally came into view. The pink Corvette had barely come to a stop when Vanya yanked on the passenger door-handle, threw open the door, and marched defiantly toward the entrance of the bar. She stopped then, trying to sense him, Saber and the human female. Yes, they were still inside the club, but no longer across the room, no longer by the bar. They were very close to the front door. Whatever for?

Refusing to hesitate, lest she lose her courage—*or regain her senses*—Vanya smoothed her skirt, glanced briefly at her own white boots, and strolled through the door.

Saber saw her immediately.

He stood up from the tall, circular table, where he was now *sharing a drink* with the human, and took a surprised step to the side, his eyes locked in fierce challenge with Vanya's.

"Princess?" he said, his voice revealing his astonishment. "What are you doing here?"

Vanya could hardly get her tongue to work. "I could ask you the same thing, Dragon." She turned to glare at the human female. "And this? What is *this* about?"

"This?" the woman said sharply. "Who are you calling *this*?"

Vanya rolled her elegant eyes and snorted. "Don't you have a pole to go dance around or something?"

The female jumped up from her perch at the table and squared her shoulders to Saber. "Sweetheart, is this your wife or something?"

Sweetheart? Vanya practically seethed. This woman didn't know a scorpion from a puppy. What a fool!

Tessa Dawn

Saber caught sight of Vanya's expression and gawked. He was momentarily speechless. Finally, he sought a telepathic connection and in a deep, psychic tone said: *Princess, I have to feed. And you are interrupting.*

Vanya spun around on him like Wyatt Earp at the OK Corral. *Feed? Feed! Oh, is that what you call it?* She took a measured step forward and waved her hand through the air in a reckless fashion, indicating the human female. *You feed with your fangs, Vampire, not with your hands...or your mouth...or your lips! And you certainly don't need to dress like a gunslinger to do it.* She practically scowled then. She knew she looked unbalanced, but she just didn't care. *Yet here you are, dressed like some dark, dangerous drifter—* she huffed with indignation—*looking for all intents and purposes like...like...*sex on a stick, *trying to sink your fangs into some two-bit street walker.*

Saber cocked his head to the side slowly, inadvertently. His severe coal-black eyes grew even darker with understanding, and his cruel mouth turned up in a smile. *Sex on a stick?* he repeated, his tongue darting out to moisten his bottom lip. *I see.*

"You see?" Vanya retorted, forgetting to speak telepathically. "What do you see?" Before he could answer, she fumed: "No, you don't see, Dragon. You don't see anything!" She turned to glare at the brunette once more—*dearest lords, she had finally gone completely off the deep end.* "It's a wonder you can see anything with those obnoxious breasts in your face. And just how much silicone did you have to buy to inflate those balloons, anyway?" she added, glaring at the human.

Now that was petty and beneath her dignity, but oh well—it was too late to take it back.

Saber looked positively thunderstruck.

"Bitch," the human snarled, raising her hand to waggle her finger in Vanya's face. "Unless you have some claim on this man, I suggest you get the hell out of my face."

Vanya recoiled. "Excuse me?"

"You heard me," the woman said.

Vanya cleared her throat. "This...this male...you are so

289

smitten by has a six-week-old child: Did he tell you that?"

"What!" Saber exclaimed, clearly unable to hold his tongue any longer. "A child you refuse to let me see!"

"That is hardly the point!" Vanya retorted.

"So what," the human said brazenly. And then she took a calculated step forward and looked Vanya up and down with contempt. Although she tried to appear haughty and self-assured, she faltered the moment she took a good hard look at Vanya, and it was obvious by the wilted expression in her eyes that she was intimidated by what she saw. After all, there was beauty, and then there was *beauty*. And this human female could not hold a candle to a celestial princess on her best day...or Vanya's worst.

"So what?" Vanya repeated.

"So, I don't care what he has at home," the female retorted, recovering beautifully. She looked Saber slowly up and down and smiled licentiously. "What I'm after isn't sleeping in a crib." She stared blatantly at Saber's groin and practically purred. "And unless this grown-ass man has changed his mind about giving it to me, you need to just go home to the little brat and deal with it. Maybe he'll be home later." She smirked and stuck out her chin. "Maybe he won't."

Kristina Silivasi snaked up to Vanya's side and gasped. Apparently, she had just entered the bar and caught the tail end of the conversation. She looked at Saber with more than a little trepidation in her eyes and tried to gain control over her fear. And then she turned back to the human female and obviously remembered what she had just heard. "Oh, hell no," she said, tossing her generous s-curls behind her back and reaching up to remove an earring. "No this tramp didn't. You want me to slap the sense God didn't give her into that feeble mind, Vanya?"

The woman rolled her eyes in an exaggerated motion. She reached up to run a long, painted nail down the front of Saber's chest, switched her hips seductively from side to side, and leaned into him in an exaggerated fashion. "Are we still going out to your truck, sweetie, or what?"

"Your truck?" Vanya parroted sarcastically. "What truck? So we are practicing grand theft auto now?"

Saber pushed the human female aside and stared at Vanya with molten savagery. As his eyes flashed dangerously crimson, he snarled in warning. "I *rented* a Ford F350 a month ago, something to drive while I figure out what I'm going to do next, not that I owe you an explanation." His eyes roamed from the bottom of her feet to the top of her head as he took her full measure. "You don't know anything about my life, Vanya, what I have or don't have, and that was *your* choice—no, your *demand*. And for a dark, soulless bastard, you might not have noticed, but I have honored that demand every second of every day. I have honored you. And Lucien!" He lowered his voice to a haunting, silky purr. "And not because it's been easy. So, I'll ask you one more time: *What are you doing here?*"

Vanya felt like Saber's words had been delivered with a dagger, and maybe it was because there was so much truth in them. They swirled around her head like bats in a cave, failing to find a purchase, and the confusion only made her more agitated. She reached out to touch Kristina's arm, sensing that the volatile redhead was only one heartbeat away from assaulting the human female—and wouldn't that just provoke Napolean into locking them all up as nut cases? "Kristina," she said coolly. "Do you attend Jocelyn and Nathaniel's self-defense course?"

Kristina wrinkled her brow. "Yeah, of course; I have to. Why?"

"Then you carry the required dagger?" She looked down at Kristina's bright pink handbag and waited for an answer.

"Uh…yeah?" Kristina said. "V, where do you think you're going with this?"

"Give it to me."

Kristina looked at Saber and shivered. "Uh, not a good idea, Princess."

"*Give it to me.*"

All at once, the human female turned pale and took a judicious step back, raising both hands in the air. "Whoa, honey...hey, I didn't realize it was that serious. He's yours, okay?"

Kristina reached into her purse and withdrew the dagger cautiously, passing it as inconspicuously as possible to Vanya, while watching Saber's every move like a hawk—she clearly expected the vampire to spring at any moment and rip all of their throats out. Turning to regard the human female, she whispered a clear command, laced with blatant compulsion: "Sit down, and shut up."

The woman instantly obeyed.

Vanya accepted the dagger, held it close to her heart, and spun on her heel, marching angrily out the front door. As bitter tears of confusion streamed down her face, she headed directly for the large, shiny F350, parked near the front of the lot, and proceeded to promptly puncture all four tires, one at a time, like a full-fledged lunatic.

Who cared at this juncture?

Who cared about any of it anymore?

Saber followed her outdoors and watched as she took her considerable angst out on his truck. But to his credit, he did not interfere or try to stop her. In fact, he didn't say a word. And truth be told, he looked like the cat had stolen his tongue, long ago in the tavern: He couldn't have formed a sentence if he had wanted to.

"There," Vanya said, handing the blade back to Kristina, who had also followed them outside. "It would appear as if your...mobile hotel...is no longer viable, Dragon." She tossed her long, flowing hair behind her shoulder, feeling like an utter fool. "So if you want to go back inside and get your *prey*, then I suppose you'll have to get better acquainted somewhere else."

Now that was just nonsensical.

Perhaps even borderline...feeble-minded.

What difference did it make if his tires were flat?

No matter.

Turning once again on her heel, Vanya marched back to the pink Corvette. "Come on, Kristina. We're going home."

Kristina practically ran to catch up, and then she quickly drew ahead, all the while fumbling frantically for her keys. *"Holy shit,"* she whispered.

Once at the car, Vanya yanked wildly at the passenger door, quickly ducked inside, and sank morbidly into the pale leather seat. She felt as if she were going to be sick. As Kristina groped wildly, trying to get her keys in the ignition, Vanya turned to regard Ciopori, who was sitting, like she had just seen a ghost, in the backseat: Her golden eyes were enormous with shock; her arms were folded tightly around her body; and her mouth was gaping open in disbelief.

After a pregnant moment, Ciopori finally swallowed her shock and cleared her throat. "Sister." The regal female spoke quietly, deliberately. "You do know that I love you, correct?"

Vanya wiped a burning tear from her eye and nodded. "Yes, of course."

"Then you know that what I'm about to tell you truly comes from the heart, don't you?"

"Yes, I suppose," Vanya said.

Ciopori nodded. "Good." She smoothed her own hair back into place. "Because I have to say that in all my years of living, whether in Romania or North America"—she sighed for emphasis then—"hell, whether with celestial beings or vampires, that had to be the single most *undignified* thing I have ever witnessed."

"Yes," Vanya said, sinking even further down in the seat. She wished she could just disappear, perhaps dematerialize right out the cosmos. She scrubbed her hand over her face and winced.

"And if you were going for…subtlety…with regard to the fact that you still have some unresolved, perhaps conflicting, feelings for that male—for whatever reason—I think the secret is out."

"Oh, gods," Vanya mumbled. "What should I do?"

"Do?" Ciopori echoed. "Um, I believe you should not *do* anything more." She shook her head like an exasperated mother.

BLOOD REDEMPTION

"As it stands, Saber has not killed any of us…yet. Napolean has not killed Saber…yet. And the truck will heal…in time. Perhaps we have all done enough for one night."

Vanya groaned. She bent over in the seat and placed her head between her knees. "I think I'm going to be ill."

No one said a word.

"Great Cygnus," Vanya continued to lament, "I'm supposed to be a princess."

"Indeed," Ciopori said.

"Yep," Kristina offered, finally turning the key in the ignition and starting the engine.

"I think I just…lost it," Vanya whispered softly.

"Ya think?" Kristina said, checking her rearview mirror to make sure the path was clear. When Vanya didn't reply, she continued thoughtlessly: "Honestly, V, I'm no fan of Saber's— we all know that—but truthfully? I don't think he was really gonna *do her*, that tramp. I think he was just getting her all hot and bothered so she wouldn't object to him feeding from her neck."

"Kristina," Ciopori chastised sweetly, "perhaps that is not very helpful right now."

"No," Vanya said. "She's right. I'm crazy. I jumped to a horrible conclusion, one that shouldn't even matter; after all, I've completely banished the male from my life. And to make matters worse, I acted…abominably."

"Yeah, you acted a damn fool," Kristina mumbled, chuckling as if the whole situation was just *girls being girls*, a night out on the town.

"*Kristina…*" Ciopori repeated.

"This whole situation has simply driven me to the brink of madness," Vanya added. "Oh, no!" She sat up abruptly. "What if the human does something rash? What if she's been traumatized? What if she—"

"Saber will erase her memory and make sure all is well. He is a lot of things, but he is not stupid," Ciopori said.

Vanya nodded, and then she slumped back in her seat. "Do

294

you think he will still…take her home?"

"To a cave?" Kristina blurted, incredulous. "I mean, she was kind of *skank*. But still, at some point, self-preservation has to kick in. If some guy had tried to pick me up in a bar and take me back to a *cave*? Uh…*no*. Can you say serial killer?"

"Kristina!" Ciopori snapped, her voice growing sharp with reprisal. She leaned forward in the backseat and placed a loving hand on Vanya's shoulder. "Perhaps you shouldn't—"

"Go there," Kristina supplied.

"In your mind," Ciopori clarified.

"You don't do so well there," Kristina added.

"Clearly," Vanya admitted. And then she stretched back, reclined the seat so she could lie down, and shut her eyes, cringing, while Kristina pulled out of the parking lot.

Saber Alexiares stared fixedly ahead as the pink Corvette tore out of the Black Bear Tavern lot, kicking up gravel in its wake. He could have used his superior hearing to eavesdrop on the conversation before the females departed, but he had chosen to decline the temptation: He wasn't at all sure he wanted to know what was being said.

He glanced over his shoulder and sighed. No doubt, there was a confused human female sitting at a raised table inside, probably trembling, perhaps throwing up, but definitely glued to her seat by the weight of Kristina Silivasi's compulsion; and he still needed to go wash her memories and set the whole thing straight. And soon.

True; he still needed to feed, but perhaps there was a young adult male who would serve him better.

For the sake of darkness! Vanya had truly lost it.

He eyeballed his deflated tires and winced—before smirking—who knew she had that kind of fire in her? And over him—the fact that he had touched another woman.

BLOOD REDEMPTION

Saber felt a primal growl rise in his throat, the call of a male predator staking his territory.

Vanya Demir had somehow known he was with another woman; and she had reacted like a territorial animal, claiming what was hers.

She had cared.

Deeply.

She had been devastated.

She had reacted like his...*destiny*.

And didn't that just make an entire world of gray suddenly black and white: It didn't matter that Saber was a dark soul, raised in the house of Jaegar. It didn't matter that Vanya was a celestial princess, perhaps raised by the residents of heaven itself. It only mattered that her soul knew his, and vice versa. They were part of each other now, for better, for worse...

And forever.

Napolean could kill him if he wanted to.

And Vanya could threaten him, *refuse him*, until the stars all burned out and the Dark Ones found souls.

It didn't matter.

The dark lords of hell could no longer keep Saber Alexiares from doing the one thing he had been killing himself not to do: *claiming what was rightfully his.*

His *destiny*.

And his son.

twenty-four

Vanya pulled her knees up to her chest and rocked back and forth on the guest room bed, staring at Ciopori's back. "Do you think he will try to contact me…approach me…now that I've made such an egregious error?"

Ciopori pulled back a white wooden slat from the blinds and peered out the window. "He's already here."

Vanya jumped up from the bed. "No!" She rushed to the blinds, peered out next to her sister, and cringed when she saw the darkly clad male, still arrayed in black and red from head to toe—and wasn't that just a striking visage against his wild hair—climb out of the hefty F350. "What should I do?"

"What do you want to do?" Ciopori asked.

Vanya shrugged helplessly. "What do you want me to do?"

Ciopori moaned. "I want you to call Napolean and ask him to behead the male once and for all, so we can go on with our lives, peacefully. However, after witnessing that scene earlier, I no longer believe that's within your best interest." She sighed. "Go talk to him." She glanced at the pristine bassinette beside the bed and added, "I will take good care of Lucien."

Vanya pressed an open palm to her chest and worried her bottom lip. "Back into the dragon's lair then?"

Ciopori shrugged and shook her head. "I suppose so."

Vanya nodded. Of one thing she was quite certain: It was probably better to meet with Saber, briefly, than risk Saber and Marquis reuniting at the front door. The last time the two had exchanged words, Marquis's hand had been buried in Saber's chest, about to dislodge his heart. "Very well," she said. "I'll let you know what happens."

Ciopori's eyes grew misty, but she showed no other sign of distress. "Vanya…"

"Yes?"

"If, for even one moment, you feel like you're in danger, call out to me, okay?"

"I will."

"Promise?"

"I promise."

The two sisters hugged, and then Vanya stepped back stoically and closed her eyes, trying to concentrate. As a recently turned vampire, Vanya should not have possessed the skill to dematerialize this soon, but her absolute command over magic and the ancient ways had imbued her with many of the vampiric powers earlier than usual.

She materialized on the front lawn, just beneath a large ponderosa pine. Less than five feet away from Saber's truck, on the passenger side.

If Saber was relieved or happy to see her, his face didn't show it. "Get in," he commanded, his deep voice holding a dark, perilous edge.

"Get in?" Vanya echoed. She stared at the door and frowned. *Where did he think he was taking her?*

"To my cave," he said, reading her thoughts effortlessly. *"Get in."*

Vanya licked her lips, noticing that they were all at once chapped and dry. The door to the truck was now like a gateway, a haunted entry that led beyond a shadowed crossroad, and once she stepped beyond the line, there would be no turning back. Every doubt, every fear, *every desire* she had ever entertained settled into the pit of her stomach, turning over in roiling waves of uncertainty. She took an unwitting step back.

The ground shifted subtly beneath them, and the dragon flexed his back. He stretched his sinewy arms and rolled his head on his shoulders; a low, almost indiscernible growl rose in his throat. *"Get in, Princess."*

They road in deafening silence all the way to the Red Canyons, heading toward the cave where Saber had been living, until Vanya almost considered opening the door and jumping from the vehicle just to escape the awkward tension. Perhaps her new vampiric body could sustain the fall. When at last Saber pulled up in front of a dark, arched entrance, the opening to his cave, she hesitated to get out of the vehicle.

"You're here now," he said, climbing out of the truck. He strolled around the cab with the stealth of a predator, the grace of a cougar—and didn't that just make her heart skip more than a couple of beats—and then he opened her door. "Welcome," he drawled silkily.

"Back up," she said, unwilling to come that close. She still wasn't sure if he was angry, revengeful, or just...being Saber.

Saber took a careful step back. "I am not going to harm you, Princess." He met her eyes in a steely gaze. "And you know it."

Vanya swallowed a lump in her throat. "Then what are you planning to do?"

He purred, throwing off an enormous amount of heat and feral energy. "Everything," he whispered. "Anything...all you have ever desired."

Vanya drew up short. "Is that supposed to make me feel at ease?"

"No," Saber said. Gliding as much as walking, he took an unflinching step forward. He reached into the cab and leaned into her until their chests were nearly touching, his heart beating wildly, only inches from hers; and then he placed his powerful hands beneath her arms and slid them down to her waist. His thumbs absently brushed the sides of her breasts as they passed by, and he lifted her out of the seat.

He set her down on the ground in front of him.

He ran the backs of his fingers along her neck and then her collarbone.

He dropped his head to nuzzle her ear and whispered: "It's supposed to make you feel...alive."

Vanya drew in a sharp intake of breath. She placed both hands firmly on his chest and shoved him back, desperately needing air. "Did you feed?" she asked nervously.

"Yes," he answered, his eyes boring holes into hers. The dark, savage pupils were molten with heat, glowing almost iridescent with raw, unrestrained passion; and the longing they reflected in their liquid depths was so great, so all-encompassing, it shook her to her soul.

She shivered, but she managed to maintain her composure. "On her?" she asked. Her voice sounded distant.

"What?" Saber whispered, sounding confused.

"On her," she repeated, feeling like a fool. "When you fed, did you feed *on her*?"

Saber's cruel mouth turned up at the corners, revealing the barest hint of ivory fangs. "No," he drawled lazily. He reached out and swept his thumb along her cheek. "It was far too displeasing to my *destiny*."

Vanya felt herself sway. She clutched at his shoulders to keep from falling over. "But you were going to," she muttered. And then she looked up into his eyes and almost swooned. "What else were you going to do, Saber?"

He shrugged with indifference. "I don't know…not that."

"But you wanted her?" Great Cygnus, why couldn't she just leave it alone?

Saber licked his bottom lip, slowly. "Princess, please…you know who I am. What I am."

She shook her head, staring at his chest, too disconcerted to continue looking him in the eyes.

"Raised in the house of Jaegar," he said. He brushed a lock of her hair behind her shoulders, placed two fingers beneath her chin, and gently raised her head. "Even if I didn't want you— *which I do*"—his voice held a dark promise of something so primitive she felt it in her toes—"she was nothing more than chattel to me."

Vanya rolled her eyes, reacting to his calloused words. "And that's supposed to make it better," she said, "endear you to me?"

"No," he answered sharply. "It's simply the truth."

She peered at him beneath heavy lids and noticed that his face was flushed with heat. Great lords, he was already summoning a dragon's fire.

"Luckily for me," he added, "you already hold me dear."

Vanya blinked in surprise.

"Shh, pretty woman," he cajoled. "Do not deny it." He bent to her ear, traced the contours with his tongue, and gently nipped at her lobe with his fangs. "*You slashed my tires*, Princess."

Vanya squirmed. She ducked from beneath his hungry advances and glanced over her shoulder at the truck. "And you already fixed them? So quickly?" Her voice was unsteady, her hands trembling, visibly.

"I'm a vampire."

She nodded, still looking away. "So am I...now."

"I know," he whispered huskily in her ear. And then he stepped back, extended his arm toward the mouth of the cave, and inclined his head. "My lair."

Vanya shook her head. "No."

Saber nodded his. "Yes."

Vanya raised her voice. "*No.*"

Saber lowered his. "*Yes.*"

Vanya panted, her breath coming in short bursts of anxiety. "Saber...Saber, please."

"Please, what?" he asked. With that, he stepped forward, grasped the back of her head in the palm of his hand, and tightened his fist in her hair. "Please, what? Please don't do what I've been burning to do since the moment you showed up at the bar? Please don't take your innocence again—I think you can only lose it once. Please don't taste you, touch you, bury my body inside of yours? Too late, Princess. You came to me; *and you slashed my tires.*" He covered her mouth with his and began to kiss her hungrily. The moment she began to return the passion—*gods help her, she was putty in his hands*—he pierced her bottom lip with his fangs, swirled his tongue over the blood, and then abruptly pulled away. "Please, what, Vanya?"

"Please...we...we need to talk." She moaned.

"We will talk." He dropped his hands to her hips and gently, expertly, pulled her forward until their groins were touching and she could feel the rock-hard evidence of his arousal straining through his jeans. "*Later.*" He rotated against her shamelessly while slowly unbuttoning her blouse to expose her milky breasts. When he dipped his head to suckle each of the rose-colored buds in turn, first the left, then the right, she whimpered with helplessness.

Her hips began to roll against his, as if by their own accord, and her right leg bent at the knee as she anchored her soft, creamy thigh over his muscular, hard one.

He groaned against her chest, and his sex kicked in his jeans. *"Gods, Vanya..."*

She gasped. "Saber...Saber...please."

"Please, what?" he repeated, rasping a sound so deep in his throat that it rumbled along her spine. As if a torrent of turbulent water, held agelessly behind a faltering dam, had finally broken, Saber could no longer restrain himself. He sank his smooth, piercing fangs deep into her breast, drawing nourishment from her heart, before forcing himself to withdraw, to lave, kiss, and linger over the bite, slowly rising upward to her collarbone, her neck, and at last, her jugular.

His fangs sank deep again, only this time, his hips worked in perfect synchronicity, rotating with urgency against her mound, sending currents of electricity streaming down her abdomen, radiating out along her thighs, and culminating in her core.

Saber fumbled with the buttons on his jeans, finally ripping the denim like it was no more than a piece of parchment in his haste to free his need. "Take me," he implored, "inside of you." It was a command, a plea, and a promise all at once.

Vanya felt like she was falling, plunging, spinning out of control. She clutched at his wild hair, harder than she should, reveling in the silken feel of the unnatural locks, luxuriating in the sensation as it slid through her fingers.

He growled into her ear. He lifted her up from the ground and held her in his rugged arms, even as he bunched the material of her skirt in his hands, drawing it up to her waist. "Wrap your legs around me," he commanded.

She gasped for breath. *Oh dear gods!* "My panties," she cried, suddenly aware of the obstruction.

Tessa Dawn

Saber set her down. He dropped to his knees before her and quickly removed the satin undergarment from her hips, tugging it down her long legs and tossing it aside on the ground. With a wicked snarl, he parted his lips, nuzzled her core, and began to devour her heat.

His lips sought her apex of pleasure, his teeth nibbled gently along her flesh, and his tongue delved deeply inside her heat. All the while, he coaxed her, teased her, and inflamed her until she began to moan.

Then scream.

By all that was holy, what was he doing!

Vanya squirmed above the feverish vampire, crying out from one orgasm after another, her body trembling in violent waves of release as Saber continued to devour her body.

When at last he stood up and raised her to his hips, supporting her weight on his muscular arms, she thought she might just pass out. She wrapped her arms around his neck for support. She was exhausted, spent, unable to even speak.

Saber entered her like a primordial dragon taking flight into a pitch-black sky, shooting ravenously upward in one powerful, primitive thrust, and staking his claim with absolute authority. His huge, pulsing organ tunneled wide and deep, forcing her to stretch to accommodate his length and his girth as he sank deeper and deeper into her very soul. "Daughter of rapture," he panted.

She groaned in response.

And then he began to thrust, to move like the wild, passionate creature he was: rocking, driving, urging, until there wasn't an ounce of her core that remained untouched.

Vanya hooked her ankles behind his back and arched wantonly, wanting and needing so much more. All of him. Every dark, uncivilized inch.

And he gave it to her. Like a ferocious beast.

When at last he threw back his head and shouted his release, she clung to his shoulders for dear life, wishing they could stay exactly as they were...forever.

303

BLOOD REDEMPTION

"Oh, sweet Princess," he finally murmured, his head falling forward to rest against hers.

"Dragon," she responded in kind, laughing in his ear. "No more pregnancies, please. I don't think I could bear it."

Saber laughed aloud then. "You slay me," he teased. And then he lifted her once more in his arms, this time cradling her to his heart as he strolled into the cave. "Come to my bed."

Vanya gulped. *He wasn't finished? Great Serpens,* she might just die from exhaustion—or satiation—before this wild one was through.

She blinked in reaction to the dim atmosphere of the torch-lit cavern, and the moment her eyes adjusted to the light, she couldn't help but be amazed. It was nothing at all like she had imagined: a damp, foreboding hideaway for a lost, bestial animal.

The cave was a masterpiece of both ancient and modern architecture. A sanctum of art and splendor. A haven built for a prince. And then her eyes grew wide. On the far, back wall of the cave, just below the ceiling, but still above a jutting platform which held his bed in its cradle, was a hand-painted work of art that would have rivaled the detail in the Sistine Chapel. "Put me down," Vanya commanded, captivated beyond words by what she saw. "Please...put me down."

Saber obeyed instantly. He lowered her to her feet, stepped back, and watched as she approached the platform and the life-size mural that hovered above it. There were ancient ships sailing across the Black Sea on their way to war, each one a masterpiece of detail and wonder; and painted on the largest one was the face of a woman—a hauntingly beautiful woman—and it was obvious, immediately so, that all of the ships were going to war for her.

Saber sidled up behind her, wrapped his arms around her waist, and nuzzled his chin in the crook of her shoulder, unable to resist dragging his fangs enticingly back and forth several times along her carotid artery. "Helen of Troy," he whispered in her ear, his voice huskier, raspier, than she had ever heard it before. "The face that launched a thousand ships."

Tessa Dawn

Vanya wiped a tear from her eye and blinked several times in rapid succession. Indeed, it was the legendary princess, the lover of Paris, and he had captured the essence of her infamous beauty perfectly, with one exception: The face that graced the walls of Saber's cave was not Helen's.

It was Vanya's.

Vanya stuttered, struggling for words. "W…w…when did you do this?"

Saber breathed heavily against her neck. "When I was starving…for blood. When I was angry…at the house of Jadon. When I remembered my father's…and my brother's…executions. When I thought about you and Lucien and wanted to kill some innocent soul in retribution for my own sins. When I loathed my existence…and when I worshipped yours."

Vanya spun around to face him. "*Dragon.*" It was all she could say.

"Vanya," he whispered, his eyes brimming with something she had never seen before: deep, unfettered emotion. "I am not the warrior you deserve. I am a soldier, a fighter, a conqueror in my own right, only purged in the blood of a dark deity, ushered into the world in deception and black magic. Nothing in my soul will ever match the purity of yours. Nothing in my existence will ever make me worthy; but I am wasted, devastated, ruined before you—and *that* I will give you for the rest of my life, if you will have me…teach me." He held her gaze in an unwavering appeal. "Forgive me for the pain I caused you—the pain I will cause you."

Vanya stared back and forth between the painting on the cave wall and the raw, unguarded soul before her. Indeed, he spoke the truth more eloquently than he had ever spoken it before: Saber Alexiares was a dark paradox, but he was also fierce and brave and capable of brutal honesty, and more than that, more than any of that, he was hers.

Fire and ice.

Two lost souls without a home.

BLOOD REDEMPTION

Brought together by the fate of a Serpens Moon.

Saber waited anxiously the next morning as Vanya returned to the cave in his truck, only this time, she carried the most important cargo of all.

Swallowing his trepidation, he cautiously strolled forward and waited, barely able to breathe, as she climbed out of the extended cab and opened the back door. The infant seat was large, seeming to dwarf the child; and there were more buckles and straps than a body knew what to do with. *For Serpens' sake,* he thought; the kid was a vampire. Sturdy. *Immortal.* Was all this really necessary?

Saber ran his hand through his thick crimson-and-black hair several times, growing increasingly impatient as Vanya finally wrested the kid free, lifted him delicately out of the seat, and rounded the hood of the cab in order to approach Saber.

He drew in a sharp intake of breath.

The child was spectacular.

Handsome, strong, and vibrant.

His coal-black hair was shimmering in the sun—and wasn't that just the greatest impetus Saber had ever had to risk stepping out into the ominous rays—and Lucien's eyes, those stunning, curious eyes, they were the oddest mixture of Vanya's and his own, a deep, dark hue that was just slightly *off*, not exactly black, but not rose-colored, either. They were a burnished coal with a hazy bronze overtone, almost as if the two colors had sought to find a way to merge and stopped somewhere in the middle. His nose was arrow-straight, with the same slightly rounded ridge on the end as Saber's; and his mouth was the mirror image of the princess's, heart shaped, with full lips and soft edges.

Saber took a tentative step forward, fighting his urge to wince as the seeking rays of the sun enveloped his head, his shoulders, and his torso: He was still amazed, every time this happened, that he didn't simply burst into flames. He swallowed a lump in his throat and met Vanya's eyes. "This is Lucien?" Now that was the stupidest thing he had ever said. Of course it was Lucien.

Vanya chuckled proudly. "Yes, Dragon. This is *your son*." She held the child out to Saber, and the vampire took him proudly, bracing his large hands as gently as possible beneath the child's armpits and around his back. He hoisted him up at eye level and studied every single detail, memorizing each unique characteristic and trait. "Hello, Lucien."

The child kicked his perfect feet in the air and wriggled excitedly.

Saber laughed, a deep sound of contentment rising in his throat. And then he cradled the child in his arms and held him to his heart. At last, there was something in this world that was *his*.

Certain.

One soul to whom he truly belonged. And always would.

He looked up at Vanya and realized with incredulity that perhaps, just perhaps, there might be two…in time. "So, you haven't had a change of heart?"

Vanya reached out to smooth a lock of Lucien's hair. "It was never my heart that was the issue."

"You haven't changed your mind then?"

Vanya shrugged. "I am taking it one day, one moment, at a time."

Saber grew deathly serious then. He glanced down at his son to make sure he was content before locking eyes with the elegant female before him. "Not good enough, Vanya." He sought to find words in a situation that was as foreign to him as Mars might be to a human. "I need to know you're committed." By the surprised look on her face, the admission was as alien to her as it was to him.

Vanya folded her arms over her chest. "There is so much that still remains unknown…unresolved."

"Like what?" Saber asked bluntly.

Vanya rubbed her arms with her hands. "Like where would

we live?" Before he could answer, she gestured toward the cave. "Napolean Mondragon will never let me live in a cave, out in the Red Canyons, no matter how modern...or beautiful." Her pale eyes softened. "And my work is still in Romania."

Saber measured her carefully. "There are caves in Romania." He winked to soften the mood. "And I can do an apartment...okay, so not an apartment, but a house...a suite at the University." He shook his head, dismissing the details. "Point is: I don't think accommodations are really the issue." He sought her gaze for a deeper truth: Did she actually want him?

"There is the matter of citizenship," she said.

"Citizenship?"

"Yes, Dragon." She pointed to his right hip pocket and raised her eyebrows. "The Crest Ring of the house of Jadon still remains in your pocket"—she held up her hands in question— "not on your right hand."

Saber nodded. There was no point in blowing smoke up her beautiful derriere at this juncture. "That's going to take time, Vanya."

"How much time, Saber?"

"Don't know."

She looked away pensively.

"I do know," he said, commanding her attention once more, "that I no longer belong in the house of Jaegar. That has to count for something." He looked down at Lucien and beamed. "I do know that I belong with this male in my arms. Always." And then he looked at her, really looked, his eyes searching hers for signs of something—what?—confirmation, maybe hope. "And I want to belong with you."

She spoke her next words quietly, solemnly. "And I, you, Saber. Truly, I do."

He nodded. "Then give me the time that I need to adjust to my circumstances, but don't do it from a distance. Be with me."

Vanya frowned. "And what of your family...and mine?"

"What of them?" he asked.

"Ciopori is my sister...*my heart*. Nikolai is my nephew, and I fully intend to participate in his upbringing, to make sure that he and Lucien grow up as more than just cousins, as friends. And Marquis—well, he is often a thorn in my side, but I love him dearly; and I would never spend my life apart from the ones I love."

"They will never accept me or welcome me; and perhaps they shouldn't."

"So, where does that leave me then? And Lucien?"

"Vanya," Saber said emphatically, "I am not a child to be coddled, nor am I a male to be intimidated. I can hold my own. Besides..." He rolled his shoulders as if shrugging the weighty idea off his back. "I spent eight hundred years completely unaware that I even had feelings; I doubt I will let the fear of someone hurting them influence me now." He chuckled slyly. "I can...try...with your family. For you."

Vanya softened. She seemed to understand what a major concession he had just made, but she still appeared concerned. "But that is just the point: I cannot be your *everything*, Saber. I cannot be your identity, or your self-esteem, or your only substantial ally, save Lucien."

Saber felt his mouth turn up in a sneer, that signature smile of his that was as much a scowl as a grin, causing the right side of his lip to ascend in a subtly cruel visage. "My identity was forged in blood and fire over eight hundred years. While it might not be the identity you would have chosen for me, it is mine just the same. I may not be a soldier in the house of Jaegar anymore, but I am still a warrior." He looked over his shoulder at the mouth of the cave. "And those talents, those skills I possess, the knowledge I have acquired over so many lifetimes, who can take that away from me now?" He leveled his gaze directly at her. "As for self-esteem, *dear Princess*: Is it not my stubborn pride that rankles every male in the house of Jadon?" He laughed sarcastically. "I do not abhor what I am." He waved his hand in dismissal before she could protest or, worse, list all of the deficient qualities he should take a closer look at. "Perhaps I just need to *refine* it. At any rate, I am not wanting for an ego."

Vanya smiled then. "I believe a truer statement has never been spoken."

"And there is Lorna," he said, his voice barely more than a whisper. "And Rafael." Before she could get too excited, he added, "I don't know if anything can come of such a tragic, fragmented past; but they are at least...there...and I know that now."

Vanya's eyebrows shot up, her kind eyes searching his for signs of promise. "You went to see your mother," she said, revealing nothing of how she knew, or what she knew.

"I did. And I actually called her *mother*," he said. The admission was as vulnerable as it was frank.

Vanya pursed her lips while considering his words. "And Rafael?"

Saber looked away.

"This will take more time then?"

He nodded. "I don't...I don't despise him." For Saber, that was a huge progression.

"No," Vanya agreed, "I don't believe you do." She stepped forward and placed a soft, elegant hand against his cheek, gazing up into his eyes with nothing but compassion. "You *loved* Damien, Saber; and you thought of him as your father, right, wrong, or indifferent. And you are nothing if not harshly loyal. You may never be able to call Rafael father, for no other reason than out of devotion to the male who raised you; but that doesn't mean you can't get to know him, give the relationship a chance."

"Perhaps," Saber said, astounded by how well she knew him already. How well she had always seemed to know him.

"And as for love?" she whispered, her thumb rotating softly against his angled jaw. "Will our pairing ever include *love*?"

Saber secured Lucien in his left arm, bringing him even tighter to his chest in an effort not to drop him, and then he brought his right hand up to cover Vanya's. He owed her honesty, and that was what he intended to give her. "I do not know...this love...you speak of, but Rafael believes that I just...that I have not yet made the connection between the emotion and the word. So, I will describe to you what I experience, and you can be the judge."

Vanya held her breath, her pale-rose eyes deepening with anticipation.

"Breathe," Saber whispered.

She inhaled sharply and smiled uneasily, still waiting.

"That very first night, when you came to me in the holding cell, you were like an angel of light; and it hurt my eyes to look at you. I felt like a caged animal...angry, restless, lost. And I struck out against you, against the captivity, against the house of Jadon. Against the internal cage I was also living in." He drew in a deep breath of air, gathering the courage to continue. "I wanted to take you, to punish someone for the sins of the world; and I might have if you had not fought back. But when you tossed me across the cell, something awakened. I could have killed you *so easily*. So quickly. *So cruelly*. But I didn't. And not because I thought it through or made a calculated decision. There was never anything to decide or think about. Harming you was simply not an option. The impulse wasn't there. The rage was...subdued." When she didn't respond, he struggled to find a better way to say it. "Vanya, the impulse to kill, to destroy, has *always* been with me, from as far back as I can remember—hell, *it was me* for eight hundred years. But in your presence, it grew still...quiet. And when you left that night, when you told me not to tell anyone of your visit, that I would be dead in thirty days and the world would be a better place for it, I could think of nothing else. No one else. I could still see your face, smell your hair, hear your voice; and they haunted me like a child's monster in the closet, always close by, always threatening to emerge from the shadows."

His eyes trailed over her mouth, her neck, and her shoulders, before returning to her eyes. "When you walked with me in the forest, I felt almost desperate to get through to you...*I wanted*...your attention, your respect, *your trust*, as crazy as that sounds. And not just to manipulate you to my own ends." He sighed in frustration. "It's hard to explain, but it was like I had become a three-corded rope, and the rope was unraveling. And I had to bring the three pieces back together: you, me, and whatever connection I knew, *felt*, to exist between us. It was like there was no purpose, no meaning, no air to breathe unless that rope was intact. There was only darkness and this strange, undefinable lifeline. I needed you to meet me on a level beyond what was happening with Napolean and Ramsey, the house of Jadon *and* the house of Jaegar. Beyond my own rage and confusion. And you did. *You saw me*, in spite of the horror of the situation; and you approached me with civility and truth."

He looked away, and she squeezed his hand. Shut her eyes, briefly.

He looked back at her again. "And I saw you, too, Princess. So clearly. All of you. I saw the woman no one else in the house of Jadon had ever seen before. I saw a sister who had been betrayed by her brother and a princess so honor-bound to serve her people that she was living for duty alone. I saw the ice you had packed around your heart so long ago in Romania and the woman who was toying with a fire-breathing dragon, at the very real risk of being burned, just to feel alive. I saw the fear that kept you at bay—and the courage that pushed you forward in spite of it." He bent to brush a strident kiss on her forehead. "*I saw you*, Vanya. And you were the most beautiful, authentic thing I had ever seen."

Vanya leaned her head into his hand and nuzzled it. "*Dear gods*, Dragon. You were a scourge to the house of Jadon, the most lethal and predatory being I had ever encountered; yet your very soul was like water in the desert to me. And I kept reaching out to touch you because I was so—"

"Thirsty."

"And yet I knew in my heart it was only a mirage. I kept getting burned."

"I was dead inside," Saber said softly. "And you were never truly alive. And then we came together, under the most brutal circumstances, and the sparks breathed life into us both. Look into my eyes, right now, and tell me it isn't so."

She stared at him, as helpless as the newborn baby in his arms. "You know it is," she whispered longingly.

He bent down and placed a soul-stirring kiss on her lips this time. "Then you must know that the night we spent in my cell, the night you came to me after my family had been executed, was as real to me as it was to you, in spite of my grief and need. Perhaps I could not articulate it, or show it, beyond the animal instincts that drove me, but it was…earth-shattering just the same. And I never intended to hurt you, to kill you with a pregnancy. I was drowning, and you were my lifeline. I reached out for it, and almost took you under with me. But never on purpose."

Vanya hiccupped a sob. "I believe you. I do. I felt it in your hands, your kiss. Your hunger. I felt it when you took my pain away; and I knew it to be true in Kagen's clinic when you offered your life to Serpens in exchange for my own, and Lucien's." She stepped back then and cupped his face in her hands, no longer appearing lost or uncertain. "You are such an enigma, Saber Alexiares. Such a dark, dangerous, beautiful enigma."

"A real bastard," he whispered.

"A fire-breathing dragon," she clarified.

"Yes," he said honestly. "And all of it—all of me—is yours."

Vanya closed her eyes. "So what now?"

Saber offered his forefinger to Lucien's seeking fist, sensing that the child was growing restless. When Lucien immediately grabbed hold and tightened his grip, Saber felt like he was home. "We take it one day, one moment, at a time. But not without commitment, not without each other."

"A marriage ceremony?" Vanya asked.

"If that is your desire," Saber said. "I don't require a ceremony to know where my loyalties lie; but if you ask me to bring you the moon and the stars, then I will do my best to get them for you."

"Your best," Vanya echoed.

"Such as it is," Saber said.

BLOOD REDEMPTION

Vanya smiled unabashedly then, and the brightness of her features rivaled the noonday sun, warming his awakening heart even as it cast a halo over the perfect child they had created together. "There really is no question," she muttered softly. "I don't think there ever was." She winced. "I think that was blatantly apparent the moment I slashed your tires."

Saber laughed with abandon then. "You did slash my tires, you wicked, wicked female." He shook his head in appreciation. "And you couldn't have touched me deeper if you had sent me flowers."

"If I had asked Lorna to pick them out for me, first," she teased.

"Touché," he said.

Just then, Lucien stirred in his arms. The child hiccupped, and then he smiled at his father for all he was worth.

Saber stared at his son, amazed to see a half sneer, half scowl emerge as the right side of Lucien's mouth turned up in a grin. Looking down into his mirror image, Saber couldn't help but think he had finally gotten it right. He had created something worth cherishing.

A future that might include love.

A family that no one could take away.

A reason to get up in the morning, despite all of the pain and betrayal.

Relaxing into the newfound sensation of warmth, Saber glowed inside. By all the gods and goddesses—those he had heard of, and those he had yet to learn of—he was finally holding his own *redemption*.

Epilogue

Kagen Silivasi reclined in an elegant, rust-colored armchair, staring up at the ceiling in his twin's vaulted Great Room. He was waiting, along with the other members of his family, to welcome Nathaniel's guests. Well, in truth, Vanya Demir and Saber Alexiares were hardly what one could call *guests,* and they weren't so much coming to see Nathaniel as all of the Silivasi brothers at once: It was more than just a little bit cryptic, this urgent, impromptu meeting.

Unsettling to say the least.

He glanced out the floor-to-ceiling windows, taking in the magnificent mountain view, before regarding his eldest brother Marquis inquisitively. "And you have no idea what this is about?"

"None," Marquis responded. He shuffled restlessly in his own armchair. "To tell you the truth, I'm still a bit shocked that the male had the brass to ask for this meeting, to step foot in this house"—he regarded Nachari's mate Deanna as well as their newly acquired little sister Kristina with deference—"to show his face around either of these females, willingly, after what he did to them."

"Agreed," Nachari Silivasi said, leaning back against the wall beside the fireplace. "It does seem like a bold move." He crossed his arms over his chest. "On the other hand, I also have to concede that the male is trying."

"Hmm," Marquis grumbled, refusing to say any more.

"It seems like only yesterday when we went through Vanya's conversion at the clinic," Kagen commented.

"Hell, it seems like only yesterday when the bastard didn't burn in the sun," Marquis retorted.

"Marquis," Kagen chastised. "At some point, we may have to let bygones be bygones."

Nachari shrugged. "The way I see it: If Vanya wants to be with him—and it's pretty evident she does—then that's her call; and we all have to get used to it."

"The way you see it," Marquis growled. "Who asked you how you saw it?"

Nachari winked at the burly Ancient Master Warrior. "Love you, too, bro."

"Whatever," Marquis grumbled.

Kagen sat forward then. "I just don't understand what this is about—what could Saber possibly have to say to all of us that is this important?"

Nathaniel, who was sitting next to his mate on the sofa, shrugged with indifference. "Perhaps, there's an apology coming."

Jocelyn rubbed her temples. "Maybe."

Deanna shifted uneasily in her seat next, sharing a knowing glance with Kristina, who was nestled on the soft beige sofa beside Jocelyn. "I hope not," she said insistently. "I'm not sure I'm quite as...forgiving...as my mate."

Nachari strolled languidly to her side and sat on the arm of her chair. He took her hand in his and softly kissed her knuckles. "Not forgiving, love. Just...evolving."

Deanna nodded and squeezed his hand.

As far as Kagen could tell, something important had passed between his little brother and the newly redeemed vampire not so long ago in the Red Canyons. Saber's dark brother Diablo, along with two soldiers from the Dark Ones colony, had tried to kill Saber; and Nachari and Ramsey had shown up to defend the recalcitrant male, to try and save Saber despite the bad blood that existed between them. Whatever had taken place in that valley had quenched some of Nachari's anger and begun to forge at least a tentative truce between the two males. As far as Kagen was concerned, Nachari was a wise and intuitive wizard. If he was beginning to see things in a different light, then perhaps a different light existed. He was just about to make a comment to that effect when Alejandra, Nathaniel's live-in housekeeper, stepped into the living room.

"Mr. Silivasi," she said in her thick Latin accent. "Your guests have arrived. Should I show them in?"

Nathaniel stretched fluidly in his seat to relieve some tension, and then he placed a protective arm around Jocelyn's shoulders—Jocelyn had her own history with Saber Alexiares; and none of the males seemed too keen on allowing their women to face the dangerous vampire alone. "Of course, Alejandra," Nathaniel drawled in his typical, laid-back fashion. "Show them in."

The maid retreated, and everyone in the room waited with bated breath.

Vanya appeared first, the regal beauty commanding instant attention as always. Saber was not far behind, his hand resting conspicuously, if not possessively, on the small of Vanya's back. Now that was one visually jarring sight if Kagen had ever seen one: the devil in blue jeans staking claim to an angel of light.

Kagen watched the ensuing interaction unfold with interest: The moment Nathaniel and Saber's eyes met, an undeniable spark of tension flashed between them, and the temperature in the room rose a couple of degrees.

"Dark One," Nathaniel spoke in greeting.

The term *Dark One* was a bit confusing as Saber was no longer a Dark One, at least, not technically. In truth, he never really had been. He was a son of Jadon who had been stolen by the Dark Ones at birth, raised as a member of the house of Jaegar, and only recently returned to his true lineage. Still, he had been one obstinate nut to crack; and with all his defiance, rebellion, and just plain meanness, the term *Dark One* had stuck to him like glue. It might be years before the sons of Jadon stopped referring to him that way.

If ever.

Saber seemed to take it in stride, maybe even wear it like a badge of honor. With a gait as weighted in stealth as it was in swagger, he sauntered toward Nathaniel and inclined his head. "Nathaniel."

BLOOD REDEMPTION

Nathaniel rose like vapor from a steaming cauldron, all at once ascending to his feet; and Jocelyn immediately took a place at his side. "Sweetheart," she murmured, placing a gentle hand on Nathaniel's arm. She turned to face their guest. "Hello, Saber."

Nathaniel couldn't help it. He sidestepped between them and growled in warning, his watchful eyes darting back and forth between the pair. In truth, it wasn't meant as a challenge: It was simply an unconscious signal—a way of saying, *Caution!*—from one male predator to another. In other words: *Back up. You're too close.*

Kagen held his breath, waiting to see what would happen next. Both Jocelyn and Saber stepped back, their collective response so perfectly timed it almost appeared to be choreographed, a primordial waltz.

Nathaniel visibly relaxed, his powerful chest rising and falling with deeper breaths.

Peeking from behind the barrier of Nathaniel's shoulder, Jocelyn forced an uneasy smile and tried again. "Hello, Saber."

Saber looked her over with more than a small measure of scrutiny. He obviously remembered her. "You," he whispered. "How have you been?"

Seemingly surprised, Jocelyn's eyebrows shot up. "I've been...good."

Saber nodded. "Still jumping into your mate's battles?"

Jocelyn smiled then. "Not so much." She smirked at him. "Avoiding guillotines?"

Saber laughed without restraint, and the sound seemed almost alien coming from such a ruthless male, bizarre in its unexpected nature.

Deanna Silivasi rose softly from her seat, placed her hand on her lower stomach, and quietly announced, "I can't do this." Her stately, five-foot-ten frame seemed to fold inward, constricting in Saber's presence. "I thought I could, but I can't." She was just about to leave the room when Nachari slid effortlessly behind her and placed both arms firmly around her waist.

"You *can* do this," he whispered in her ear. When she started to shake her head, Saber stepped forward, and she visibly flinched, drawing back in surprise. When he descended to one knee in front of her, Deanna looked at him like he had grown a second head. She glanced over her shoulder at Nachari and frowned. "What is he doing?"

"He is trying to appear as nonthreatening as he can," Saber answered for the Master Wizard. He bowed his head and shook it slowly back and forth. "Deanna, you have nothing to fear from me. Not now. Not ever again."

Deanna tried to take a cautious step back but ran into the brick wall of Nachari's chest. "I have much to...*remember* with you," she said bitterly.

Saber stood slowly then. He reached as gingerly as he could, as slowly as he was able, and retrieved a burnished dagger with serrated edges from the waistband of his jeans. He flipped it deftly in his hand and extended the grip to Deanna.

Marquis stirred restlessly. His eyes flashed red, but he didn't rise or interfere.

"In the house of Jaegar," Saber said, "when someone has a wrong to redress, it's done in blood, and then the matter is closed...forever."

Deanna blanched. She shook her beautiful head, her exotic bluish-gray eyes clouding with distaste. "I...I can't cut you, Saber."

Kristina Silivasi rose from the sofa, took four long strides across the room, her hips swaying in an effort to balance her petite frame above her three-inch stilettos, and snatched the blade from Saber's hand. She swung it neatly across his face, slicing from his left ear to the corner of his mouth, then, once again, from his right cheek to his temple, cutting deep into the bone. "I can," she snapped.

Saber didn't flinch, although Vanya did. "Should I leave it as it is...unhealed?" he asked.

Vanya sighed in exasperation. "Please, Kristina. I have to look at him for the rest of my life."

Kristina stared at Vanya and frowned. "Fine. He can heal it...*later.*"

Saber nodded. "Very well. Later then."

Kristina looked startled by his compliance, more than a little off balance. Searching for a way to regain control, she smirked. "How are your flat tires, Dark One?"

Vanya dropped her head in shame.

"No longer flat," Saber said. The corners of his mouth turned up in a smile, or a predatory scowl, depending on how one looked at it, and he winked at her.

Kristina drew back in surprise, and a tiny glint of respect registered in her eyes. "Cool." She turned to face Deanna. "Are we good now, Dee? The second one was for you."

Deanna nodded tentatively at Kristina. She forced herself to meet the vampire's eyes once more, and something unspoken passed between them. "I don't want your blood, Saber. I just want to know *why.*"

Again, Saber stood strong against the scrutiny. "I was a soldier in the Dark Ones' colony. I was ordered to hurt the enemy, and I obeyed. I didn't think; I didn't feel; I didn't reason. It may not be what you want to hear, but it's the truth."

Deanna frowned. "And now?"

Saber glanced at Vanya. "And now I am learning how to think and feel...and reason. Or at least I'm trying." He shrugged then. "It's all I've got."

Nachari tightened his arms around his mate and waited. When she still didn't speak, he whispered, "Deanna?"

"I'm still—"

"For what it's worth," Saber offered. "I am sorry."

Deanna nodded and Marquis snorted. "Enough!" He waved his hand through the air, as if to dismiss the whole silly scene, and scowled. "You were a soulless bastard who deserved to die. We tried to kill you, but you wouldn't burn. And now you're in love with the princess. So you've come here to talk to us about something: Get on with it."

Kagen rolled his eyes. Leave it to Marquis to put things in

perspective. Of course, the Ancient Master Warrior did conveniently leave out the part where he almost removed Saber's heart for getting his mate's sister pregnant; but all in all, it was a fairly good summary.

Saber regarded Marquis thoughtfully and inclined his head. "Very well." He eyed an empty chair next to the fireplace and sat down. "May I?"

"Looks like you already did," Marquis snorted. He gestured at the chair. "Sit, stand, hang upside down if you like. Just talk."

Saber leaned forward and braced his arms on his elbows, looking as if he were bracing himself for the conversation. When Vanya made her way to his side, placed a supportive hand on his shoulder, and squeezed it reassuringly, Kagen tensed with anticipation.

What in the world was this all about?

Saber cleared his throat. "I don't want to take up any more of your time than is necessary, and I really don't know how to start, how to say this, so I'll just put it out there as succinctly as I can."

Nathaniel leaned forward, looking both leery and intense. "Go on."

Saber drew a deep breath. "In the colony, I did a lot of things other than fight, for the house of Jaegar. Mostly woodwork, iron work, shit with my hands." He eyed the females apologetically. "*Stuff* with my hands." When Marquis gave him an impatient stare, he hurried on. "And on a few occasions, I put data into our computers for the council—I fed the historic annals." He glanced upward as if searching for a better way to put it. "The historic annals are kind of like the colony's version of an electronic library, where we keep our important records, demographic information, our history." He sighed, frustrated by the recurring slip. "Where *they* keep *their* history."

Vanya stroked his shoulder with her hand as if to say, *You're doing fine,* and the whole thing made Kagen restless, uneasy deep down in the pit of his stomach.

Where in Hades was this going?

321

BLOOD REDEMPTION

He shifted anxiously in his seat. "So?"

"So, about four hundred and eighty years ago, when the Lycans attacked the valley, there were about thirty Dark Ones killed."

Marquis's jaw stiffened and he clenched his fists, cracking all ten of his knuckles in unison, before relaxing once again and staring blankly at Saber.

Kagen inhaled deeply: The Silivasis had intimate knowledge of the Lycan attack—how could they not? They had lost their own mother at the hands of the werewolves, and their father had been lost soon after.

Nathaniel cleared his throat, and Nachari pursed his brows. "Continue," the Master Wizard said, his voice lacking its usual charisma.

Saber made eye contact with Vanya, and the princess nodded.

"At the time," Saber said, "Salvatore and the other sorcerers spent an enormous amount of time and energy trying to locate our common enemy. Needless to say, we wanted revenge pretty badly. But more so, we wanted to find out where they lived, so we could eliminate them once and for all."

"They live all over the planet," Nachari said thoughtfully. "Embedded in their Council of Nations; disguised as national headhunters; meeting on occasion with human militia leaders."

"That's true," Saber agreed, "but there's more to it than that. A lot more to it."

"Like what?" Marquis asked.

"The sorcerers were able to discover something new, something really odd, something previously unheard of." He took a deep breath and just put it out there. "Another dimension."

"Another dimension?" Kagen asked.

"Yes," Saber replied. "A world apart from our own, the origin of the werewolves."

The entire room inhaled as one.

"What do you mean?" Nathaniel asked.

322

Saber looked off into the distance for a moment as if trying to *see* the right words. "I mean another dimension, a realm parallel to this one, but apart. A place called Mhier." Before one of the Silivasis could interrupt him again, he explained: "There's a reason none of us have ever been able to locate anything more than a regional headhunter here or there, a reason why we've never been able to ferret out an entire community or civilization of Lycans and exterminate them. It's because they're not here. Not the majority of them, anyhow. Not in this dimension." He sat back in his chair, apparently deep in concentration. "The sorcerers said that Mhier was like, I don't know, a lost civilization from somewhere back in time, complete with salt mines, slaves, and some pretty gnarly animals. And from what I could garner from Salvatore's entries in the annals, any Dark Ones that had been taken by the Lycans were long dead, and the challenge of trying to get there was a greater risk than it was worth—it was better to just wait for their periodic attacks and fight them here."

Marquis exhaled slowly then. "Okay, so no one is going to deny this is important information. *Very important information.* You should be sharing it with Napolean. Why did you come to us?"

Saber scrubbed his face with his hand and swallowed hard. "Because it affects your family more than most."

Kagen did not like the sound of that...wherever this was going.

Not one bit.

"How so?" he asked, his heart beginning to beat rapidly with a brash, resounding thud.

"Indeed, how so?" Marquis repeated.

Saber closed his eyes briefly. When he reopened them, they were dark with regret and deathly serious. "Because of a small entry I came across, written as no more than a footnote in the text."

"Well?" Marquis Silivasi bit out impatiently.

Saber met the Ancient Master Warrior's stare head-on. "It

was the name of a vampire, a slave still living in Mhier, at least at the time of Salvatore's last entry."

"And?" Nathaniel Silivasi demanded, his voice growing harsh with anticipation.

"And the name was Keitaro Silivasi."

Nachari released his hold on Deanna and took two steps back, his stunning features flushing absent of color. He ran a rigid hand through his thick, wavy hair, and shook it out in disbelief. The wizard had only been twenty-one years old when their father disappeared; he had barely had a chance to know him.

Nathaniel's fangs slowly extended in his mouth, and his eyes burned a deep crimson red; yet he said nothing. For centuries, he had believed Keitaro was still alive, and he had searched from one end of the globe to the other before finally giving up and laying the male's memory to rest.

Marquis sat back in his chair, far too casually.

His piercing eyes dimmed from deep phantom blue to eerie shark black, the depths going vacant with barely concealed anguish—and rage—and then he began to tremble.

Uncontrollably.

Kagen sat forward on the edge of his seat, watching Marquis carefully, fully expecting him to plunge over the edge of sanity at any moment: Marquis and Keitaro had been the best of friends, bar none. And their father's loss had affected Marquis more tragically than any of the others, hardening his heart, changing his personality, molding him into the brutal, impassive male he was today. Kagen couldn't help but wish Ciopori had come with him, that the other females had found someone else to watch their kids, because by the look on Marquis's stony face, the male was slipping further and further away by the second, perhaps going somewhere from which he would never return.

To Kagen's immense surprise, the huge male seemed to simply snap out of it. That is, in a truly creepy, *five-faces-of-Eve* kind of way. It was almost as if another personality had simply taken over for him, run his emotions through a paper-shredder, and discarded them in a bin on the other side, leaving him free to process the information. "That was almost five centuries ago," Marquis grumbled in irritation. "Even if he was alive then, he's unlikely to be alive now. Especially if he was surviving as a...a slave." He stumbled over the last word despite his self-control.

Vanya took a deep breath then. "I don't believe that to be true, brother-in-law," she said. "I have reason to believe he might yet be living."

"What reason, Princess?" Nachari asked, his tone also carefully controlled.

Vanya swallowed hard. "Before I met Saber, I had a dream about him, a dream that vexed me horribly and would not give me a moment's peace. I dreamed that there was a fire-breathing dragon in the house of Jadon, and that our paths would cross inexorably. In the dream, he always burned me when I approached him; yet I couldn't stay away. *I simply couldn't.* Because he was guarding something so precious, so valuable to the house of Jadon. A treasure. One that had to be returned to the people." She sat back and sighed. "Last night, I told Saber about the dream, and it sparked his memory. He believes—and I agree—that the treasure he was guarding was not his own return to the house of Jadon, but his knowledge of that single footnote: that marginalized entry. Your father's name."

Whatever...*whoever*...was guarding Marquis Silivasi's emotions stepped aside. He shot out of his chair like a rocket, fueled by highly combustible energy, ready to launch to the sky, and roared like an angry lion. "Son of a bitch!"

Nathaniel and Nachari immediately flanked him on either side, both males placing a firm hand on his shoulders. "Settle down, Marquis," Nathaniel warned, alluding to the powerful impact a male vampire's emotions had on the earth around them. The last thing they wanted was to trigger an electrical storm or create a flash flood.

"Be calm," Nachari said, immediately weaving an intricate pattern over the male's head, no doubt some spell or another to catch his rage.

Kagen stood to face Saber then, his own heart practically beating out of his chest. "Do you know where the portal is, the entrance to this...this other dimension?"

Saber shook his head. "No, I never saw that information."

Nachari shook his head adamantly. "Perhaps not, but if Salvatore Nistor could divine it with his sorcery, then I can find it using wizardry."

Saber held up his hands in question. "I don't know if that's true or not, but I do know this: If you guys can find the portal, I can draw you a map of the territory."

About The Author

Tessa Dawn grew up in Colorado where she developed a deep affinity for the Rocky Mountains. After graduating with a degree

in psychology, she worked for several years in criminal justice and mental health before returning to get her Master's Degree in Nonprofit Management.

Tessa began writing as a child and composed her first full-length novel at the age of eleven. By the time she graduated high-school, she had a banker's box full of short-stories and books. Since then, she has published works as diverse as poetry, greeting cards, workbooks for kids with autism, and academic curricula. The Blood Curse Series marks her long-desired return to her creative-writing roots and her first foray into the Dark Fantasy world of vampire fiction.

Tessa currently splits her time between the Colorado suburbs and mountains with her husband, two children, and "one very crazy cat." She hopes to one day move to the country where she can own horses and what she considers "the most beautiful creature ever created" -- a German Shepherd.

Writing is her bliss.

Books in the Blood Curse Series

Blood Destiny

Blood Awakening

Blood Possession

Blood Shadows

Blood Redemption

Blood Father (Coming Soon…)

If you would like to receive notice of future releases,

please join the author's mailing list at

www.TessaDawn.Com

CPSIA information can be obtained at www.ICGtesting.com
Printed in the USA
LVOW06s0640071113

360211LV00002B/14/P